ABBEYFORD
ABBEYFORD INHERITANCE
&
ABBEYFORD REMEMBERED

Born in Gainsborough, Lincolnshire, Margaret Dickinson has spent most of her life in that county, moving at the age of seven to the coast where she still lives today. She began writing at the age of fourteen and her first novel was published when she was twenty-five, followed by seven others. Married with two grown-up daughters, Margaret combines her writing career with a busy working life.

ABBEYFORD
ABBEYFORD INHERITANCE
&
ABBEYFORD REMEMBERED

Margaret Dickinson

PAN BOOKS

Abbeyfield first published 1981 under the title of *Sarah*
First published as *Abbeyford* 1998 by Severn House Publishers Ltd
Abbeyford Inheritance first published 1981 under the title of *Adelina*
First published as *Abbeyford Inheritance* 1998 by Severn House Publishers Ltd
Abbeyford Remembered first published 1981 under the title of *Carrie*
First published as *Abbeyford Remembered* 1999 by Severn House Publishers Ltd

This omnibus edition published 2002 by Pan Books
an imprint of Pan Macmillan Ltd
Pan Macmillan, 20 New Wharf Road, London N1 9RR
Basingstoke and Oxford
Associated companies throughout the world
www.panmacmillan.com

ISBN 0 330 40064 9

1 3 5 7 9 8 6 4 2

A CIP catalogue record for this book is available from
the British Library.

Printed and bound in Great Britain by
Mackays of Chatham plc, Chatham, Kent

ABBEYFORD

Author's Note

I have been asked to tell you something about myself and my work. My writing career falls into two 'eras'. I had my first novel published at the age of twenty-five and between 1968 and 1984, I had a total of nine novels published. Because of personal circumstances I then had an enforced seven year gap, but began writing again in the early nineties. There then occurred that little piece of luck that we all need at some time in our lives. I found a wonderful agent, Darley Anderson, and on his advice I began to write saga fiction – stories with a strong woman as the central character and with a vivid and realistic background as the setting. The old adage 'write about what you know' never fails and now I am setting my novels firmly in my home county of Lincolnshire – the place I know best. Older, and with a maturity those seven 'fallow' years has brought me, I recognise that I am now writing with a greater depth and daring.

So it was with a sense of nostalgia that I recently re-read this novel which, I hope, you are about to read. Originally published in 1981 under the title *Sarah*, it was the first in the Abbeyford Trilogy, comprising *Sarah*, *Adelina* and *Carrie*.

This trilogy has a chequered history and took four years to complete. I actually wrote the second book, *Adelina*, first, as one long, rambling 150,000 word novel. On advice, this was cut drastically to about 60,000. Whilst this was going the rounds of the publishers, I started a sequel, *Carrie*, and this, from the start, was much better.

It was suggested that this book should be submitted instead of *Adelina*, but to me that would have been wasting the first part of the story. I decided to put the two novels together and to write an earlier piece to start it all off, thereby forming one long novel again, but in three separate parts. This was then sent out to publishers and found acceptance. But – wait for it – the publisher wanted it split into three separate books!

Whilst *Sarah* must be described as light historical romance, re-reading the novel, I can see that all the seeds are there for the writer I have now become. I have always loved writing a kind of 'sins of the fathers' theme, following the characters through several years, generations even, sharing their joys and sorrows, identifying with their mistakes and all the tragedies that come from those human frailties, and, finally, seeing the people they have become by the end of the story.

I am delighted that Severn House are re-publishing these three novels, the first of which is now called *Abbeyford*. I hope that you will enjoy it and want to look out for the next two.

Happy Reading!

M.D. 1998

ONE

Abbeyford, England, 1795

"Smallpox!" Joseph Miller gaped at his wife, Ellen, in horror. "Oh no! *No!*"

He sank down on to the wooden chair at the side of the hearth. With her usual stoical acceptance of life's hardships, Ellen Miller continued to stir the gruel in the huge cooking-pot suspended from an iron crane over the fire.

"I was afeard of it when she fell ill three days back, but I kept it to mysel'." She paused, then said flatly, "Now I'm sure."

"There's a rash?"

Ellen Miller nodded. "All over 'er face, an' spreadin'."

Joseph Miller groaned and dropped his head into his hands. "Poor bairn. Poor Beth." Then he raised his eyes and looked at his wife, his voice a hoarse whisper of fear. "What of Sarah and little Ella?"

Ellen shrugged her shoulders, not because she did not care, but because there was nothing she could do.

"Time will tell," she said sadly and began to ladle the hot

liquid into a wooden bowl for her sick daughter.

"You've some red flannel?"

"Aye, an' I'll wrap her in it. But . . ." She left the words unsaid and moved towards the other room of their small cottage where her fifteen-year-old daughter lay shivering with a high fever.

Joseph hovered in the doorway for a moment watching the tortured twistings and delirious mumblings of his child. Then he turned away, helplessness bowing his strong shoulders.

He left the cottage to return to his work. There was still work to be done. No matter what affliction hit his family, there was always work to be done!

From his cottage Joseph Miller crossed the village green and took the path leading to the common land where the villagers grazed their own few livestock. A stream ran through the common land and beyond that, higher up the hill, stood the Manor House, a square, solid building with farm buildings behind it. Joseph Miller's face hardened. The Manor—and the Trents who lived there—ruled their lives. There was a deep-rooted bitterness in Joseph Miller's heart.

Hardship was no stranger to his family. Generations ago, under the open-field system, his forefathers had tilled their own strips of land, working only on the lord's land as payment of rent. But a Bill of Enclosure had changed all that. Now all the arable land, all the buildings, even the cottage which Joseph Miller called home, belonged to the Earl of Royston of Abbeyford Grange. And he preferred to

6

let his land to one tenant farmer, Sir Matthew Trent, who in turn employed some of the villagers as his farm labourers. Now they worked the land that had once been their own for a weekly pittance. True, each villager had a strip of land behind his own cottage, but it was scarcely big enough to grow more than a few potatoes, support a few chickens or maybe a pig. They were becoming dependent upon the self-appointed 'squire', Sir Matthew Trent.

But a few—like Joseph Miller—still clung tenaciously to their self-sufficiency. They still had the right to graze their livestock on the common waste-land, and his wife, Ellen, and daughter, Beth, worked at the spinning-wheel to bring a little extra money into the home.

He stood a moment at the edge of the common watching his eldest daughter, black-haired, rosy-cheeked Sarah, tending their few sheep, two cows and ten geese. She wore a low-necked bodice, a coarse woven skirt hitched up to her knees and she had kicked off the clogs her father had made for her and ran barefoot.

"Sarah, oh Sarah," Joseph Miller whispered in anguish. "Not my pretty Sarah." Stout-hearted though he was, the burly countryman felt a lump in his throat and tears prickle his eyelids at the mere thought of pretty, lively Sarah scarred to ugliness by smallpox—Sarah whom he could not help but love best of all of his three daughters.

For Beth he had a natural fondness and for little Ella an added feeling of protectiveness for she had not grown and developed as she should have done. Already Ella had brought Joseph and his wife sadness though through no

7

fault of her own. She was a pretty ten-year-old with golden curls, but in her eyes there was a vacancy and a lack of understanding and when she did speak—which was rare— it was in the words of a five-year-old.

It was Sarah who brought Joseph joy, in whom he placed his trust and his hopes for the future. Her pertness enlivened his day, her willingness gladdened his heart and her beauty was his pride.

But now! What now?

"Come on, Pa," she was calling to him with mock impatience as he neared her. "It's time we wur milking. That un over there can 'ardly walk, her udder's that heavy."

"Sarah," he called, but already she was darting away from him, rounding up the straying cow. "*Sarah!* Come here, girl, I've something to tell you."

"Aw, Pa!" She came reluctantly and he could feel her impatience to be off again.

"It's our Beth."

"Beth? Is she worse?"

"Aye, I'm afeard so."

"What—is it?" Now there was anxiety in Sarah's voice and her youthful restlessness was stilled by a chill of fear.

"Your ma says it's the smallpox."

"Oh no!" Her violet eyes widened. Father and daughter stared at each other. At last Joseph Miller sighed and moved stiffly. "Ah well, we've work to do, girl. While us can."

"Aw Pa. Poor Beth."

"Aye, poor Beth indeed," he said bitterly and he glanced

8

back over his shoulder towards the village. "An' poor Abbeyford if it spreads among us all."

Abbeyford nestled in its own shallow valley in rolling countryside some fifteen miles south of Manchester. Not that the cottagers knew much about life outside their own enclosed community. Most of them were born, grew up, fell in love, married, became parents themselves, grew old, died and were buried in the small churchyard in the centre of the village without ever having travelled more than a mile or two beyond the valley.

"Come on, let's get these cows milked," Joseph said roughly to hide the growing terror in his heart.

Soberly now, with the carefree lightness gone from her step, young Sarah went about her work.

"You mun come an' stay with us, Sarah, out of harm's way."

"I'll do no such thing, Henry Smithson," Sarah snapped at the tall youth who stood over her, frowning heavily. Then regretful of her sharpness, for after all he was only thinking of her welfare, she said more gently, "It's kind of you, but I mun stay with Ma and Beth and help where I can."

"Aw Sarah, but if you should catch it . . ." Henry's eyes roamed over her clear skin, her rosy cheeks, her bright violet eyes and shining long black hair and the thought of her with that dreadful disease made him feel sick in the pit of his stomach.

"Sarah . . .?" His hand was on her arm. "Let me speak to your Pa about us. I know you're young yet, but we could be

9

promised."

Sarah wriggled under his touch. She knew—it seemed as if she had always known—that Henry had a special feeling for her. Instinct had told her he was waiting for her to grow up. He wasn't exactly her cousin but their families were related way back.

Now he had put these feelings into words and Sarah wished that he had not. She had no desire to be tied by a promise at sixteen.

"Sarah—please . . .?"

"No, Henry. You know Pa wouldn't agree."

The young man's frown deepened and he said moodily, "He'd agree if it wur what you wanted, Sarah."

"Then you dunna know him as I do. Pa's got a right temper on him if things dunna go his way."

Henry made a clicking noise of disbelief. "Ach, you can twist him round your finger if you've a mind, Sarah."

"That's where you're wrong, Henry," Sarah replied quietly.

"Ah, an' it seems to me you're as stubborn as your Pa, an' all. All right, go home, go and catch the smallpox an' see if I care!"

Swinging his arms, Henry Smithson marched off up the lane towards his own home, his back rigid with anger. Despite his denial, the trouble was that he cared far too much for young Sarah!

Sighing, Sarah opened the door of the Millers' cottage, eager to see how her sister fared and yet reluctant to become involved in the atmosphere of sickness and worry. In the

10

corner the spinning-wheel stood idle. Her mother was not in the one main room which served as kitchen-cum-living-room, but Sarah could hear sounds from the adjacent small room—her parents' sleeping quarters. Normally the three girls slept in the attic bedroom of the tiny cottage, directly under the thatch, but in times of sickness they were moved to their parents' room. Sarah stood in the doorway, almost recoiling from the sight of her poor sister.

Beth's face was blotched with small, hard pimples. For three days before the appearance of this rash she had been unwell with shivering fits and vomiting and had complained constantly of pains in her back and legs.

Now she lay quietly, her eyes closed as if sleeping.

"Ma?" Sarah whispered.

Ellen Miller turned. "Don't come in here, Sarah."

"But isn't there anything I can do to help?"

Ellen walked through to the kitchen, her movements slow and stiff as if she carried a great weight. She was a thin woman, slightly round-shouldered from the hours she spent at her spinning-wheel to augment the family income. Her hair, beneath her bonnet, was grey, her hands red and always a little swollen for there was never an idle day in Ellen Miller's life.

"Not for Beth—no," she answered Sarah. "But for yoursel'—keep away!"

"Ma, she's not . . .?"

"No, no, child. She's feeling better for the moment now the rash has come out." Ellen glanced back towards the sickroom and sighed. "But in a few days she'll be bad again

11

when all those spots turn into abscesses. Here, help me tear this flannel into strips. It's an old remedy my own grandma told us—to wrap her in red flannel might stop her being so badly scarred."

Silently Sarah tore the red material into strips.

"You know, Sarah, you could be safe from it."

"Me? Why?"

"You had cowpox last year when you started helpin' milk up at the Manor."

"So I did, but . . ."

"They reckon anyone who's had cowpox dunna get the smallpox."

"Oh." Sarah was thoughtful whilst she took in the full meaning for her. "But Ella—she's not had the cowpox."

"No, I know."

"What about you an' Pa?"

"I reckon I had it as a child, but I dunna know about your Pa."

"I hope it dunna spread round all the village," Sarah murmured, but with little hope.

Beth's spots grew larger and became blebs of milky fluid; still growing, the fluid became a yellow pus and her face and body were covered with abscess-like spots. Round each tell-tale pock was an inflamed ring. The fever returned and Beth twisted and cried in pain, tearing the red flannel from her face and scratching in anguish at her swollen eyes.

Patiently Ellen nursed her daughter through the crisis. Her life was saved but not her smooth, childish complexion.

12

Beth's face was hideously marked with cruel pocks.

A little over two weeks after Beth, Ella fell ill too. Placid, docile Ella lay quite still, close to death and yet never a cry of complaint did she make. Meekly she submitted to being wrapped in red flannel and, when the worst was over, it was obvious that she was not to be so badly scarred as poor Beth who had repeatedly torn away the covering in her delirium.

As the Millers had feared the disease spread through the village, but no one else in their own family caught it.

Two babies, three older children and an elderly woman died and then came the shocking rumour—shocking to the villagers who believed that their own troubles and hardships never touched their betters.

Joseph brought home the news.

"Lady Caroline has the smallpox!"

Three pairs of eyes regarded him in surprise; Ella in her corner crooned softly to her rag-doll, lost in her own little world.

"Never!" exclaimed Ellen, whilst Beth fingered her own disfigured face.

"She'll not be so high 'n mighty if she ends up like me!" Since her illness, Beth's tongue had sharpened with bitterness.

Sarah was silent thinking of the girl she had seen so often in Lord Royston's open carriage around the lanes of Abbeyford. A pretty child. No, more than pretty, Sarah thought without envy. Lady Caroline was beautiful. Was that beauty to be lost for ever? Beth had not been what would be called pretty even before the smallpox. And now . . .

13

Sarah reached for her shawl from the hook.

"Where are you going, girl?" her father asked.

Sarah wrapped the shawl closely around her thin shoulders and lifted the latch on the door. "To the Grange."

"The Grange!" Her mother was scandalised. No villager ever approached Lord Royston's home without a very special reason. "Whatever are you wantin' there, child?"

"I mun see how the li'le lady fares. Maybe there's summat as I can do to help."

"Help! Help, is it?" Beth screamed, her blotched face growing purple. "Who was there to help *me*?"

Sarah looked at her sister with pity, then without a word she turned and left the cottage.

Sarah crept along the edge of the gravelled driveway of Abbeyford Grange, not feeling quite so bold in her errand of mercy now she was in the shadow of the awesome building and the powerful gentry who lived there.

To her left stone steps led down into a sunken rose garden. She paused a moment to admire the profusion of pink roses. No other colour broke the mass of flaunting pink. Already the gardener was sweeping the fallen petals and cutting off the overblown blooms.

He looked up and stopped his sweeping. "What you doin' here, young Sarah Miller?"

"I've come to see—to see . . ." she faltered and then took a deep breath and finished boldly, ". . . her ladyship about Lady Caroline."

The gardener said soberly, "The little maid has the

14

disease."

"I know—that's why I'm here."

He resumed his brisk sweeping movements. "It's an unhappy house. They'll not want to be troubled wi' likes of you."

"We'll see," Sarah said, confident that she would be heard if she brought hope for their beloved daughter.

Moments later she was facing the forbidding figure of the housekeeper at Abbeyford Grange. Mrs Hargreaves folded her hands neatly in front of her severe black dress and looked down upon the village girl who had presumed to present herself at the Grange.

"Well, and what do you want, girl?"

Though her knees trembled beneath her long skirt, Sarah said, "I wish to see Lady Royston, if you please?"

The housekeeper's gasp of surprise was plainly audible. "Do you indeed? And what makes you so certain that her ladyship will condescend to see *you*?"

Sarah stuck out her chin defiantly. "Because I've come to help her—to help Lady Caroline."

Mrs Hargreaves gave a snort of contempt. "If the best physicians in the county can do naught for the poor child, what can a chit like you hope to do, eh, miss? Tell me that?"

Sarah's clear violet eyes met the cold gaze of the housekeeper unflinchingly.

"Besides," Mrs Hargreaves continued, "her ladyship is far too distraught to talk to *anyone*, let alone . . ."

"Then I'll speak to his lordship. I'm not afeard."

"No, and more's the pity! A bit more respect for your betters, my girl, that's what . . ."

Sarah ignored the tirade of abuse and her sharp eyes spotted the staircase leading from the kitchens to the upper landings of the house. With the swift suddenness of youth, she dodged around Mrs Hargreaves and darted up the stairs before the housekeeper had realised what she was doing.

As the door swung to behind her, cutting off the indignant screech of the housekeeper, Sarah found herself in a vast, high hall, the staircase curving round and round, up and up. Ancestral paintings lined the walls, their cold, staring eyes reproving her bold entry into their world.

A young footman, hovering in the hall, almost dropped the tray he was carrying at the sudden arrival through the door of a village milkmaid.

At that moment the double doors leading to one of the rooms off the hall opened and Sarah found herself staring open-mouthed at the tall figure she knew to be Lord Royston. He, too, stopped in surprise to see her there, but there was neither the anger nor contempt on his face that she had seen in the expressions of the housekeeper and, even now, the footman.

She ran forward and bobbed a curtsy. "Beggin' your pardon, m'lord," she began breathlessly, "but I heard Lady Caroline has the smallpox and I had to come, you see, perhaps I can help . . ."

At that moment a flustered Mrs Hargreaves arrived through the door and the footman too hurried forward and grasped Sarah roughly by the shoulder.

16

"I'm sorry, m'lord, I can't think how she got in . . ." he began, whilst behind them Mrs Hargreaves cried apologetically, "Oh your lordship, I . . ."

Lord Royston raised his hand to quieten them both, his eyes upon the clear unwavering gaze of the girl standing before him. "No—wait," he said, his deep, soft tones instantly demanding respect and obedience. "I wish to hear what this child has to say."

"But, your lordship, she's naught but a village girl . . ."

Lord Royston's eyes burned fiery for a moment and the housekeeper fell silent.

"I will listen to anyone—*anyone*—who can perhaps help my daughter. Come, girl, come in and let me hear what it is you have to tell me."

Standing in front of a blazing log fire with Lord Royston seated in front of her, Sarah explained.

"M'lord, my two sisters have had the smallpox an' me ma wrapped them both in red flannel, like her own grandma told her, to stop the scarring, m'lord."

"And?" he questioned softly. "Did it—help?"

"Well—Beth, she was that bad she tore off the binders and scratched at her face and, m'lord, she's terribly marked."

"Poor child," his lordship murmured, but Sarah knew his thoughts were more for his own daughter than for Beth Miller.

"But Ella, the youngest, she's a good li'le thing, she lay quiet and never moved the flannel me ma put on her."

"And?" There was a note of pathetic eagerness in the

17

earl's tone.

Sarah smiled. "She's scarcely a mark on her, m'lord, not that won't fade given time, an' yet she had just as many spots as Beth at the start."

"Red flannel, you say?"

"Yes, m'lord."

He pondered a moment and then, with sudden decision jumped up and pulled violently on the bell-cord, shouting at the same time. "Mrs Hargreaves—Mrs Hargreaves. Red flannel—have we any red flannel?"

Mrs Hargreaves appeared in the doorway. "Why yes, m'lord. I believe so, but . . ."

"Wrap Lady Caroline in red flannel. See that her face is covered—particularly her face—but her hands and arms too. All must be wrapped in red flannel!"

"Yes, m'lord." Mrs Hargreaves, peeved by her master's enthusiasm for this peasant girl's wild notion, nevertheless hurried to obey his orders.

More calmly, his lordship turned back to Sarah. "And you—did not catch this dreadful disease?"

"No, m'lord. Me ma thinks it's because I caught the cowpox when I began working as milkmaid for Sir Matthew Trent. She's heard say as those as gets cowpox dunna get the smallpox."

"Ah yes, yes. Indeed, I've heard of Mr Jenner who—now what do they call it?—vaccinates against this smallpox—and uses cows to do so. Ah, if only I had known in time, had thought . . ." Then he added, "You're not afraid of catching the disease then?"

18

Sarah answered truthfully. "At first I wur, m'lord. But now—well, I reckon if I wur goin' to get it I'd have it by now."

"Yes, yes. Now listen, you have been a thoughtful girl to come here. Whether or not your idea works, I appreciate your concern for my daughter. Now—how would you like to become her personal maid, eh?" The earl even managed to smile, despite the heavy weight of anxiety he carried. "She's been pestering me these last few months to allow her to have her own maid, just like her mother, instead of a governess."

Sarah's mouth dropped open and she gaped in astonishment at Lord Royston. Never in her wildest daydreams could she have imagined herself, a lowly milkmaid, being offered such a position.

"Now, what do you say?" the earl prompted.

TWO

"No, no, *no!*" Joseph Miller thumped the table with his clenched fist. "She's not going up there. I won't have her going into service. She'll mix wi' bad company."

Ellen Miller's spinning-wheel whirred all the faster. "Joseph Miller, you're a good husband and father, I'll not deny, but do you want to see your daughter a milkmaid all her life? Dun't you want a better life for her? Why, at the Grange as Lady Caroline's personal maid, she's almost equal to Mrs Hargreaves. Just think—she's stepping straight into a good position, when most girls would start as kitchen-maid."

"She'll still be a servant," he muttered. "We Millers call no one 'master' . . ."

Ellen sighed. She'd heard all this before.

"We hold our heads high, we're our own masters." He thumped the table again. "But between the pair o' them," he gestured to one side of the valley towards Abbeyford Grange and then the other way towards the Manor. "Between the two, they're trying to make lackeys out on us,

21

on land we used to call our'n!"

"Joseph—it's better this way. The crops is better than when all the land was divided into strips. I remember me pa for ever complaining his land was ruined by couch-grass spreadin' from his neighbour's strip . . ."

"But it don't *belong* to us."

"We still have the common land and . . ."

Joseph thumped the table again. "Not for much longer it seems."

Ellen's eyes widened and the rhythmic whirr of her spinning-wheel faltered. "What do you mean?"

Joseph's voice became a low growl. "Not content wi' robbin' us of our strips of arable land, they're going to enclose the common."

"No!" Ellen gasped and the wheel stopped completely. "I dunna believe it."

"Well, it's true. But this time they've a fight on their hands! We didn't fight last time because a lot o' the villagers thought Trent's arguments for increased production were sound. But we'll not let it happen *this* time!"

Ellen was silent. The arable land had been enclosed long before her marriage to Joseph, when they had been village children together, but she well remembered the anger of her own father and of Joseph's and the meetings they had held in their cottages to try to get all the villagers to unite against the Bill of Enclosure. But opinion had been varied. Some believed that they would be better off working for the Trents and the rebellion Joseph's father had tried to bring about had not happened.

22

Now she was to go through all that again.

They were silent for a moment, then his wife said tentatively, "But you'll not stop Sarah going to the Grange, Joseph, will you?"

"I'd like to, but they'd turn us out of our home if I go agen them in every way. I reckon I dunna have no choice but to let her go," he said bitterly, then added, clinging to a last, vain hope, "Mebbe she'll not take to the life anyway."

Sarah lay tossing and turning in the bed trying not to disturb her two younger sisters sleeping alongside her. She was far too excited for sleep! More than once she reared up on her elbows to look at the new grey dress and white lace cap and apron spread neatly over the box at the foot of the bed.

Tomorrow she was to begin working at Abbeyford Grange as Lady Caroline's personal maid. Of course, at sixteen—almost seventeen as she was quick to emphasise— it was not her first job. Since the age of nine she had worked in the fields gleaning after the harvesters; picking potatoes; bird-scaring; tending her father's livestock on the common land or driving them into the woods at the top of the hill. Then she had become a milkmaid at the Manor. But now . . .!

Sarah, in her shared bed, wriggled again.

"Go to sleep, our Sarah," murmured Beth sleepily. But Sarah could not sleep. Tomorrow she would be up there with the gentry, part of their life-style. Never again would she have to suffer the backbreaking fieldwork, shed tears of pain over cold hands, chapped until they bled, or be driven half-mad by stinging chilblains, or risk being kicked by a stubborn cow. No longer for her, life in a farm-labourer's cottage.

From tomorrow onwards she would be sleeping in a soft feather-bed and have a room of her own. No longer would she bear the indignity of sharing a bed with her younger sisters.

Tomorrow she was to become a lady's-maid.

She was up before dawn, creeping across the cold floor of the attic bedroom in her bare feet to dress herself in the uniform of her new life, her fingers trembling with excitement.

She couldn't swallow any of the usual thick breakfast porridge and for a time she stood in the quiet confines of the small kitchen listening to the sounds of the cottage. She could hear her father snoring in the next room, the thrum of the wind in the chimney.

Sarah looked ruefully towards the almost cold grate of the kitchen fireplace. She ought to blow the fire back to life, but dressed now in her finery, her hands scrubbed to an unusual cleanliness, she refused to scrabble about with ashes and faggots.

She pulled her cloak around her and bit her lip with indecision. She was ready to go, anxious to be off, but knew she should say 'goodbye'. Not that she wouldn't be coming down to see them every week but her mother would never forgive her if she left without a proper farewell. Her pa, too, would want to warn her yet again to be a good girl and not to allow herself to be led astray.

24

She heard a movement in her parents' room and moments later her father appeared in the doorway, scratching his head and yawning. His bare feet stuck out below the shirt he wore day and night.

"Lord! You up already, me girl?"

"Yes, Pa. I couldna sleep."

He yawned again and grinned at her. "You're lucky! I reckon I could sleep for a hundred years and then some." He paused and his eyes roved proudly over her heart-shaped face with its smooth rosy skin, the pert nose and generous mouth. Her violet eyes were shining with excitement and her cascading unruly black hair was gathered neatly now beneath the white lace cap. Then, as he noticed her new finery, his smile faded. "You're off then?" he said gruffly.

"Aw Pa, dun't spoil it for me."

He sat down on the hard chair and began to pull on his working boots. "You'd do better to settle down and marry Henry."

"I dunna want to marry Henry, Pa, nor anyone else. Not yet."

He wagged his finger at her. "Don't you go gettin' fancy ideas about yoursel', me girl."

"No, Pa. I'll work hard—and I'll be good," she added impishly.

"Aw," Joseph Miller doubled his fist and landed a gentle mock blow upon her chin, but now he was smiling. "Go on wi' you! You'd best say 'goodbye' to your ma," he jerked his thumb towards the next room, "then you can be off."

25

As she pulled the cottage door shut behind her, Sarah breathed deeply in the fresh morning air. Directly in front of her was the village green with its duck-pond and on the far side the vicarage and the church and churchyard.

She turned left and walked along the lane, past the line of cottages which bordered the green. The lane curved to the right and then swung sharply left away from the green. More cottages lined the road on either side now and amongst them on the right-hand side was the village's one inn, the Monk's Arms. Sarah walked on, the road curving left towards the bridge over the stream. The last two buildings of the village, close beside the stone bridge, belonged to the smith and his brother, the village wheelwright. Already she could hear the clanging sounds of the smith's heavy hammer. Beyond the bridge the trees overhung the lane, almost touching at the top and forming a shadowy, natural tunnel.

Sarah took another deep breath and gave a little skip of sheer delight. More sedately, as befitting her new position, she walked on, climbing the hill on the eastern side of the valley towards Abbeyford Grange standing proudly just below the summit of the hill, sheltered from the cold easterly winds.

She paused at the huge wrought-iron gates leading into the grounds of the Grange and gazed in awe at the black and white mansion, with four gables at the front and one over the porch entrance. The house was built of wood and plaister, reminiscent of the Tudor age, but had been built in the early part of the seventeenth century by the first Earl of Royston.

Sarah turned to look back down into the valley. Her own home looked minute now, almost lost to the eye amongst the row of cottages nestling around the village green.

Directly opposite the Grange about halfway up the western hill stood Abbeyford Manor. It was a square, solid house with stables to one side and farm buildings at the rear, and had been built by the fourth Earl of Royston for his younger son and his bride and completed in 1741, but the young couple had died without heirs. Then, after the Bill of Enclosure, the house had become the home of the Earl's tenant farmer. To young Sarah the Manor was a fine house, but nothing like as grand as Abbeyford Grange.

Robert Elcombe, the sixth Earl of Royston, owned Abbeyford Grange and all the surrounding farmland and woodland upwards of a thousand acres. He owned all the cottages in the village, even the vicarage and the Monk's Arms. His tenant farmer, Sir Matthew Trent, who occupied Abbeyford Manor, now farmed the land, though the earl himself took an active interest in the running of the estate and employed a forester and a gamekeeper to tend the woodland, the game-birds and trout-streams. Only the common waste-land belonged by feudal right to the cottagers—and now it seemed even that was to be taken from them.

But Sarah was not worrying about such things on this most important day. Her mouth curved in a small smile as she surveyed the valley beneath her, her eyes fondly following the twisting paths of the streams, one which ran down the hillside on which she stood, the other running from the

27

north-west corner of the valley and through the common. The lane leading from the village up to the Manor ran through this stream, literally, for there was only a narrow footbridge across the water at this point. Farm carts, or the gentry's carriages, had to splash through the ford in the lane, which in times of heavy rain could become treacherously deep. At the southern end of the valley the two streams joined together and ran as one out of the valley through a natural pass between the hills to join a river some miles away.

Above the Manor and a little to the south, gaunt and black against the skyline stood the abbey ruins on the very top of the hill. Sarah's gaze finished its roving and with a last glance towards the tiny cottage she called home—as if to draw courage from it—she turned her back upon the valley and entered the gates of Abbeyford Grange.

"So you are to be Lady Caroline's personal maid, Sarah Miller?" Mrs Hargreaves, the housekeeper, stood before her.

"Yes'm," Sarah whispered. Mrs Hargreaves's hair was stretched tightly back from her face beneath a white muslin cap with a ruffled frill. Her cold grey eyes bulged slightly and beneath her small mouth her chin sloped sharply inwards so that her overlarge nose dominated the whole of her face. She launched into a seemingly endless list of a personal maid's duties, most of which flowed directly over Sarah's head. The night's excited anticipation was giving way to dread now.

". . . And finally, you will be allowed one half-day off a week and every fourth Sunday." The housekeeper paused and looked keenly into Sarah's pert face. "Servants are not allowed followers. Do you know what that means?"

"Yes'm."

"And don't get above yourself, just because his lordship thinks your idea worked for Lady Caroline. He can't see that it was just a way of trying to better yourself." Mrs Hargreaves thrust her sharp features close to Sarah's face with undisguised malevolence. "It didn't help poor Lady Royston, did it, Miss Clever? You're nothing more than a cowgirl and never will be!"

She straightened and sniffed contemptuously. "But there's no dissuading his lordship. You're here, so you'd better follow me and I'll take you to Lady Caroline."

It was two months since Sarah had come boldly to Abbeyford Grange. Lady Caroline had recovered from the smallpox and, to Lord Royston's mind thanks to Sarah Miller, would be very little scarred. But three weeks after Caroline had first become ill, her mother, Lady Royston, had contracted the smallpox and, despite the attendance of three physicians and the further use of red flannel, on the ninth day of her illness Lady Adeline Royston had died.

Meekly Sarah followed the housekeeper up the back stairs and through a door on the first-floor landing which divided the servants quarters from the rest of the house. Silently now on the thick carpet they walked along the gallery overlooking the main staircase. Heavy chandeliers hung from the ceiling and tapestries lined the walls. In the north wing of the house Mrs Hargreaves paused, rapped sharply on a door and when she was bade, "Come in", opened the door and ushered Sarah into the most beautiful bedroom the girl had ever seen.

Sarah Miller, born and raised in a cottage, had never imagined such luxury even existed. The white plaster ceiling was embossed with figures of cherubs playing various musical instruments, the pink-flowered wallpaper complemented the pale pink flower-sprigged silk of the bed canopy and drapes. The fireplace was marble with embossed decoration picked out again in pink. The chairs and dressing-stool were upholstered in pink silk brocade and the whole effect was utterly feminine and luxurious.

"This is Sarah Miller, Lady Caroline. Your—er— personal maid."

The young woman sat up in bed, yawned, stretched and smiled a little wanly at Sarah. "Thank you, Mrs Hargreaves, that will be all."

"I have explained her duties to her, and . . ."

"Yes, yes," Lady Caroline said a little impatiently.

"Lady Caroline," Mrs Hargreaves said stiffly and, as the door closed behind the rigid figure of the housekeeper, Lady Caroline held out her hands towards Sarah.

"I'm so glad you're here," she told the surprised girl. Closer now, Sarah could see for herself that, though at present Caroline's skin was not as clear and smooth as it had once been, the pock-marks were such that would soon fade and she would bear only one or two scars—easily disguised—on her lovely face.

30

"This is the first time I've been allowed a maid of my very own," Lady Caroline was saying, stretching and running her fingers through her tumbling auburn hair. "Until now my life has been ruled by nannies or governesses. Of course, my mother . . ." Her voice broke a little for the loss of her mother was still very new and painful. ". . . always had her own maid. Do you know it has taken me a whole *year* to persuade Papa to allow me a maid of my very own?"

Sarah smiled. Lady Caroline was only a year or so older than Sarah herself and she was relieved that her attitude towards her maid was, though perhaps a little unconventional, more friendly than Sarah had expected. It helped to lessen the hostility in the housekeeper's eyes.

"Well—you might as well start right away. Did Mrs Hargreaves show you your room?"

"No, m'lady. She b-brought me straight up here."

"Never mind," Caroline waved her hand airily. "Take off your cloak and put it over there."

As she did so, Sarah listened to Lady Caroline's instructions. "I take a bath every morning at eight o'clock. The housemaids bring up the water, but you should be here to see that everything is prepared just as I like it, and all my garments ready for the day. I usually go riding most mornings before I have breakfast at nine-thirty, but recently, since my illness, I've risen later. Papa thinks I am well enough to go out a little now and this afternoon I shall drive over to Lynwood Hall. Lady Lynwood is—was—a dear friend of Mama's and—and I should like to see her." There was a wistfulness in the girl's voice. Then, with a

31

determined effort to be more cheerful, she added, "And yo
shall come with me. After all, you'll be replacing old Rope
as my companion."

"Who—who was old Ropey?" Sarah dared to ask.

"Miss Roper—my governess." Caroline sat down on th
silk-covered stool before the dressing-table, picked up
hairbrush and began to brush the tangles from her lon
hair. "Here, you should be doing this now."

Sarah took the brush her mistress held out to her and wit
trembling fingers began to brush Lady Caroline's hair wit
tentative strokes.

"Harder, Sarah, harder. It must be smooth and shining
One hundred strokes a day, old Ropey used to say."

Sarah obeyed.

"That's better," Lady Caroline murmured and with he
first words of praise Sarah's confidence began to grow.

That afternoon Sarah found herself seated in the gig, bowl
ing along the country lanes, the reins in the confident, expe
hands of Lady Caroline. As they neared the ford in the roa
Sarah's tongue ran round her lips fearfully and she foun
her hands gripping the side of the vehicle. But Lad
Caroline merely gave a sharp slap of the reins, the hors
quickened pace and they splashed through the water safel
Then they were climbing the hill.

"That's the road leading to the Manor." As they reache
a fork in the lane, Lady Caroline pointed to the left. "But w
take the right-hand road to Amberly and then on t
Lynwood Hall." They reached the top of the hill and passe

beneath the trees of the wood. "Have you been this way before, Sarah?"

"Only to Amberly, m'lady. I walked it once with Henry."

"Who—is Henry?"

Remembering Mrs Hargreaves's warning against 'followers' Sarah imagined Lady Caroline's question to hold an ominous note. Swiftly she assured her, "Oh, he's only a distant cousin, m'lady."

Beyond the wood they left the boundary of Lord Royston's lands and entered the Lynwood estate. They passed through the village of Amberly. On either side now Sarah saw fields of waving, golden corn. In one field she could see a line of reapers rhythmically swinging their sickles as they moved slowly forward, the corn falling with each cut. Then other men were loading it on to a waggon, pulled by four huge shire-horses, their harness glinting in the sunlight. Several children followed the reapers and Sarah allowed herself a small smile of satisfaction to think that she was riding beside her mistress instead of bent double in the cornfield.

Skilfully Lady Caroline turned the gig through the gates leading to the parkland of Lynwood Hall and they followed the winding driveway leading to the house itself. Deer, grazing in the meadows on either side, raised their heads to watch the gig rattle past.

Ahead of them Sarah could now see a vast, square mansion of three storeys, the ground floor being set halfway below ground level. A straight balustrade of pinnacles surrounded the flat roof. The smooth lawn before the main entrance was completely encircled by the driveway and, to the side of the house, the ornamental gardens led down to a lake where swans swam upon the water, their white plumage shining in the sun. Fountains played in the gardens, the shimmering water cascading like silver.

"It's even bigger than Abbeyford Grange," Sarah said, forgetting her shyness in her wonder.

Lady Caroline laughed, for the moment her recent suffering and bereavement banished from her mind. "Don't let my Papa hear you compare Abbeyford Grange unfavourably with Lynwood Hall. He and Lord Lynwood used to argue constantly about the relative merits of their estates and houses. But they were the best of friends really," she added, jumping down from the gig as they came to a halt outside the main steps of the Hall. Awkwardly, unused to riding in such a grand manner, Sarah climbed down and followed her mistress.

They were shown into Lady Lynwood's small sitting-room, Sarah hovering uncertainly in her mistress's wake.

Briefly, with a wave of her hand, Lady Caroline dismissed her. "Sarah, go with the footman. He'll take you somewhere you can wait until I'm ready to leave."

"Yes, m'lady." As she turned to follow the liveried footman, Sarah saw Lady Lynwood rise and move forward to greet Caroline.

"My dear Caroline, how wonderful to see you well again!" Lady Lynwood was a handsome woman, with bright, merry eyes and black hair with a single streak of white rising from the centre of her brow and sweeping over

he crown of her head. Her figure was still slim and surprisingly youthful. As Sarah followed the footman, she
passed a young boy of about fourteen hurrying to enter the
room she had just left. He was a good-looking, fair-haired
boy, but he spared not a glance for Sarah.

"Who was that?" she whispered to the footman.

"That was Francis Amberly, Lord Lynwood. He's a bit
partial to Lady Caroline. Very forward for his age, is young
Francis!"

"Is he a 'lord'? He dun't seem old enough for a title."

"Young Francis succeeded to the title three years ago
when his father died. Age has nothing to do with it." The
footman laughed derisively. "You don't know much about
the nobility, do you, miss?"

Sarah coloured and said, hotly defensive, "I am Lady
Caroline's personal maid."

The footman bowed towards her mockingly. "Pleased to
make your acquaintance, ma'am!"

He opened the door leading to the servants' domain and
they clattered down the stairs, the warmth and noise from
the busy kitchens rushing up to envelop them.

"Here's my Lady Caroline's personal maid come to
honour us with a visit," he announced as he ushered her into
the main kitchen. Three pairs of eyes were turned upon her,
but the work did not pause for an instant. The cook continued to beat batter in a large bowl, the kitchen-maid
continued to chop vegetables and the housemaid's duster
never faltered over the spoon she was polishing so vigorously.

35

"Come away in, my dear," the cook smiled kindly. "Take no notice of young William, he's a big tease, ain't he, Martha?"

The housemaid nodded ready agreement. "A sight too ready with his tongue, if you ask me." And she cast a withering glance towards the young footman, but he only laughed, bowed mockingly once more but this time to include all of them and left.

"Sit you down, me dear. What's your name?" the cook continued, still slapping at the batter in her bowl with uninterrupted rhythm.

"Sarah. Sarah Miller."

"You been with Lady Caroline long?"

"This is my first day."

"Is it now?"

"Yes. To tell you the truth," she felt the urge to confide in the friendly cook, "it's all a bit strange."

"Ah well—you'll soon settle in. We've all got to start somewhere." She nodded her head towards the silent kitchen-maid. "I started as a kitchen-maid, like young Annie here. You think yoursel' lucky to have got a job as personal maid already. How old are you?"

"Seventeen. Well—nearly."

"There you are then! Lucky, you are. Annie's a year older 'n you and still a kitchen-maid. A bit slow, she is, but she's willin', aren't you, Annie?"

The girl nodded and smiled, not in the least insulted.

"You work hard and you'll go up in the world, young Sarah, mark my words. And Lady Caroline—she's a lovely girl. Ah, but we was that sorry to hear poor Lady Royston had gone. As I tell Annie here, mebbe we sometimes envy the folks we works for, but for all their riches it don't stop 'em havin' troubles sometimes just like the rest of us, do it now? But you're lucky, an' no mistake, young Sarah."

Yes, thought Sarah, she was lucky, very lucky, but she couldn't help wishing that this kindly body was in charge of the staff at Abbeyford Grange instead of the sour-faced Mrs Hargreaves.

The days passed into weeks and the weeks into months and, once the period of mourning was over for Lady Royston, Sarah began to find out what it was really like to be a 'lady's-maid'. Even when, on her days off, she visited her family, she could hardly wait to climb the hill once more back to Abbeyford Grange.

Her mother revelled in her good fortune, but Joseph Miller said little. Henry would tease her about her lofty position.

"I mun doff my cap when I speak to you soon, young Sarah.".

At first his teasing was good-humoured, but gradually, as her family were subjected on her every visit to her ceaseless recounting of what Lady Caroline said or did, how things were done at the Grange and how her mistress depended upon her so, Henry's words began to take on an unfortunate ring of truth.

"You're getting above yoursel', young Sarah," he told her soberly as he walked her up the lane in the dusk of evening

37

on her return to Abbeyford Grange after a visit home.

Sarah tossed her head. "I'm sure I don't know what you mean, Henry."

"Look," he stopped and took her by the shoulders forcing her to stop and turn to face him. "It's time we got things straight 'atween us. You're seventeen now and I want to speak to your pa about us."

"About us? What d'you mean?" She pretended not to understand him.

He gave her shoulders a little shake. "You know very well, Sarah. Don't play fancy games wi' me. It's time there was an understanding 'atween us. You know I want to marry you . . ."

Sarah's eyes widened and she blurted out. "They don't allow no followers, Henry. You know that."

He gave a little click of exasperation. "They needn't know. They've never said anything about me seeing you back at night on your days off, have they?"

"No," Sarah said doubtfully, "but . . ."

"Well then, they wun't know no more than that. Come on, Sarah, what about it?"

Sarah wriggled to escape his grasp. "I'll think about it, Henry. I'm fond of you, you know that, but . . ."

"But what?" His face darkened with hurt pride. "Not good enough now, aren't I? For Lady Caroline's lady's-maid!"

Sarah was silent. She could not deny that since living at the Grange she had begun to notice the vast difference between her own background and that of Lady Caroline's upbringing.

Sarah's own rough edges were automatically being smoothed by her new environment, so much so that her family's coarse manners, rough ways and poor circumstances grew daily more apparent—and more abhorrent—to her.

"Don't despise your own folk, Sarah," Henry said as a parting shot as he swung open the wrought-iron gate for her to pass through into the grounds of the Grange. " 'Pride goeth 'afore a fall' as Parson's allis tellin' us," he added darkly and swung the gate shut with a heavy clang.

He stood watching her walk up the drive realising that not only the ironwork of the gate physically between them separated their two lives now.

THREE

Sir Matthew Trent leaned back in his leather chair, and, fingertips to fingertips, eyed the red-faced Joseph Miller standing before him.

The difference between them was marked. The 'master' was elegantly dressed in tight-fitting pantaloons, a striped silk waistcoat over which he wore a tailed coat. A silk cravat nestled against his throat and his own hair, still a rich red colour with scarcely a speck of grey, was worn long and tied at the nape of his neck.

In contrast Joseph Miller wore rough knee-breeches, a loose, open-necked shirt and stout, home-made boots. His wiry hair, once black, was now completely grey; his face was weather-beaten and lined by the years of hard work. Whilst the master's hands were pale and smooth with a signet-ring on his fourth finger, Joseph Miller's hands were gnarled and dirty.

But he stood before Sir Matthew with no feeling of inferiority. Joseph Miller was a proud man, despising Sir Matthew for the way he made his living—by the labour of

41

others.

"You've already taken away the land we cultivated, now you're trying to take away our grazing rights on the common waste."

"Not quite, Miller, not quite. The wastes must be enclosed. Each man must pay his share of the legal expenses and enclose his own allotment with fences or hedges and ditches."

"Not one of us villagers could afford to do that," Joseph Miller growled.

Sir Matthew shrugged his shoulders and spread his hands, palms upwards. "That is hardly my concern. Lord Royston is willing to buy out any man who cannot afford to do the necessary . . ."

"You know well enough there's not one amongst us who can," Joseph Miller stormed. "It's just a way to get ownership of *all* the land around here, to say nothing of our homes."

"The war with France has compelled us to increase food production—quickly. Now, be reasonable. This area is excellent for cattle-rearing and I propose to increase the size of my herd considerably. What do you say to becoming my head cowman, Miller?"

"Bribery, is it?" Joseph Miller thundered, forgetting the need for caution. "You take away my livelihood with one hand and offer me work with the other."

"So? I fail to see what is so wrong with that." Sir Matthew, with a supreme effort, retained his patience. "'Tis nothing to be ashamed of to be a good, honest working

42

man."

"What of those men who lose their grazing rights and yet have no work? I canna see you being able to employ all the menfolk of the village."

"Perhaps not, but there is work a-plenty in the cities. The textile trade in Lancashire is undergoing a vast change. Exciting changes, my man . . ."

"These are country-bred folk an' want naught to do wi' cities and manufactories."

"Well then, I'm sorry," Sir Matthew said curtly, his pale blue eyes hard and cold. "There's work to be had if they're enterprising enough. But as for the enclosure of the common land—it will become law very soon and there's nothing you nor I—nor anyone else—can do about it."

"Nor do you want to, I'm thinkin'," Joseph Miller muttered.

Sir Matthew was on his feet, the anger he had purposely held in check overflowing. "I'll see you get no work here-abouts, Miller. I'll not have trouble-makers amongst my employees."

"I'd sooner starve first!"

The two men glared at each other and Sir Matthew said tightly, "Your attitude may well bring you to it, Miller. It may well bring you to it!"

Once more, as his father had before him, Joseph Miller found himself without allies against the enclosure of the common land.

"But 'ee pays good wages, Joseph," Seth Brindley argued.

"Better'n some as I've 'eard tell."

"That's only to get you into his employment, to get you entirely dependent on him. Then what? We'd be no better than those black slaves they bring into Liverpool by the boatload!"

"Well . . ." Seth cast about for some reasoned argument. He liked working for Sir Matthew, knowing that at the end of each week he would have a regular income. The uncertainty of grubbing his own living from meagre strips of land and his own scrawny three or four cows had been replaced by a comforting sense of security. "Well, 'ee seems fair to me," he ended lamely. "'Ee gave me a good price for me cattle."

Joseph brought his fist down upon the scrubbed table. "Mebbe so—now. An' to those whom he offers employment." Joseph leaned towards Seth, who backed away. "What of all those who he don't employ? What's to become of them?"

Seth was silent. He had not the intelligence nor the foresight of Joseph Miller. Amongst the simple country folk, Joseph Miller was something of an individual. Though, like them, he could neither read nor write, his intelligence and logical reasoning far outstripped that of the ordinary labouring man.

Seth—and all his kind—lived for today, but Joseph Miller could visualise tomorrow—and he did not like what he saw!

Autumn gave way to winter and with the harvest over the villagers began to plan for their Christmas celebrations. Every year Sir Matthew held a festive gathering in his huge

44

barn at the back of the Manor for all the villagers—an event anticipated with pleasure by everyone. Even Joseph Miller would put aside his resentment and join the merry-making.

Lady Caroline said, "Sarah, I shall join the villagers' celebrations this year."

Sarah looked up, her action in folding Caroline's undergarments stilled. "Will your Papa allow it, m'lady?" the young girl asked doubtfully. Though Lord Royston doted on his vivacious daughter and spoilt her in many ways, lavishing gifts on her and arranging the life of the Grange around her, Sarah could not believe that he would allow Caroline to mix socially with the workers on his estate.

Lady Caroline shrugged her smooth shoulders and thought for a moment. "I'll ask Guy Trent to escort me."

Sarah thought about the wild young man she frequently saw galloping about the district on his horse, usually at a distance. But only the previous week he had spoken to her for the first time. She had been walking home down the lane from the Grange on her free afternoon when the sound of thudding hooves behind her had made her scurry to the side of the road. Guy Trent had pulled his temperamental chestnut stallion to a standstill, whilst he grinned down at Sarah, who drew further back on to the grass verge away from the restless animal's pawing hooves.

"Good-day, Miss Miller."

Sarah gave a startled gasp, surprised that he should know her name. Then, as if reading her thoughts, he laughed, showing white, even teeth. His red hair was fashionably long and tied at the nape of his neck, but he spurned the

45

wearing of a hat. His blue eyes had twinkled roguishly down at her. He was short and stockily built, but for a man who led the life of an idle gentleman his shoulders were broad and his muscles powerfully developed. She had heard he joined in with the village youths—wrestling, bare-knuckle fighting and other such contests of strength.

"Don't look so frightened. What have they told you about me, eh Sarah? Have they told you what a wicked fellow I am?"

Sarah had taken another step backwards. "Yes—I mean, no, sir."

Guy's laughter had rung out, then his expression had softened. He had steered his mount close to her, reached down and touched her cheek with the tips of his fingers. "Don't be afraid of me, Sarah, I wouldn't want to hurt a pretty little thing like you."

His touch had seemed to burn her cheek and, with a swift intake of breath, she had leapt back yet again. "I mun go," she had muttered and turned to hurry on down the lane, her heart beating alarmingly.

"I'll see you again, lovely Sarah," he had called after her and seconds later she was obliged to step again into the grass at the side of the lane as he galloped past, the panting horse's thudding hooves so close.

As she emerged from the shade of the overhanging trees, at a bend in the road she had seen him leap a hedge into a field and gallop wildly down the steep-sloping meadow towards the stream. Madly he had plunged his mount into the water, splashed through the stream and climbed up

46

the opposite bank. He had pulled on the reins, bringing his horse to a standstill. Then he had swung round and waved to her again.

"We'll meet again, Sarah," he had shouted, his words reaching her faintly on the breeze. She had looked about her anxiously, afraid that someone would hear his wild promise.

When she had looked back at Guy Trent, he was galloping across the common, through the herd of cows grazing there and across the second stream and up the opposite hill towards the Manor.

Remembering her meeting with him brought a faint blush to her cheeks as she recalled too the rumours she had heard about Guy Trent concerning two or three village girls; the warning her father had given her so many times, "You keep away from Master Guy, our Sarah. He's a wild one and no mistake. Don't let him charm you wi' his fancy talk. He's a rogue."

In the next breath Lady Caroline herself confirmed this. "He's a philanderer, of course, but," she sighed, "since I am to be stuck here in the country until the next London season, he's the nearest there is to a suitable escort. And Sir Matthew and Lady Penelope will be there, so perhaps Papa won't object."

At first Lord Royston did object, but Caroline wheedled and coaxed until he relented.

If only he could have foreseen the disastrous consequences which were to follow this one, seemingly innocuous, merry-making event, he would have locked his precious daughter

47

in her pink room and thrown away the key!

Sarah arrived at the barn with her own family. She was wearing the finest dress she had ever possessed—a discarded gown of Caroline's altered to fit the smaller, thinner Sarah. It was a full-skirted pale pink gown with a pleated flounce at the hem and also on the sleeves. The neckline was low with a black velvet bow at the bosom.

Henry Smithson was both admiring and yet suspicious. "You look the right lady now," he said, an edge of sarcasm to his tone.

Sarah laughed and her eyes sparkled, intoxicated by the excitement and the atmosphere. The barn was lit by numerous rush-lights and warmed by the earthy smell of the animals who normally wintered there.

"Come on, Henry, let's dance," Sarah begged, eager to join the red-faced sweating villagers jigging about to the surprisingly tuneful noise issuing forth from the motley selection of instruments which the villagers always managed to produce on these occasions.

Reluctantly he allowed himself to be dragged into the mêlée of the boisterous villagers. Whilst Sarah was light on her feet, a natural dancer, Henry was clumsy, growing red with embarrassment at every faltering step.

"Aw, I ain't no good at this, our Sarah," he puffed, but Sarah merely laughed and continued to skip lightly around him on her toes. Out of the corner of her eye she saw Lady Caroline dancing with Guy Trent and envy flooded through her. They made such a handsome couple, dancing so

48

expertly together that they outshone everyone else.

Lady Caroline's entrance a few moments earlier on Guy's arm had surprised and confused the villagers. They were a little shy of continuing their celebrations in her presence. Guy Trent's arrival did not disturb them, for he was frequently in the company of the young men of the village —and of the young girls too, much to their parents' chagrin! They were all used to the Trents' attendance, but not that of Lord Royston or his daughter. But when they realised that she meant to join in their festivities whole-heartedly, they forgot their shyness and the chasm between their social positions. When the spiced ale had inspired confidence, they ceased to be embarrassed.

Whilst Sarah danced with the clumsy Henry, casting envious glances at her young mistress, Guy Trent led Caroline towards the corner of the barn where his particular friends had gathered.

"No bad language, you fellows," Guy laughed as he presented Caroline to them. "We have a *lady* amongst us."

Caroline shot him a look of annoyance. She did not want to be marked out as someone different. Tonight she wanted to be one of them. She smiled brightly at the four faces before her, all of whom she knew by sight.

There was Joe Robinson, the village smith; Will Briggs, the son of the landlord of the Monk's Arms; Patrick O'Reilly, the forester on the estate, and Thomas Cole, the estate's bailiff and Abbeyford's parish constable. They all rose and greeted her pleasantly and Thomas Cole offered her his place on a bale of hay.

49

"Thank you." She bestowed upon him her most brilliant smile and the quiet Thomas Cole, shy of women, was utterly captivated. He was scarcely taller than Caroline with soft, wavy brown hair and a skin tanned to a pale bronze from being out riding around the estate on his horse in all seasons. He was not a conventionally handsome man, but his face mirrored the kindness and gentleness that was his nature and his smile made deep furrowed creases in his cheeks and around his eyes.

"What a noise!" Caroline laughed and leant towards him. "But they seem to be enjoying themselves enormously."

Thomas Cole's shyness intrigued Caroline. The young men of her acquaintance, of the same social standing as herself, dandies all, were over-confident, superior beings, treating her with an air of charming condescension. Now this quiet, thoughtful man was looking at her with such admiration in his tender eyes that it made her girlish heart turn over. And despite his air of diffidence there was an earthy strength and virility about him that excited her as no other man had ever done.

"I've seen you riding about the estate," she told him, herself feeling an unaccustomed self-consciousness under his steady, bemused gaze. For some reason she could not herself explain, Caroline wanted this man to think well of her.

She need not have worried. Thomas Cole could hardly believe his good fortune to be here talking to this lovely creature, the goddess he had only ever seen before from a remote distance.

50

"Yes, m'lady."

"Oh please call me Caroline—for tonight at least," she added swiftly, lest her bold suggestion that they forego formality would offend his idea of propriety. She patted an empty place at the side of her. "Please tell me about yourself," she asked, Guy Trent quite forgotten as Thomas Cole sat down beside her.

The smile creased his face and Caroline found herself smiling in response—that was what his smile did to people. They just had to smile in return and Lady Caroline at this moment was the very last person to wish to fight against the natural instinct.

"There's not much to tell, really," Thomas Cole began, in his soft, deep voice, and for something to occupy his nervous hands he fished out his pipe from his pocket and began to fill it. Fascinated, Caroline watched his strong fingers packing the brown tobacco into the bowl of the pipe shaped in a fox's head.

"I've never seen a pipe like that before."

He held it out towards her and she took it from him and held it, cradling it in her soft hands. The tangy smell of the tobacco rose to her nostrils, but it was the intricate, perfect carving of the fox's head which intrigued her.

"It's beautiful," she murmured and handed it back to him. As he took it their fingers brushed, the merest touch like a butterfly's wings, but it was enough to make their eyes meet each other's steadfast gaze and to feel the tingling run from the touching fingers through the whole of their bodies.

Thomas was the first to break the spell, as if realising

51

suddenly that he had no right to look at the earl's daughter in such a way. Just because she had come amongst them at Christmas to join in their festivities was no reason to suppose that that closeness could continue once Christmas was over.

But Caroline was feeling acute disappointment as he cleared his throat and looked away from her.

"I was born in Amberly," he was saying. "My father was bailiff on the Lynwood estate and I began work under him."

"You said *was* Lynwood's bailiff?" she prompted softly.

"He died last year."

"I'm sorry," and her tone held genuine sympathy, not merely the utterance of obligatory condolence. "You didn't take over in his place then?"

"No. I was already employed here and well settled. And there was no reason to move back. My mother had died two months before him."

"Oh how dreadful for you!" Caroline said. "To lose both of them in such a short space of time."

She glanced down at her hands lying in her lap. The pain of her own loss was still fresh. She raised her green eyes to look into his gentle ones. "I don't know what I should have done if I'd lost them both—like that—so quickly."

"I think it was my mother's death that caused my father's. They were very devoted to each other and he—well—he seemed to fade away after her death." Thomas clamped the pipe between his teeth and lit it, inhaling deeply on it.

Caroline was thoughtful, trying to understand the bond

52

of love that so tied two people together that the death of one could break the other's will to go on living. In her own society a marriage between two people was usually arranged by their respective parents who believed the match to be 'suitable' either by way of an amalgamation of properties, or a title married to wealth, or for some such mercenary reason. If the marriage partners were fortunate, an affection grew between them later. Occasionally—though rarely—they fell deeply in love with each other and were doubly blessed. That could not be said of her own mother and father, Caroline thought, though she did believe that they had been fond of each other and that a mutual respect and genuine friendship had existed between them. And certainly they had been united in their devotion to her, their only child. But now, as Caroline listened to Thomas Cole's deep voice speaking of the love between his parents, she realised that perhaps her own parents had missed experiencing the dizzy heights of a grand passion and a deep abiding love. Her romantic, girlish heart yearned to experience such a love.

The fact that Guy Trent danced with Sarah Miller four times during the course of the evening whilst only once with any other village girl escaped the notice of the ale-bemused villagers. All, that is, except one. Glowering resentfully, Henry Smithson observed his Sarah dancing so lightly, so expertly, with Guy Trent. There was nothing he could do about it. Guy Trent was the young master and Sarah was not betrothed to Henry. At least, not yet.

But she will be before this year is out, Henry vowed, and since there was scarcely a week of the old year left he would speak to her father the very next day.

Unaware of, or at least determinedly ignoring, Henry's sullen mood, Sarah danced on. Her eyes sparkled and in the flickering lights her white teeth glistened. Her cheeks were pink with the exertion of the dance and with excitement and pleasure. Watching Caroline dance with Guy Trent, Sarah had longed to change places with her, knowing that she too could dance just as well. And now here he was, Guy Trent, the handsome young master, looking at her as if she were the prettiest girl in the barn that night, and his sweet words of flirtation whispering into her willing ear. She was intoxicated by his flattery. It was the first time any man—except Henry and he didn't count being almost a cousin—had paid her such attention.

"Where've they been hiding you, Sarah Miller? You're the prettiest girl in the village. How is it I haven't seen you before a week or so ago when we met in the lane?"

Pertly she smiled and said, "Oh I've been there, Master Guy, but you just haven't noticed me, that's all."

Guy clasped his hands to his heart and threw back his head, giving a mock cry of agony. "Oh, all that wasted time! You were there and I didn't see you! Sarah, my lovely Sarah!"

Gaily Sarah laughed, accepting his madcap compliments lightheartedly, and yet her heart quickened to see the look in his eyes, to feel the pressure of his fingers upon her hand. She tossed her flowing black hair and danced on, swaying,

54

skipping, curtsying, flirting with the handsome young master. And all the time Henry Smithson watched them, the jealousy in his heart festering into hatred.

FOUR

Joseph Miller said, "Aw Henry, she's too young yet to be promised to anyone. She's nobbut a lass. Besides, what have you to offer her, eh?"

Henry's scowl deepened. "You've changed your tune all of a sudden. A bit back you'd have let 'er marry me to stop 'er goin' to the Grange."

"Mebbe so. But you're Trent's man now, aren't you?" Joseph said scathingly.

"Ah—so *that's* it!"

Henry Smithson had been offered—and had accepted much to Joseph's disgust—the job Miller himself had refused, that of head cowman.

"But you're wrong, Joseph Miller, trying to fight the Trents. It's progress. Sir Matthew's building up his herd. One day he'll be famous for his cattle."

"Ach!" Joseph flung out his arm in a gesture of dismissal. "An' it'll be *your* labour that makes him famous—and puts money in his pocket!"

"An' if I'm well paid for it, why not?"

Joseph growled and turned away.

"An' if that is why you wun't let Sarah marry me," Henry shouted after him. "Because I work for the Trents, well, you want to watch out. Young Master Guy has his eye on her."

Joseph spun round and walked back towards Henry, his fists clenched by his sides, menace in every step. Henry faced him fearlessly. He was younger, stronger, fitter than Joseph Miller.

"Just what d'you mean by that?"

"What I says. Didna you see him last night—at the barn? Four times he danced with Sarah. *Four times!*"

"I'll not have you speak her name in the same breath as his," Joseph spat.

Henry shrugged. "Well—I'm warning you. That's all."

"Our Sarah's a good lass. She'd not be led on by 'im."

Henry guffawed. "She's had 'er head turned already by them up at the Grange."

"Mind your tongue, Henry Smithson, when you speak of my Sarah."

"Aw, Joseph. I've no wish to quarrel wi' you. You know how I feel for Sarah."

Joseph's expression softened a little but he was still on the defensive.

"I don't want no harm to come to 'er, that's all," Henry added.

"It won't. I'll see to that."

Henry sighed. Joseph Miller was a stubborn man, he thought, far-seeing in some things, but where his beloved Sarah was concerned he was completely blind!

58

Caroline could not forget the shy Thomas Cole. She was intrigued by him. Starved of any company of her own age and class in Abbeyford, his obvious, yet unspoken, admiration for her was an oasis in the desert of loneliness.

Her early-morning rides, which had for some time been routine, now took her down the hill to the bridge near the smithy, for the cottage beyond the smith and the wheelwright was where Thomas Cole lived. She found that he left home at eight o'clock each morning to begin his day's work. Late by some standards, but as estate bailiff and parish constable he varied his times of work according to the needs of the estate and village.

That first morning he saw her on the bridge seated side-saddle on her horse which pawed the ground restlessly, Thomas could not believe the good fortune that had brought him out of his cottage in time to see her pass. She was wearing an emerald green velvet riding habit, the jacket close-fitting whilst the full skirt fell in soft folds.

With a shock, Thomas realised she was not passing by, she was waiting on the bridge. He hesitated, uncertain what to do.

It could not be for him she waited, surely?

Caroline waved her riding-whip and Thomas Cole was drawn, unresisting, towards her. He raised his hat and bowed.

"Good-morning, Lady Caroline."

"Good-morning, Mr Cole," and then she added in a low whisper, *"Thomas!"*

He felt a jolt somewhere in the region of his heart as she

59

murmured his name with such urgency. Then he heard her merry laugh.

"How formal we are this morning, Mr Cole! 'Twas not so that night at the barn." She leant down from her horse and touched him lightly on the shoulder. "Don't say you have forgotten that night already?"

"Oh no—no, my lady. I shall never, *never* forget that night," he said softly.

Conscious that they were in full view of half the village, Thomas raised his hat again. "I'll bid you a pleasant ride, m'lady," and he made as if to move away.

"Thomas—I—I thought you rode about the estate?"

"That's right, m'lady."

Smiling coquettishly she said, "Then may I ride with you?"

He managed to answer, "Yes—of course," but his mind was in turmoil.

Every moment he spent in her company, he knew himself to be falling more and more in love with her. But where could that possibly lead? It could only end in unhappiness.

Still, he contented himself as he quickly saddled his own horse and joined her once more, a few hours in her company was better than only seeing her from afar.

Unassuming, modest Thomas Cole did not for one moment think that Lady Caroline could fall in love with him!

Every morning for the first two weeks of the New Year, Caroline rode away from the Grange, down the hill to the bridge to meet Thomas Cole. Together they rode around the estate for an hour or so and with each day that passed Thomas's love for Caroline deepened. But still he could not believe she cared for him.

'She's lonely', he told himself. 'She just wants a companion on her rides.'

But he was wrong. Caroline decided that she loved Thomas Cole.

Soon one meeting a day was not enough. She began to take another ride in the afternoon around the hillsides and fields of Abbeyford searching for Thomas as he went about his duties as Sir Matthew Trent's estate bailiff.

And then—the snow came!

If Lady Caroline did all the running in the love-affair between herself and Thomas Cole, then the opposite was true in the case of Guy Trent and Sarah Miller. After the night of the celebrations in the barn at the Manor, she did not see him for over two weeks. Not that there were many times when he had chance to see her for she had very little freedom and, when she did visit her family in the village, suddenly Henry, or her father, seemed to be keeping a close watch upon her.

"You keep away from Master Guy," her father had warned, worried by the doubts Henry's words had put into his mind. "He's no good. He's got two young lasses from the village into trouble already."

Sarah gasped. "Pa! How can you say such a thing? You don't know."

"Don't I, me girl? Why's Nell Potter and Meggie Owen

disappeared all of a sudden then?"

"Well," Sarah floundered, trying to find some explanation, some excuse. "Mebbe they've gone into service—away from the village. Not all of 'em are as lucky as me to find work close by," she reminded him artfully.

"Huh!" her father scoffed. "Aye, that's the tale their families tell. But I knows different, see. You just do as I say, me girl, an' keep away from him. You attend to your work an' if you wants a young man you need look no further than young Henry."

Sarah tossed her head. "Anyway, I don't know why you think Guy Trent would ever look at the likes of me." But even as she spoke the words she could not prevent the hope stealing into her mind that he would indeed look at the likes of her. She remembered, indeed clung to the memory of, the look in his eyes when he had danced with her.

Only two weeks into the New Year the snow came, falling steadily through a day and a night. Joseph Miller and Henry were out with the other men of the village rescuing the in-lamb ewes from the snowdrifts and bringing all the animals down to the buildings at the rear of the Manor.

Even Joseph Miller put aside his resentment against Sir Matthew when it came to rescuing animals.

On her half-day off, in the dusk of the winter afternoon, Guy Trent waited for Sarah beneath the snow-laden trees bordering the lane leading to the Grange.

Sarah trudged through the deep snow on her return to the Grange, her clog-encased little feet leaving deep gullies in the snow, her skirts soon sodden and clinging to her legs.

She bent her head against the cold and concentrated on keeping to her feet.

She gave a cry of fright as she came up against something solid and looked up to find herself gazing into the laughing face of Guy Trent.

"Did I startle you, lovely Sarah?"

She gasped from the fright and from the cold, her breath like a puff of steam from her lips. "Yes—yes you did."

He took her hand in his and tucked her arm through his own. "Come, there's a sheltered spot under the trees where we can—talk."

Sarah made a half-hearted attempt to pull away. "No—I must be getting back, I'll be in trouble if I'm late."

"Just five minutes, Sarah," he pleaded. "Besides, you can't be expected to hurry through all this snow, now can you?" he added, reasonably enough.

Sarah allowed him to lead her to a shady spot under the trees, half of her wanting to stop and talk to him, the other half afraid of the consequences if her pa should find out.

"I've thought about you all the time since that night in the barn at Christmas."

She gave a nervous laugh. "That you haven't, Master Guy!"

"Indeed I have, lovely Sarah. I've been trying to see you. I've watched for you every week, but always your father or Henry Smithson has been with you." He frowned. "What is young Smithson to you, Sarah? Are you betrothed to him?"

"No—no," she shook her head quickly. "He's my cousin

—sort of."

"Good." Guy was smiling again. "Then you're not promised to anyone?"

"Me?" she laughed and blushed. "Of course not."

"Why 'of course not'? I'm surprised half the village lads aren't pounding on your door, lovely Sarah."

Her blush deepened every time he called her 'lovely Sarah'. Was he mocking her, or did he, could he, really mean it?

"I mun go." Now she did pull her hand away, but he caught her again.

"Meet me again, Sarah, please!" he begged urgently.

"I canna—I mustn't. I don't know how I could," she added, weakening.

"Of course you can. Before you go home, come to the abbey ruins. The snow may have gone by next week. Look, I'll be waiting for you in the ruins midday every Wednesday."

"No, no, I canna." She pulled herself free of his grasp and floundered away from him through the snow.

"I'll be waiting, lovely Sarah," he called after her.

I can't go, I mustn't go, she told herself fiercely, but with the sound of his voice ringing in her ears calling her 'lovely Sarah' she knew she would go!

FIVE

"Oh—this wretched snow! Will it never go?" moaned Caroline, restlessly pacing up and down in front of the long windows of the morning-room. "Just look at it!"

For a whole week she had been unable to go riding— unable to meet Thomas. She had grown irritable, feeling a prisoner, trapped by the bad weather.

Then she stopped and peered out of the window. "Goodness—whatever is this coming? Why, it's Lynwood!" She clapped her hands in delight. "Oh do look, Papa, he's driving a sledge pulled by two ponies. Oh, how clever of him!"

She whirled around, picked up her skirts and ran from the room. "Tell him to wait for me . . ."

The young Lord Lynwood was shown into the morning-room. Lord Royston greeted him warmly. "Why, Lynwood, how good to see you!" His eyes twinkled merrily. "My daughter instructs me to ask you to wait for her. I think she rather fancies a ride in your—er—new mode of transport."

Lynwood laughed. "That's why I came—I was rather hoping she might."

Lady Caroline appeared dressed in a dark blue velvet coat and holding a warm fur muff. Perched upon her head was a hat with three fluttering plumes.

"Good-morning, Caroline." Lynwood's blue eyes were full of devotion. "I came to see if you would care to come skating. Our lake is completely frozen over."

"Oh Francis—I'd love it!" she cried, but Lord Royston frowned.

"Are you sure it's safe, Lynwood? The ice is not always as thick as it seems."

"Yes, my lord. I've already tried it out."

"Very well then. But take care."

Minutes later they were in the sledge.

"Francis—this is wonderful," Caroline laughed as the sharp air stung her face bringing a rosy glow to her cheeks. "How clever you are to think of such a scheme! I have not been out of the Grange for over a week and I've been so *bored*!"

They flew across the snow, the sure-footed ponies never faltering. As they passed by the village, Caroline scanned the snow-covered fields, but to her disappointment there was no sign of Thomas.

As Lynwood had said, the lake in front of Lynwood Hall was frozen over.

"I'll have to hold on to you, Francis," Caroline said, as Lynwood bent to tie on her skates for her. "I remember skating here once—but I was only eight or nine. Your poor papa took me on to the ice."

Lynwood stood up, his face sober.

Caroline squeezed his arm. "I know how you must miss him, for I miss my dear mama. But come, let's not think such morbid thoughts today. You must teach me to skate. Show me first what I should do."

Lynwood stepped on to the ice and skated steadily around in a circle, then he returned to Caroline and held out his hands. "Take hold of my hands."

Caroline giggled and stepped on to the ice. It was a peculiar sensation, feeling not quite in control of her feet. She clung on to Lynwood whilst he pulled her round the ice.

"Now you try sliding each foot forward—that's it."

"Oh Francis—this is fun!"

Young Lynwood slipped his arm about her waist to guide her, for, although he was four years her junior, already he was half a head taller than Caroline.

"Oh, oh I'm falling," she cried and clutched at him.

"I've got you—you're all right."

It was one of the happiest afternoons Lynwood could remember. He had Caroline all to himself. She laughed and talked with him as her equal, clinging to his arm for support.

As the bright winter day faded into gloom, Lynwood took her into the Hall for a glass of hot punch before taking her back to the Grange in his sledge.

"Thank you, Francis. It was sweet of you to take me skating."

Lynwood smiled and gallantly raised her fingers to his lips.

67

As he watched her go into the Grange, he thought that in four or five years' time when he came to manhood the difference in their ages would not seem so great.

Lynwood returned home with a secret hope locked within his heart.

The snow was slow to clear and Sarah passed the week following her meeting with Guy in the lane in a ferment of indecision. She wanted the snow to melt away so that she could go to the abbey ruins to meet him and yet she half-wished that more snow would fall so heavily that she could not possibly get there!

But by the following Wednesday most of the snow had gone. Frozen patches still blotched the fields but the way to the abbey ruins was clear.

A little after midday Sarah left Abbeyford Grange but instead of taking her usual way home down the lane she ran down the slope in front of the big house and crossed the stream by a footbridge. Skirting the village she walked through the meadow and joined the lane leading out of the village up towards the Manor. She came to the ford in the road and to the narrow footbridge, the only means by which a traveller on foot might cross the water. The stream was swollen with melting snow and the wooden boards of the bridge were only just visible above the water and every few moments the water lapped right over them. Sarah swallowed and glanced about her fearfully. There was no one about, no one who had seen her come this far. She looked up towards the abbey ruins standing black and gaunt and lonely against the lowering sky. Was he there? Was Guy waiting for her? Or was she making a complete fool of herself?

She bit her lip and stepped gingerly on to the bridge. Holding tightly on to the handrail she picked her way carefully across, but the water splashed against her boots and caught the hem of her skirt. Again she looked about her and, seeing no one, she bent her head and hurried up the lane towards the Manor, but instead of turning into the stable-yard she scurried past, on up the hill and into the wood. Here beneath the shadow of the trees Sarah breathed more easily. But there was still the open space between the wood and the abbey ruins to cross. At the edge of the wood she paused. If she ran across the space to the ruins she was clearly visible from the valley though, at this distance, scarcely recognisable. If she walked a little further to the right, she thought, she would not be so easily seen for, although the land did not actually slope away on this side but continued in an undulating plateau until it dropped again into the village of Amberly, at least she would be out of sight of the village. And on this side were the Lynwood lands, so anyone in these fields seeing her would not be interested.

Picking up her skirts and drawing a deep breath she ran from the edge of the wood in a wide arc and eventually came into the abbey ruins from the opposite side to that overlooking Abbeyford. Breathless she leant against the crumbling walls, drawing the cold air into her lungs in huge gasps. As long as her pa or Henry hadn't seen her!

She peered into the ruins and shivered. The wind howled around the broken-down walls, moaning like the ghosts of long ago, and Sarah, fanciful and superstitious, would have turned and run away if she had not seen Guy Trent's chestnut horse tethered by the far wall.

Her heart gave a leap. He was here. He was waiting for her. Then she saw him, standing on one of the low walls, looking out over Abbeyford, watching for her.

She drew her cloak around her and stepped into the ruins, over the ground littered with stones and boulders. He heard her crunching step and turned round. Seeing her, he grinned, leapt down from the wall and ran towards her.

"You came!" he said placing his hands upon her shoulders and smiling down into her dark, fearful eyes.

"Yes," she whispered. "But I shouldn't have."

"Oh Sarah, who's to know?"

"I canna get away so easily. Me ma will be expecting me."

"Say you were delayed."

"But what if anyone saw me coming up here?"

"They didn't—did they?"

"Not that I know of, but . . ."

"Lovely Sarah, don't frown so." He smoothed her forehead with his fingers, as if to brush away her worries. "Come—over here. It's warmer."

He drew her into a small, cell-like room, the only one left whole in the ruins, with only a narrow window, high up, and the doorway to let in any light.

Sarah swallowed her apprehension as she saw that there

70

were dried rushes upon the floor. Guy must have prepared this place for her—for them.

"Here—sit down, Sarah." He spread his own cloak over the rushes and as she sat down he dropped down beside her. He put his arm about shoulders and pulled her to him. "There, that's warmer, isn't it?"

She nodded. She was where she wanted to be—with Guy. Yet she could not still the fear, the knowledge, that she was doing wrong. She was afraid of what he might do. But Guy just sat with his arm about her shoulders, holding her close for warmth, making no attempt to kiss her, just talking to her, so that gradually she began to relax against him.

"Do you like it up at the Grange? Are they good to you?"

"Oh yes," Sarah told him eagerly. "Lady Caroline's lovely. He's nice, his lordship, but a bit severe, an' I don't see much of him anyway."

Guy sighed. "What a pity it's not my mother you work for, then I could see a good deal more of you." He gave her shoulders a squeeze and again Sarah felt that peculiar thrill run through her—half fear, half delight.

"I should be going," she murmured, but she made no effort to move.

"Not yet." Guy's face was close to hers in the half-light of the tiny room.

Time passed more quickly than she realised in his company and, when next she thought about leaving, she looked towards the slit of a window and saw to her horror that it was already growing dusk.

She scrambled to her feet. "Oh it's late. I'll be missed. I'll

71

be in trouble."

Guy too got up. "Sarah, Sarah, don't run away."

"I must, I must!" Wildly she pulled away from his reaching hands and squeezed out of the doorway and began to stumble across the rubble-strewn ground.

"Sarah! Sarah!" He caught up with her and grasped at her arm. "When will you come again?"

"I don't know, I don't know!" she cried, unable to think clearly, the only thought in her head being to get home before it grew dark, before her pa and Henry came home. Henry would come to their house tonight straight from his work, knowing it was her half-day off.

As she hurried out of the ruins and began to run across the intervening space towards the wood, completely forgetting this time to hide herself from the valley, she heard him call.

"Next week, Sarah. Please!"

Sarah hurried on, her head bent against the blustering wind which now blew flecks of snow against her, stinging her cheeks and catching her breath.

Through the wood and down the lane past the Manor. She hurried towards the footbridge and then stopped in dismay. The water now completely covered the planking of the footbridge. In that short time the water had risen that last vital inch or so and now covered the wooden boards of the bridge. Panic rose in her throat and her knees began to tremble. She was trapped on the wrong side of the stream and it was already growing dark. This was the only way across the stream into the village.

It couldn't be so very deep, she tried to reason. She

glanced back up the lane. If only someone would come along with a cart, she could beg a lift through the ford. But now, when she wanted someone to appear, the lane was still empty.

Sarah bit her lip and glanced at the threatening sky; the flecks of snow had turned to rain now and it was coming faster. Soon there would be even more volume added to the already swollen stream. Sarah took a resolute breath and picked up her skirts almost to her knees and stepped into the water. She gasped as it swirled above her ankle-boots and clutched icy fingers at her legs. She reached for the handrail and breathed a sigh of relief as she felt its roughness beneath her fingers. Slowly she inched her way along, feeling with each foot for the hidden boards beneath. She was about halfway across and thinking she was going to make it when her foot slipped and almost before she realised she had fallen she was floundering in the freezing stream, gasping for breath. The stream bowled her over and over, bruising her arms and legs, and a stone cut her chin. She spluttered and gulped and then, feeling the bottom, she managed to stand upright. It wasn't as deep as she had feared, only to her thighs, but the shock of falling into the cold water and the unusual swiftness of the flow of the stream had made her think she was in more danger than she actually was.

Sobbing, she dragged herself out of the water, her clothes clinging to her in a sodden mass. She squelched the rest of the way home and fell thankfully through the door into the warmth of the cottage kitchen.

Her mother, lifting bread from the brick oven, threw up

73

her hands in horror.

"Oh my dear child! Whatever's happened? I thought you weren't coming today, it bein' so late now. Where have you been?" She hurried towards the shivering Sarah and drew her towards the fire. "Here, strip these clothes off an' I'll get you a blanket. You'll catch your death, else."

"No, Ma, I canna. Pa an' Henry . . ."

"Never mind them. They can stay out till you're finished. I'll not have you catch cold, me girl."

Soon Sarah was sitting with a rough blanket wrapped around her, whilst her mother rubbed her wet hair. Guiltily Sarah accepted her mother's ministrations.

"What happened?" her mother asked again, towelling her dry with skin-reddening briskness.

"I—I fell in the stream. The water's over the bridge."

Her mother stopped her rubbing and stared at her in amazement. "What, Smithy's Bridge?" Mrs Miller referred to the stone bridge near the smithy.

"No—no."

"I didna think it could be. Why, if that were under water then the whole village'd be flooded!" She thought for a moment then added. "You weren't daft enough to come by the field bridge—the one behind the village?"

"Well—yes, I did. But it weren't that one."

"Well then?"

"The—the footbridge—near the ford."

"Lord, girl! What were you doin' near that un? It dunna take much to put that un under water—you *know* that!" she added scathingly to a girl born and bred in Abbeyford.

74

Miserably Sarah nodded.

"What were you doin' that way, anyway?"

Sarah took a deep breath. "I—er—had to take a message to—to the Manor."

"Huh!" Mrs Miller resumed her vigorous rubbing. "'Tain't right. Askin' a young girl to go traipsin' round the countryside in weather like this. I've a mind to . . ."

"No, Ma, please!" Sarah cried, frightened that her lie would lead her into deeper trouble. "Dunna say nothing—please."

"Well," said her mother doubtfully, "I don't want to do anything to make you lose that good job you've got, but still . . ."

"Please, Ma," Sarah begged.

"Very well, then, but I dunna know what your pa will say." Sarah was silent. She too was worried what her pa would say!

Joseph Miller had plenty to say—but not what his wife had expected.

"She's lying!" he exploded, thumping the table with his fist, whilst Sarah jumped physically and her mother gasped in astonishment. "Joseph . . .!"

"I tell you, she's lying. They wouldn't send a young maid on such an errand. They've footmen and stable-boys for that. Just where did you go, girl?" he demanded, leaning towards her menacingly.

"I—I told you," Sarah stammered.

Beth said slyly, "I reckon I saw Master Guy Trent riding

75

across the brow of the hill towards the abbey ruins this afternoon."

That was all she needed to say for the colour that swept into Sarah's face gave her away.

"You little bitch!" Jospeh Miller spat and raised his hand to strike her across the face, but his wife stepped between them.

"Joseph, I will not have such language in this house. And don't strike the girl till you know the truth." She rounded on Beth. "And you, miss, I know your vicious tongue. As for you . . ." She whipped round to Sarah now and grasped her by her long black hair. "We'll have the truth now. Well?"

When Sarah did not answer at once, her mother pulled her hair hard. "Answer me, girl."

"Yes—yes—*yes*!" The admission was torn from her and then she sank to the floor in a sobbing heap.

Her mother stood over her, her lips pursed, whilst Joseph growled, "There, I knew it!" and Beth merely smiled, maliciously satisfied. In her corner, Ella, the youngest sister, crooned softly to her doll oblivious of the drama taking place in front of her uncomprehending eyes.

"You're a little fool, Sarah. You'll not meet him again. You promise me now? He's no good, d'you hear me?"

Still sobbing, Sarah nodded.

Mrs Miller turned towards her husband, taking charge of the situation now. "You or Henry will meet her each week from the Grange and see her back." She glanced down at her eldest daughter, then looked at her husband. "Say no more about it now. I reckon she's learnt her lesson."

She stepped over Sarah and began laying the table for supper, but Joseph's face still scowled.

He was not so sure his wayward daughter would obey.

SIX

When the snow cleared, Lady Caroline resumed her own
secret meetings—with Thomas Cole. Soon all the village
were aware of the growing attachment between them. Only
Lord Royston remained in ignorance. The villagers shook
their heads over the matter, foreseeing only tragedy at such
an unsuitable liaison.

"Someone should tell his lordship!" was the general
opinion. But who? Who would dare to tell the Earl of
Royston that his beloved only daughter was keeping
company with his tenant farmer's bailiff?

Caroline played a meticulous game of hide and seek.
Seeking out Thomas whilst at the same time hiding from her
father, who himself frequently rode about the estate offering
advide to Sir Matthew, or giving orders to his own gamekeeper.

Always she had an excuse ready in case she should be
questioned. She made frequent visits to Lynwood Hall in the
hope of being able to meet Thomas on the way back. But this
ploy was often thwarted for Lynwood would escort her home

and spoil her plans.

At one time she had enjoyed basking in Lynwood's obvious adoration of her. Now she found his devotion irksome. His insistence on accompanying her prevented her from seeing Thomas!

"There's really no need for you to come all the way back to the Grange with me, Francis. I am quite able to take care of myself."

"We still get vagabonds and paupers along the roads— even in Abbeyford and Amberly," Lynwood told her seriously.

Caroline laughed rather cruelly. "And if we were set upon—just what do you think *you* could do? You're only a boy!"

She slapped her riding-crop against her horse's flanks and galloped ahead of him, into the woods above Abbeyford.

She could not have hurt young Lynwood more if she had plunged a knife into his heart!

He reined in and sat watching her gallop away from him, her wide skirt billowing, her long auburn hair flying free.

As she disappeared amongst the trees, he turned his horse around and returned home, the secret hope in his heart shattered.

Caroline found a further excuse for riding down into Abbeyford with the arrival in the village of her cousin, Martha.

Martha was indeed 'the poor relation'. She was the daughter of Caroline's mother's sister and so the connection with the Earl of Royston was rather distant. But that did not prevent Martha feeling resentful that her cousin Caroline should be a lady of quality whilst she herself was a mere curate's wife. Lord Royston had been prevailed upon by his late wife's sister to offer the living at Abbeyford to her son-in-law, the Reverend Hugh Langley.

So the recently married Langleys had moved into Abbeyford Vicarage.

"It's a lovely house, Martha." Caroline viewed the rooms critically.

Martha sniffed, folding her hands in front of her. "It will no doubt be cold and draughty. These huge vicarages always are."

"Oh come now, my dear," Hugh remonstrated gently. "Pray don't let your cousin think us ungrateful." He turned his pale eyes on Caroline. "I am indebted to your father. I never thought to gain such a living so soon."

"It's no more than you deserve, Hugh," Martha snapped. "Why must you always belittle yourself so?"

Hugh Langley was a mild, gentle, rather fussy little man. At thirty he already stooped slightly from the long hours he had spent poring over his books, studying hard. His mousy-coloured hair was thinning and his face was pale from lack of sunshine and fresh air.

Hesitantly he said, "There was just one more thing—er—I was wondering if there are any boys locally who might benefit from—well—private tuition?"

Caroline wrinkled her brow thoughtfully. "Guy Trent's a little old now." She laughed. "And he's scarcely the studious type anyway. There is Francis, Lord Lynwood.

81

He's about fourteen."

"No doubt they'll already have some arrangement for his education," put in the pessimistic Martha.

"His father's dead, but I'll ask Lady Lynwood the next time I see her."

"Thank you—thank you," Hugh said fussily, almost bowing towards Lady Caroline, but Martha merely pursed her already thin lips.

"As a matter of fact, that's an excellent idea, Caroline," Lady Lynwood beamed. "I have been looking for a tutor for Francis. I must confess, Caroline, that although I should send him away to school I fear I am far too selfish to rob myself of his company. Your cousin's husband sounds admirably suitable."

Caroline laughed. "Oh, Mr Langley is the typical 'professor' type. Very muddly over everyday living and completely dominated by my cousin, Martha." Caroline wrinkled her nose a little. "She's a bit of a shrew, but I believe he's really quite clever academically."

"Good—good. Ah Francis, there you are," Lady Lynwood greeted her young son as he sidled into the room, his blue eyes intent upon Caroline.

Caroline smiled at him. "Good-day, Francis."

"Lady Caroline," he murmured and listened politely whilst his mother said, "Caroline has found you a tutor. The new vicar at Abbeyford is her cousin's husband."

Francis nodded, but his gaze did not divert from Caroline's face. Though he still looked upon her with adoration, now there was a haunted, hurt expression deep within his eyes. The fact that it was Caroline who had found a tutor for him was yet a further reminder of the difference in their ages. He was still regarded as a schoolboy, whilst she was out of the classroom, an adult young lady.

Lady Lynwood, sensitive to her son's feelings for Caroline, was immediately aware of the subtle change in him. She could see in an instant that in some way Caroline had hurt her son.

Caroline stood up. "I must be going. There's a meet of the hunt next week, I believe, now the snow has gone. Will you be following in your carriage as usual, Lady Lynwood?"

The older woman nodded. "Most definitely. Francis is to be bloodied. I mustn't miss that."

"Neither must I." Caroline turned to the boy. "I'll be sure to watch out for you," she told him and the colour rose faintly in his cheeks and the pain in his eyes lessened a little.

Lady Lynwood sighed within herself. There was nothing she could do to help him, but she wished that her son were not so easily affected by Caroline's volatile moods. One kind word from her could make him happy, one cruel word could make him miserable.

Lynwood accompanied Caroline to the front door and down the steps. He watched her mount her horse and canter away down the drive.

Behind him he heard two of the stable-lads sniggering together. Then clearly their conversation drifted to his ears.

"My Lady Caroline off to meet her lover. Master Thomas Cole aims high!"

Lynwood turned, rage flooding through him. He couldn't understand the full meaning of their words because he knew nothing of her affair with the bailiff. But he recognised by the inflection in their voices that they were insulting Caroline.

Without hesitation, Lynwood launched himself towards the two boys, fists flying. Caught unawares, one fell beneath his blows, his nose bloodied. The other received a blow beneath the ribs which doubled him up and he sank to his knees.

"You are dismissed from my employ and will be off the Lynwood estate by nightfall!"

Breathing hard, Lynwood turned and marched back into the house. The two boys, nursing their injuries, stared after him in amazement.

"What did us do? What did us *say*?" they asked each other.

Caroline rode away from Lynwood Hall, back through Amberly towards Abbeyford. But once in the wooded shade at the top of the hill she left the track leading through the wood to Abbeyford, turning in the opposite direction from the abbey ruins. She followed a rough footpath as far as possible and then slid from her horse's back and tethered him to a tree. Delicately lifting her skirt she ran lightly down a steep narrow path, twisting and turning through the trees until she came to a waterfall bubbling down a steep rock face into a deep pool and then tumbling on down the hillside until it became the stream which meandered through

Abbeyford valley.

Caroline sat down upon a rock, watching the waterfall. With all the recent snow added to its normal flow, it was fast-flowing and the pool deeper than ever. Caroline shivered and drew her cloak around her and hoped Thomas would soon join her.

They met in different places around Abbeyford. Sometimes here at the waterfall. Sometimes in the abbey ruins. Sometimes they each rode out of Abbeyford, well away from the prying eyes of the villagers, meeting in the fields and lanes, in tiny copses or derelict shepherds' huts.

She heard a rustle on the pathway and jumped up to meet him as Thomas appeared through the trees. She ran towards him flinging her arms around him with passionate abandon.

"Thomas, oh Thomas. It seems an age since I saw you and yet it was only yesterday. Kiss me!" She clung to him, winding her arms around his neck.

Never ceasing to wonder why this adorable creature should imagine herself in love with him, Thomas held her close, kissing her tenderly and then finding himself responding ardently to her feverish desire.

"Thomas, oh my Thomas! If only we could be together for always," she murmured.

Thomas smiled gently but a little sadly. He could not believe that her love for him would last. He told himself that loneliness had driven her to seek him out, that once the London season began again he would be swiftly forgotten. He loved her, he knew, but he could not believe that there would be a future for them together.

Caroline was determined that it should be otherwise.

"Thomas, listen!" She took his hand and led him to the rock. Together they sat down side by side. "I've been thinking. We cannot go on like this."

There, he knew it! And although he had always told himself it would end he could not stop the swift, painful stab in his heart.

"I think I should tell my father that—that we love each other."

Fear washed over him. "Caroline, my love—no!"

Caroline's eyes widened. "Why ever not? Thomas—you do love me, don't you?"

"Oh my darling." He reached out and touched her cheek wonderingly, adoringly. "You'll never know how much."

"And you do want to marry me, don't you?"

The turmoil of emotions showed upon his face. Torn between the exquisite longing to make her his wife and the knowledge that it was impossible. His voice was a hoarse whisper. "Caroline—it can never be."

"Why ever not?" she demanded fiercely, her pretty mouth pouting as it did when she was about to be thwarted in something she wanted. She jumped angrily to her feet. "You're making excuses. You don't want to marry me. You—you don't love me! You're—you're just playing with my affections!"

Thomas rose to his feet, holding out his arms pleadingly towards her. It was the first time he had seen her angry and it frightened his gentle, loving nature. "Caroline—you know that is not true. You know I love you more than life itself, but your father . . ."

Caroline flung herself against him again. "Oh Thomas, I'm sorry." She covered his face with kisses. "Forgive me. Don't let us quarrel, I can't bear it if we quarrel. I know you mean to protect me. But he will have to know sometime."

Thomas sighed. He knew what would happen. Caroline would be confined to her home and he would be dismissed and sent away from Abbeyford. He voiced none of these fears to her. She could not see that her father would deny her anything, but Thomas knew that Lord Royston, despite his indulgence towards his daughter, would never countenance this liaison. His anger would fall upon his daughter as never before, though she could not realise it.

"I must go." Reluctantly she withdrew from the shelter of his fond embrace. "Till tomorrow, my love. We'll meet in the abbey ruins tomorrow—the same time."

Once more she kissed him, pressing her young body to him, causing Thomas's head to reel and driving all sensible thoughts from his mind.

"Till tomorrow," she whispered, turned away and ran up the path.

Thomas waited for some minutes before he too left the shelter of the glade and returned to Abbeyford by a round-about route.

The hunt met in the stable-yard at Abbeyford Manor.

Lady Lynwood, with Caroline beside her, watched from her open carriage.

It was a fine sight—the scarlet coats and high top-hats of

the huntsmen, the horses groomed to shining perfection. The hounds, which were kennelled at the Manor, were fine brown and white dogs, strong and eager for the chase to begin, their tails held high, their pink tongues lolling.

"There's Francis! Oh doesn't he look splendid?" Caroline waved eagerly to the young boy, who was seated, straight-backed, on his mount. "You must be very proud of your son, Lady Lynwood. I'm sure he'll break a few hearts when he grows up."

Lady Lynwood laughed—a delicious cackling sound, quite unladylike but infectious to anyone hearing it. She patted Caroline's hand. "'Tis a pity he's not older for I know he admires you greatly."

Caroline laughed too. "He'll be a fine man one day and she'll be a lucky girl who catches him, but I'm afraid I can't wait that long."

Her eyes strayed to where Thomas Cole sat astride his horse. How elegant he looked, how solemn and so aware of the privilege he had been given in being allowed to join the hunt which was, after all, made up mainly of wealthy landowners or their respected tenant farmers! For Thomas Cole to be one of their number was an unusual compliment to the man.

Lynwood, ever acutely aware of Caroline's nearness, saw her watching Thomas Cole. Young though he was, because of his own feelings for her Lynwood easily recognised the expression of love upon her face as she watched Thomas Cole.

Lynwood frowned. So, he thought bitterly, the stable-boys' gossip had not been without foundation.

The cry went up, "They're moving off!" and then the horses and hounds moved out of the yard, watched by the half-dozen or more grooms and stable-lads who looked after Sir Matthew's horses and the hounds belonging to the hunt.

Down the lane they cantered and into the fields, the hounds streaming out ahead of the huntsmen, trying to pick up the scent of a fox.

Guy Trent, reckless as ever, galloped ahead, to the annoyance of his father, but young Lynwood, though this was his first meet, had been well-schooled in the etiquette of the hunting field and stayed well to the back. He rode well and easily, but his mind was not on the chase. Before him was the picture of Caroline's face when she looked at Thomas Cole!

Over hedges and ditches the horses flew, through the two streams and up the hill, the hounds spreading out. Suddenly there was a shrill barking and the dogs streaked forward. The hunting-horn sounded and they were off up the hill past Abbeyford Grange and over the brow.

Lady Lynwood flicked her reins and the carriage moved forward. "We'll follow at a more sedate pace, my dear," she said.

Sarah Miller saw the hunt pass the Grange. Leaning out of a second-floor window, she saw Guy Trent, his head down, his body pressed close to his horse, galloping like a mad thing after the baying hounds. She watched him, admiring his daring but at the same time fearing for his safety because she loved him. She saw them all pass by and reach the top of the hill above the Grange and then they were gone out of sight, only the sounds of the dogs and the drumming hoofbeats were left, growing fainter and fainter.

She leaned her face against the cool casement of the window. Yes—she loved Guy Trent. But what a hopeless, foolish love it was!

Guy Trent, eager to secure the brush as his trophy, rode, knife in hand, amongst the hounds as they closed upon the fox, after a long and gruelling chase.

"Damn the boy!" Sir Matthew muttered. "Has he no sense? He'll cripple my best hounds."

Lynwood, though he would dearly have loved to secure the brush to present to Caroline, held back.

As Guy triumphantly held aloft the severed tail, his father beckoned him. Extricating himself from the excited, barking dogs was not without hazard and Guy felt more than one nip on his legs. But his prize of the day justified a little discomfort.

Sir Matthew held out his hand towards his son.

Guy's face darkened. "The brush is mine, sir."

"I think not. As Master I have the right to bestow it upon whosoever I choose in the field."

Father and son glared at each other; Sir Matthew with his hand still extended waited.

With a growl of annoyance, Guy almost flung the brush at his father and turned away. He mounted his horse and galloped—hot-headed as ever—away from the field.

90

"Here, my boy," Sir Matthew turned towards Lynwood. "This is yours. You have carried yourself well today. Your father would have been proud of you—very proud."

The boy smiled and accepted the brush.

Lady Lynwood and Caroline caught up with the hunt just after the kill, in time to see young Francis initiated. They watched as Sir Matthew passed the bloody head of the decapitated fox across the boy's forehead and down each cheek, the brilliant red blood stark against the paleness of the boy's skin. He stood erect, proud, almost haughty, making not a sound.

Lady Lynwood smiled with pride at her son as he re-mounted his horse and rode over to her carriage. How mature he looked today, far older than his fourteen years!

"Well done, my son, well done!" She reached over and squeezed his hand.

Caroline smiled at the boy. "Indeed, Francis, you are a credit to us all."

Shyly he held out the brush to Caroline. "I—would like you to have this."

"Why, Francis, how sweet of you to give me your very first trophy!"

She took the brush and smiled at him. She could see his adoration for her in his eyes. "Why, Francis, you're quite the gallant."

Lady Lynwood looked on but said nothing. Her son's feeling for Caroline was a fragile, vulnerable thing and young Lynwood could be so easily hurt—desperately hurt —if Caroline were to ridicule his devotion to her.

Fond though she was of the daughter of her dear friends, Lady Lynwood was sensible enough to see the selfish, even ruthless, streak in Caroline's nature and knew the girl would always want her own way and care little for the feelings of others who might try to thwart her desires!

SEVEN

Winter gave way to Spring reluctantly, but at last the days grew warmer and Nature's life-cycle began again. As the trees blossomed so did the love between Guy Trent and Sarah Miller. Perhaps it was because it was a forbidden love that it made their stolen moments all the more precious, the excitement of furtive meetings, the danger of further discovery fuelling their passion for each other.

For several weeks after Joseph Miller had found out that Sarah was meeting Guy, she had no opportunity of seeing him, for every week on her days off either Joseph or Henry would meet her from the Grange, escort her home and accompany her up the lane again in the evening.

She knew Guy was trying to reach her. Twice, as she returned to Abbeyford Grange, her father striding along at the side of her, she heard the soft whinnying of a horse hidden amongst the trees which bordered the lane. She felt her father's eyes upon her, but he said nothing and she, head down, walked on in silence, but her heart was leaping wildly within her, her legs trembling at the thought of Guy's

93

closeness.

As the days lengthened, work on the estate increased—and the fences began to go up on the common waste-land. Jospeh Miller watched with resentful eyes.

"I mun sell my cows an' sheep, Ellen," he told his wife, hardly able to keep the savagery he felt inside from showing in his tone.

"Oh no, Joseph!" Her eyes were wide with fear.

He shrugged. "We've still got your spinning and perhaps . . ."

"Joseph—there's—there's something I've been meaning to tell you, but—but—I hadn't got around to it." Her fingers plucked nervously at her apron.

He had never seen his wife act this way before, as if she were afraid of him. Gently he took her by the shoulders. "Why, Ellen, what is it, wife? Aw, I know I've been difficult of late—it's the Trents . . ." With an effort he swallowed his own anger and spoke tenderly to his wife. Tears welled up in her eyes. His Ellen, who never wept whatever harsh blows life inflicted upon her!

Joseph was shocked.

He gave her a gentle little shake. "Come, tell me what ails you?"

"It's the spinning work, Joseph. There's a new man been round. A Mister Lewis. He—he says they're installing some new-fangled machinery in the factory an' cutting down on the cottagers in this district doin' the work. He said it's—un—uneconomical—yes, that was the word he used."

Joseph's fingers tightened on her shoulders and his eyes

94

flashed with renewed indignation. "An' its a sight more 'uneconomical' for us! Him an' his fancy words! Dun't he know he's robbin' us of our livelihood? Just how much are they cutting down?"

"Well . . ." Ellen hesitated and avoided meeting his gaze, then she whispered. "Next month'll be the last he brings any."

"You mean he's stopping all of it?"

Ellen nodded. "Joseph—I'm sorry."

"Aw Ellen, it's not your fault. But—what are we to do?"

Ellen, always the family's will of iron, its rock, was for once lost.

Joseph loosed his grip on her shoulders, turned away and sat down heavily in the chair at the side of the hearth. "I'll have to look for work away from Abbeyford. I canna get work here. Not now. Trent as good as told me." Bitterly, his mouth tight, he added, "I shouldn't be surprised if Trent hasn't had a hand in this other business an' all."

"Oh Joseph, surely not. Why, Mr Lewis is naught to do with the Trents."

Joseph shrugged. "Aye, but them 'n all their kind are in league agen us and Trent as good as threatened me with it!"

"Joseph—what are we to do?" Ellen whispered.

"As long as he dunna turn us out of our home, I can find work."

"There's Sarah's money. She's very good, Joseph, she only keeps a penny or two for hersel'."

Joseph's face was grim. He still did not like to be reminded of Sarah's employment at the Grange, but for the moment it was all they had to live on.

The next morning—very early—found Joseph trudging up the hill out of the valley in the hope of finding work away from Abbeyford. He would not be able to meet Sarah on her half-days off, he thought, as every step took him further and further away from his family. Henry too would be too busy now that Sir Matthew was increasing the size of his herd, but Jospeh comforted himself with the belief that with the lapse of time since she had last seen Guy Trent he would have forgotten all about little Sarah Miller and found himself fresh amusement.

Joseph was wrong. The very fact that Sarah was being kept from him only served to make Guy want her more. If he had but understood the nature of Guy Trent, Joseph's action was the very one to inflame the young man's interest. Had he left things as they were, perhaps Guy's ardour would have quickly waned. As it was, her elusiveness was a challenge—a challenge the madcap Guy could not resist.

Sarah skipped down the lane from Abbeyford Grange on her own for the first time in weeks.

She gave a little cry of fright as she heard a rustle amongst the trees and saw the stealthy figure of a man. Then, as he emerged into the lane, happiness flooded through her. It was Guy! He held out his arms to her and without a moment's hesitation she ran into his embrace.

"Sarah, oh Sarah. They shouldn't have kept you from me. They shouldn't have!" he murmured with a rare insight into his own character.

"Oh Guy, I missed you so," Sarah whispered, completely

without guile or affection. He was raining kisses on her face, on her smooth brow, her eyelids, her soft, rosy cheeks and her delicious mouth. She clung to him, yielding herself to him.

"Where can we go?" he murmured against her mouth. "How can we meet? I can't go on living without you."

Breathless, Sarah said, "They'll come with me whenever they can. I don't know why one of them isn't here today." Almost fearful that either Joseph or Henry might suddenly appear, she glanced over her shoulder.

"Can you slip out—at night—from the Grange?" Guy asked urgently. "I could be waiting—anytime—anywhere."

"I don't—know. I could try," she said eagerly. "The servants all go to bed about ten o'clock. Sometimes Lady Caroline wants me later, but—not often."

"Can you get out without being seen?" Tenderly he stroked her black hair away from her forehead, looking down into her upturned face.

"I'll try, oh I'll try," she breathed.

"Tonight. Behind the stables at the side of the Grange. I'll be waiting," he told her. Reluctantly he let her go, watching her hurry away down the lane towards the village.

"See what your precious Guy Trent and his father have done to us now?" Beth was the first to meet Sarah with the news of the recent disaster which had overtaken the Miller family. "We'll be out on the street next!"

Sarah did not answer. Nothing—but nothing—could dim the glow in her heart at the thought of meeting Guy that

97

very night.

That night and many nights following, Sarah crept from her warm bed, out into the dark night and into the arms of her lover.

Towards the end of April the maypole was set up on the village green and on the evening of the last day of April an excited, laughing party of village youths and girls set off for the wood at the top of the hill to gather green branches and spring flowers to weave into garlands to decorate their homes and the maypole. Mayday was a day of celebration in the village. It marked the beginning of summer for the country folk, of warmer days, of new life and growth.

Among the revellers were Sarah Miller and Henry Smithson. Henry was in a particularly jovial mood. Tonight and for the whole of the next day he and Sarah could be together and by the end of that time, he vowed, he would have made her promise to marry him.

The woods soon echoed with laughter, with squeals and furtive giggles as the young men stole kisses from their sweethearts. Many a new courtship began at Mayday and resulted in marriage before the year was out.

Henry slipped his arm around Sarah's waist and felt her stiffen.

"Oh, come on, our Sarah. No one can see us here. Just a little. kiss!"

Roughly he pulled her towards him and planted his wet mouth upon her unwilling lips. She struggled against him, but Henry held her fast. She twisted her face away, but still his arms held her. She felt guilty, and disloyal to Guy, whom she loved, and yet there was guilt too in her secret affair with Guy Trent. Beside him Henry was rough and uncouth, yet he was sensitive enough to feel her revulsion. His arms locked about her more fiercely and his dark eyes searched her face in the shadowy half-light. "We'll be married, Sarah, 'afore this year is out."

Angrily, Sarah replied, "That we won't, Henry Smithson!"

"And I say we *will*!" He made as if to kiss her again, but with one desperate push against him she fought herself free and ran from him, dodging between the trees, losing herself in the shadows.

"Sarah! Sarah! Come back!" Angrily Henry crashed his way through the undergrowth in search of her, but Sarah, hiding behind a bush, breathed a sigh of relief. He was going in the opposite direction.

A hand closed over her arm and Sarah gave a cry of fright, but turning she found herself looking into the laughing blue eyes of Guy Trent.

"Guy, oh Guy," she breathed his name in a whisper of thankfulness and laid her head against his chest. His arms were about her, his lips against her dark hair.

"Let's escape from them," he murmured.

Hand in hand they slipped through the shadows, amongst the trees to where Guy had tethered his horse.

"Tonight, you are mine and mine alone," he told her as he lifted her on to the horse and swung himself up behind her. In the moonlight they trotted out of the wood away from Abbeyford.

"Guy, where are you taking me?" Sarah gasped. "I must get back soon, or else I'll be missed. Henry . . ."

Guy only laughed aloud and spurred his horse to a canter, his arm tightly around Sarah's waist.

"Oh lovely Sarah—we should run away, you and I, and never come back."

Some distance away from Abbeyford, high on a hillside near a derelict shepherd's hut, Guy pulled up and dismounted. He held up his arms to Sarah and she slid into them. Then, without warning, he picked her up in his arms and carried her towards the hut.

Inside it was surprisingly warm. Once more she made one feeble effort for reason, but his lips were upon hers silencing her protest. "Sarah, oh Sarah. Be mine, Sarah, be mine!"

His hands caressed her until, shivering with delight, she allowed him to unfasten her dress.

Reverently his eyes roamed over her nakedness bathed in soft moonlight.

"Oh you're lovely, lovely Sarah! I knew you would be."

Her own hands ran through his hair, pulling his head down towards her and together they lay down. The tumbledown shack became their palace, the rough, makeshift bed their bower of love.

Softly she moaned his name like a prayer. "Guy, oh Guy, my love."

Willingly, lovingly, foolishly careless of the consequences, Sarah gave herself to him.

As the dawn crept palely into the shack, Sarah stirred and then sat bolt upright, terror-stricken. Beside her Guy lay sprawled in sleep, his arm flung carelessly across her.

"Guy—wake up!" She shook him and then fumbled to dress herself, to cover her nakedness—in the stark light of early morning sanity—her shame!

She began to sob and her fingers shook so that she could scarcely fasten the buttons of her dress.

"Oh what will they say? What will I do? Pa'll kill me!"

"Sarah?" Guy sat up, rubbing his eyes.

"Guy—Guy, take me back. No—you mustn't. Oh—I don't know what to do . . ." Her teeth were chattering with cold and fear.

"Sarah, Sarah, my love." His hands held hers, warming her. "Don't be afraid. I love you, Sarah."

Still weeping, she shook her head muttering, "I shouldn't have, oh I shouldn't have . . ."

"Sarah, look at me." He cupped her chin and turned her face towards his. Her eyes, brimming with tears, met his steady gaze. "I love you. I'll not let them harm you. I'll take you back to the Grange."

"But I'm supposed to be at home—for Mayday."

Guy sighed. "Oh," he said heavily. He thought for a moment. "Couldn't you say you got separated from the others and—and went back to the Grange?"

Miserably she shook her head. "From where we were—in the woods—it's further to the Grange than—than home."

"But do your parents know exactly where you were?"

"Henry did."

101

"Well—I still think you'd better say you've been at the Grange all night."

"They'll not believe me," she whispered.

They did not believe her. Later that afternoon, her knees trembling and her mouth dry, Sarah lifted the latch and let herself into the cottage.

Already the green was buzzing with the village folk on their days' freedom from work. The bright ribbons on the maypole fluttered gaily in the breeze. Laughter and jollity filled the air.

But in the tiny cottage Joseph Miller, home for the day's holiday, and his wife waited, grim-faced, for their daughter.

"Where were you last night?" Joseph demanded.

Sarah squared her shoulders and stuck to the story she had planned. "At the Grange." And added with an outward show of defiant haughtiness, "Where else should I be?"

Joseph Miller and his wife exchanged a glance. "How did you get back there? And why? I thought you were comin' home for the night?"

Sarah shrugged, but inwardly her stomach churned. "Lady Caroline needed me first thing this morning. I prepared her bath as usual and laid out her clothes. Ask her—if you don't believe me."

Joseph made a sudden movement towards her as if to strike her but his wife's restraining hand was upon his arm.

"Wait. Sarah—is that the truth now? Were you at Abbeyford Grange last night?"

"I told you—I had to go back to help Lady Caroline."

102

It was the truth—but not the whole truth. She had indeed returned to the Grange. Guy had taken her there, leaving her behind the stables. A fresh shiver of fear ran through her as she remembered how she had hidden there, waiting her moment to slip into the house, hiding again in the wash-house and then running stealthily through the main kitchen when the cook went into the pantry and the kitchen-maid bent over the range. Up the back stairs she had raced to the sanctuary of her own room, her heart thumping, her knees trembling. After a few moments to calm herself, she had changed her dress, splashed her face with cold water, tidied her hair and emerged as if she had spent the night in her room. She was fortunate none of the numerous servants had seen her return and lucky too to be back in time to appear at the usual hour to attend her mistress.

Now, holding her breath, she watched her parents look at each other. Joseph sighed and raised his shoulders in a weary shrug.

Mrs Miller's eyes were upon her daughter. "Well then, we'll say na' more about it. You'd better go 'n join Henry. He's waitin'. He was worried to death last night. You'd better apologise to 'im."

Sarah tossed her head, her confidence returning now that her story seemed to be believed. "Huh! It's him that needs to apologise. His behaviour last night wasn't exactly perfect!"

Joseph started up again, "What d'you mean . . .?"

But Sarah had gone, flinging open the cottage door and crashing it to behind her.

103

Ellen Miller sighed. "What's to become of her I don't know."

"I'm beginning to think perhaps Henry's right. She'd be better married to him—and soon!" Joseph growled.

Henry was sullen and Mayday quite spoilt for them both.

"Why did you run off, Sarah?" he asked.

"You *know* why, Henry Smithson," she said scornfully. "We're not promised. You'd no right . . ."

He grasped her wrist. "I've *every* right!"

"Let go—you're hurting me!"

"It's time you came to your senses. You can't have 'im, you know. He'll not *marry* you."

"I—I don't know what you're talking about."

Henry nodded grimly. "I reckon you do. He's just amusing hissel'."

Angrily Sarah twisted herself free. "You dun't know anything about it, Henry Smithson, so hold your tongue!"

Sourly Henry watched her go.

EIGHT

Although there was no one amongst the village labourers who would dare tell Lord Royston of his daughter's secret meetings with Thomas Cole—and they had all known for some time—there was one person who was not afraid, indeed was gleeful to have the opportunity for personal spite against her envied cousin.

Word of Caroline's affair had come to the ears of Martha Langley!

Two days after Mayday Martha Langley walked up the lane towards Abbeyford Grange, determination in every stride.

She stood before Lord Royston in his book-lined library, her hands folded in front of her, her lips pursed to their customary thinness.

"I thought you should know, my lord, I thought it my duty to tell you—for her own sake—that Caroline is meeting frequently with the Trents' bailiff, Thomas Cole. Far too often for it to be a mere casual acquaintanceship."

Lord Royston glared at her, but, not in the least deterred,

Martha stared back at him.

Lord Royston prided himself on being a good judge of character. He had never liked Martha Langley or her mother, his late wife's sister. Early on in their marriage he had detected the jealousy in Martha's mother, who had been unable to make as good a marriage as her sister. That jealousy had been bred into Martha and she directed it at her wealthier, more beautiful cousin, Caroline. Nevertheless her malicious gossip was disturbing. He was also uncomfortably aware of the wilful nature, the strength of character, of his own daughter and had known that when she grew to womanhood he would have to find the right suitor for her quickly lest she choose for herself someone entirely unsuitable. Without his wife to guide him he had failed to realise that at nineteen his daughter was already a woman grown.

He had left it too late!

With a growl of anger, directed not only against himself for his tardiness but against Martha Langley for being the bearer of such ill news, he said grudgingly, "Yes—I should be told." But he could not bring himself to express words of thanks to her!

Lord Royston decided his best approach was not to confront his daughter about her meetings with Thomas Cole, not even to let her know that he knew of them. Instead he would whisk her away to London, give her a generous allowance to spend freely on all the things women loved: new clothes, jewellery—anything she wanted.

The season did not end until the beginning of June—time enough left for a busy round of routs, balls and parties to obliterate all fanciful thoughts of Thomas Cole. Indeed there might even be some eligible viscount ready to offer his hand, if Lord Royston let it be known in society circles that Caroline was the sole heiress to his estate.

He would prise her away from Thomas Cole without her realising what was happening.

But Lord Royston had misjudged the strength of his daughter's will and miscalculated the extent to which the affair had already gone. By pretending no knowledge of it, he allowed Caroline to believe herself undiscovered.

She agreed quite readily to go to London, even though being parted from Thomas for even a short while caused her pain. She anticipated a few weeks in society happily, ignorant of the scheming which lay behind the proposal. She did not even suspect when she found herself accompanied wherever she went, either by her father himself or by one of his servants appointed to accompany her, so that clandestine meetings with Thomas became imposssible. She thought it coincidence and her only worry was that she was obliged to leave for London without having seen him, without having had chance to explain the reasons why she had not met him recently.

In desperation she had taken Sarah into her confidence. Her maid had listened wide-eyed whilst Caroline had pressed a letter into her hand.

"Now listen carefully, Sarah. This afternoon is your half-day off, is it not?"

The girl had nodded.

"Good. Then I want you to deliver this note to Thomas Cole, who lives in the cottage next to the wheelwright. You know where I mean, don't you?"

Again Sarah had nodded, dumb with amazement that Lady Caroline should be sending letters to an estate worker. Perhaps, she thought, her mind clinging to any excuse, it is a letter about estate matters, but Caroline herself dispelled this illusion with her next words.

"You must not let this letter fall into anyone else's hands. You understand? No one must even know about it, let alone see it."

"Yes, m'lady."

But Caroline's plans were thwarted, not, this time, by her own father, but by Sarah's father who met her from the Grange and accompanied her back there the same evening. Sarah dared not deliver the letter in her father's presence. In his present ever-suspicious mood he would be sure to question her closely.

Sarah was almost in tears the following morning as, with trembling fingers, she held out the letter to her mistress.

"I couldna take it, m'lady. Me pa was with me all the time."

Caroline snatched the letter from her and snapped, "Oh you useless girl! Get out of my sight! Can you not even deliver a letter for me? I've a good mind not to take you to London with me!"

Sarah crept from the room. It was the first time Lady Caroline had spoken so sharply to her.

So Caroline had to leave Abbeyford without having been able to send Thomas any explanation, but she was sure he would be there, still waiting for her when she returned to Abbeyford.

Thomas Cole, when he heard of her departure, sadly thought she had grown tired of him, as he had believed she would eventually. Though he had warned himself to expect it, her sudden seeming rejection of him cut deeply, wounded him and tore away his happiness.

Thomas Cole began to think of leaving Abbeyford, of seeking a new life in America, as far away from Caroline as he could get!

Caroline did not carry out her threat to leave her maid behind, though Sarah almost wished she had. Once she would have been excited by the visit to the big city, but now, now she had met Guy and she could not bear to leave him. Miserably she imagined that as soon as she was away from him Guy would swiftly forget her and amuse himself with another village girl. Or worse, he would marry one of his own kind and be lost to her for ever!

It was quite an entourage that set out for London, for Lord Royston, whilst accompanying his daughter himself, felt the need of advice and help from his dear friend, Lady Lynwood, and he had prevailed upon her to go with them.

"I have to take you into my confidence, my dear Elizabeth. Caroline is consorting with my estate's bailiff!" Lord Royston marched the length of Lady Lynwood's morning-room whilst she watched him from her sofa. As he turned

109

to walk back towards her, she nodded and said, "I didn't know, but I cannot say that I am surprised. I noticed on the day of the hunt that her eyes continually sought out a young man who was unknown to me. I wondered then—partly because of my own son's reactions. He is excessively fond of Caroline, you know."

Lord Royston agreed. "'Tis a great pity he is not a little older—I would have willingly arranged a marriage between them. Of course," he shrugged, "four years is no age difference to speak of, once Francis reaches maturity. But, Elizabeth, I dare not wait that long. Caroline is a wilful, headstrong girl and I—I fear the consequences of further delay. Already it seems I have waited too long."

"So what do you propose to do?"

"Take her to London. There are still some six weeks of the season left."

"And you hope that in that time she will forget this bailiff?"

"I'm convinced she will. Once amongst her own kind, she will see her own folly. Here she has no company of her own class of her own age. Elizabeth—will you come with us? Please? I ask you as an old and valued friend. Now Adeline is gone—I . . ." He passed his hand wearily across his forehead. "I hardly know what to do for the best."

Lady Lynwood smiled. "Think no more of it, Robert. We shall leave for London as soon as we can be ready. And Francis shall come too. Although he is still a trifle young for society life, he looks older than his years and perhaps if he were to have the chance to see other delectable young ladies

110

in society, maybe it would help him to overcome his obsession with Caroline. Perhaps we can help both our children at the same time."

Lord Royston looked at her in surprise. "I had realised he was extremely fond of Caroline, but is it really so deep?"

Soberly Lady Lynwood nodded. "I fear so, Robert. I am afraid his feelings for her are much too deep for his own good." A wistfulness came into her eyes. "And, if he is anything like his father, then those emotions will be difficult to change. It will take an exceptional girl to make him forget Caroline!"

Lord Royston turned away, a little embarrassed. He knew a little of his old friend's romantic love-affair with Elizabeth—how he had married her against his parents' wishes, who had objected to her birth and background. Yet their marriage had been superbly happy and Elizabeth had proved herself to be far more of a 'lady' than many born to that position. He had pondered on the wisdom of confiding in her—knowing of her own story—and yet there was no one else to whom he could turn.

So they set out for London in three carriages—Lady Lynwood, Lord Royston, Caroline and Francis in one, their servants in a second and the third was piled high with their trunks and boxes.

Sarah Miller found the city life totally different from anything she could have imagined.

The roads, as they neared London, were thronged with coaches and carriages and riders on horseback. The country girl who had never even visited a large town, let alone a city,

111

was appalled by the narrow crowded streets, the bustle and noise, the cries of the street-merchants, the dirty ragged urchins begging for money, or picking pockets when they could.

She shuddered and longed for the tranquillity of the country. She grew pale and wan and was physically sick with longing to return to the familiar surroundings—and people—of Abbeyford valley.

She was afraid of the servants at Lord Royston's town house in London. They ridiculed her strange way of talking —though to Sarah their speech was just as peculiar. They laughed at her coarse dress and heavy clogs.

But Lady Caroline blossomed in the different environment, though she too, in her innermost heart, longed to return to Abbeyford and to Thomas—and she was determined that before very long she would do so!

It took Sarah some time to become accustomed to the new and strange routine. Lady Caroline now rose very late in the morning. After a light breakfast she would make social calls with Lady Lynwood or visit the dressmakers and milliners. Dinner was in the early evening and then she would dance until the early hours of the following day.

The weeks passed during which, young though he was, Lynwood accompanied his mother and Lady Caroline to many of the functions and he was obliged to stand and watch with envious eyes whilst Caroline danced and flirted with every dandy in sight. One Viscount Grosmore paid her particular attention and soon he was Caroline's constant escort.

One evening, when attending a very important ball where many influential people would be present, Caroline decided to follow the daring new fashion which was all the rage in revolutionary France. She instructed Sarah to dress her hair very simply in the style of Ancient Greece, with curls at the back of her head held in place with a ribbon.

As she laid out the new gown only delivered from the dressmaker that morning, Sarah gasped in horror. It was a straight gown, girdled just below the bosom, but what shocked the country girl was the low-cut of the neckline, the short, puffed sleeves and the transparency of the material. After being accustomed to the full-skirted heavy silk ball-gowns Lady Caroline had worn until this moment, Sarah held up the diaphanous garment in perplexity.

"M'lady, has there been some mistake? Is—is this an under-garment?"

Caroline turned from the mirror. "No—you silly goose. *This* is the petticoat." Caroline giggled and her eyes held mischief. "I want you to dampen it slightly for me, Sarah, just the skirt part."

Sarah's violet eyes were still puzzled. "Whatever for, m'lady?"

"You'll see. Just do as I say."

By the time Caroline was dressed, Sarah was even more shocked and by now really anxious. "Oh m'lady, I don't think your papa will—will approve."

The dampened petticoat clung to Caroline's body, emphasising her shapeliness, barely concealed by the transparent gown over it.

113

Caroline tossed her head and her eyes glinted. "*He* brought me to London. He must want me to involve myself with society and all its ways," she said defiantly and added, "If he doesn't like it, then perhaps we shall return to Abbeyford all the sooner."

Sarah watched her go, her long cloak covering the daring gown. Perhaps, Sarah thought shrewdly, it was Caroline's way of getting what she wanted. Sighing, Sarah began folding all her mistress's discarded clothing and tidying the bedroom. She would then snatch a few hours sleep before she would have to awake in readiness for Caroline's return.

But Sarah was awakened suddenly by the early return of her mistress who fell on to her bed, her face buried in the pillow, her whole body shaking.

Caroline had concealed her gown from Lady Lynwood, her father and Francis until their arrival at the ball. As she removed her cloak in the room set aside for the ladies, she heard Lady Lynwood's gasp and turned to see her staring almost open-mouthed at Caroline's gown.

"My dear—whatever is that?"

"Why, Lady Lynwood, this is the latest fashion. Don't tell me you have not observed that this is what all the ladies of fashion are wearing. Why, only last evening . . ."

Lady Lynwood felt the laughter bubbling up inside her. The little minx! she thought, but could not help being more amused than angry at the girl's daring. It was so like the sort of thing she herself would have done at the same age, she had to admit.

114

With a great effort Lady Lynwood retained a straight face; indeed for the sake of her dear friend, Lord Royston, she attempted to adopt an expression of severe displeasure. "I doubt your father will appreciate your—er—devotion to fashion, my dear. I think it would be wisest if you were to return to the house and put on something a little less—er—revealing."

"I shall do no such thing," Caroline retorted and she repeated the words she had spoken to Sarah. "Since it was Papa's idea for me to come to London—I'm sure he must want me to participate fully in the ways of society." She slanted her green eyes, full of mischievous cunning, at Lady Lynwood, but this time she added nothing about returning home to Abbeyford. Without waiting for any reply, Caroline left the room and made a grand entrance into the ballroom.

Her arrival caused little stir amongst those who did not know her family well, but Lord Royston and those of his acquaintance were appalled by her appearance.

Lady Lynwood, entering a moment after Caroline, saw Lord Royston marching purposefully across the room towards his daughter.

Young Lynwood watched, his eyes unfathomable depths.

"What is the meaning of this, Caroline?" her father thundered, quite oblivious to the whispers and mocking smiles of those nearby.

Caroline turned innocent eyes upon her father. "Why, Papa, 'tis the latest rage, have you not noticed . . .?"

"How dare you appear in such—unseemly attire? Leave at once, do you hear me?"

115

"My Lord Royston, pray forgive my intrusion . . ." Lord Grosmore began, but Lord Royston turned on him in fury.

"This is no concern of yours, Grosmore, you'll oblige me . . ."

"I was about to offer my carriage to convey Lady Caroline —and of course my Lady Lynwood—home, where she may change and return . . ."

"We have our own carriage, Grosmore," he muttered gruffly, "and my daughter will most certainly not return here tonight—nor for that matter any other night. We shall be returning to the country."

"Oh my Lord Royston," Lord Grosmore bowed ingratiatingly, "I had no wish to offend you. Pray believe me . . .?"

Lord Royston dismissed him with a wave of his hand, took hold of his daughter by the elbow and propelled her from the ballroom. Lady Lynwood and her son followed.

So it was that Lady Caroline arrived home in a great flurry to be found on her bed by Sarah.

The girl touched her mistress lightly on the shoulder. "Oh, m'lady."

Caroline rolled over on to her back and Sarah was astounded to see that she was rocking with laughter!

"It worked—oh Sarah, it worked! We are to return to Abbeyford tomorrow!"

Sarah wept with relief.

"Sarah—what has happened to you, child? Are you ill?" Ellen Miller spread her arms wide and enfolded her

116

daughter to her bosom. Then she held her back at arm's length and looked critically into her face.

"No, Ma—well . . . I dun't like the city, Ma." Tears welled in her eyes. "I were that homesick."

"Well, dun't fret no more. You're home now. Beth—welcome your sister home. Let her warm hersel' by the fire."

Beth moved forward reluctantly. "Wish I'd been given the chance to go to London. You dun't know how lucky you are, our Sarah."

Huddling near the fire, cold and shivering after the days of travelling over rough and dangerous roads, Sarah didn't feel at all lucky. She was thankful to be home, back in Abbeyford, back with her family. And soon—she might see Guy!

Somewhere in the pit of her stomach she felt a fluttery feeling of excitement at the thought of seeing him again.

"We'll soon have you rosy-cheeked 'n blooming again, our Sarah," Ellen Miller smiled. "Dun't you fret."

On the same day that Sarah returned from London, late at night a weary Joseph Miller walked down the hill from Amberly towards Abbeyford village. He paused on the footbridge near the ford.

Clearly in the moonlight he could see the lines of fencing criss-crossing the common land.

Without giving conscious thought to what he meant to do, he walked slowly towards where the fencing started. He stood a moment, just looking at it. Then he pushed at one of the posts. Newly erected, the post moved in the soft earth

117

and almost before he had realised what he was doing Joseph had pulled up the post and flung it away as far as he could. He moved on to the next upright and began to pull at that too.

Anger and resentment gave him strength and soon much of the new fencing lay scattered on the ground. He uprooted the young saplings which had been planted at intervals along the fencing and with his heavy boot he crushed the young roots.

Breathing hard, Joseph stood in the bright moonlight and surveyed the havoc he had wrought single-handed. Never in his life before had he committed an act of destruction on something that was now someone else's property. But his rage against Sir Matthew for robbing him of his rights on the waste-land, and now too his anger against Guy for turning Sarah's head, had temporarily robbed him of his sanity.

Joseph Miller retraced his steps across the footbridge and returned up the hill out of Abbeyford.

He did not want to be in the village when the damage was discovered the following morning.

"Have you any idea who could have done it?" Sir Matthew demanded of Thomas Cole who had brought him the news of the destruction of the fencing.

"No, sir."

"Hmm." Sir Matthew grunted and added brusquely, "Find out where Miller was last night."

"Joseph Miller?" Thomas's surprise showed in his voice. "I don't think he would commit such a crime, Sir Matthew."

"He harbours resentment against the enclosure of the common land."

"Yes—I know, but . . ."

"Don't argue, man. Do as I say!"

Thomas Cole, as parish constable as well as bailiff, made enquiries throughout the village, but all he could learn was that Joseph Miller had been away from Abbeyford to find work and had not been home on the night the damage had been done.

Sir Matthew received the news with scepticism. "Well, on this occasion we can prove nothing, but I still think it was Miller. There's no one else who would dare!"

A week later Joseph returned home and feigned surprise when Ellen told him of the damage done to the new fences.

"Mr Cole came askin' about you, Joseph, but I told him as how you was away seeking work."

"Aye, you did right," was all Joseph would say.

The fences were repaired and more saplings planted and this time they were not touched!

The days passed after Caroline returned from London and still she had no chance of meeting Thomas. Always there seemed to be someone near, someone watching her every move. Late one night, when she believed everyone at the Grange to be asleep, Caroline slipped from her warm bed and dressed. She stole along the moonlit landings. The shadowy portraits of her ancestors seemed to look down upon her with disapproval.

Out of the side door, Caroline made her way to the stables where, with much tugging and heaving, she managed to saddle her horse. She was accustomed to having such menial tasks done for her. Nor did it occur to Lady Caroline to *walk* to the village to see Thomas!

Leaving her horse tethered near the stone bridge, her heart beating fast, she hurried past the smithy and the wheelwright's cottage. The cottage next to that had a soft light shining out from the ill-fitting curtains.

Caroline crept forward and to her relief saw Thomas seated at the table, bending forward as if he were writing something, his brown wavy hair almost touching the lighted candle on the table. Her heart turned over at the sight of him. She knocked on the door and when it opened she flung herself against him, almost knocking him over.

"Thomas, Thomas! How I've missed you. My father sent me to London and I couldn't get word to you, couldn't see you. Oh I was so afraid you would think the worst . . ."

"Caroline, Caroline." Gently he eased himself from her clinging arms and closed the door.

"Oh Thomas, it wasn't my fault. You must believe me. Say you believe me? Say you still love me, as I love you, darling Thomas?"

Wistfully, Thomas hushed her near-hysteria. "My dearest Caroline, I still love you. I shall always love you. But," he sighed, "these weeks have shown me that—that our love can never be."

"Why?" she cried passionately.

120

"My darling, your father must have heard something about our meetings. If not everything, then enough to make him suspicious. Enough to make him take you away from Abbeyford for a time."

Caroline gasped. "You really think so?"

"Yes, my love, I do. You must realise that he—he will never allow anything to—to come of it."

Defiantly Caroline tossed her head. "Then we must run away. For I declare I won't marry Lord Grosmore. He's a conceited dandy and I hate him!"

Already Thomas had heard the village gossip concerning Grosmore who had become a frequent visitor to the Grange ever since Caroline's return from London.

"My darling—he is of your world and I—I am not."

"Thomas! Don't say such things." She wound her arms about him. "I will *not* marry Lord Grosmore—and I shall marry you."

Thomas drew her close, desperately savouring every moment he could hold her in his arms, knowing that their love could never be, that it would be wrong of him to take her away from the only life she knew—a life of comfort and luxury and security.

Caroline threw back her head and gazed up into his eyes. "We must go on seeing each other, but we'll have to be very careful, that's all."

But Caroline was not careful. Indeed she was very thoughtless.

Whilst she slept late the following morning, Lord Royston

121

found her horse in the stable, still saddled and caked with mud. Angered by her ill-treatment of an animal, he also guessed that his wayward daughter had resumed her meetings with Thomas Cole. And at night too! It was unthinkable.

Lord Royston returned to the house, rage in every stride. His loud voice rang through the hall. "Fetch Lady Caroline to me at once!"

Mrs Hargreaves appeared, flustered and anxious at the anger in Lord Royston's tone. "She—she's still sleeping, m'lord."

"Then wake her, woman, wake her!" his lordship roared. He flung open the double doors into the morning-room where he paced the floor until Caroline appeared, her eyes heavy with sleep, her rich auburn hair in tangled disarray.

"What is it, Papa?"

"Come in and close the door behind you," her father said grimly as he stood with his back to the fire, facing her.

She did as he bade and then came to stand before him. As she saw the fury in his eyes, even Caroline's resolute heart faltered and for the first time in her young life she feared her father's wrath. He began to speak slowly, as if weighing each word deliberately before it was spoken. "I would have preferred not to speak of this matter to you—but it seems I must.'

"Papa, I . . ."

"Be quiet, I have not finished. You have disgraced yourself. The whole village knows of your—your liaison with Cole. You will not see him again. You will not leave this house unaccompanied and at night, since you obviously cannot be trusted, your bedroom door will be locked."

"Papa!" Caroline cried in anguish and flung herself against him, crying. "But, Papa—I love him. And he loves me!"

"What do you know of *love*? And as for him—he's nothing better than a fortune-hunter."

"That's not true!" Angrily Caroline stood back from him. Tears shimmering in her eyes, she faced her father defiantly. "I wanted to tell you myself, but he said you wouldn't understand, he said . . ." she faltered, reluctant to repeat exactly what Thomas had said—that Lord Royston would dismiss him and send him away from Abbeyford, in case her father should pounce on that very idea as a solution.

"Well, at least he seems to have shown a little sense there," Lord Royston murmured.

"But I told him you would only want my happiness, that you could not possibly be so—cruel as to . . ."

Lord Royston gave a wry laugh. "Really, my child, don't you realise the foolishness of your conduct? Did you ever *really* suppose anything could come of it? My estate bailiff!"

Caroline tossed her head. "I don't care. I would still love him if he were a—a beggar!"

Lord Royston's eyes glinted. He leant towards her and said slowly and deliberately, "Would you indeed, my dear?"

Caroline drew breath swiftly in horror at the implied threat in his tone. "Oh Papa—you wouldn't. You *couldn't*!"

"Oh couldn't I?"

Caroline turned and fled from the room in tears. Lord

123

Royston watched her go, his anger giving way to sorrow now. Of course he wanted his daughter to be happy, but not for one moment could he countenance Caroline marrying the estate bailiff!

NINE

Sarah's paleness and sickness did not disappear even after she had been home a few weeks. The rosiness was gone from her cheeks and beneath her once-bright eyes were dark shadows.

"Oh Sarah, my lovely Sarah—what have they done to you?"

She was in his arms again. Guy had not forgotten her.

Her reply was muffled against his chest. "I didn't like the city, Guy, and—I missed you so."

He stroked her black hair. "Oh Sarah. Listen, you must not meet me for a while at night, not until . . ."

She looked up into his face, her violet eyes wide and fearful, her heart hammering. "Why—why not?"

"You must get yourself well again."

"I am well. Please Guy—don't say that . . ." She wound her arms around him. "Please don't. Let me see you!" she begged.

"I'm thinking only of you. I want to see you too, but . . ."

"Do you? Do you really? I was so afraid you would have

forgotten me."

"Sarah, oh my Sarah!" His mouth came down hard upon hers and she allowed herself to be consumed in the fire of his passion.

So their nightly meetings began again and Sarah grew more pale and listless and exhausted for she still had to be up early to do her work as usual.

On one of her Sunday visits to the cottage in the village Mrs Miller asked, "Are you ill, child? I'd hoped to see you better by now. That city were no good for you, but I thought once you'd been home a bit . . ."

Three pairs of eyes turned upon Sarah—only Ella, sitting in her usual corner, took no notice.

"I'm a bit tired and—I keep being sick. Must be the rich food up at the Grange."

Her mother bridled. "I'm sure I don't know what you mean. You've always been well-fed at home."

"How long have you been feeling badly?" Her father's question was sharp.

"A couple of weeks or—or so."

"How long—*exactly*?"

Her voice was a whisper. "Nearly six weeks."

Her father moved suddenly and came to stand over her. He gripped her chin with his strong fingers and forced her head back till her neck hurt.

"Look at me! Have you been a bad girl while you've been in London, Sarah?"

"No—no—I . . ."

"The truth!" he thundered. "You've lied before—

remember?"

Sarah closed her eyes. She felt him release her, felt the draught of air as he drew back his hand. Then he hit her twice, once on each side of the face, with such force that she was knocked first one way and then the other.

"You're with child, aren't you? *Aren't you?*"

"No—no," she screamed from the floor where she had fallen, but now he grabbed hold of her arms and hauled her to her feet. He shook her like a limp rag-doll.

Her mother looked on, making no attempt to interfere this time. Beth smiled smugly.

"Who is it? Who's—the father? Someone in London?"

Dumbly Sarah shook her head.

"Who then? *Who?* Not—not *Henry?*"

Again Sarah shook her head, this time even more vehemently.

"I know," piped up Beth. "It's him, isn't it, our Sarah? It's Guy Trent."

"Oh my God!" groaned Joseph Miller. "I thought we'd put a stop to *that*!"

"Oh I've seen 'em," Beth continued gleefully. "Meetin' in the woods or the ruins. An' I'll tell you some'at else an' all. Me Lady Caroline'll be ending up the same way as our Sarah, if she dun't watch out, with that Thomas Cole."

"Hold your tongue, girl," her father growled. "That's no concern of ourn, but this'n is!"

Again he shook Sarah savagely and then flung her away from him in disgust and stormed out of the cottage slamming the door behind him.

127

Sarah crumpled into a sorry heap upon the floor.

"Oh Sarah. How could you?" her mother mourned. "How *could* you?"

"What'll happen?" Beth asked pertly, seeming to enjoy the situation, though Ella, sitting in the corner rocking her doll, said not a word. Much of what was happening passed completely over her head, did not penetrate her private little world.

"'Cos he won't marry her!" Beth continued. "They're arranging for him to marry a girl from Manchester way. Louisa somebody."

Sarah raised her tear-streaked face to look at her sister. "What? What did you say?"

"I'm friends with Mary Tuplin, aren't I?" Beth retorted cockily, "and Mary Tuplin's Lady Trent's maid, ain't she? An' she overhears things, doesn't she?"

Sarah's tears flowed afresh. So, all his sweet words, all his promises, had been idle flattery to make her give herself to him.

Sarah bowed her head in shame.

Joseph Miller did not return home until the early hours of the following morning.

"Where is she?" he demanded of his wife as he flung open the door of the bedroom they shared. Ellen Miller, awakened from her sleep, sat up, bleary eyed and startled. "Oh Joseph, what a fright you gave me! Where have you been?"

"Where's Sarah?" he asked again, ignoring his wife's question.

"She—she's gone back to the Grange."

"God in Heaven, woman! You let her go?"

Ellen flinched in the face of his wrath. Her man was rarely moved to violent anger but when he was he was fearsome. He slammed the door behind him making the whole cottage shake. Grumbling to himself he began to take off his boots. Ellen lay back and let her eyes close, seeking the oblivion of sleep once more. But she was aroused again by her husband's voice.

"She's to be brought home. Henry'll have her. I've fixed it all. They're to be married quick."

Ellen was silent. It would be for the best, she told herself, but knowing Henry's nature she could not predict a happy future for her daughter as his wife.

Joseph Miller went to Abbeyford Grange the very next morning and explained the situation to Lady Caroline in person. He did not spare Sarah, nor himself, in telling her the full story of their family's shame. Later Caroline faced Sarah.

"Oh Sarah, you're a fool. Why—why did you let yourself be taken in by him?"

Fresh tears spilled over on to cheeks already puffed from a night's weeping. Dumbly she shook her head.

Caroline sighed. "You know he's a rogue, don't you? You were a plaything to him."

Lady Caroline was confirming Sarah's worst fears, fuelling the doubts against him which her family had already put into her mind.

"You cannot possibly have thought he would—or could *marry* you?" Caroline's tone was incredulous that such a thought might ever have been entertained by a girl of Sarah's birth. Caroline, in her blind selfishness, could not see that she herself was treading on as equally dangerous ground as Sarah, in her affair with Thomas Cole.

Sarah gulped. "He—he said—he loved me." But the words spoken aloud in a last desperate effort, sounded unconvincing even to Sarah's own ears.

In the harsh light of day, and in the face of cruel reality, Guy's murmured words of love seemed only a lovely dream.

Lady Caroline sighed. "Your father tells me you are to marry your cousin Henry."

Sarah nodded.

"Then you had better pack your things and leave today," Caroline said coldly, all trace of the friendliness she had previously shown her maid gone in an instant. Dejectedly Sarah left the room. Caroline clicked with exasperation. She was angry with Sarah, not so much for the girl's sake but for her own selfish reasons. With Sarah gone, how could she send messages to Thomas?

Lord Royston had carried out his threat. Caroline was never alone and at night her bedroom door was locked. The only way she had been able to keep contact with Thomas Cole had been to send notes to him through Sarah.

Never once, though, had Thomas replied and although Sarah had repeatedly assured her mistress that Thomas was still here in Abbeyford, still employed as the bailiff, Caroline was so afraid that suddenly he would leave either by his own choice or on dismissal by her father and she would lose him.

And now even that link with her lover was broken.

"Damn Sarah Miller!" Caroline muttered crossly, her concern solely for herself. Not one moment's thought did she spare for the unhappy Sarah and the life of misery that lay before her.

Sarah carried her bag down the lane away from Abbeyford Grange, reluctantly returning to the cottage in the village. She came to the place where the trees overhung the lane. She heard the hoofbeats behind her and his voice calling urgently, "Sarah! Sarah!"

Her heart gave a leap, but she continued walking, head bowed. Guy drew level with her and flung himself from his horse. *"Sarah!"*

Still she did not stop to look up.

He caught her by the shoulders and spun her round, almost throwing her off balance. His eyes were wild.

"Why, Sarah? Why?" Torment was in his voice.

So—he had heard already! Heard she was to be made to marry Henry Smithson.

"Look at me, Sarah!"

Slowly she raised her eyes and looked into his face and her heart turned over. She loved him still. Wild, reckless, irresponsible—wicked, some would say—though he was, she would always love him.

"I must. It's all arranged," she said flatly.

"But—but *why*?"

131

She hung her head and murmured almost inaudibly, "I'm with child."

He was motionless. For a moment he seemed to stop breathing. Then harshly he asked, "His?"

Her head snapped up, her dark eyes wide. "No—oh no!"

His anger softened. "Mine?"

She nodded and allowed him to draw her towards him, her head against his chest, his chin resting on her dark hair.

"You *can't* marry Smithson. Sarah—we'll be married. I love you. I told you that! Didn't you believe me?"

"They—they said you didn't mean it. Even Lady Caroline said you wouldn't marry the likes of me."

"Well, we'll see about that!" Guy said firmly. "Just trust me, Sarah. Trust me!" He held her close, fiercely protective, and she melted against him.

Without his strength, she was lost, lonely and afraid. But as soon as she was once more in his embrace, everything seemed to come right.

"Never!" Sir Matthew Trent shouted, his face purple with rage. "A common village slut and you want to *marry* her? And a *Miller* too."

Guy Trent faced his parents squarely: his father's anger and his mother's tears, as she lay back upon a sofa almost at the point of fainting.

"Yes—I do. I love her and she loves me."

"Pah! Love! What has that got to do with it?" Sir Matthew bellowed. He prodded his forefinger towards his son. "You'll marry Louisa Marchant, boy, and be glad her father's willing that you should!"

"I shall not. I shall marry Sarah."

"*You—will—not!*" roared his father. "You're a disgrace to the name of Trent. I'll arrange for the girl to be sent away to have it." Grimly he added, "She's not the first to bear your bastard, is she? But, by God, she'd better be the last!"

"This time it's different. The other two—well—they were nothing to me. But Sarah . . ."

"Have you no *shame*, boy? You dare to stand there and admit you've wronged three young girls and yet you show no remorse, no feeling . . ."

"I *do* care—about Sarah," Guy shouted heatedly. "Not about the other two—I admit. Besides, they weren't virgins . . ."

Lady Trent gave a little cry and her head lolled back.

"Hold your vulgar tongue, boy, in front of your mother."

But Guy ignored his warning. "But Sarah was. She belongs to me and only to me. I won't have her married to Smithson."

"What? What's that?"

Sullenly Guy explained. "Her father's arranged that she should marry Henry Smithson."

"Smithson—my cowman?"

"Yes."

Sir Matthew's anger subsided and he almost beamed to realise the problem had already been half-solved for him by the girl's father.

"There you are then. That's the answer to everything. I'll see young Smithson right. They must be given a cottage

133

and . . ."

"No—no—*no!*" Guy yelled. He turned and almost ran from the room. "I won't let her marry him—I *won't!*"

The door slammed behind him, rattling Lady Trent's fine china in its cabinet. Sir Matthew sank into a chair and exchanged a look of sheer defeat and helplessness with his wife.

Guy Trent hammered on the door of the Millers' cottage.

"Sarah! Are you in there, Sarah! I want to talk to you." Again he thumped on the door with his clenched fist.

The door was flung open and Guy almost hit Joseph Miller in the face as he raised his hand to strike the door again.

"Good-day, Mr Trent." Joseph's face was a grim mask.

Guy was panting hard for he had galloped, angry and distraught, from the Manor after the heated exchange with his father.

"I want to see Sarah."

"Sarah is—not available."

"She is—to me!" Guy made as if to enter the cottage by force, but Joseph's strong arm against the door frame stopped him.

"Mr Trent—we'll settle this trouble ourselves, if you dun't mind."

"I've a right to see her."

Joseph shook his head. "My daughter is to marry Henry Smithson."

"Sarah! *Sarah!*" Guy shouted and thought he caught the

134

sound of muffled sobbing from within the cottage.

"Let me in!" He caught hold of Joseph's arm but the older man was bigger, tougher, stronger even than Guy Trent.

"Mr Trent," Joseph said yet again, his patience ready to snap, "I don't want to quarrel with you, and God knows I've just cause, but I've me home and family to think of." He held the younger man easily at arm's length and, though fit and strong, Guy Trent was no match for the burly farm-labourer.

"You've brought shame to this family and me and mine'll not forgive you."

"Miller, listen to me. I love Sarah. I want to marry her. Please . . ."

Joseph Miller shook his head. "Your sort don't marry the likes of us, Mr Trent. You know that," and added bitterly, "You'll use our young lasses for your pleasure, but when it comes to marrying," he gave a bark of wry laughter, "you'll marry your own kind."

"I must see her, talk to her," Guy persisted.

"She dun't want to see you. She's agreed to marry young Smithson."

Guy closed his eyes and groaned and his hands fell away from Joseph's arm. As he felt the younger man give way, Joseph relaxed his hold. Even he was surprised by the look of utter misery on Guy Trent's face. Perhaps he did care for Sarah—but no, marriage between them was out of the question. They were trapped by the accident of birth which separated their lives.

As Guy turned away, defeated on all sides, Joseph was

135

moved to add, "Sarah'll be all right. I'll see to that."

They were all against him. The whole village were ranged behind the Miller family against Guy Trent. Even his own parents. He didn't even catch a glimpse of Sarah, let alone have a chance to talk to her.

If only they had let him see her, he could have persuaded her to run away with him. He knew he could! Perhaps that was the very thing they were afraid would happen.

As it was, the days slipped past towards her wedding-day.

Guy made one last desperate effort to see her. He went again to the Millers' cottage and was met at the door this time by both Joseph Miller and Henry Smithson. They would not listen to his arguments. Henry stood clenching and unclenching his fists, conscious of the desire to knock Guy Trent to the ground, to beat his face to an unrecognisable pulp, to kill him!

Already it was growing dusk as Guy Trent turned away from the Millers' cottage and flung himself on to his horse and turned, not westwards towards the Manor but across the common and up the hill out of the valley. Away from Abbeyford—he had to get away from Abbeyford; from the Millers, from his parents—away from everyone who stood between him and Sarah.

Henry Smithson watched him go, resentment festering in his heart. Quietly he too left the Millers' cottage, walked up the lane and across the footbridge near the ford and on up the hill, taking the right-hand fork which led to Amberly.

Although Guy Trent had galloped off in his frenzy towards the north, shrewdly Henry guessed that in his present mood he would seek the solace of drink. But he would not return to the Monk's Arms in Abbeyford—not this night. The most likely place he would go eventually would be the inn at Amberly and, if so, then Guy Trent would return home by this route.

Silently Henry Smithson slipped into the shadows of the wood and there he lay in wait for Guy Trent.

Darkness came completely, but anger and hatred kept Henry Smithson oblivious to the cold, the damp and even his own bodily weariness after a day's work in the fields. One thought filled his mind.

Guy Trent! He would kill Guy Trent!

Hour after hour he lay in in wait. The eeriness of the woodland by night held no fears for him; he scarcely heard the rustling undergrowth, the hooting owls, nor the incessant waterfall. His ears strained for only one sound— the sound of hoofbeats from the direction of Amberly.

In the early hours of the morning Henry moved stiffly, stamped his feet and then listened. Faintly, growing louder with each moment, came the sound for which he had waited through the long cold hours.

He slipped off his jacket and crouched low behind a bush at the side of the track through the wood as nearer and nearer came the steady rhythmic cantering hooves.

Louder and louder, nearer and nearer.

Henry leapt out from his hiding-place, flapping his coat and yelling. The horse whinnied and shied, rearing up above

137

Henry, but he dodged to one side. The rider toppled from its back and the terrified animal bolted.

Henry stood over the motionless form on the ground, bent down and grasped him by his clothes. Twice as strong, Henry Smithson hauled him to his feet and without even giving Guy Trent time to recover his senses, to defend himself, he smashed his fist into his young master's face.

"Take my Sarah, would you?" Henry was weeping with rage, each blow punctuated by a verbal insult. "You pig! You—rotten—bastard! I'll kill you . . .!"

Each time Guy fell to the ground, Henry pulled him up again and again. Guy Trent was senseless, could not even put up his arms to protect himself from the vicious onslaught, let alone put up any kind of defensive fight.

Finally exhausted, Henry let him fall to the ground and stood over him, swaying and panting. He aimed one last vicious kick into his victim's groin and then turned away and stumbled through the wood, back to the sanctuary of the village leaving Guy Trent bleeding and unconscious on the cold ground.

TEN

They found him six hours later.

When Sir Matthew became aware that his son's horse had returned home riderless, he sent some of his own household to search.

They carried him home, more dead than alive, and Sir Matthew called in the apothecary.

"Well?" he demanded as the apothecary, William Dale, came into his study after attending to Guy Trent's injuries. He was a portly, middle-aged man, with a hearty manner.

"A-hem, well now, it seems to me that the young man's injuries have not been caused by a mere fall from his horse. Oh dear me, no! They have been *inflicted* by some person or persons—I am convinced of it."

William Dale sipped the brandy the footman handed him and watched Sir Matthew Trent's face darken.

"Some brawl, I suppose," Sir Matthew muttered and sighed. "The young devil's always in some scrape or another."

"Possibly, possibly. Remarkably good brandy this, if I

139

may say so. But if you want my opinion, Sir Matthew, *this* time it was not of your son's making."

"What do you mean by that?"

The apothecary shrugged. "It seems to me—and I've seen a good few of these cases, mark you . . ."

"Get on with it, man," Sir Matthew rapped testily.

William Dale continued in his own time, not in the least daunted by Sir Matthew. The power he wielded in this neighbourhood as employer and magistrate did not intimidate William Dale, who regarded himself as a professional man, safe in the knowledge that there was no other physician for miles around with his expertise. No—he had naught to fear from Sir Matthew's temper. But those who had harmed his son would be in grave danger.

"To my mind," he continued, sipping the brandy between phrases with irritating slowness. "To my mind, your son has been set upon. Perhaps by thieves—or perhaps by someone who bears him a grudge."

"What makes you think that?" Sir Matthew growled menacingly.

"Your son does not appear to have defended himself. He was too drunk for one thing," he added baldly. "There are no lacerations or bruises on his hands." He doubled his fist and punched the empty air to demonstrate. "See what I mean? In an equal fight there would be such evidence—and also I would expect to see bruising on his forearms where he'd put up his arms to protect himself. Where d'you say he was found?"

"In the wood on the road to Amberly."

"And his horse returned home riderless?"

"Yes, yes."

"Hmmm. Seems to me," the apothecary mused shrewdly. "He—or they—lay in wait for him in the woods. Probably frightened his horse and it threw him. Then they set upon your son." He finished the brandy with a flourish and got to his feet.

Sir Matthew put up his hand, palm outwards. "Just a minute. What *exactly* are my son's injuries?"

"A broken nose, severe bruising to all areas of his face, particularly his eyes. Two teeth broken, a cut lower lip and a damaged ear. He'll probably be deaf in one ear for the rest of his life. Add to that severe bruising in the groin and the risk of a severe chill since we must presume he lay in the open for most of the night."

"I—see."

"I'll call again tomorrow, Sir Matthew. Good-day to you."

"Good-day," Sir Matthew murmured automatically, but already his thoughts were elsewhere.

He knew who had attacked his son and that man would be made to suffer for it.

Not for nothing had Sir Matthew become magistrate for this district. It gave him not only power over the villagers as their employer, it gave him absolute power over every aspect of their lives!

Ironically, it fell to Thomas Cole to arrest the man Sir Matthew believed had attacked his son.

141

Sir Matthew had consulted Lord Royston who was also a magistrate and considered senior to Sir Matthew by way of position, wealth and power.

"I want this man arrested and tried for attempted murder," Sir Matthew had told him bluntly.

Lord Royston had sighed and waved his hand towards Sir Matthew in a gesture of dismissal. "Do whatever you have to, Trent. It's no concern of mine. I've got my own problems," he muttered.

Thomas Cole knocked at the door of the low, squat cottage. It was opened by Beth Miller, who, with no premonition of the disaster which was about to fall upon her family, politely invited the bailiff to step inside.

Joseph Miller, who had not been able to find casual work that week, was at home. He rose from his chair at the table. Mrs Miller looked up but did not rise. Ella continued to eat her meal without noticing Thomas Cole.

Of Sarah there was no sign.

"Is there something wrong, mister?"

"I'm afraid so, Miller," Thomas Cole sighed. He had no stomach for the task he had to do. He had not wanted the job of parish constable along with that of bailiff on the estate, but he had been desperate for employment not too far from his parents in Amberly and, knowing Abbeyford to be in the main a law-abiding community, he had agreed.

Now he regretted becoming keeper of the peace.

"Joseph Miller—I am instructed by Sir Matthew Trent as magistrate of this parish to arrest you on a charge of attempted murder of his son, Guy Trent."

Ellen Miller screamed. Joseph's mouth gagged open and he sat down heavily in his chair as if his legs had given way beneath him. Beth's sharp eyes darted from her father's stricken face to Thomas Cole.

"It weren't me pa, it were Hen . . ."

"Hold your tongue, girl!" Joseph Miller snapped, recovering his senses swiftly. Slowly he rose again from his seat at the table. Bemusedly he looked around the small, dingy room, as if feeling this might be the last time he saw it.

"You'll come peaceable-like?" Thomas Cole asked.

"Aye, I'll give you no trouble, mister. Seems as if I'm in enough already!"

Ellen's customary composure deserted her. She fell to her knees and clasped her husband about the legs. "Joseph—tell him! Tell him it weren't you. Tell him the truth!"

Joseph Miller bent down towards his wife. "Hush, woman. It's better this way. Think on Sarah."

Still Ellen clung to her man. "Sarah! Sarah!" Her voice rose to hysterical pitch. "Why must you always think of her? After what she's done? She's the cause of all this. All these years we've been an honest, hard-working family with naught to fear from the justices. And now—now . . ." She choked on the words, could not speak of the fear that was in her heart.

Justice, metered out by the squire or the lord, was swift and severe. If Joseph Miller walked out of their cottage now, Ellen knew she might never more see him back there!

At best it would be prison, at worst swinging from the

143

gibbet!

Gently Joseph released himself from her clinging, care-worn hands, stood and squared his shoulders. His face was ashen, but his voice was steady as he said, "I am ready to come wi' you, mister."

As they left the cottage, Henry Smithson met them. He stopped, his eyes glancing from one to the other as they passed him.

From the doorway Beth shouted. "He's takin' our pa, Henry Smithson, for summat you done!"

Thomas Cole hesitated, stopped and turned round. Joseph stopped but did not turn about.

"Is that true, Miller?"

"You 'ad orders to arrest *me*, didn't you, mister?" Joseph muttered, looking steadfastly ahead.

"Yes, but . . ."

"Then you're arresting me."

Once more Thomas Cole looked towards Henry Smithson, standing there, not moving, saying nothing.

"It's a bad business," Thomas murmured, "a bad business." And, turning, took hold of Joseph Miller's arm and made to lead him away.

Then Joseph did look back, his dark eyes boring into Henry. "Look to our Sarah, lad. You know what you mun do, dun't you?" The two men stared at each other, then slowly Henry nodded.

Satisfied, Joseph turned and walked away without a backward glance.

In the attic bedroom beneath the thatch Beth leant over her sister lying on the bed.

"Do you hear, the bailiff's taken Pa—accused of murder, he is? All because of you."

Sarah's violet eyes flew open and the last vestige of colour in her already pale and sickly face drained away.

"Pa? Oh no! Why do they think it were Pa?"

Beth smiled wryly. "They knows Pa has no love for the Trents an' because of *you* they think he done for Master Guy."

Sarah struggled to sit up. "Guy—he—he's not dead?"

Beth screeched and lashed out at her sister, the palm of her hand striking Sarah's cheek. "You still think of *him*— even now. Think on Pa! What'll they do to Pa? They'll likely *hang* him!"

At eight o'clock on an early September morning in the year of 1796 Sarah Miller married Henry Smithson. No one attended the ceremony except the Reverend Hugh Langley and sufficient persons to witness the ceremony legally.

They married because Joseph Miller demanded it. Sarah, because he was her father and there was no other way to cover the shame of her swelling body, and Henry Smithson agreed because Joseph Miller stood accused of the crime he, Henry, had committed. In tacit agreement made in those few moments when Thomas Cole arrested Joseph Miller, Henry had understood what was expected of him.

Joseph would keep silent if Henry would marry Sarah and take her bastard as his own.

Grimly Henry walked beside Sarah from the church back to the Millers' cottage where he would now live with his bride.

Once he had loved this girl in his own rough way, but his heart was filled with hatred—against Guy Trent, even against Joseph Miller for forcing him into a position where he was obliged to marry Sarah when she had belonged to another man. And most of all he hated Sarah for betraying the love he had had for her, for giving herself to young Trent, for lying with him, for . . .

Each time he thought of them together he felt the violence creep over him again and knew that though they had to spend the rest of their lives together, he would never forgive and never forget!

They entered the Millers' cottage. Ellen Miller sat in front of the cold hearth, her hands lying idle in her lap, her eyes staring and vacant. Ella in her corner rocked to and fro, clutching her rag-doll close to her thin chest.

Beth was tying a shawl about her head.

"Seems I mun become milkmaid now," she greeted them resentfully, "else we shall all starve."

"Is there any news?" Henry asked, whilst Sarah lowered herself into a chair opposite her mother and bowed her head.

Beth's eyes met Henry's. "But for you Henry Smithson, he'd be here where he belongs, not standing 'afore the magistrate."

Roughly Henry grasped Beth's arm and twisted it cruelly. "I'll not take that from you or anyone else. Your father knows what he is about."

146

Beth glanced at Sarah. "Aye, an' so do we all. He's sacrificing himsel' for *that*!" She flung her arm out in a gesture towards Sarah.

"An' he's not the only one, an' don't you forget it," Henry said grimly.

They stood staring at each other, the man with bitterness in his heart, the girl with her badly pock-marked face, full of resentment. Then Beth shook herself free of his grasp and left the cottage. Ellen Miller had not stirred, had not seemed to notice the heated exchange of conversation. She contintued to stare into space.

"Well, Sarah Smithson. You'd best start being a wife. Seems your ma has given up. I'll be away to me work."

As the cottage door banged behind her husband, Sarah covered her face and wept, the sobs racking her body. But no comforting hands reached out to her. Guy's embrace was lost to her for ever, and even her mother, who sat only a few feet from her, did not reach out to comfort her conscience-stricken daughter.

ELEVEN

Joseph Miller squared his shoulders and faced Sir Matthew across the wide expanse of the leather-topped desk in Sir Matthew's study at the Manor.

As local magistrate, Sir Matthew was entitled to hold the 'court' at his home.

Thomas Cole cleared his throat and attempted, from his scant knowledge of such proceedings, to carry out his duties correctly.

"Joseph Miller, you are hereby charged that on the night of August thirtieth last you did wilfully assault Mister Guy Trent with the premeditated intention of causing him fatal injury. How do you plead? Guilty or not guilty?"

There was silence in the room whilst Sir Matthew and Thomas Cole waited for the accused man to reply. Joseph fixed his gaze upon the window behind Sir Matthew's chair, clamped his jaw firmly shut and said nothing.

"Well, man, speak up, did you do it or didn't you?" Sir Matthew Trent thundered.

Still Joseph did not speak.

Thomas Cole sighed heavily. He didn't like all this. Not one bit. Ever since the moment he had arrested Joseph Miller he had doubted that the man accused had had anything at all to do with the attack on young Trent. And now the fool refused to speak in his own defence.

"Sir Matthew," Thomas Cole murmured. "I think Miller is protecting someone, I think . . ."

"Nonsense. If he won't speak up, then his silence must be taken as an admission of guilt. Well, Miller, have you naught to say?"

Joseph continued to stare steadfastly above Sir Matthew's head.

Sir Matthew viewed the accused man standing before him through narrowed eyes. He knew he had to be careful. He would have liked to have rid himself of Joseph Miller for ever, to have seen him at the end of a rope or at least transported to Botany Bay, but to turn the charge into a capital offence would mean the trial would have to be held in a higher court—and then he could not be sure that Miller would be found guilty, particularly if the whole sorry story of Guy's involvement with Miller's daughter—of the bastard she would bear him—were to come out.

Sir Matthew shuddered. He could not afford the scandal. No, he would keep the whole matter within his own power—especially since he had so far had the luck that Lord Royston did not wish to be involved.

He decided to pretend leniency.

"Now look here, Miller—in view of the unfortunate—er—circumstances concerning your daughter, which we

150

both know about . . ."

Joseph's face remained impassive.

". . . and because you didn't use a weapon on my son—only your own murderous fists . . ." Sir Matthew clenched his own fist in an attempt to hold his own temper in check. ". . . I am prepared to change the charge to a 'common law misdemeanour' with a maximum sentence of two years' imprisonment with hard labour . . ."

Joseph gave no sign, but Sir Matthew heard Thomas Cole's shocked, swift intake of breath, but he ignored it.

". . . and when you return to Abbeyford, I hope you will have learnt your lesson and . . ."

Thomas Cole was leaning across the desk, anger blazing in his usually docile eyes. "Why, man, it's a death sentence you're giving him. In those gaols . . ."

"Nonsense, Cole. What would you prefer? To see him on the end of a gibbet?"

"It might be kinder . . ."

"It's not within my power to try a capital offence, he'd have to be tried in a higher court."

"Well, let him be. Yes, let him. He might stand a better chance . . ."

"No!" Sir Matthew snapped. "No—we'll deal with this ourselves."

"I don't see anyone else present—only you!" Thomas Cole muttered. In desperation, he turned to Joseph. "For God's sake man, speak out. *Did* you do it?"

He felt this was all wrong. Sir Matthew was using his power to rid himself of a troublesome element in the valley.

151

Thomas Cole believed Miller innocent, but at least, even if guilty, the man should have had a proper court trial, with jury and a properly conducted hearing. This way, Sir Matthew was using his power—to Thomas's mind—unjustly.

Thomas groaned deep within himself. Joseph Miller remained stubbornly silent.

Thomas turned back to Sir Matthew, rage bubbling up inside him. "You can't *do* this—it's wrong!"

Sir Matthew glowered at him and said in a dangerously controlled voice, "And why not, pray? Am I not squire and magistrate of this valley?"

"Aye, and I'm beginning to see why! You have no proof of this man's guilt and I tell you I have strong suspicions that he's definitely *not* the man! And yet you still send him to his death . . ."

Sir Matthew attempted to laugh. "Imprisonment is not death."

"Oh yes it is, and you well know it!" Thomas Cole thundered. "*If* he survives the hard labour, *if* he survives amongst the criminals and rogues he must live with, you know as well as I do that the gaol-fever will get him. You know all that and yet you still send him—I say—to his death."

"I'll have no trouble-makers in my valley," Sir Matthew growled. "I still hold him responsible for those damaged fences."

"But you've no *proof*—either about that or this attack on your son. You're just using this as an excuse to get rid of

152

someone who has dared to stand up to you. A man who was only trying to protect his livelihood and his family. You reckon you can rob a man of his land, use his young lass for your pleasure and still expect him to touch his forelock to you. You're a dictator—a bloody murderer!"

Sir Matthew was on his feet. "How *dare* you speak to me like that? Take care I don't dismiss you . . ."

"I'll not give you the chance. I won't work for you a minute longer!" Thomas Cole shouted.

For the first time Joseph Miller opened his mouth. "Nay, Mister Cole, I don't hold you to blame for a' this. I wouldn't want you to lose your job 'cos 'o me."

Thomas swung round, his soft brown eyes now blazing with indignant fury. "Miller—why don't you speak up, man?" he demanded again.

With quiet resignation, Joseph said, "I have me reasons, mister."

"Aye, an' they must be good ones. Man, you're throwing your *life* away!"

Stubbornly, Joseph Miller's jaw hardened and he remained silent.

Thomas Cole's shoulders sagged in defeat. "I can do no more if you won't defend yoursel'."

His eyes met the cold, hard stare of Sir Matthew Trent. He made one last desperate effort. "What of his family? Will they be turned out of his cottage to starve?"

"No. If I understand things correctly," Sir Matthew looked towards Joseph for denial. "Your daughter is by this time married to young Smithson and he will move into

153

your cottage? Is that correct?"

Joseph Miller's eyes came at last to rest upon Sir Matthew's gaze. For a long moment they glared at each other, a challenge of strong wills between the man who knew himself master and victor and the underling who knew himself beaten, yet still could not deny the pride in his blood.

Released from the necessity for silence, the flood of passion poured from Joseph's lips. "Aye, they'll be wed by now. Your son's bastard will bear the name of Smithson." He pointed his finger at Sir Matthew, "And he'll be raised to bring revenge to you and yours for this day's work . . ."

"That's enough, Miller. Get him out of here, Cole."

"No—I'll play no more part in this," Thomas said doggedly.

Sir Matthew glared at him but Thomas Cole—so quiet, so gentle—had never felt such a violent anger against any human being until this moment. Nor was he going to let the matter rest there. He took a deep breath and said, "I'll see Lord Royston . . ."

Sir Matthew gave a wry laugh. "I doubt you'll be welcome there, Cole."

Thomas Cole reddened. "You'll find no one in this valley will lay a hand against Miller to help you put him in gaol."

Sir Matthew smiled and said quietly, "I had already foreseen that possibility."

He moved and pulled the bell-cord. Instantly there was the sound of shuffling and rattling outside and the door flew open to reveal four tough, evil-looking men, completely unknown to either Thomas Cole or Joseph Miller.

154

"There's always those who'll undertake *any* kind of work, Cole, for a guinea or two," Sir Matthew said smoothly.

Helplessly Thomas watched whilst the four men made to take hold of Joseph Miller and bear him away. Now he realised fully just how deep was Sir Matthew's hatred—and fear—of Jospeh Miller.

As the men half-dragged Joseph from the room, he turned and now looked Sir Matthew full in the face, his final threat echoing in Sir Matthew Trent's ears.

"Tha'll rue the day your son defiled my girl, my Sarah . . . There'll be a curse upon the Trents! A curse . . .!"

"You can't come in here, my man," the butler said loftily.

"I can—and I will!" Thomas Cole shouldered aside the butler and stepped into the spacious hall of Abbeyford Grange.

He paused a moment. Anger and a sense of outrage had brought him this far and would still carry him to face Lord Royston—but for the moment he paused, conscious of the fact that he was standing in Caroline's home.

As if his longing had transmitted itself to her, miraculously she appeared at the top of the wide, sweeping staircase.

"Thomas!" she breathed his name and started down the stairs towards him but at that moment the double doors to the morning-room were thrown open and Lord Royston appeared.

His surprise at seeing the estate's bailiff standing there swiftly turned to anger as he saw Caroline hovering on the stairs. The impudence of the man! Daring to come here! He was about to open his mouth to speak, but Thomas Cole turned and completely ignoring Caroline strode purposefully towards him.

"I must speak with you on a very urgent matter, my lord."

Misunderstanding, the earl said stiffly, "I do not think there is anything we have to say to each other, Cole."

Ignoring his dismissive air, Thomas persisted, "My lord, please hear me out. There has been a serious miscarriage of justice. Sir Matthew Trent has sentenced Joseph Miller to two years imprisonment with hard labour for an alleged attack upon his son. I believe the man to be innocent."

Lord Royston's eyes were hard, his mouth a thin line. Slowly, with deliberate emphasis, he said, "I would trust Sir Matthew's judgement rather than yours. Whatever action he has taken has my full approval."

Thomas Cole stared at him in disbelief. He had known the Earl of Royston to be a hard man, but had always believed him to be just. Now it seemed that Lord Royston could be as corrupt as Sir Matthew. His next words confirmed that he too would use this situation to bring about something he wanted. "And since you have ranged yourself on the side of this villain I think you had better leave this district without delay, Cole, *without delay*!"

Thomas heard Caroline's cry of despair, but he did not look up. Instead he faced her father, fearless now, his resolution firm. "And gladly, *my lord*," he said with heavy sarcasm. "Perhaps the Americas will treat a man more

156

justly."

He turned and walked towards the door.

"Thomas, oh Thomas!"

He heard her cry, but he neither looked back nor even hesitated.

The door closed behind him to the sound of Caroline's distraught weeping.

For Caroline, help came unexpectedly.

Lady Lynwood and her son paid a visit to the Grange and, whilst the old friends talked together, eagerly Caroline suggested that she and young Lynwood should go riding.

Lynwood noticed Lord Royston's hesitation but could not guess at the reason for it.

"I'll take good care of her, my lord."

The earl's expression softened. The young boy, in his adoration of Caroline, could know nothing of the doubt in the older man's heart.

It was five days since Thomas Cole's visit to the Grange, during which time Lord Royston had scarcely let Caroline out of his sight.

Surely Cole would be gone by now? Surely he would not have dared to linger in Abbeyford?

"Very well then, but be back here before dusk."

Gleefully Caroline ran to change into her riding-habit. "Hilton, Hilton, have my horse saddled, will you? And bring Lord Lynwood's mount too."

A short while later they were cantering down the grassy slope towards Abbeyford village.

157

Caroline reined in and breathed deeply at the fresh, clean air. "Oh Francis, you don't know how good it is to be free, to get away from that house."

Lynwood frowned, puzzled. "I don't understand you." He was disturbed to see that Caroline looked pale, with dark shadows beneath her eyes.

"Did you know that my father is arranging a marriage for me—to Lord Grosmore?"

The boy's face coloured. "No, no I didn't."

Caroline grimaced. "Well, he is."

"You—you're not—pleased?"

"I most certainly am not! 'Gros' by name and gross by build. Ugh, he's fat and ugly, Francis."

All the time she was speaking her worried eyes were searching the fields and hillsides. Francis could feel her agitation.

"But, surely, your father only wants your happiness?"

Caroline's pretty mouth pouted. "It seems in our social sphere one marries suitably—it doesn't signify whether or not one loves—or even likes—one's husband."

Lynwood burst out, "How I wish I were older!"

Caroline smiled and leaned across to pat his arm. "Oh Francis, how sweet you are! Things don't seem so bad whilst I have you to champion my cause."

Together they rode down into the valley, over the bridge near the smithy. Here Caroline slowed her horse to walking pace and looked down at him anxiously.

"I fear Captain is lame, Francis. How fortunate we are near the smith! I think he had better take a look at him."

Lynwood dismounted, tethered his own horse to the rail outside the forge and held up his arms for Caroline to dismount. She slid into his arms. For a moment the young boy held her in his embrace. Though he was some four years younger, he was already taller than Caroline.

Coyly Caroline tossed her head and laughed. "My, Francis, I hadn't realised how tall you've grown."

Reluctantly he let his arms fall from about her waist, knowing that because of the years that separated them, because she would not wait for him to grow up, his love for her could never be returned.

She was moving away from him, calling to the smith. "Smith, are you there?"

A tall, broad-shouldered man appeared, his face red from the heat. "M'lady." He touched his forelock.

"I fear my horse, Captain, is lame. Will you take a look?"

"Certainly, m'lady." The man caught hold of the bridle and led him into the forge. "Steady, boy, steady," he murmured soothingly to the animal. "Now, let's take a look at you."

Lady Caroline and Lynwood followed the smith and stood watching. Caroline began to fidget. "Oh Francis, the heat is too much. I must get a breath of air!"

He turned and would have accompanied her outside again, but Caroline laid her hand upon his arm and smiled her most winning smile. "No, I shall be all right, you stay. The smith may need you to hold Captain's head." She turned and walked away. Lynwood hesitated, wanting to follow her, to stay with her, but she had asked him to remain

159

here . . .

Caroline walked swiftly away from the forge and along the lane until she came to the cottage where Thomas Cole lived. Her heart was thumping wildly and she glanced back frequently to be sure Lynwood had not followed her. If only Thomas had not gone!

She tapped on the door and waited anxious moments, biting her lip. The door opened and he was standing before her.

"Caroline!"

She held her fingers to her lips and stepped inside the cottage. "Thomas, oh Thomas, my love! I have only a few moments—Lynwood is at the smith's with my horse . . ."

As she stepped into his cottage and saw that the room was in a state of turmoil, packing-cases and trunks standing open, Caroline turned wide, frightened eyes upon him. "Thomas—you really are going away!"

"I must, my dear. I can no longer stay here—you know that." His mouth was tight, his eyes bright once more with remembered anger.

"Yes . . ." she whispered.

"The man—Miller—was innocent, Caroline, I'm certain of it. But Trent wanted to be rid of him because he was a disturbing influence amongst the villagers."

Caroline's eyes filled with tears. "And my father? He would not help, would he?"

Sadly Thomas shook his head. "No. It grieves me to think ill of him, my love. But—he would not." Thomas sighed. "I think he too saw a chance to rid himself of *my* presence."

Caroline bit her trembling lip and held out her hands to him. "Oh Thomas, I was so afraid you would have gone already."

For a moment they were silent, staring at each other, their love for each other flowing between them.

"Thomas—Thomas—take me with you," she begged, desperate because he was leaving her.

His arms were about her fiercely, his lips against her hair. "Aye, b'God, an' I will! I'll play them at their own game!"

Caroline did not understand the bitterness behind his words—all she knew, all she cared about, was that he would not go away without her.

He held her away from him, his strong hands gripping her shoulders, his brown eyes boring into hers.

This was a new Thomas Cole—a masterful, decisive Thomas Cole. "We must talk, make plans. How can we meet?"

Eagerly she said, "The waterfall—I could get away from Lynwood and meet you there soon. He's at the smith's with my horse. I pretended Captain had gone lame so I could slip along here. I *had* to see if you were still here—I was so afraid . . ."

"Yes, yes," Thomas Cole kissed her swiftly. "Go now—quickly . . ."

Lynwood was already leading her horse out as Caroline hurried back towards the forge.

"The smith could find nothing amiss, Caroline."

She forced a bright smile. "Perhaps I was wrong. Come,

help me mount and we will continue our ride."

They skirted the village and rode up through the pastures towards the abbey ruins.

Caroline's merry laugh came bouncing across the breeze to him. "Come, Francis, I'll race you to the woods."

She spurred her horse to a gallop and was away across the grass before Lynwood had realised what she was doing.

When he reached the edge of the wood, she had disappeared amongst the trees. He could neither see nor even hear her horse. Lynwood groaned. After his confident promise to Lord Royston to take care of her, he had lost her.

"Caroline, Caroline!" At walking pace he rode amongst the trees, following a track, then doubling back and trying a different direction. He came to the roadway leading to the Manor and followed it until he stood at the edge of the wood overlooking the valley. He scanned the hill slopes, the lanes and pastures. There was no sign of Caroline.

"Caroline, *Caroline!*" he called in desperation, his heart pumping fearfully. Through the wood again he continued northwards until he came to the road leading from Abbeyford through the trees to Amberly. There was no one on the road, no one to ask if they had seen her. All was silent and still save for the distant sounds of the waterfall. Ducking beneath the trees, Francis rode on towards it and felt relief flood through him as he saw Captain tethered near some bushes at the top of the cliff overhanging the fall. Then swiftly, he felt a stab of terror. Had she fallen? Was she lying injured below, or worse, in the pool?

"Caroline!"

Young Lynwood flung himself from his horse and ran to the edge of the cliff. He was about to scramble down the rough pathway when he stopped.

Below him, near the pool, oblivious to his presence, stood Caroline. With her was the Abbeyford estate bailiff—Thomas Cole—his arms around her, his lips against her neck.

Unobserved by either of the lovers, standing on the very edge of the sheer drop, Lynwood stood motionless. Transfixed, unable to leave, he watched them, the pain growing in his chest, the hurt that Caroline, so lovely, so pure, could be meeting someone in clandestine furtiveness. Now he realised the reason for Lord Royston's reluctance to allow Caroline to go riding that morning. And worse, Caroline had used him, Lynwood, to escape from her father's watchful eye and meet her lover. The use she had made of him, the deceit she had practised upon him, hurt almost more than seeing her in the arms of Thomas Cole. He had not wanted to believe ill of her, but now there was no escaping from the truth.

Young Lynwood turned from the edge of the cliff and retched upon the grass.

He had idolised Caroline, worshipped her as an untouchable goddess. But his goddess had fallen from the pedestal on which he had placed her and the boy suffered the first pain of total disillusionment and disappointed love.

In those few short moments the Earl of Lynwood grew to manhood.

TWELVE

The village was stunned by the news of the sentence Joseph Miller received. Justice was swift and severe—they all knew and accepted this—but in Abbeyford very few people ever broke the law and only the very oldest inhabitant could remember the last hanging in the village and that had been for sheep-stealing by a young man desperate for food with a young and starving family after the Bill of Enclosure had taken his land and livelihood.

Sarah wept. It seemed as if these days her eyes were constantly red-rimmed. The rosiness was gone from her cheeks. As her body became swollen with child, her youthful bloom was lost for ever. Her black hair became lank and lifeless, her face puffed and blotchy. Wearily she dragged herself about the cottage, but the home that had once been warm and comforting was now a dismal and unhappy place.

Joseph Miller never saw his family again, for, just as Thomas Cole had predicted, seven weeks after his committal to prison, Joseph died of gaol-fever. From the day he was taken from his cottage, Ellen Miller had sat in a chair by the cold hearth, her eyes vacant, her hands idle. She neither spoke nor could she be persuaded to eat.

A week after the news of Joseph's death had reached them, she died in her sleep. Beth found her in the morning, the life gone out of her body as it had gone from her spirit the day her husband had been snatched from her.

Ella, who had depended solely upon her mother's care, pined, developed consumption and followed her mother to the grave in a few short weeks.

Beth wrapped her few belongings into a bundle and took the road out of Abbeyford, vowing never to set foot in the valley again.

"There's work to be had in the manufactories in Manchester and such cities for the likes o' me. Why, amongst them city girls, even *my* face won't be out o' place!"

Now there was only Henry Smithson and she in the cottage as Sarah came near the time to give birth to her child—Guy's child.

When Guy Trent had recovered sufficiently to leave his room, it was to find that things had changed vastly. Sarah— his lovely Sarah—was married to Henry Smithson and beyond his reach for ever.

Joseph Miller was gone from the village and the Miller family broken. Sir Matthew's tyrannical treatment of Miller had stirred resentment in each and every villager. Realising this, he planned steps to restore himself in the eyes of the simple village folk as their benevolent squire.

"Well, my boy, after this escapade, 'tis time you settled

down and took yourself a wife. I have arranged a marriage between you and Louisa Marchant, the daughter of a clothing manufacturer near Manchester. He has promised a generous settlement upon his daughter . . ."

Guy Trent rode his horse like a maniac away from Abbeyford towards Manchester, his heart filled with fury. The marriage was fixed for November and all the village would be invited to attend a grand feast in the barn at the Manor to celebrate their master's son's wedding. In this way, Sir Matthew hoped to banish the bitter memories from the minds of his tenants and employees. He would feast them and entertain them and make them forget that he had ever been anything but the kindly, charitable master he fondly imagined they had always believed him to be.

On the very day of Guy's marriage to Louisa Marchant, in the cottage in the village Sarah Smithson gave birth to his child. Though two months premature, the boy survived. There was no rejoicing at the birth of Evan Smithson. In the pain of her labour, Sarah cried out for Guy. Her cries for her lover finally destroyed the last shreds of Henry's affection for Sarah. He would never forgive. He would never forget. Henry looked upon the bawling, red-haired babe with loathing and vowed to sow the seed of revenge within the child against his own sire!

"Papa, we are invited to Guy Trent's wedding," Caroline had told her father some weeks before the proposed date. Lord Royston smiled tenderly upon her. For the past few weeks she had been good-humoured, obedient and a most loving daughter towards him.

He congratulated himself.

Thomas Cole was gone from Abbeyford—he had checked on that. And Lord Royston now presumed—indeed hoped —that the young man was already safely out of England bound for America.

As Lord Royston had confidently expected, Caroline seemed to have realised her foolishness when she had had more chance to observe the differences between Lord Grosmore—a man of unquestionable high birth and wealth —and Thomas Cole, the estate's bailiff.

Grosmore had become a constant visitor to the Grange and, though at first Caroline had been most ungracious towards her suitor, during the past few weeks Lord Royston had noticed a marked change in her attitude. She received Grosmore more kindly and seemed animated in his company.

Only the previous day Grosmore had sought out the earl and, with great pomposity, had asked for his daughter's hand in marriage. Royston had agreed at once, relieved that his strong-willed daughter would soon be safely married and out of danger from entering into any more such unsuitable liaisons. Royston shuddered and his thankfulness at the happy resolution to his worries made him say now, in a generous and expansive mood, "No doubt Trent will organise entertainment for the villagers in his barn, but perhaps we should offer for them to hold the wedding reception and ball here—at the Grange. After all, Trent, and I believe Marchant too amongst *trade* circles, are both well thought of."

"Why, Papa—that is an excellent idea."

"And—er—would it not be an opportune moment to announce your own engagement to Lord Grosmore?"

Caroline hesitated and for a moment there was, deep in her green eyes, a flash of anger, of rebellion. Fear stabbed at Lord Royston. More sharply than he intended to speak to her, he said, "I trust you do intend to accept him?"

For a moment a bleak, desolate expression flickered across her face. Then quietly Caroline said, "It seems I have no choice."

Inwardly Lord Royston sighed with relief. Outwardly he beamed once more upon his daughter. "Good, good. You shall have a new ball-gown. And I have a surprise in store for you, my dear, but that is to be my own special secret."

Caroline seemed to be lost in her own thoughts and merely murmured some reply. Lord Royston patted her shoulder and smiled to himself.

No doubt it was quite usual for a young bride-to-be to be a little dreamy and distant, her thoughts already on the future life she would share with her wealthy, aristocratic husband.

It seemed the whole county attended Guy Trent's wedding —though that was not strictly accurate. Because of the Earl of Royston's involvement, the wedding was attended by many aristocratic people who would not normally have condescended to be present at the marriage of a squire's son to the daughter of a man in trade—wealthy though he may be!

The small village church was overflowing with guests and the Reverend Langley was flustered with the honour, the importance, the responsibility!

Guy Trent stood facing the altar as his bride entered the church on her father's arm. He neither turned to watch her walk towards him, nor even looked down to greet her as she stood uncertainly at his side.

It was the first of many heartaches Guy Trent was to inflict upon the young girl. Louisa Marchant had come to Abbeyford as a young and attractive bride, full of hope and shy affection for her handsome, virile husband.

But her illusions, her hopes, were to be swiftly shattered, for Guy would never, could never, love Louisa when that love belonged for ever to Sarah.

Why he had ever loved—and would continue to long for —the black-haired, vivacious village girl, instead of the cool, serene, well-bred beauty of his wife, neither Guy Trent nor anyone else could ever explain.

Guy would spend the rest of his life in the Manor only a mile or so away from Sarah in her peasant's cottage and yet they were as lost to each other as if half the world separated them.

Louisa would shed many tears and, although Guy would do his duty as her husband and she would bear him a son, over the years her misery would grow into a cold bitterness.

But on this day of merry-making only Guy—and his Sarah alone in her labour giving birth to his son—could foresee what desolation the years ahead would hold.

The rest of the village caroused in the barn at the Manor, whilst their master's entertainment at the Grange was a little more refined.

After a sumptuous banquet Lord Royston rose to make the usual speech of good wishes to the bride and bridegroom and then added, "And it is my happy duty to announce the engagement of my beloved daughter, Caroline, to Peter, Viscount Grosmore."

There were cries of delight and surprise amongst the guests and Caroline found herself being gazed upon with fond eyes.

Only Lord Lynwood, seated beside his mother, turned ashen at Lord Royston's words and kept his eyes averted. He could not bear to see Caroline's unhappiness. Even though she had used and abused him, had destroyed his trust in her by her secret affair with Thomas Cole, which must now have been at an end, in spite of all that, Lynwood could not bear to think of her being obliged to marry a man she disliked, the odious, pompous, gross Grosmore!

When he did dare to look at her, Lynwood was surprised to see a faint smile upon her lips and calm acceptance in her eyes. He watched as Lord Grosmore, with a great fuss and flourish, placed the ring upon her finger—a huge ruby, far too large and gaudy for Caroline's slim fingers.

Then Lord Royston gave his daughter a silver locket set with a ruby surrounded by smaller diamonds. As he fastened the delicate chain around her neck and stooped to kiss his daughter's smooth brow, Caroline opened the locket and saw the two tiny miniature portraits of her dear mother and

171

father. Lynwood saw her mouth quiver, her eyes fill with tears, saw her clasp her father's hand and hold it against her cheek for an instant. But then she was in control of her emotions once more, graciously receiving the congratulations and good wishes of those present with a gentle smile upon her lips. But Lynwood wondered . . .

He only had a chance to speak to her briefly as they danced.

"Caroline—are you—happy?"

Her eyes were shining, her lips parted. "Oh yes, dear Francis—I am going to be so happy."

As the dance ended she held both his hands in hers for a moment and looked up at him her green eyes beseeching him, "Francis—you will always think well of me, won't you? You will always—understand?"

Thinking she was in some way asking for his forgiveness for her past foolishness, he answered, "Of course, of course I will. Need you ask?"

She touched his cheek lightly with her fingertips. "Dear Francis—don't ever forget me, will you?"

Then she was moving away from him across the crowded floor and slipping quietly behind a heavy brocade curtain and through a door.

Only Lynwood, whose eyes had followed her all evening whilst she had danced and curtsyed and smiled at her fiancé, saw her go. Perhaps she is fatigued, he thought, for even after Guy Trent and his bride had left the company the dancing had gone on and on and it was now well after midnight.

172

Tired himself of the noise, the music and laughter, Lynwood went out on to the terrace overlooking the rose-garden. It was a mild November night, the moon and stars amazingly bright in the dark sky. Lynwood leant against the balustrade in the shadows, listening to the muted strains of the music and thinking of Caroline.

He must have been there some time when a small sound disturbed his thoughts.

He shrank further into the shadows as he saw a figure hidden by a dark cloak and hood glide along the terrace towards him. As she neared the steps only a few feet away from him, she paused and glanced back over her shoulder. For a moment the hood of her cloak fell back from her face and Lynwood recognised her.

He almost cried her name aloud: *"Caroline!"* but no sound came from his lips.

He saw her falter, saw her fingers touch the locket at her throat, saw her glance back towards the lighted windows where her father's guests still danced away the night, where Lord Grosmore searched amongst the dancers for his fiancée.

In the bright moonlight, Lynwood fancied he saw a shudder pass through her slender frame, then she turned and, pulling the hood over her face once more, ran lightly down the stone steps into the rose-garden. Silently she flitted like an ethereal shadow along the twisting paths until she came to the door in the wall at the end of the garden which led into the field beyond.

As she slipped through it, Lynwood moved from his

173

hiding-place and ran to the door. He reached it in time to see her running swiftly down the slope towards the foot-bridge.

From the shadow of the bushes beside the bridge, Lynwood could just discern the figure of a man emerge, saw him open his arms to her as she flew towards him and watched as she was enfolded into his loving embrace.

For a timeless moment the lovers clung together and then Thomas Cole lifted her on to one of the two horses tethered near the bushes.

As they rode away into the darkness, only Lynwood saw them go.

ABBEYFORD INHERITANCE

ONE

New York Harbour, 1815
Adelina Cole rubbed away the grime on the window with
her fingers and peered into the tavern. She could see her
father sitting in the far corner with three of his so-called
friends, drinking and gambling as usual.

She sighed and shivered as a gust of wind blew along the
wooden verandah. Pulling the torn shawl closer around her
shoulders, Adelina glanced fearfully towards the harbour.
She could see the forest of ships' masts lining the piers,
swaying more than normal. The black sky overhead warned
of a gathering storm. Adelina bit her lip. She did not know
which frightened her the most – the threatening
thunderstorm or the inmates of the waterfront tavern!

But, to get to the room where she and her father lived
above the bar, she would have to go in. If only Sam, the
owner, did not see her and insist that she serve his
customers as payment of rent arrears.

She leaned her head against the rough wood and closed
her eyes, momentarily overcome by the weariness of the
daily struggle – hour by hour – to survive.

She opened her eyes again and they focused upon her
father. Even from this distance she could see the hand in
which he held his cards shaking. His eyes were bloodshot

and bleary, blinking rapidly, and he stretched his face from time to time as if he could not see clearly. Nor could he, she thought, not without a little impatience, for one eye was half-closed and surrounded by purple bruising from last night's fight.

Every night it was the same. The drink, the gambling – and then the quarrels. Drunken, ugly brawls and always Thomas Cole, weak and sick and vulnerable, came out of them bruised and beaten. Adelina was frightened. Not for herself, but for him. Frightened that one night, one drink too many or one punch too hard, would really harm him.

Life was hard on the New York waterfront and lives were cheap. There'd be no one to care – except his daughter.

Adelina fingered the silver locket about her neck. It was the only thing left in their harsh life that reminded her of earlier, happier days. She had worn the locket for the past four months, ever since she had found it.

One night while helping her father on to the shake-down on the floor of their room, as she had removed his jacket – struggling with his helpless, sprawling limbs – she had felt something hard sewn into the lining of his coat. When she had examined it closely, she found the stitching, though ill-formed and untidy, was tight and strong as if concealing more worth than the whole threadbare coat itself. As she had fingered the small, hard object, her eyes had lingered upon the prostrate form of her father, his head lolling to one side, his mouth wide open, snoring in uneven, rasping bursts. Adelina had sighed and shaken her head sadly. What an ugly sight he had become, and yet he was so pathetic.

It had taken her three days to prise the truth from her father, to persuade him to cut open the stitching and show her the object. His shaking fingers dropped the heart-shaped silver locket into her hands. "It was your mother's, she always wore it." He sniffed. "It's the only thing I have left of hers." He paused, then said reluctantly, "I suppose you'd better have it."

Adelina thought cynically that it would be safer in her possession, so she did not persuade him to keep it. Silently she fastened the tarnished chain about her neck. Then she opened the locket and twisted it to look at the tiny pictures within.

"Who are they? Not – not you and Mama?"

"No – her people. Her parents." He jabbed a grubby finger at the locket. "My Lord and Lady Royston, they are."

"Who?" Adelina's green eyes widened.

"Robert Elcombe, the Earl of Royston, of Abbeyford – a little village near Manchester in the Old Country." Thomas Cole's bleary eyes watered at the memory of far-off days. "He's her father. Her mother's dead – died before I even knew her."

"And – and her father?"

He shrugged and then flopped back on the shake-down and closed his eyes. "How the hell should I know!" he muttered.

Within seconds he was snoring loudly, whilst Adelina still gazed at the faces in the locket.

Now as she stood peering in through the dirty window, fingering the locket, her thoughts were interrupted as the swing doors flew open and a man came hurtling through the air to land in a sprawling heap almost at her feet. Another figure sprang through the doors and leapt on top of the man on the ground and began smashing his fists into his face. Such drunken fights were commonplace and Adelina was untroubled by it. She saw the disturbance only as a means by which she might succeed in slipping through the saloon and up the stairs unobserved.

She was about halfway to the stairs when she felt someone grip her arm and, turning, found young Sammy's blue eyes gazing up at her.

If there was anyone in this awful place who was a friend to her then it was the tavern owner's young, ill-treated son, Sammy. The fourteen-year-old boy looked only eleven, his tattered clothes hanging loosely on his thin body. He worked hard but received nothing for his efforts but abuse and his father's fist. Right now his eye was beginning to colour from yet another vicious cuff.

"What is it, Sammy?" Adelina asked him gently.

"Your Pa's sure gettin' himself in deep trouble, Miss Adelina. He ain't no match for those card-sharps."

Adelina sighed and glanced through the haze of smoke towards her father. She hesitated between reaching the safety of their one room and rescuing her befuddled father from the men who would cheat him out of the ragged shirt on his back.

She hesitated a moment too long.

"Aha, Miss Adelina." Big Sam was approaching. A fat, cruel-looking man, his only aim in life was to make money with no scruples as to how he made it. His right arm swept in an arc and knocked young Sammy off his feet, but he did not even glance down at his son.

"Leave the boy alone," Adelina faced the big man angrily, but he only laughed.

"Ah, you're sure lovely when you're angry." His grip fastened upon her arm and he pushed his ugly face close to hers. "You'll serve my customers their drinks, miss, and make like you kinda want to, or," he jerked his thumb towards her father in the corner, "I'll see him in the jail."

Big Sam's threat was no idle one, for he'd put her father in jail twice before for debt and kept her working for him to pay off twice the amount which was owed.

As always, his threat brought her rebellion under control, but strengthened her iron resolve to escape from this man's clutches, even if she had to drag her father bodily with her. She would not – could not – desert Thomas Cole, for in her heart there were still the memories of better times.

The memory of her mother's lovely face and her father's smile; of a warm bed; of food and new clothes; of soft hands and a gentle voice; of happiness. For the most part the memories were faint, elusive, obliterated by the harsh reality of the present, yet at times they came flooding back into her mind strong and clear to revive her spirit and help her to fight all the harder for their existence. She had to struggle for the both of them, for Thomas Cole had lost the will to live with the death of his beloved Caroline some nine years earlier. Only Adelina's will-power kept him alive. From a genteel, sheltered little girl, she had, of necessity, had to become a fighter, a survivor and protector of her father. From her parents, Adelina had inherited their best qualities – strength without selfishness, gentleness and compassion without weakness.

There was a commotion in her father's corner. The table overturned and drinks were spilled.

"You're a liar and a cheat, Thomas Cole!"

Her father sat in his chair, slumped forward. Four days' growth of beard upon his chin, his hair long and dirty, his eyes bloodshot. Adelina's heart turned over at the sight of him. Objectively, she couldn't understand why she stood by him, supported him, worked for him. Yet he was her father. He was all she had right now. She moved towards him, but the man who had yelled abuse at him now caught hold of the neck of his shirt and hoisted Thomas to his feet. For a few seconds he held him aloft. Thomas, stupified, hung there limply, his head lolling to one side, his eyes rolling. The man brought his right arm back and clenched his fist.

As Adelina cried out, "No, oh no!" his fist smashed into her father's face, snapping his head back with a sickening crack. The man loosened his hold on him and Thomas Cole fell backwards hitting his head on the table with a dull thud.

Several other men now rose to their feet, their shouts only adding to the confusion. Adelina tried to push her way through them to reach her father, but they pressed round the scene, blocking her path.

Suddenly, their raucous shouts died away and there was an uncanny silence.

"*Jesus!*" someone said, "you've killed him."

Frantic now, Adelina fought her way through. The man was standing over her father, who was lying in a twisted heap at his feet. Blood trickled from Thomas Cole's mouth and from a gash on his temple. Adelina threw herself upon her knees beside him. She took hold of his hand and chafed it. Her eyes flashed angrily towards her father's assailant.

"You're a brute, Jed Hawkins. You'll swing for that fist of yours yet."

"Seems like he will now," muttered someone. "Yer sure seen him off."

Jed stood there looking stupid. "I didn't mean to kill him, Miss Adelina. It's just that the silly old fool was playing his cards all wrong. I guess he was too drunk to see them ..."

"Oh, shut up and help me carry him upstairs. I must bathe his head and ..."

"'Tain't no use, Miss Adelina." Another of the men put his hand upon her shoulder with a rough tenderness. "Don't you understand what we're sayin'? He's a gone. He's dead!"

For a moment Adelina stared at the man.

"No – oh, no," she whispered and then slowly turned to

look down at the still form. She was rigidly motionless for some moments, while the men watched with uneasy silence.

Trembling a little, she reached out her hand and slid it beneath his shirt. There was no heartbeat.

As they had said, her father was dead.

Adelina bowed her head on to his lifeless chest and wept. Tears of bitterness, tears of remorse, tears of grief.

She became aware of feet shuffling near her and of the mutterings.

"That sure weren't no fair fight, no sir!"

"You oughta be hanged, Jed."

"Hittin' the poor ole begger and him drunk and senseless."

"What about the girl?" "Guess Sam'll take care o' her." There were a few half-hearted guffaws.

Death came quickly and often in this neighbourhood and was swiftly forgotten by those not directly involved.

Sam! The name penetrated her distraught mind and Adelina scrambled to her feet. There was nothing more she could do for her father.

Now she must save herself ...

Too late, for Sam himself was shouldering his way through the throng. Wildly, she looked about her for a way of escape but there was none. He stood, legs apart, over the corpse and laughed, his great, fat belly shaking with mirth.

The tears dried in Adelina's eyes as grief gave way to rage. With a shriek she hurled herself at Sam and pummelled her fists against his chest, but he gripped her wrists and held her easily. So she kicked his legs and bit his hand. She screamed and kicked and scratched, venting her anger and grief upon this hateful man who had been the supplier of the drink which had ruined her father and had held her captive by the subsequent debt.

How she hated and feared this brute who could not even

treat his own son properly.

"You've a handful there, Sam," someone shouted.

Sam laughed. "I'll tame the she-cat. She'll come a-crawlin' soon enough." He dealt her a vicious blow with the back of his hand. "I'll lock you in your room, miss, until you've come to your senses."

Huddled on the shake-down, the bruise on her temple swelling rapidly, Adelina fingered the locket about her neck.

England, she thought, if I can get away from Sam, I'll go to England and seek out Mama's home.

There was a scrabbling at the door and the rusty key turned in the lock and young Sammy's spikey hair appeared round the door. "Quick, Miss Adelina, he's out the back. You can get out while he's gone."

Adelina scrambled to her feet, snatched her shawl and the bundle of her few items of clothing from the corner and followed Sammy down the stairs, through the now empty saloon bar and out into the wild night.

He took her hand and dragged her along the street. The wind whistled, plucking at her skirt, threatening to tear away her shawl, but bending her head against the storm she followed Sammy.

Breathlessly, they fell into a sheltered corner near the harbour. The storm was overhead and Adelina's teeth began to chatter with fear. She hated storms.

Sammy cupped his hands around his mouth and spoke close to her ear. "If you can get on a ship, you could get right away from here. It'd be the best way. By road, he'd catch up with you."

Adelina nodded. "I could go to England, but I've no money."

Sammy shrugged. "No problem. Stow away." He

suggested in a matter-of-fact manner.

"But – but how do I know which ship is going to England?" Adelina's eyes flickered down the long line of swaying masts.

Sammy said, "Look, you stay here, I'll go along the harbour an' see if I can find out if there's one bound for England."

He was gone a long time, so long that Adelina began to think he had deserted her and returned home. She crouched behind a stack of barrels, trying to find a little shelter. Then the rain came, soaking in minutes her thin shawl. She shivered from cold and fear, and delayed shock. She groaned aloud, the picture of her father's still form horribly fresh in her mind.

Sammy was back, squeezing his thin frame between the barrels. "Miss Adelina, where are you? Oh, there you are. I've found one," he told her gleefully. "Come on, I'll take you. It sails on the tide. If we go now, there's no one about, the crew are all having a last fling ashore. If you slip on now and hide yourself in one of those longboats they have on deck, no one'll find you."

"But – but I can't stay hidden under there all the way to England. It takes weeks!"

"I've thought about that," answered the practical Sammy and gestured towards a bundle in his hand. "I've gotten you some food. Stay hidden as long as you can, then if they find you when they're at sea it'll be too late anyway," he said triumphantly. "They'll not turn back just to put you ashore."

"I suppose not," Adelina said doubtfully, "but – but what do they do to stowaways? Flog them?"

"Naw," scoffed Sammy, "not a pretty girl, anyway. Likely as not they'll make a fuss of you," he added with a confidence Adelina did not share. The young boy, old for his years though his hard life had made him in many ways, could not be expected to understand the fears of a young girl amongst a group of rough, tough sailors.

Adelina swallowed her fear. The prospects of a life under big Sam's rule were even worse. She would take the risk. She would do anything, risk anything, to get away from Big Sam.

"What about you, Sammy, aren't you going to come with me?"

"No, Miss Adelina. I'll get away from him one day, but I want to head west. I gotten it all figured out. When I'm a bit older ..." He grinned at her, for a moment no longer the half-starved waif, but a boy with determination and toughness. Adelina felt relief. Sammy would be all right.

Adelina remained hidden for the first four days of the voyage. Luckily she did not suffer sea-sickness and, though the small, stuffy space beneath a tarpaulin covering a long-boat was cramped and unpleasant, there she stayed.

On the fourth day, when the sun was high in the sky, two sailors pulled back the tarpaulin.

Adelina blinked in the sudden bright light.

"Gawd love us! Look what we 'ave 'ere!" cried one.

The other one gaped. "A stowaway!" Then he grinned with blackened teeth. "An' a mighty pretty one too, ain't she?"

"I saw 'er first, Black Wilf," said the first.

"Mebbe, but you owes me for savin' yer miserable life in that fight we 'ad in New York harbour, don't forgit."

Suddenly a knife blade flashed in the sunlight and Adelina watched with horrified eyes as the two ruffians faced each other, circling like two wary fighting cocks.

"She's mine, I tell 'ee."

"You owes me."

"What's this?" roared a deep voice. It was the First Mate

bearing down upon the sailors. "No fightin' aboard this ship." He stopped in astonishment as he caught sight of Adelina.

"Good grief!" He stared at her open-mouthed.

"She'm a stowaway, Mister Mate."

"An' I saw 'er first. She's mine. Warm my hammock a treat."

As Black Wilf growled again, the First Mate said, "She'll warm no one's hammock. She'll be dealt with by the Cap'n."

"Aw, come on, Mister Mate ..."

"*Silence!*" the Mate roared and even Adelina jumped and began to feel more afraid than she had at the mercy of the two seamen.

"Come on, out with you," the Mate flicked his hand towards her.

Stiffly, her limbs cramped and cold, she climbed out of her hiding-place. Not one of the watching men stepped forward to offer her his helping hand.

"Come with me." The Mate turned abruptly and Adelina followed him meekly. The sailors, now united in their disappointment in losing her to their superior, shouted after her.

"Lucky Cap'n with you in his bed the night!"

Adelina bit her lip, regretting her hasty, thoughtless flight from New York just to escape from Big Sam. Doubtless the world was littered with the likes of Big Sam! Perhaps the Captain ...

Below, the Mate knocked upon a cabin door and pushed her in front of him.

"Cap'n. We have a stowaway." The man who looked up from the chart he was studying spread out on the table in the centre of the small cabin, was tall, broad, but with a tell-tale middle-aged paunch. His face was half-covered by a beard and moustache, but his eyes were sharp and bright in the weatherbeaten, leathery face.

He grunted and straightened, his cool eyes looking Adelina up and down. "Well, missy, and where did you think you were going?"

With a brave defiance she did not feel inwardly, Adelina held her head high. "England! My grandfather is the Earl of Royston."

A huge bellow of laughter welled up inside the man and he threw back his head and roared. "Hear that, Mister Mate? We have a *lady* aboard!"

"Aye, Cap'n," the Mate grinned.

Adelina glared resentfully at the Captain.

"Well, missy, I admire your courage. 'Tis a pity you're not a man. You'd make a fine seaman, eh, Mister Mate?"

"Aye, Cap'n."

"Well, now," the Captain said, controlling his mirth at last. "What to do with you?" He pondered for a moment, looking at her reflectively. "Can you cook, girl?"

"Yes – yes I can."

"Good. Our ship's cook's gone down with the fever this very day. You," he prodded his finger at her, "can take his place."

So Adelina passed the voyage as ship's cook! She had been very fortunate to find a Captain, not only with a sense of humour who treated her presence aboard his ship as a huge joke, but one who was also a god-fearing gentleman who minded that she was kept safe from his lusty crew!

TWO

"'Ere you be, miss." The tinker pulled his laden cart to a jingling, tinkling halt. "This 'ere's Amberly. I stops 'ere. O'er yonder, see that wood?"

Adelina shaded her eyes against the summer sun. "Yes – yes, I see it."

"Go through that there wood, and down t'hill and you'm in Abbeyford. Lord Royston lived at Abbeyford Grange on t'opposite side. Big place, you'm can't miss it."

"Thank you for the ride," she said, climbing down from the cart and giving his mangy old mule an affectionate pat. The flies buzzed around the animal's head so that his ears were constantly twitching and his tail swishing, but in vain in the August heat. "Poor old thing, you're sure hot, aren't you?" She sighed. "So am I." She looked down at her old skirt, dusty and badly stained. "I can hardly meet my grandfather like this," she murmured, "but I guess there's not much I can do about it."

Although she had been confiding her thoughts to the mule, the tinker's sharp ears missed nothing.

"'Ere, ain't you no other dress but that 'un?"

Adelina grinned up at him. "I'm afraid not. He'll just have to take me as I am."

The tinker sniffed and rummaged in a box behind him. He pulled out a pale blue silk dress, high-waisted with puffed sleeves and a low neckline. "Will this fit you?" He pushed it at her.

She held it up before her, her eyes sparkling. It was crumpled and had a small tear at the hem, but it was a vast improvement on the garments she wore. "Yes – but I've no money." She held it out to him. "I'm sorry – I can't pay you."

"G'arn," he sniffed. "You'm been company on the road here from Liverpool. Tek it."

"Are you sure?" Adelina said doubtfully, but still holding the garment, secretly longing to keep it, but the tinker looked scarcely any wealthier than herself!

He grinned toothlessly at her. "Well, I ain't no use for it, an' folks round here won't buy it, it's a sight too fancy for country women."

"Well – if you're sure – thank's a lot."

The dry dust rose in little puffs as she walked along the meandering lane and Adelina was thankful to reach the shade of the wood. She was so hot and sticky and thirsty. She dropped down into the grass, leant against a tree and closed her eyes, but her mouth and throat were so dry. In the quiet of the wood she listened intently.

Amidst the birdsong and the rustling of scurrying little creatures through the undergrowth, Adelina could hear the sound of water. She licked her dry lips and swallowed, her throat sore. The sound seemed to come from her left so she rose and followed the narrow, winding path through the trees until the way fell steeply downwards. The noise of the waterfall was louder now. Eagerly, Adelina slipped and slithered down the path and gasped with sheer delight as she came upon the waterfall and the rocky pool.

Scrambling feverishly over the rocks, she cupped her hands beneath the sparkling water and drank and drank. Then she splashed it over her hot face. Thirst satisfied, she sat down upon a rock and watched the waterfall in fascination. It was cooler here, beside the water and beneath the shade of the overhanging trees, but she still felt hot and dirty. She spread out the dress the tinker had given her on a rock and eyed the deep, inviting pool longingly. Without really making a conscious decision, she peeled off her clothing and jumped into the water. She gave a little squeal of surprise and pleasure, the water was colder than she had expected, but lovely, deliciously cooling! She splashed and dived and shook her head like a playful puppy, enjoying the freedom, the freshness.

Riding through the wood on his way home, Francis Amberly, seventh Earl of Lynwood since the death of his father twenty-three years earlier, heard faintly Adelina's squeals of delight. Quietly, he swung down from his horse and leaving the trustworthy animal, he ran softly between the trees until he came out at the edge of the rock face overlooking the pool. For some moments, he watched the lovely naked water nymph splashing in the water. In a patch of sunlight filtering through the trees, she raised her wet face to the warmth, hair plastered darkly to her head, eyes closed, lips parted in sheer ecstasy.

Lynwood felt a strange constriction in his chest, the scene reeling before his eyes. He grasped hold of the branch of a tree to steady himself.

No! No – it wasn't possible!

He passed his hand across his eyes as if in disbelief. But when he looked again, she was still there. This girl – was real!

Caroline had come back!

No – no, he told himself firmly, half angry with himself for such whimsical thoughts. That was twenty years ago. This was a young girl – but so like Caroline it was hardly credible.

He watched as she climbed from the pool, her lovely body glistening, her long hair wet and shining. He watched as she dried herself with her shawl, and dressed. He saw her stand, half clothed in her chemise, holding the blue dress up, inspecting it critically. To Lynwood's eyes it was a poor rag of a gown, but the girl seemed pleased by what she saw, and a small smile curved her lips as she slipped the garment over her head and wriggled into it. Still he watched as she found a rock to sit on where the sun shone warmly through the trees, and began to rub her hair dry. Unable to move, he gazed in fascination, knowing even before it happened, that as the seemingly black, wet hair dried, it would become the lovely auburn colour of Caroline's hair!

The nymph stood up and, as if feeling his eyes upon her, she turned and slowly surveyed the edge of the rock face above her.

As soon as she saw him, her lips parted in a gasp and the colour slowly crept up her neck and suffused her face. Then embarrassment was replaced by indignation. Hands on hips, she demanded, "How long have you been standing there?"

Her voice was not Caroline's, though everything else about her, from her auburn hair, her green eyes, now sparkling angrily, to her lovely, curving body was Caroline. It was incredible! Not possible!

But the voice was different. Caroline's had been high-pitched, rather affected. This girl's was low and husky and her speech held the faint drawl of the Americas.

"Quite some time," he said.

They stared at each other. Adelina – in spite of her discomfort – noticed that he was a handsome man, obviously a gentleman with a broad brow and a long, aquiline nose. He wore a short riding-jacket, with a high-collared shirt and a casually tied neckcloth, close-fitting breeches and black, knee-high riding-boots. His tall hat was set at a jaunty angle and as he stood looking down at her, a sardonic smile curving his lips, he idly slapped his riding-crop against his boot.

"Well, if you've quite finished?" she said drily, smoothing down the skirt of her recent acquisition, and picking up the bundle of her old clothes, "I'll be on my way."

She climbed up the path and as she made to pass, close by, he reached out and his fingers closed about her arm.

Her green eyes flashed contempt into his blue, mocking gaze.

"Don't run away, my lovely water-nymph," he smiled.

"How *dare* you?" she cried, knowing now that he had most certainly observed her bathing. Against her will, her blush deepened.

"Where are you going, anyway?"

She flung back her head and retorted, "To Abbeyford to meet my grandfather – the Earl of Royston," she added grandly, hoping to impress him.

His grasp upon her arm tightened, his fingers digging into her flesh. He pulled her closer to him. Looking down into Caroline's eyes, Caroline's face – and yet it was not Caroline – he demanded harshly, "Who *are* you?"

"Adelina – Adelina Cole."

Although he was half expecting such an answer, the shock still showed in his face.

"Her daughter!" he muttered.

"I beg your pardon?"

"Nothing!" he snapped and released his hold on her abruptly. He seemed about to turn away from her, but hesitated saying, "You'll find no welcome at Abbeyford Grange."

Adelina waited, the questions tumbling about her mind,

but something about this man's attitude silenced her – almost frightened her. He seemed to be battling with some inner conflict..

She watched him, her head on one side then said quietly, "You know him?"

"Yes. Yes, I do. And he'll not want to see you. You're too like your – mother!"

Adelina's eyes shone and she asked eagerly, "My mother? You knew my mother?"

Lynwood glanced at her and then looked quickly away. "Oh, yes – I knew her." There was bitterness in his tone.

The sight of Adelina – so like Caroline – had brought back a tumult of emotions Lord Lynwood had thought buried along with his boyhood. It was as if a ghost stood before him, the object of his boyhood affections, the subject of his adolescent dreams – the one who had, by her cruel deceit, destroyed his adoration, and his belief in women. And yet he could not turn away from this girl, so obviously alone and impoverished. She was Caroline's daughter – he should turn and flee! Grudgingly, half knowing as he did so that he was lost, he said, "Look – I'd better take you home with me, to Lynwood Hall, for the time being. Perhaps my mother will know what's best to do with you."

"Lordy me, Francis, what on earth have you picked up here? A scarecrow?" Then Lady Lynwood peered more closely at the girl her son had brought into her luxurious sitting-room. The same surprise Adelina had seen in Lynwood's eyes was mirrored in his mother's, but this time there was no pain accompanying it. "I don't need to ask who *you* are!"

The old lady's eyes appraised her from head to foot. Adelina held her head defiantly high and met Lady Lynwood's gaze boldly. She seemed, to Adelina, to be incredibly old – a tiny figure dressed entirely in black with a wide, voluminous skirt, a jet necklace and ear-rings. Her hair was completely white and her olive skin very wrinkled, but her eyes were bright and alert and now twinkled with sudden mischief as she looked at her son. "I dare say she'd be quite presentable properly dressed. Has he seen her?"

Lynwood shook his head.

"My word – he's in for a shock! What's your name?"

"Adelina Cole."

The old lady nodded slowly and murmured, "Named after her mother – Adeline."

"I beg your pardon?" Adelina was becoming tired of being the subject of their musings which she could not understand. Impatiently, she said, "I've come from America to find my grandfather. My parents are dead and …"

The old lady gasped and Lord Lynwood twisted round to face Adelina. "What?" they both cried together.

Adelina looked from one shocked face to the other.

"Er – m-my parents are – dead," she repeated.

Lynwood gave a groan and sank down into a chair. His face turned a deathly white. As for Lady Lynwood, she seemed to accept Adelina's news more calmly, but there was a sadness in her eyes that had not been there a few moments ago.

"You'd better ride to Abbeyford Grange and see Lord Royston, Francis," Lady Lynwood murmured, her gaze still upon Adelina. "Tell him – tell him what has happened and …" She paused and directed her question at Adelina. "When – and how – did your mother die?"

"About ten years ago," was Adelina's husky reply. "In childbirth. The baby died too."

"And your father?" There was gentleness in Lady Lynwood's tone.

"Just before I came to England." Adelina lowered her head, not wanting to tell them the sordid details of her recent life, of her father's death. Thinking her reluctance to say more stemmed from the newness of her grief, Lady Lynwood probed no further.

"Go to Abbeyford, Francis, and see him," she told her son.

"I'm sorry," Lord Lynwood told Adelina on his return from Abbeyford. "But – Lord Royston cannot bring himself to see you." Pain flickered briefly in Lynwood's own eyes, as if he understood her grandfather's feelings only too well.

Adelina said, "May I ask why not?"

Lynwood's shoulders lifted fractionally. "He has not forgiven your mother, I suppose."

"Forgiven her? What for?"

He looked at her then, fully. "Don't you know what happened here twenty years ago?"

Adelina almost laughed, but the hurt in his eyes stopped her. "I didn't even know of Lord Royston's existence until a few months ago. I found this locket."

She opened the locket at her throat and Lynwood bent forward. The miniatures were faded but still recognisable. He straightened up.

"Lord Royston gave that to his daughter – your mother. He held a grand ball at Abbeyford Grange in honour of Guy Trent's marriage, but, in the midst of it, she slipped away and eloped with the bailiff on the estate – one Thomas Cole!" The bitterness was back in his tone. "I presume he was your father, since you bear the same name."

Adelina nodded.

"Afterwards – Lord Royston became a recluse. He never forgave them. Nor does he want to see you now!"

"I see." Sadly, Adelina turned away.

"But he's not a vindictive man. He realises that what happened is no fault of yours," Lynwood was saying, whilst Adelina waited, her back still towards him, her head lowered. "He has asked me to see Martha Langley – Caroline's cousin – to see if she will take you in. Her husband is the Reverend Hugh Langley, Vicar of Abbeyford. They live at Abbeyford Vicarage."

Adelina twisted round, her green eyes flashing. "I don't want charity!" she snapped. "I can take care of myself. I've done it for the past few years ..." The words were out before she could prevent them.

Lynwood's eyebrows lifted fractionally, but he did not question her. One glance at her clothing told him that life could not have been one of ease and comfort for her.

"Give Lord Royston time. My news was a shock. He may – I'm not saying he will – but if he knows you're close at hand still, he may relent." Lynwood smiled. "His curiosity to see his only grandchild may work in your favour, Miss Cole."

"Very well, but only for a short time. I'll not stay where I'm not wanted," she told him determinedly.

"I don't see why we must take her in," Martha Langley muttered as her own daughter, Emily, ushered their unexpected guest from the room and took her upstairs.

"Oh, come now, Martha my dear," Hugh said. "It was a shock for you, I know, seeing her and so like your poor, dear cousin."

" 'Poor, dear cousin', my foot!" countered Martha. "I'll not deny her daughter's sudden arrival out of the blue has caused me considerable unease. But not," she added vehemently, "in the way you mean."

Leaning towards her husband, she said, "You realise what this means, don't you?"

Agitated, Hugh Langley clasped and unclasped his womanish hands. "I – I don't understand you, Martha."

"She's a threat to Emily's inheritance. *That's* what I mean!"

Hugh Langley looked shocked. "Martha – how can you think of that when the poor child is a homeless orphan? I would not have thought you so uncharitable." It was the closest he ever came to remonstrating with his wife.

"Uncharitable? It'll be a sight more than 'charity' if *she* inherits from Lord Royston now, instead of our own daughter!" Martha Langley said tartly.

Mr Langley shook his head sadly. He'd tried, oh how he'd tried over the years to soften Martha's mercenary streak, her bitterness against her wealthier relations. Then, after Caroline's elopement and the birth of their own daughter, Emily, Lord Royston had altered his Will and had made no secret of the fact that he had cut out his own wayward daughter and had made baby Emily Langley heiress to his entire estate.

Martha's vindictiveness had been mellowed somewhat by his action. But now, threatened again by the arrival of Caroline's daughter – Lord Royston's own granddaughter, a close blood relative whereas Emily was only distantly connected to him and that by marriage – all Martha Langley's jealousy was rekindled.

Emily led Adelina up the stairs and along the dark landing to a room at the rear of the Vicarage.

"This," she said, sounding almost apologetic as she opened the door, "is your room."

Adelina stepped inside. To anyone else the bedroom would have appeared poorly furnished. There was a high, hard single bed, a dressing-table and wash-stand and a tall, narrow wardrobe. The bedspread was obviously old and patched here and there, and the faded blue curtains scarcely covered the window. But to Adelina, who had more than once slept on bare boards with only one moth-eaten blanket as a cover, it was comfort indeed!

"There's some water in the ewer and clean towels nearby," Emily said. "I'll leave you to freshen up. Please," she begged, lacing her fingers together nervously, "don't be too long. Dinner will be served very soon, and Mama dislikes unpunctuality." Then she gave Adelina a quick, hesitant smile and left the room.

Adelina went over to the window. Immediately below her window was part of the Vicarage garden and the village green, then the road and a row of cottages. Behind them was a strip of meadow-land and the stream and then the ground rose. Adelina's gaze travelled up the hill until she saw a mansion standing just below the top of the hill.

"That must be Abbeyford Grange," she murmured, "where Lord Royston lives." She found it impossible to think of him as her grandfather. He was only a remote image created in her mind. Sadly she turned from the window and left the bedroom. Emily was waiting for her in the hall.

The meal was passed in an uncomfortable silence. Covertly, Adelina appraised her new-found relatives. Martha Langley sat stiffly at one end of the dining-table. She was thin with angular features, a pointed chin, a long nose and narrow, almost non-existent lips. At the opposite end of the table, Mr Langley stooped over his plate, his shoulders permanently rounded. He was bald except for tufts of wispy white hair over his ears. His manner was diffident, rather fussy, and yet Adelina could sense his kindliness towards her.

Emily, seated opposite Adelina, was small and slim, but rather plain. Her brown hair was pulled tightly back from her face into a coil. Her dress – though of good material and well-made – was a drab grey.

At any moment Adelina expected to be questioned about her parents, but Martha Langley remained obstinately tight-lipped and silent.

After casting several glances towards his wife, and then sighing softly to himself, Mr Langley turned to Adelina and said, "What happened to your mother, my dear?"

Martha Langley's head snapped up, but resolutely he ignored his wife. "And your father?"

"My mother died ten years ago, in childbirth – the baby too. My father ..." she hesitated, reluctant to be disloyal to her father, yet she could not hide the truth for ever. "My father," she continued firmly, "suffered much after her death. He never fully recovered. Eventually, we lost everything. He – he died shortly before I came to England."

"So," Martha put in waspishly, "you thought you'd look up your wealthy relative, did you?"

"Martha!" Mr Langley's tone was gently warning, but his wife would not be silenced.

"Well, let me tell you, my girl, Emily is Lord Royston's heiress and nothing and no one is going to change that!"

Emily blushed scarlet and hung her head, whilst Adelina's own heightened colour came from an indignant anger. She sprang to her feet, the chair falling backwards with a crash at the violence of her sudden movement. She faced Martha Langley squarely. "If I'm not welcome by my mother's own folk, I'll go – at once!" Impetuously, she made as if to turn and leave the room and the house that very instant.

Mr Langley's soothing voice spoke up. "Adelina, Adelina. Sit down, child, do. You shall stay with us for a short while, until his lordship has had time to – to make up

his mind. This has all been a great shock for us, my dear,·
you must realise that."

Adelina saw him glance at his wife again. "We were not
even aware of your existence, nor of your mother's death.
You must give us all time to adjust to the situation."

Anger still smouldered in Adelina's green eyes. "I'm not
a fortune-hunter, if that is what you are thinking," she
declared.

"No, no, my dear, of course you are not." Once again the
gentle eyes were directed at Martha, but with a note of
firmness in his tone now, he added, "You shall stay here
until after Christmas at least. Then we shall see what is to
be done."

Martha Langley shot him a look of malice, her thin lips
tight, but she said no more.

Later, alone in her room, after she had undressed down to
her chemise, Adelina went over to the window and opened
it. She leaned out and breathed the night air deeply. Her
fingers touched the leaves of an ivy tree which covered the
outside wall and wound itself round her window. High up
on the hill she could see Abbeyford Grange where her
grandfather, Lord Royston, lived in lonely splendour.

If only she could see him, could meet him, just once. She
touched the locket around her neck, her fingers tracing the
ruby set in the centre and the smaller diamonds
surrounding it. As she gazed through the darkness at the
house her mother had once called home, Adelina felt the
yearning to belong – really belong – to someone. She
resolved that somehow she would find a way of meeting her
grandfather – no matter who stood in her way!

THREE

The following day Emily took Adelina for a walk to show her the village.

Abbeyford lay in its own shallow valley in gently rolling countryside some fifteen miles south of Manchester. In the centre of the village was the church and the Vicarage, the green and the duckpond, and clustering around them were the villagers' cottages. On the hill-slope to the east, just below the summit, stood the half-timbered Grange, built in the Tudor style. On the opposite hillside was Abbeyford Manor, a square, solid house with stables to one side and farm buildings at the rear. Above the Manor and a little to the south, on the very top of the hill, the abbey ruins rose gaunt and black against the sky.

From the waterfall where Adelina had first met Lord Lynwood, a stream ran through the wood, channelling a deep gully, down the hill and into the valley and on through the common. The lane leading from the village up to the Manor ran through this stream, literally, for there was only a narrow footbridge across the water at this point. Farm-carts and the gentry's carriages had to splash through the ford in the lane. Another stream ran from the eastern hill-side through the valley and at the southern end the two streams joined together and ran as one out of the valley through a natural pass between the hills to join a river some miles away.

The two girls looked in the church with its grey stone and shining wooden pews and then walked across the green. A few children played in the roadway and here and there a woman sat in her doorway spinning. Adelina was shocked to see that the children ran barefoot and that their clothes were ragged and dirty. The low, squat cottages, too, were tumble-down. Doors hung off their hinges and broken windows were stuffed with sackcloth to keep out the cold.

Emily linked her arm through Adelina's. "I'm glad you've come, Adelina. I hope we shall be friends."

After Mrs Langley's open hostility, Emily's gesture was all the more surprising. "I've to take a message to Mrs Smithson," Emily said. "She helps out at the Vicarage sometimes."

She stepped towards one of the cottages and knocked upon the door. It was opened, somewhat tentatively Adelina thought, by a woman.

"Mrs Smithson, I have a message from my mother ..." The woman's stare travelled past Emily and saw Adelina. "Oh, this is Miss Adelina Cole. She's from America. Our mothers were cousins, you know."

The woman's eyes widened as she looked at Adelina. Then she gasped and one hand fluttered nervously to her throat while the other gripped the door fiercely as if to gain support.

"What is it, Mrs Smithson?" Emily asked. "Are you ill?"

"No, no. But it's like seein' a ghost, miss." She continued to gaze at Adelina.

"You mean Adelina is like her mother? Yes, Mama, was saying so."

"I can scarce believe it, Miss Emily!"

"Mrs Smithson, Mama says can you come to the Vicarage tomorrow afternoon?"

The woman nodded absently, hardly seeming to hear

Emily, her attention still upon Adelina.

Sarah Smithson must once have been very pretty, beautiful in a natural way, Adelina supposed, but now she wore the lines of defeat and bitterness upon her tired face. Her mouth was drawn into a tight line, her shoulders drooping, and her movements were slow and lethargic as if life held little interest or meaning for her. She was dressed in a shapeless blouse and a coarse brown skirt. Her eyes were dull and sorrowful and her hair, once black and shining, was now grey.

Sarah Smithson blinked and seemed to recover her senses. "What – oh, yes. I'll be there, miss."

As Emily and Adelina walked back to the Vicarage they passed several villagers. Each one smiled and bade Emily 'good-day'. Then their eyes strayed to the stranger at her side. Their reactions were varied. A young girl merely smiled and passed on. A youth grinned cheekily, his admiration of Adelina apparent. But two older women, walking together, stared at Adelina with open astonishment, and as they passed by they whispered to each other.

"It seems," Adelina remarked, "that my appearance has a strange effect upon some of the villagers."

"The older ones – yes. Those who remember seeing your mother. Mama says your likeness to your mother is uncanny."

Adelina was silent. Just what could her mother have done to arouse such deep resentment that it had lasted all these years? First Lord Lynwood, then Martha Langley – and of course Lord Royston, who would not even meet his own granddaughter!

They walked on. Adelina asked suddenly, "Lord Royston – he owns all this?" She waved her hand to encompass not only the farmland on the surrounding hill-sides and the cattle grazing there, but the tumble-down cottages too.

"Why – yes." Emily turned her wide eyes upon Adelina. "Why do you ask?"

"I just wondered why he doesn't do a little more for his tenants?"

Emily blushed. "Lord Royston has nothing to do with the day to day running of his estate."

"Then who has?" Adelina demanded sharply, growing more disgusted at the poverty she saw where there was no reason for the people to be so poor.

"The Trents. I suppose Wallis Trent really, since his father, Squire Guy Trent," she paused as if searching for the right words, "takes little active part in running the estate."

"Hmm, I should like to meet this – Wallis Trent," Adelina murmured.

"You'll meet him tomorrow night," Emily was saying softly.

Adelina turned to look at her. Emily's face wore a dreamy expression and two bright pink spots of colour burned in her cheeks.

"Will I indeed? How?"

"He'll be dining with us tomorrow evening." Emily spoke reverently. Adelina raised her left eyebrow in surprise, but asked no more questions.

The following evening Adelina viewed her one gown critically. The old skirt she had worn before was beyond salvation, but now the dress the tinker had given her seemed tawdry beside Emily's neat, finely stitched gowns. Adelina sighed and pursed her lips grimly as she pulled it over her head. She refused to give Martha Langley the satisfaction of hearing her ask for anything. She would sooner wear this one dress until it fell from her back! Adelina thought.

She was very soon ready. She knocked on Emily's door and entered. As she turned from her dressing-table, Emily appeared prettier than usual. There was the light of happiness shining in her eyes, a rosy blush to her cheeks. Her gown, though plain and demure, was of good material and fitted her slim figure well. Her soft brown hair shone.

"Oh, Adelina – haven't you any other gown but that one? Oh I'm sorry," she added swiftly. "I didn't mean to hurt your feelings."

Adelina smiled ruefully.

"I expect you lost all your clothes on the voyage, did you?" Adelina did not contradict Emily's kindly invention and the girl hurried on, "If it won't offend you – there – there are one or two of my gowns we might alter to fit you, though you are a little more – shapely than me." There was a wistful note in Emily's voice.

Despite the poor, faded gown, Adelina was still strikingly lovely with her clear skin, auburn hair and green eyes. Adelina smiled. Emily's offer held none of the resentment her mother harboured.

"Thank you, Emily. That would be sweet of you."

Wallis Trent rose from the sofa as the two girls entered the drawing-room. He was, Adelina thought, the tallest man she had ever seen. His hair was jet black and his eyes grey. His presence seemed to fill the room. There was an aura of power and authority about him.

Mrs Langley made the introductions grudgingly. "This is a distant cousin, Wallis." There was a distinct accent upon the description 'distant', but there was a fleeting surprise in Wallis's cool eyes, quickly hidden. He took

Adelina's hand in his and his voice as he greeted her was deep but lacked warmth.

During the evening Adelina found herself studying Wallis Trent. She noticed every tiny detail about him – a fine-cut tailcoat and a frilled shirt beneath a low-cut waistcoat. His hair was short, but, unlike Lord Lynwood's, without a trace of curl.

At the dinner-table, the Reverend Mr Langley and Mrs Langley sat at either end while two places for Wallis and Emily had been set on one side with one place opposite for Adelina.

Wallis Trent, seated on the right hand of the Vicar, turned to him for conversation. "How is your historical research on the Amberly family progressing, sir?" He asked politely during the soup course.

"Oh, admirably, my boy. It really is fascinating. I'm sure you would be interested. Lord Lynwood's family have a fine record, you know. Oh, of course, there have been a few black sheep ..."

Was it Adelina's imagination that she saw Wallis's jaw harden at his words? Perhaps not, for Mr Langley himself seemed suddenly embarrassed and hurried on swiftly.

"A-hem! Did you know that one of Francis's uncles, his father's younger brother, fought with Cornwallis in the War of American Independence? Why, Adelina, my dear, this would interest you. He was killed at Yorktown, just before the final surrender."

Adelina smiled but she had little knowledge of the subject. Her fight had been for mere survival. She had had no time to worry about the wars and battles of history. But she did not wish to appear ignorant, so she listened intently, and said, "You mean Lord Lynwood's uncle?"

"Yes, my dear," Mr Langley replied.

"You know Lord Lynwood?" There was surprise in

Wallis Trent's tone and she could feel his eyes upon her dowdy gown.

"Yes – I – er – met him when I arrived here."

"Are you staying here long, Miss Adelina?"

"I – don't quite ..."

Mrs Langley interrupted. "Adelina must find employment. Her parents are dead."

There was an awkward silence around the dinner-table. It was as if Wallis Trent were waiting for Mrs Langley – or someone – to tell him more about Adelina, and Mrs Langley's short, clipped sentences gave the impression that there was certainly more to tell, but that she had no intention of telling it.

"I see ..." Wallis murmured, but his tone implied that he did not.

Then a thought came to Adelina. Wallis Trent was her grandfather's tenant-farmer. Perhaps he was on friendly terms with Lord Royston. Perhaps a man like Wallis Trent, with his authoritative manner, could help her. Impetuously, she said, "I thought perhaps, that if only – I could meet my grandfather ..."

"Be quiet, Adelina," Mrs Langley snapped.

Wallis glanced quickly at Mrs Langley and frowned slightly. Ignoring her command he addressed Adelina. "Your grandfather, Miss Adelina? And who might that be?"

Everyone was motionless, the silence tense and watchful.

Adelina hesitated. She realised she had spoken out hastily, but it was too late to draw back now.

"Lord Royston."

"*Lord Royston*!" Wallis repeated, his frown deepening noticeably. "I see," he added slowly, this time with more obvious understanding.

"Lord Royston does not acknowledge her as his grand-daughter," Mrs Langley said pointedly. "He disowned her mother twenty years ago when she eloped with the bailiff of the estate."

"But you're hoping your grandfather might relent now, are you?" Wallis was still speaking directly to Adelina.

"I only – wanted to meet him. To – to see where my mother had lived. Is that so very wrong?"

Wallis shook his head. "No – no I suppose not. If that is all you *do* want."

The meal was finished amidst embarrassed silence, and conversation in the drawing-room afterwards was stilted and strained. Wallis Trent appeared to be thoughtful, as if deliberating with cool calculation, and often Adelina could feel his gaze upon her.

As he took his leave, he turned to Adelina and, smiling now, asked, "Do you ride, Miss Adelina?"

"I ..." she hesitated. She had not, of course, ridden for a long time and yet, hazily, she seemed to remember having done so as a child.

Boldly she answered, "Yes, yes, of course."

"Then my stables are at your disposal. I should deem it an honour to take you riding and show you the countryside."

She heard Mrs Langley's swift intake of breath and a gasp from Emily.

"Why, thank you, Mr Trent," Adelina replied politely. "That – that would be most kind of you."

He took her hand and kissed it. Then he said 'goodnight' to the others and was gone.

As soon as the front door closed behind him, Emily burst into tears and fled upstairs to her room. Bewildered, Adelina turned to meet the hostile eyes of Martha Langley.

There was hatred in the woman's expression and, strangely, a look of fear. "Why did you have to come here?" she hissed.

"I – don't understand why Emily is so upset?"

Mrs Langley thrust her thin, angular face close to Adelina and said, "Emily is betrothed to Wallis Trent."

"What has that to do with me?" Adelina asked.

"Nothing – and everything!" was Martha Langley's puzzling reply.

The next morning – Sunday – Adelina, heavy-eyed, found herself being aroused even earlier than usual.

"You've to go to early service at the church, miss," the housemaid explained, "with the mistress and Miss Emily. They always go."

Adelina groaned but roused herself.

Much to her surprise she found that the bright, clear morning air invigorated her. The dew was still on the grass and the birds twittered in the trees and hedgerows.

Adelina found herself the centre of attention even amongst the devout few who attended such an early service. No doubt, she thought wryly, word of her arrival would have passed round and those who remembered her mother would have revived all the old scandal and gossip.

As they returned home together, Adelina tried to draw Emily from her quiet mood. The girl's eyes were red with weeping and her mouth still trembled, but she uttered no word of reproach to Adelina.

"There weren't many in church, Emily."

"No – it's very early. Matins and Evensong are better attended, you'll see."

Adelina stopped and turned to face her. "Do you mean we have to go again today?"

"Why, of course."

"To *both* services?"

"Yes. That's what the Sabbath is for," Emily said primly. "Besides, it brings the whole village together in an act of worship right from the Squire of the Manor down to the labourers and their families."

"Does – does Lord Royston attend church?" Adelina asked hesitantly.

"No," Emily replied with uncharacteristic harshness in her voice. Then she sighed and, in a rush of tender feeling towards Adelina, put her hand upon her arm. "I wish you would forget the idea of meeting your grandfather. He has said he does not want to see you, and – and …"

"Yes?" Adelina prompted.

"And my mother will see to it that you don't meet him!"

"I see," Adelina murmured, her tone flat with disappointment. "So everyone is against me."

Emily did not answer.

Evensong, as Emily had predicted, was far better attended than the earlier services. Mrs Langley, Emily and Adelina were already seated in their pew when Wallis Trent entered the church with his mother on his arm. As they took their place in the Trent family box pew, Adelina was aware of the glances and whisperings exchanged amongst the villagers. She was surprised, after what Emily had implied, that there were no smiles of welcome for their employer and his mother, their faces were resentful. Instead of uniting employer and employee it was as if they felt the Trents had intruded upon their one social event of the week.

Lady Louisa Trent was a tall, stately woman. Once she must have been very beautiful, with a flawless skin and grey eyes, but time and life had etched bitterness into her face. Her mouth was tight and unsmiling, and her eyes held some deep sadness. She was dressed in a pale blue pelisse trimmed with braid and tassles. She carried a matching reticule and parasol and her bonnet was trimmed with a darker shade of blue velvet ribbon.

Suddenly a hushed whisper and a stir ran through the congregation, and the few who dared, turned to see Lord Lynwood enter the church with his mother, the Dowager Countess of Lynwood.

The Earl glanced from side to side as he progressed slowly up the aisle, the Countess leaning heavily on a stick in her left hand and with her right arm through her son's. He appeared to be looking for someone.

Then the Earl saw Adelina and his eyes stopped their restless roaming. He smiled slowly at her and Adelina smiled in return, suddenly realising how very glad she was to see him again.

The Earl and Lady Lynwood took their places in a box pew on the opposite side of the aisle to the Trents, to whom they nodded in greeting.

Once more, Lady Lynwood was dressed entirely in black, her hat giving the only relief to her sombre outfit, being topped with three large white plumes, and the crown encircled by a white ribbon and bow.

Throughout the service, Adelina was acutely aware of the presence of both Lord Lynwood and Wallis Trent. They stood in front of her, tall and straight, Wallis a head taller than the slim and elegant Earl.

The service ended and the Earl and his mother left the church first, followed by the Trents. There was much reluctant curtsying and forelock-touching from the village folk, but at last Mrs Langley, Emily and Adelina were able to leave. Outside, the Dowager Countess was waiting.

"Mrs Langley." Her ladyship's voice rang out. Adelina was amused to see the haughty Martha Langley obliged to curtsy to her superior. "You're looking well," Lady

Lynwood said and then her sharp eyes fell upon Adelina. "Ah, Miss Adelina, we meet again." Her eyes, twinkling with mischief, met Adelina's. Then Lady Lynwood gave her strange cackle of laughter, and pointed her stick at Adelina with a sharp prodding movement.

"You'll have your work cut out with this one, Martha Langley. She'll not be as docile as your own little foal. *She's too much like her mother!*"

Mrs Langley's mouth pursed and the fingers of her hands clenched. Adelina guessed that Mrs Langley would dearly love to answer the old lady with some sharp retort, but dared not.

"Come and visit me, Miss Adelina, whenever you wish. You're a girl with spirit – I like that. Your mother used to visit me often – it'll be like old times." She nodded, turned and once more leaning heavily on Lord Lynwood's arm, she moved towards her carriage. Adelina saw Lynwood bend towards his mother as he helped her into the carriage and say something to her. Again Lady Lynwood's cackling laugh rang out, then she patted her son on the arm and glanced across at Adelina and nodded knowingly. The Earl did not climb into the carriage, but closed the door and bade the coachman 'drive on' to leave him standing on the roadside.

Lady Trent, too, stepped into her carriage alone, Wallis remaining at Emily's side.

Lord Lynwood was standing before Adelina. "Miss Cole." He bowed towards her but there was mockery in his action. Not to be outdone, Adelina curtsied pertly. "My lord."

"I have seen your grandfather again this morning." Concern for her and some hidden pain seemed to be fighting for control of his features. "But he is still of the same mind."

"It was kind of you to try," she smiled up at him.

His eyes searched her face, boring into her soul, but he did not return her smile.

"You're so incredibly like her," he murmured. "It's hard to believe ..."

Adelina sighed. "But I am *not* her. I am Adelina."

For an instant his face cleared of his inner anguish and she glimpsed how differently he – and everyone else – might treat her if she were not the living image of her mother.

"Yes, yes, of course you are." He smiled and his face became suddenly more boyish, more roguishly handsome. He held out his arm to her. "May I escort you home, Miss Cole?"

She was about to accept his offer graciously when Wallis Trent approached them. The two men nodded curtly to each other, and Wallis said to Adelina, "Mrs Langley has asked me to escort you and Emily to the Vicarage."

Adelina almost laughed aloud. How foolish all this was! Why, here were two men exchanging hostile looks over who was to escort her home, when the Vicarage was only a few yards away, right next to the church. It was ridiculous!

Lord Lynwood dropped his arm and the brooding expression was back in his eyes. "I'll bid you 'goodnight' then, Miss Cole," he said tersely and without meeting her gaze again, he strode away. Adelina watched him go, wondering at his strange, erratic changes of mood.

"... If you are free tomorrow," Wallis Trent was saying.

"I'm sorry. What did you say?" Adelina dragged her attention from Lord Lynwood's disappearing figure to concentrate on what Mr Trent had been saying.

"I said, 'I should be happy to take you riding if you are free tomorrow'."

"Oh – I – er, yes, thank you. And Emily too?"

The smile faded a little from Wallis Trent's face. "Of

course, if she wishes to come. But I thought she did not ride."

"I – don't know. I haven't asked her."

At that moment Emily moved towards them and with a determined cheerfulness stepped between them and linked her arms through theirs. So, with Wallis on her left arm and Adelina on her right, Emily drew them down the narrow churchyard path towards the Vicarage.

Wallis and Adelina walked in silence and, though Emily chattered about the weather, her father's sermon and the presence of the Earl of Lynwood and his mother, it was with a forced gaiety, a pretence that nothing was wrong.

"It's unusual for them to come to our church, isn't it, Wallis? The Dowager Countess is wonderful, though I must admit to being a little afraid of her. They say she was a great beauty in her day and had all the gentlemen falling at her – her feet!" There was a catch in her voice as if the longing to be beautiful herself was too much to bear.

As they reached the Vicarage gate, Wallis said, "I shall expect you at the Manor at three tomorrow afternoon, Emily. I shall take Adelina riding. You may come with us, if you wish," his tone was uninviting, "or stay and talk to my mother. She's always glad to see you."

"Yes, Wallis," Emily said meekly.

He gave a small bow. "I'll say 'goodnight', then." And he was gone.

Three o'clock the following afternoon found the two girls walking up the lane towards Abbeyford Manor. Adelina was dressed in a riding-habit borrowed from the tight-lipped Martha Langley, who would have liked to have refused but dare not, since it was Wallis Trent who had issued the invitation. The habit must be twenty years old, Adelina thought, and it was far too tight for her figure, but at least it was a riding-habit. Emily walked beside her in silence. They crossed the wooden footbridge near the ford and took the left-hand fork in the lane towards the Manor. Emily led the way through a small gate from the lane directly into the stableyard so that they did not go near the front of the house.

Suddenly, Emily stopped, her eyes widening and her cheeks blushing furiously. "Oh dear!" she whispered.

"What is it?" Adelina, who had walked a few paces ahead, stopped too and turned to look back at Emily. Then she followed the line of Emily's wide-eyed gaze and saw a man walking the distance of the hundred yards or so from the house to the stable and slapping his riding-boots with his whip as he walked. Adelina's eyes narrowed as she took in his appearance, and at Emily's whisper, "It's Squire Trent – Wallis's father!" Adelina watched him with interest. He was rather small for a man, but stocky and powerfully built. His head was bare and showed a fine head of hair, still red though slightly greying at the temples.

Squire Trent, Adelina noticed, still wore breeches and top-boots, though these were now no longer worn by the younger men of fashion. His blue eyes were dull and blood-shot, his teeth, yellow and broken.

As he saw the two girls, he stopped and blinked as if he thought they were some drink-induced mirage.

"My God!" he muttered under his breath. "Royston's daughter!" He blinked again and shook his head slightly as if trying to clear his muddled thoughts. "No, no, it can't be! That was years ago." He put his hand to his head. "Who the devil *are* you?"

"I'm Adelina Cole. Lord Royston's *grand*daughter."

He nodded slowly as realisation dawned upon him. "There's no mistaking that. Dear God, but you're the image of her! It's as if ... God, how you bring back the memories!''

Guy Trent, wavering a little unsteadily on his feet, gazed at Adelina's face, drinking in her loveliness and her youth. And as he did so the wasted years seemed to roll away and he could almost believe himself to be once more the virile, attractive, impulsive young man he had once been.

"Oh, there's Wallis," Emily cried, relief evident in her tone, and Adelina looked up to see Wallis striding across the stableyard towards them, an angry frown upon his face.

Squire Trent gave a grunt, winked broadly, though a little tipsily, at Adelina. "I'd better be on my way if my sobersides son is about to descend upon us." He sighed dramatically. "He always seems to spoil my fun." His voice dropped to a whisper and he leant closer to Adelina, his breath hot and evil-smelling upon her face. "I do hope we meet again, Miss Cole." With that he turned and walked unsteadily away towards a stable-lad holding a horse by its bridle. He waved his hand to his son. "Just going, my boy, just going."

A moment later, Squire Trent rode out of the yard, looking none too safe on his mount, waving wildly to Adelina.

Why, she thought, he's afraid of his own son, and she felt a flash of pity for the drink-sodden, unhappy man who lived on his memories.

"Good afternoon, Miss Adelina – Emily," Wallis greeted them.

"I will – go and see your mother, Wallis, if – that is convenient?"

"Of course, my dear," Wallis smiled slightly. "You'll find her on the terrace."

"G-goodbye then, Adelina. Enjoy your ride." She turned

away swiftly as if to hide the tears.

The stable-boy was leading a horse forward to the mounting block.

"Ah, here is Stardust for you to ride, Adelina."

Now that the moment had arrived, Adelina regretted her bravado. She moved towards the horse, biting her lip and trying to remember what she should do. But she need not have feared, for as soon as she stood upon the mounting block and felt the smooth leather of the saddle beneath her fingers and touched the horse's neck, the knowledge she must have learned in childhood came flooding back instinctively. She mounted quite easily and held the reins. It surprised Adelina herself to find that she knew exactly what to do without hesitation. For a moment the longing for the lost years of her childhood with both her mother and father, the happier years, threatened to engulf her. Then she saw Wallis mounting a magnificent animal, a wild-eyed stallion, his shining coat jet black.

"This is Jupiter," Wallis called to her. "Do you like him?"

"He's superb."

Wallis patted the horse's neck, his action showing his pride in the possession of such an animal. "Come, let us begin our ride."

They left the stableyard and trotted up the lane to the wood. Winding through the trees they came to the open fields on top of the hill. Wallis urged his horse to a steady canter and, feeling more confident now, Adelina did the same. They rode towards the abbey ruins, and when they came within the shadow of the crumbling walls they reined in.

Adelina looked up at the decaying building with interest. "It's a lonely place," she said and shuddered.

Wallis frowned. "The villagers fear the place – some

stupid superstition which I think has been put about by those who wish to use it for their own purposes."

"Whatever could you use a place like this for?"

Wallis smiled a little. "A trysting place, perhaps, for lovers to meet in secret."

Adelina's eyes were drawn once more to the cold stones. Perhaps her mother and father had met in this very place all those years ago.

Suddenly there was a movement and the figure of a man appeared on one of the walls. He stood, his legs wide apart, his arms akimbo, looking down at them. The horses shied a little at the man's sudden appearance.

"What the devil are you doing here?" Wallis Trent shouted angrily. "Why aren't you working?"

"Oh, I'm working, Mr Trent, I'm working." His tone was insolent. "One of the sheep strayed. I'm looking for her."

Wallis snorted disbelievingly. "Well, be about your work, then."

The man made no move to obey, bitterness and hatred in his blue eyes as he looked down at Wallis Trent. He was stockily built, with broad shoulders and slim waist and hips. He wore a loose shirt, open to the waist and with the sleeves rolled up above his elbows, showing his tanned, muscular arms. Around his neck was knotted a red spotted neckcloth. He wore breeches with leather leggings buttoned on the outside of each leg from ankle to above his knee, and heavy boots. He had a shock of red hair and white, even teeth.

Adelina frowned slightly. He seemed to remind her vaguely of someone ...

Wallis was speaking again. "I said be about ..."

The man sprang from the wall and leapt the small distance between himself and Wallis's horse. Jupiter reared, but the young man, showing no fear, caught hold of the bridle.

"Mr Trent – *sir* ..." Instead of being a polite salutation, his tone was a sarcastic insult.

"Let go my horse," Wallis Trent hissed between clenched teeth.

"When are you going to repair my mother's cottage, to say nothing of all the other cottages in the village? You treat your animals better than your workmen!"

"*Leave hold my horse*," Wallis said with dangerous emphasis on every word.

The young man held on, his face turned up towards Wallis. "When you've answered my question – *sir*!"

Adelina saw Wallis raise his riding-crop, and a small scream escaped her lips as he brought it down with a single vicious stroke across the man's face. The man winced and turned his face away but, to her surprise, Adelina saw that he still held the bridle fast in his hand.

"Aye, you'd like to kill me, wouldn't you?" his voice was low and menacing and then he added but one more word, putting into it every ounce of the hatred that was in his heart. "Wouldn't you, *brother*?"

Then he let go of the horse, turned and walked away but not before Adelina had seen the purple weal made by Wallis's whip swelling on his cheek. She stared after him and as she did so the thought came to her that he was the first person she had met in Abbeyford who had no fear of Wallis Trent.

"Come," Wallis was saying, breathing heavily with ill-concealed anger. "We must return home."

"Who – was that?"

There was a pause before Wallis replied. "Evan Smithson. One of my employees, who seeks to rise above his station." Then he urged his horse ahead as if to prevent Adelina asking further, unwelcome questions.

FOUR

"Emily, who is Evan Smithson? Is he Sarah Smithson's son?"

"Oh, Adelina," Emily said, her eyes wide with fear. "You shouldn't be here. Mama will be angry. Go back to bed."

After she had undressed in her own room that night, Adelina had quietly unlatched her door, listened a moment to be sure there were no sounds coming from the lower rooms, and had crept along the landing to Emily's room.

Now she perched herself on the end of Emily's bed. "Not until you've answered my questions," she whispered.

Emily sighed. "Oh very well. Yes – he's Sarah Smithson's son."

"We met him this afternoon – up near the abbey ruins. Emily – he – he seems to hate Wallis? Why should that be?"

"I suppose he thinks he has good reason. He's – he's Squire Guy Trent's illegitimate son."

Adelina gasped. "Of course! The likeness is there. Why ever didn't I see it? But – surely, he's about the same age as Wallis, isn't he?"

Emily nodded. "A year older, actually. Years ago, Guy Trent was as handsome and – and attractive as Evan is now. As you've seen, though, he drinks now and – and gambles ..."

"But what about Evan? I mean – how …?"

"As a young man Guy was wild and irresistible. They say no girl was safe! He fell in love with a village girl – Sarah Miller. She – she had his child, but neither her family nor his would let them marry."

"What happened?"

"The Miller family arranged for Sarah to marry a distant cousin, Henry Smithson. But their life together has not been happy. Henry Smithson bears a grudge, and so now does Evan, against the Trent family."

"Yes," Adelina said slowly. "Yes, I guess they do. And what about Guy Trent?"

"He married Louisa Marchant, the daughter of a wealthy clothing manufacturer from Manchester way, according to *his* parents' wishes. You saw her in church."

"She didn't look exactly happy either," Adelina remarked. "But Wallis is their son, I take it?"

Emily nodded and seemed about to say more, but at that moment they both heard the stairs creak and Mrs Langley's familiar sniff.

"Oh Adelina," Emily whispered frantically. "We're caught. She always comes in here when she comes to bed."

"Hush," Adelina swung her feet to the floor. "Lie down, Emily, and pretend to be asleep." So saying Adelina lay on the floor and rolled under the bed. The coverlet fell down at the side to hide her completely. The latch lifted on the door and Mrs Langley whispered softly, "Emily?" But when, after a moment, there was no reply from her daughter except her steady breathing, Mrs Langley closed the door again. When she heard the other bedroom door close too, Adelina rolled out from beneath the bed, stifling her helpless laughter. She scrambled to her feet and not trusting herself to speak to Emily, for she knew she would laugh aloud, Adelina escaped back to her own room. She jumped into bed and pulled the covers over her head as her merriment shook her.

Adelina surmised that perhaps Wallis Trent, who seemed to wield such power in Abbeyford valley, since neither Lord Royston nor his own father took much interest in the estate, might succeed where Lord Lynwood had failed.

She made up her mind that she would ask him to approach Lord Royston on her behalf.

"One last try," Adelina told herself as she mounted Stardust in the stableyard at the Manor, "and if that doesn't work, I'll leave Abbeyford!"

A busy harvest-time had kept Wallis away from the Vicarage for some time, but he had left word that Miss Adelina was to be allowed to ride Stardust whenever she wished. Taking advantage of his offer, Adelina slipped away from the Vicarage one afternoon and went in search of Wallis Trent.

She turned in the direction of the abbey, thinking that from such a vantage-point she would be able to see the workmen in the fields and perhaps see Wallis. As she drew near the ruins she could see plainly the gaunt walls, half gone, rising up grotesquely against the grey sky. It was a stark and lonely place and yet it fascinated Adelina, for she believed that perhaps her mother and father had met here when their love had to be kept a secret. She was surprised to see how much of the building was still standing as she walked into the ruins. Within the outer shell there were numerous other walls, in various stages of collapse. There was a large, oblong-shaped room which had perhaps been the refectory, narrow passages, smaller rooms which might have served as kitchens, then tiny cell-like rooms which must have been the monks' sleeping cells. One of these – the only one – still had its roof so that, inside the tiny square

room, it was almost as it must have been before the abbey
had been destroyed. Adelina stepped inside. The stone floor
was remarkably clean – almost as if someone had swept it.
The tiny slit of a window let in little light so that the cold
stone room was dark and dismal and eerie. Adelina
shuddered. Fancy spending one's entire life walled up in a
tiny cell like this! She tried to look out of the narrow
window, but it was too high.

"May I help, m'lady?"

Adelina jumped violently and a small scream escaped her
lips as she spun round. She fell back against the wall, her
hands spread against the rough stone. The figure of a man
blocked the doorway, but she could not see his face clearly,
merely his outline. He was only a little taller than she and
thickset.

"You!" she gasped as she recognised Evan Smithson.

"Aye, 'tis me," he answered and moved towards her. "So
you're Royston's granddaughter, are you? And you've
wasted no time wi' me brother, I see. I've seen you ridin'
round wi'im."

"It's – it's not like that ..."

Evan laughed hollowly. "Expect me to believe that?
You're a sight better lookin' than Miss Emily, I'll grant you
that." His eyes roved over her face and body. "Aye, I've a
fancy for you mesel' ..."

At that moment there came the sound of footsteps over the
loose stones which littered the floor of the ruins. Adelina
ducked out of the small room and into the open again. Then
a girl's voice rang eerily through the crumbling walls.

"Evan, Evan! You here, Evan?"

Adelina glanced back over her shoulder in amusement at
the frowning young man. So, she thought, Evan Smithson
used the abbey ruins as a trysting-place.

"Over here," growled Evan, and a young girl appeared round the corner. She stopped uncertainly, her eyes widening in surprise as she saw Adelina. Adelina, too, was somewhat surprised herself, for the girl looked no more than fifteen or sixteen, though she gave every promise of womanhood. Long black hair fell about her shoulders like a cape and her coarse-woven dress was cut low at the neckline. Her face was thin and pinched, but her dark brown eyes flashed a look of jealousy plain for Adelina to witness as they rested upon her, flickered briefly towards Evan, and then returned to Adelina to take in every detail of her appearance. The girl's hands, dirty and work-worn, plucked nervously at her brown skirt. Jealous she might be, for she had sense enough to recognise a worthy rival in Adelina, the mysterious beauty from a far-off land, of whom the villagers had gossiped never-endingly since the day of her arrival.

Evan grinned, suddenly, enjoying the spectacle of the two girls eyeing each other. The girl sidled closer to him until she stood beside him. Casually, he put his arm about her waist and drew her to him. The girl looked up at him adoringly, Adelina forgotten now. But Evan's eyes were still upon Adelina's face, challengingly.

Adelina's mouth curved and she threw back her head and laughed. "I'll bid you 'good-day', Mr Smithson."

Lightly, she skipped over the rough ground and out of the ruins. Still laughing, she picked up the skirts of her borrowed riding-habit, mounted Stardust and cantered away.

Halfway down the hill, she saw Wallis riding Jupiter alongside the stream so she urged her mount forward. Seeing her, Wallis reined in and waited for her. He raised his hat and smiled as she neared him.

"Miss Adelina. What brings you out alone?"

Adelina reined in beside him. "I was looking for you," she replied with candour.

"I'm flattered."

"I – want to ask you something."

"Your wish is my command," Wallis said pedantically.

"You seem to be a man of position around here," Adelina began. "I wondered if you would speak to my grandfather on my behalf. If – if you could persuade him to – to receive me."

"Take you back into the family fold, you mean? Forgive and forget – everything."

Adelina shook her head sadly. "I can't expect him to forget, certainly. And – and I suppose he can't forgive, or he would have done so a long time ago. No, I just want to meet him. To know him. After all, he is my closest living relative now."

"And you," Wallis murmured thoughtfully, "are *his* closest relative."

They rode along side by side now and for some moments Wallis appeared deep in thought. Then he said slowly. "I see your grandfather about once a month. I'll see what I can do."

"Please – please will you speak to him the very next time you see him?"

Suddenly Wallis leaned over and to Adelina's surprise took hold of her hand. "If I do, and he agrees to see you, then I may have a great deal to say to you concerning you and me."

Then he let go of her hand, straightened up and turned away so swiftly that Adelina wondered if she had imagined his action and his words. Words which seemed almost a promise!

During the following weeks, Wallis's attentions towards
Adelina became markedly more noticeable. He took her
riding frequently and for carriage rides. All the while
Emily's face became more forlorn and Mrs Langley's more
outraged, but neither seemed to dare to speak out against
Wallis Trent. Adelina felt trapped. She could not risk
offending Wallis, for with him lay her last chance of a
reconciliation with her grandfather.

Early in November, Mr Langley announced at breakfast
that he was to visit Lynwood Hall that afternoon. "I need to
visit the library there to assist in my research. I have written
to Lady Lynwood, asking her permission and she has
graciously invited Adelina to take afternoon tea with her."

"Why Adelina?" snapped Martha Langley waspishly.
"Why not Emily?"

"I fancy her ladyship took a liking to Adelina, Martha
my dear," the Vicar replied mildly.

Martha Langley sniffed disapprovingly.

"You'd like to go, wouldn't you, Adelina?" Mr Langley
was asking her.

Adelina hesitated momentarily, shaken by the sudden
longing to see Lord Lynwood again. During the past few
weeks she had scarcely thought of him, but now his every
feature was suddenly, startlingly clear in her mind's eye.
The brooding melancholy in his eyes, then the swift boyish
smile that transformed his face. "I would love to go, thank
you."

The carriage bowled along the lane out of Abbeyford,
through Amberly and at last wound up the long drive
towards Lynwood Hall through the parkland and drew to a
halt before the house.

A liveried footman held open the door of the carriage for
her to alight and another opened the heavy front door at the

top of a flight of wide stone steps. Adelina stepped down from the carriage and daintily picked up her skirts to climb the steps into the hall.

The first time she had been here she had scarcely noticed her surroundings. Now Adelina saw that the interior was even more grand than the exterior. The oak floor was covered with Persian carpets. There were two staircases, with white balustrades, sweeping up on either side of the hall to join in a balcony at first-floor level. White busts of Amberly ancestors were set in alcoves, and the high white ceiling was dome-shaped.

"Welcome to Lynwood Hall," a voice spoke softly behind her and Adelina turned to see Lord Lynwood leaning against a door-frame, his arms folded, a small smile of amusement upon his lips.

"My lord," Adelina dropped a curtsy as she had seen the villagers do.

"Ah, there you are, my lord," Mr Langley entered through the door at that moment. "Your mama kindly asked Adelina to take tea with her whilst I peruse some of the documents in your fine library."

Lord Lynwood inclined his head. "Quite so, Mr Langley. Perhaps Miss Adelina will permit me to take her on a tour of Lynwood Hall before tea?"

The question was more a statement, for without waiting for either of them to reply, he offered Adelina his arm, his eyes never leaving her face, and when, shyly, she put her hand on his arm, he led her away leaving Mr Langley to find his own way to the library.

From the hall, Lord Lynwood took her through a seemingly endless number of rooms. Huge drawing-rooms with panelled walls, hung with tapestries, the dining-room with its long table with matching carved oak chairs, the walls almost covered with large oil paintings of the Amberly family. In the long gallery Adelina saw a portrait of Lady Lynwood, Francis's mother, as a young, beautiful woman with black shining hair and those same bright eyes which still twinkled with mischief in her now wrinkled face.

Room after room with painted ceilings, rich tapestries, priceless furniture and objets d'art. Adelina caught her breath as Lord Lynwood led her into the family's private chapel. Rows of high-backed chairs each with its own hassock. The altar was ornately carved out of white marble and rose almost to the ceiling, which was painted too. The lower half of each wall was panelled, but the upper half was entirely covered by a long mural running round the entire length of the chapel, depicting scenes from the Testaments.

"Oh, it's beautiful," Adelina's husky whisper echoed eerily.

From there Lynwood led her through more rooms to a conservatory filled not only with plants of every conceivable kind but with more marble busts on pedestals.

"Well?" he asked, "what do you think of my home, Adelina?"

"It's very beautiful," Adelina repeated wistfully.

Today he seemed determined to charm her, to be the perfect host, but then his eyes clouded briefly. "Your – your mother came here often." With a supreme effort he brought his attention back to the present, to Adelina.

It was strange to have this girl here in his home, to see her sitting in the same chair where long ago Caroline had sat. She was so like her mother and yet there *was* a difference. In her eyes there was a depth of experience, of suffering, that Caroline in her protected world of luxury had never known. At least, Lynwood mused, not when he had known her. And there was a strength about Adelina too – a determination. Caroline, too, had been strong – ruthlessly, selfishly strong. Was Adelina so self-centred too?

Lynwood didn't know. Part of him longed to find out, to test her, and yet he shied away from being hurt in the same way again. No woman, he had vowed, would ever have the power over him to inflict such hurt as Caroline had done – not even her beautiful, desirable daughter! And yet ...

Adelina, intrigued by his lovely home, was acutely aware of Lynwood's swiftly changing moods, but could not begin to understand the cause.

A footman appeared. "Her ladyship is waiting for the young lady, my lord."

As Adelina turned to follow the footman she heard Lynwood, robbed of her company, swear softly under his breath.

After her visit to Lynwood Hall, Adelina passed the following days in a fever of hope. Soon now, Wallis Trent would surely see her grandfather. Every day she looked for him in the hope he would bring her news. Life within the Langley household was becoming unbearable.

Then one Sunday evening as Adelina and Emily left the shelter of the church porch and drew their capes closely about them against the flurry of light snow which had been falling since the afternoon, they found Wallis Trent suddenly beside them.

"Come, I'll see you home." He stepped between them and offered each of them an arm.

"Oh, Wallis," Emily breathed, looking up at him with adoring eyes. "I didn't see you in church. I thought you had not come."

"I was delayed earlier and could not arrive in time for the service, but I thought I might see you if I came now."

Deliberately, it seemed, he avoided saying which of them he had come to see. There was a strained silence between the three of them as they walked the short distance from the church to the Vicarage, but on reaching the front door, Emily said, "You will come in for a while, won't you, Wallis?"

He nodded. "Of course, Emily."

They found a warm log fire in the dimly-lit drawing-room.

"I'll go and see about some hot chocolate for us," Emily said with a forced cheerfulness. "I won't be a moment."

As the door closed, Wallis and Adelina, with one accord, turned towards each other.

"Have you seen him yet?" she asked eagerly.

"I went tonight, my dear, but I am afraid I was unable to broach the subject with him. He is a little unwell at the moment and — tetchy. I didn't think it wise to touch upon such a delicate matter."

"Unwell?" Adelina asked worriedly. "It's nothing serious, is it?"

Wallis's eyebrows rose fractionally. "Why so concerned about someone you don't even know?"

"He's my grandfather. Of course I'm concerned. I want to meet him — to heal the breach, before it's too late."

Wallis smiled and, sarcasm lining his words, replied, "That I can well believe!"

"When will you see him again?"

"Shortly after Christmas."

"Not before?"

"No. Listen, my dear, I'm sure you have no need to worry. I'm sure I shall be able to persuade him." Wallis moved closer to take her hand in his. "You are a beautiful woman, Adelina, and when things *are* settled betwen you and your grandfather, then ..."

At that moment the door opened and Emily returned. Wallis and Adelina turned swiftly from each other, as guiltily as if they had been caught in a passionate embrace.

With shaking hands, Emily set the tray of cups upon the table, her cheeks pink with embarrassment and misery.

The three of them sat around the fire, the flames flickering and dancing, casting eerie shadows. With the soft light highlighting her beauty, Adelina was aware of Wallis's eye's straying towards her. There was a painful silence between the three of them.

Wallis drained his cup and stood up quickly. "It's getting late. I must go."

Instead of begging him to stay, Emily said quietly, "Yes, Wallis." She stood up and accompanied him to the door. Adelina remained seated in front of the fire.

When she returned, Emily stood in front of Adelina. "I suppose you think," she began, her voice trembling, "that you're very clever, stealing him from me. He's the only man I've ever loved, or ever will love ..." She gulped, and tears began to run down her face. At once Adelina went to her and tried to put her arm about Emily's shoulders.

"Don't touch me!" Emily cried, shaking her off.

"Emily, it's not like you think. I'm not trying to steal Wallis from you. I ..." She was about to confide the real reason to Emily, but caution told her to keep quiet. Emily would be sure to tell Mrs Langley, who would see to it that Wallis did not speak to Lord Royston at all.

"The way he looks at you," Emily was saying. "He used to look at me like that – but not any more. I know what he's waiting for. For Lord Royston to accept you and then – then Wallis will marry you."

Adelina gasped. Emily had half guessed Adelina's hope, but she had added far more to it than had ever entered Adelina's mind. Emily turned and ran from the room. Adelina sank back into the chair, feeling as if Emily had struck her. She closed her eyes and moaned softly. She hated being the cause of Emily's distress, but she could not give up – not yet!

The days seemed to pass so slowly, but finally Christmas came. On Christmas Eve the wassailers trudged through the village, singing their carols and stamping their feet to keep warm. At the Vicarage, even Martha Langley seemed touched by the spirit of Christmas sufficiently to unbend enough to make the revellers welcome.

Leaving the Vicarage the villagers disappeared up the lane their lusty carols echoing through the frosty night.

"Where are they going now?" Adelina asked Emily.

"To the big barn behind the Manor. The Trents always entertain the villagers at Christmas. The merrymaking goes on for days. Tonight they'll be drinking spiced ale from the wassail cup and ..."

Adelina gripped Emily's arm, her eyes shining. "Couldn't we go too, Emily?" She was eager for a little fun and laughter. The days spent at the Vicarage were depressingly dull.

"Oh, no, Adelina – not tonight. They get a little – well – merry, you know. But Wallis has promised to fetch us the day after Christmas Day. The villagers will be putting on their usual mummers' play then, and there will be plenty to eat and drink, beef and plum pudding. And dancing. No doubt you're hoping Wallis will dance with you," Emily added bitterly. "I'm sure you won't be disappointed."

"Emily, please ..."

But she would not listen.

The Christmas services at church seemed to bring the whole village community together – with the notable exception of Guy Trent and his love-child, Evan Smithson.

Adelina was surprised to see in the church the village girl whom she had seen with Evan in the abbey ruins, kneeling to pray and bowing her head with every semblance of piety.

Her name, Adelina had learned, was Lucy Walters.

A few pews behind the Langleys, on the opposite side of the aisle, sat Sarah Smithson and with her a man whom Adelina had not seen before. Most of the villagers were known to her now, but not this man.

Adelina nudged Emily. "Who is the man in the check coat and cap, with Mrs. Smithson?" she whispered. Emily took a hurried, furtive glance over her left shoulder.

"Henry Smithson – her husband," she murmured.

Adelina turned to stare at him. So this was the man who had been obliged by his family to marry Sarah to hide her shame and give Guy Trent's son his name. There was bitterness written upon Henry Smithson's face and a wild anger in his eyes as his glance rested upon Lady Louisa Trent and her son Wallis, sitting in the Trent family pew.

There was a stir as the church door flew open, letting in a cold blast of wintry air. Adelina's heart skipped a beat as Lord Lynwood strode purposefully down the aisle. He stopped beside their pew and bowed to Mrs Langley and the two girls.

"Your servant, Miss Adelina," he murmured, and almost reluctantly went to his own pew.

The service ended and Adelina found Lord Lynwood by her side. "I shall not be thwarted this time, Adelina." Without giving her chance to refuse, he took hold of her hand and placed it, possessively, through his arm and led her down the aisle. Adelina was aware of the gasps which ran like waves amongst the congregation.

Outside the church, Wallis, frowning heavily, faced them. "My lord, I shall escort Miss Adelina home."

"I think not tonight, Trent," Lynwood said softly.

"Have you asked Mrs Langley's permission?" Wallis persisted, still glowering.

"Have you?" countered the Earl.

"It's understood that I escort the young ladies home from church, Lynwood," Wallis drew himself up, his broad shoulders seeming massive.

"I'm sure Mama would not object – for once," Emily put in coyly, aware that for once she could have Wallis to herself.

"Oh, very well," Wallis said with bad grace and marched away, almost dragging Emily along with him.

Lynwood laughed aloud.

"Shh," Adelina tugged at his arm. "He'll hear you."

"So?"

"Well ..." then she began to smile too.

They wandered down the frosty lane and for a few moments they were alone in the dark night. He slipped his arm about her waist and drew her close to him. "Adelina!" he whispered.

"No, my lord, no," she said pushing him away, and yet her senses were reeling at his closeness, at his touch.

"Would you reject Wallis Trent's advances, Adelina?" Lynwood asked harshly.

"I – of course." Then anger made her forget caution. "There's only one thing in the world I want at this moment."

"What's that?"

"To meet my grandfather."

She heard Lynwood sigh, but he said nothing. How could he tell her that he had asked Lord Royston repeatedly to meet her, but the stubborn old man steadfastly refused. Lynwood took her hand once more and led her towards the front door of the Vicarage. There, beneath the light of the lamp, he turned to face her and looked down into her upturned, lovely face. He took her gently by the shoulders. "Don't put your hopes too high, but if you like, I'll speak to him again."

"No — Wallis said — I mean ..." The words were out before she could stop them.

Lynwood frowned. "Trent? What did he say?"

"He — he sees Lord Royston once a month. He said he would speak to him on my behalf."

"Really?" Lynwood drawled. "You're sure it was on *your* behalf and not his own?"

Abruptly he left her, his strides taking him down the path to his waiting carriage. She saw him climb into the vehicle and slam the door, making the horses shy in fright.

"Drive on!" he shouted irritably.

FIVE

During the early evening of the day after Christmas Day, the Trents' carriage drew up in front of the Vicarage. The two girls, warmly wrapped in their cloaks, were helped into the carriage by Wallis and, in only a few minutes, they arrived outside the barn at the Manor. Adelina gasped as she went in. The huge barn had been transformed. Holly and mistletoe wreaths decorated the walls and beams, and the light came from rushlights. At one end a makeshift stage had been erected and the floor was covered with rushes. As they entered the handbell ringers were playing a carol and from the onlookers – all the villagers, it seemed to Adelina – there came a soft humming.

At the opposite end of the barn to the stage a ladder led up to a hayloft and Adelina's eyes widened as she saw Evan Smithson and Lucy sitting at the edge of the open hayloft, their legs swinging over the side, watching the proceedings below them. When the bellringers had ended their carols, a motley selection of instruments was produced – drums, trumpets, pipes and fiddles – and suddenly a surprisingly tuneful, merry jig filled the barn. But amongst the rest of the villagers there was a strange reluctance to begin the dancing. They stood in small groups occasionally glancing with sullen eyes towards Wallis Trent.

They don't want us here, Adelina knew suddenly,

intuitively. Wallis Trent – and those with him – were unwelcome intruders.

Wallis ignored their hostility. "Would you care to dance, Adelina?"

"Why – I'm not sure I know how."

Wallis bowed. "As you wish." He turned to Emily and led her on to the middle of the floor instead. Gradually, almost with a sullen belligerence, the villagers joined in.

Adelina watched the dancers and tapped her feet and swayed in time to the music. The rafters rang with the noise and the dancers whirled and spun, but there was no spontaneous gaiety, no laughter.

"May I have the pleasure of this dance, Miss Cole?"

Evan Smithson stood before her, his startlingly blue eyes challenging her. Adelina glanced up towards the hayloft to see Lucy pouting moodily because Evan had left her to seek out Adelina.

"I can't dance ..."

"Of course you can. Come on," Evan said and put his arm about her waist and before she could stop herself, she was amongst the dancers.

"You see, you can dance. Was that merely an excuse to avoid dancing with the likes o' me?"

Adelina laughed. "Of course not."

He swung her round, almost sweeping her off her feet, so that she was obliged to catch hold of him for support. He laughed aloud, his eyes glinting dangerously, warningly. "I can be a good friend, Miss Adelina, but a dangerous enemy."

Adelina arched her left eyebrow. "Really?" she remarked drily, all her old instincts aroused by his threat.

"You know," Evan said softly in her ear as the dance finally came to an end. "You know, Miss Adelina, I like you. You're different. You're not afraid of me."

"Afraid of you?" she laughed. "The very idea, Mr Smithson."

Evan gripped her wrist and his handsome face was close to her own. "Don't tempt fate, sweet Adelina."

There was menace in his words and in his tone. But Adelina adroitly twisted her wrist from his grasp and dropped a mocking curtsy. "Thank you for the dance, Mr Smithson," and moved away from him to rejoin Emily and Wallis.

When the music began again, Wallis said, "Since you seem to have learnt the steps remarkably quickly, Miss Adelina, perhaps you will dance with *me* now?"

Inwardly, Adelina sighed. What a web of bitterness and tension and hatred existed in this village, she thought, and she seemed unwittingly to be caught in the middle of it. Wallis danced in silence, a frown upon his forehead. Adelina was aware of the eyes of the villagers upon them, and when, several times during the evening, Wallis demanded that she dance with him, she found herself increasingly embarrassed by his obvious attention to her. He danced only once with Emily, but Adelina was often in his arms.

"I shall be seeing your grandfather tomorrow, Miss Adelina."

"Oh, Wallis, thank you. You will – let me know what he says?"

"Of course." She felt his arm tighten about her and Adelina was acutely aware of Emily's face scarlet with misery. "I'm sure we shall have much to discuss – after I have seen him."

Before Adelina could reply, the music ended and Wallis led her back to Emily. As the noise died away, a voice rang out. All eyes turned to see Evan Smithson standing, none too steadily, at the top of the ladder leading to the hayloft, waving a tankard of ale in his right hand. Lucy, standing at his side, was pulling at his arm vainly trying to stop him.

"My friends," he shouted, his words a little slurred. "I give you a toast. To our lords and masters – our employers – our landlords – the Trents – my – my *family*! May they rot in hell!" He ended with a flamboyant gesture with his right hand, spilling beer. Suddenly he lost his footing. Lucy tried to catch hold of him, but he slipped from her grasp. Lucy and several of the women shrieked as Evan toppled head first from the loft to the floor below. Luckily, he fell on a thick heap of straw and lay there laughing drunkenly.

Wallis clenched his fists and took a step forward towards his half-brother, his face contorted with rage. Boldly, Emily grasped his arm.

"No, Wallis, no, please. Look at your father. See how distressed he is. And the Smithsons. Please – don't make it any worse."

"Very well, since you ask it, Emily," Wallis muttered. "But one of these days that fellow will go a step too far ... Come, we're leaving."

Vividly Adelina remembered the animosity which had flared between the two half-brothers when face to face.

As they threaded their way through the revellers, Adelina saw Sarah Smithson sitting in a dark corner, quietly sobbing into her hands. Nearby was Henry Smithson, an expression of hatred and resentment on his face. His hands, resting on his knees, were tightly clenched. Adelina stood on tiptoe, searching for sight of Squire Trent. He was standing on the opposite side of the barn, his shoulders slumped, his eyes steadfastly fixed upon the weeping Sarah, helpless misery etched into every line of his face.

Adelina passed the days following Christmas in a fever of

anticipation, but Wallis did not come near the Vicarage. New Year came and went and still there was no word from him.

At last, towards the middle of January, Adelina could stand the waiting no longer. She must go in search of Wallis.

So one wild January day, when the clouds were black and threateningly low, Adelina slipped away from the Vicarage towards Abbeyford Manor. The wind whistled and blew her skirts. Her heart beat faster – she hated this kind of stormy, blustery weather and yet her desire to see Wallis overcame her fear.

First she went to the Manor stables. Thomas, the head stableboy, told her his master was out in the fields on Jupiter.

Minutes later she left the Manor yard, riding Stardust up the lane, through the woods and out on to the hillside. She rode towards the abbey ruins, once more in the hope of being able to see Wallis from there. The wind blew with the force of a gale, the black clouds scudding overhead. Near the ruins she paused and looked about her. Then she saw him below her, down the hill on the far side of the stream, a dark figure on his black stallion. A group of farm labourers stood in a semi-circle around him – though keeping a respectful distance from the tossing head and stamping hooves of the temperamental horse. As she drew nearer, Adelina could see that Wallis Trent was shouting at the men, his face as dark as the storm clouds overhead. The men stared back at him – sullen obstinacy on their faces. Amongst them Adelina recognised Henry Smithson and beside him, Evan.

The young man's face was set in lines of bitterness and his eyes glittered with hatred.

"Be off with you," curtly Wallis Trent dismissed them with a wave of his hand. "And I'll stand no more of your insolence."

As the men moved away, Evan's glance rested on Adelina for a moment, standing a short distance away beside her horse, waiting to speak to Wallis.

A small smile of malice quirked Evan's mouth and then he turned and followed his workmates.

Adelina thought no more of Evan. She did not even notice which direction he took, for now her whole attention was fixed upon Wallis Trent.

He dismounted and came towards her. At first she thought that the anger still upon his face lingered from the harsh words to his men. Then she realised that he was not at all pleased to see her.

"Well, Miss Cole?" The question was sharp, unfriendly. Instinctively, she knew immediately that the reason she had not seen him recently was because he had deliberately avoided meeting her.

Before she even voiced the question she must ask, she knew what his answer was going to be.

"Wallis – I – I came to look for you because you've never let me know if you've spoken to my grandfather. I was getting desperate."

His lips curled wryly. "That I can believe. Well – I do have some news for you, Miss Adelina Cole. Your grandfather wants naught to do with you. He does not acknowledge that he even *has* a granddaughter. Emily will remain his heiress. So, all your efforts to worm your way into his affections and have him make *you* his heiress have failed. And I shall marry Emily."

Adelina gasped, staring up at him in disbelief. "It – it had nothing to do with that. I just wanted to – to meet him ..."

"But it would follow, wouldn't it? You had it all planned?"

"No, no," Adelina cried, anguished. "Is – is that want he thought?"

Wallis lifted his shoulders in a shrug. "Who knows. He was deaf to all pleas. Lynwood tried too, so I understand, and has been doing ever since he brought you here."

So Lord Lynwood had made repeated requests to Lord Royston for her. The thought warmed her cold heart to know that, despite his strange erratic moods, Lynwood had cared.

"You'd best make your way back to America. You're not wanted here," Wallis Trent told her heartlessly.

Adelina turned away sick at heart, the loneliness sweeping over her. She remounted Stardust awkwardly, Wallis Trent making no move to help her, though all the while she was acutely aware of his cold eyes upon her. She wheeled her horse round, dug her heels in and set off up the slope towards the abbey ruins, scarcely knowing where she went – nor caring!

Three people watched her go. Wallis Trent watched her until she reached the top of the slope and galloped towards the ruins, then he remounted his own horse and rode away in the opposite direction without a backward glance.

Later, he promised himself, he would visit the Vicarage and resume his courtship of Miss Emily Langley – Lord Royston's only heiress!

From the edge of the wood a motionless figure on horse-back had observed her meeting with Wallis Trent, had watched the short exchange of conversation and their parting. Lynwood's heart twisted. Was he ever destined to watch the woman he desired meet with other men?

From the abbey ruins, still breathing hard from running, Evan Harrison crouched behind a crumbling wall and watched Adelina ride towards him.

As she drew near the ruins, it began to hail. Huge hail-stones came tumbling from the laden clouds, stinging the horse and making the docile creature rear in fright.

Adelina screamed as she felt herself falling backwards. She fell upon the wet ground and Stardust bolted. For a moment Adelina was stunned, the breath knocked from her body. She lay motionless as the wind roared in her ears and the hail beat down upon her. Her dread of storms blotted out all common sense and reason and the final rejection she had just suffered destroyed her spirit. Then she felt hands lifting her up and carrying her.

As understanding returned she realised someone had carried her into the ruins, into the cell-like room which afforded the only real shelter in the derelict abbey, and had laid her on the floor.

She looked up to see Evan Smithson standing over her.

"Well, well, well!" In the dimness of the room she could scarcely see his face. "And what are you doing out on a wild day like this, my fine lady? Was your meeting with my dear half-brother *so* important?"

Adelina struggled to her feet, but with one strong push from his muscular arm, she found herself sprawling on the floor again.

"Not so fast, my pretty one. Now I've got you here, here you'll stay for a while."

Fear flooded through Adelina's limbs. She broke out in a cold sweat. There was menace in this man's tone.

All her old fighting instincts came flooding back. Fear and anger gave her strength. She watched his shadowy form and waited her moment, then with the swiftness born of terror she scrambled to her feet and made for the doorway. But Evan was too quick for her. He put out his foot and in the confined space easily tripped her so that she pitched forward, knocking her head on the rough stonework. She gave a groan of pain and lay still.

"Don't you like my company, my lady? Prefer my brother, do you? Well, we'll see how he'll like you when *I've* finished with you!"

Again Adelina made to struggle up, but now Evan grasped her arms and pulled her to her feet. His arms slipped about her waist, and his lips found her mouth in a crushing, bruising kiss – a kiss which held no affection, nor even passionate desire. It was merely a weapon of hatred and revenge. He was brutally strong. He held her easily with his left arm, her arms pinned against his chest. With his right arm Evan wrenched at the bodice of her habit, tearing away the fastenings to reveal her thin chemise. She felt herself being pushed down on to the rough floor again. In the dim light she saw his face twisted with cruel vengeance. She screamed but her cries were drowned by the gale outside and the lashing rain. And then she heard him laugh in triumph as he held her arms pinned down upon the floor above her head, while his mouth sought hers.

"No, please, Evan," she pleaded. "Please – let – me – go!" She writhed frantically, but he held her prisoner.

"No, no," she screamed in terror, and he struck her across the face with the back of his hand, rendering her senseless. Then his full weight was upon her.

Suddenly it was over and he was moving away from her, leaving her exhausted, weak and bruised and filled with shame and horror and revulsion. She rolled away from him into the corner of the cell and retched, sick with humiliation and physical pain. Then she lay panting, sweating and yet shivering.

"No fine gentleman will want you now, my lady. And let

me tell you, my brother thinks himself a fine gentleman."

Adelina's whole body shook and quivered, her teeth chattered and her icy fingers trembled as she reached for her clothes and pulled on her chemise and then her habit. She found the bodice so torn that she could scarcely conceal her bosom. She was cold and yet her body was bathed in sweat, the cold, clammy sweat of panic. Against her will, pathetic sobs escaped her throat. She whimpered like a small, bewildered wounded creature whom Evan had taken pleasure in hurting. He had wrought all his bitterness and hatred against the Trents upon Adelina, just because he believed Wallis Trent wanted her for himself.

She found her fear giving way to fury. She had survived the dangers of New York's waterfront, only to come all the way to England to be robbed of that which she held so dear in the place where she should have been secure – her grandfather's own village!

She saw that Evan, now fully clothed, was on the point of stepping through the doorway to leave her. Adelina scrambled to her feet. She stumbled blindly after him, rage robbing her of all sense and reason. The sky was dark and the rain falling heavily, but Evan was stepping casually over the stones which littered the ground. She began to run after him but tripped and fell. She screamed as the stones cut her hands. Sobbing wildly, she lay a moment and closed her eyes.

When she opened them she saw that Evan had stopped and was staring up at an awesome figure who was standing on top of one of the low, ruined walls, rigidly still, just waiting.

"*Lynwood*!" Adelina groaned. "*Oh, no!*"

Lying on the rock-strewn, rough ground, the stones biting into her flesh, Adelina closed her eyes again, the shame sweeping over her once more.

Lynwood had arrived too late and was cursing himself for his delay.

From the edge of the wood he had watched her ride away from Wallis Trent towards the ruins. Then he had seen her fall from her horse, had even made the first move to reach her, but then he had seen Evan appear, lift Adelina's limp form and carry her, with apparent gentleness, into the shelter of the ruins. For the second time in the space of a few minutes, jealousy and blind rage swept through Lynwood. He wrenched his horse about and galloped like a madman through the wood with neither a thought for his own safety nor that of his horse.

He raced towards the waterfall – the scene of his very first moment of disillusionment. Years before, in his boyish innocence, Lynwood had adored and worshipped Caroline. But, in ruthless pursuit of her own happiness, she had shattered his belief in her. Out riding with him, Caroline had slipped away from Lynwood, who had searched for her with desperate anxiety, fearing she had been thrown from her horse – was lying injured or worse! Then he had come upon her unexpectedly at the waterfall – locked in the arms of her lover Thomas Cole.

And now it was all happening again – but with her daughter Adelina.

Flinging himself from his horse, Lynwood ran down the steep path, crashing through branches and undergrowth, heedless of injury, to sink down, breathless, against a rock. He was shaking, his hands sweating, his heart thudding, his breathing painful rasps. He sat with his head in his hands for some time and then, as he calmed, reason began to return and he raised his head slowly and with unseeing eyes gazed at the rushing waterfall, a more horrible picture forming in his mind's eye.

Lynwood knew something of Evan Smithson's story,

knew of his hatred for the Trents – and the reason for it. Lynwood frowned, trying hard to pull a vision from his subconscious mind. As he had watched Adelina meet with Wallis Trent, he had been vaguely aware of the farmworkers moving away, but then his whole attention had been riveted upon Adelina and Wallis Trent, the jealousy surging through his being. But there was something else, something important ... He must remember ... He groaned from deep inside as the picture came to him. While he had watched them, with only half an awareness he had seen too a shadowy figure leave the group of workmen and set off in the opposite direction, running, running hard up the hill towards the ruins.

Lynwood sprang to his feet. Evan Smithson! He had been the running figure. He had seen Adelina meet Wallis Trent, had darted back to the ruins while they talked and had lain in wait for her. Lynwood ran up the path and threw himself at his horse, his heart bursting with sudden fear.

He had been wrong – so wrong! Adelina would not meet Evan Smithson intentionally. Wallis Trent – yes. That was probable. But not Evan!

That outcast from the Trent family could only mean to harm her. Oh God! What have I done? He prayed as he galloped back through the wood, this time desperate to reach Adelina not to flee from her. Oh, Adelina, forgive me! Pray God I'm not too late!

But Lynwood was too late. Now, as he stood upon the broken wall and looked down upon the loathsome figure of Evan Smithson, and beyond him Adelina, bruised and hurt and weeping hysterically, he knew he was too late!

For a moment the earth reeled around him and the chasm of time opened up at his feet. The features of the man before him blurred, became those of another out of the past.

As Lynwood leapt down, it was not only Evan Smithson's, but the throat of Thomas Cole that his hands grasped and held and squeezed! There was a wild, murderous look upon Lynwood's face. Evan struggled desperately and lashed out at Lynwood's face with his fists. Lynwood reeled backwards, releasing his hold. Evan threw himself on top of him, punching his face. Then Lynwood threw Evan over and he had the advantage. As the wind blew and the rain lashed about them, the two exchanged blow for crushing blow. Locked together they rolled over and over on the stones, their clothes becoming mud-stained and soaked. Adelina, too, watching, became wet to the skin, her hair plastered against her head. She saw Lynwood stagger to his feet and pull Evan up after him. With his left hand he held Adelina's attacker while his right hand smashed time and time into Evan's face until it was a raw, bleeding pulp. Suddenly Evan seemed to find a fresh surge of strength and he kicked Lynwood viciously in the groin. A grunt of pain escaped his lips, and he let go of Evan, bending double in agony. Evan took the advantage and turned to flee, stumbling over the rough ground. Lynwood looked up and saw his quarry escaping. Still holding his stomach, he limped after him. Adelina pulled herself to her feet and followed. She emerged from the ruins to see that Lynwood had caught Evan again, throwing himself full-length to catch him by the legs. They fell together and began to roll, legs and arms flailing, down the hillside, straight into the stream at the foot. Lynwood was the first to rise. He bent and from the rushing water pulled Evan to his feet. Again he smashed his fist into Evan's face, again and again, until at last, exhausted himself, he released his hold. Evan fell back into the stream. Without a backward glance, Lynwood staggered out of the water, grasping at tufts of slippery grass to pull himself up the bank. He stood a moment swaying slightly, panting heavily.

As he climbed painfully back up the hill towards her, she saw that blood smeared his nose and one eye was half closed and beginning to swell. Adelina huddled against the wall, while Lynwood stood before her, swaying, still panting, his arms hanging loosely by his sides.

His rage was spent, worked out upon Evan. As he looked down at her swollen, bruised face, at her torn clothes and drenched hair, all that was left was an infinite sadness, a desperate longing for what might have been and now could never be!

He bent down and touched her arm. "Come – I'll take you home," he said flatly.

"No, no!" She shrank against the stones. "I can't – go back – there," she whispered, hoarsely, brokenly.

"No – I know. I'll take you to Lynwood Hall."

SIX

There was nothing else either of them *could* do. Lynwood could not desert her now, for his own remorse told him he could have prevented this tragic occurrence if it had not been for his own blind, jealous stupidity in allowing bitter memories from the past to overshadow the present and this innocent girl.

How she had been made to suffer for things past which were none of her doing! Her grandfather would not even see her, would not even acknowledge her existence because of the hurt her mother had inflicted upon him. Her relative – Martha Langley – could show her no kindness because Adelina represented a threat to the fortune so nearly within Martha's grasp. And Lynwood himself – the bitterness of a boy forced to face reality and disillusionment had grown like a cancer to warp the mind and twist the heart of the grown man.

He could not desert her, but daily he still fought the battle to obliterate the images of Caroline and see only Adelina. Still she was to continue to suffer because of this conflict within him.

"I'll take you away," he told her. "To London. Perhaps there we can both forget what has happened." But, sadly, they both knew it could not be so. Abbeyford and all that had happened would for ever be a dark shadow between them.

Dazedly, her spirit crushed, Adelina allowed Lord Lynwood to organise her life. He persuaded his mother to accompany them to London as chaperon for Adelina, and their journey, which took two days, was uneventful and uninteresting, for a steady drizzle fell the whole time.

At last, travelling through the heart of fashionable London, St James's Street, Piccadilly, they passed numerous elegant carriages, the dandies fastidiously dressed in their close-fitting trousers and high starched collars, strolling up and down.

"They're on their way to one club or another to play cards at the green baize tables – whist, faro, hazard – far into the night," Lord Lynwood leaned forward, trying to rouse Adelina's interest. "Fortunes can be won or lost in a single night." But her eyes were dull and unseeing as she stared out of the carriage.

Their vehicle turned into a residential square in Mayfair and drew to a halt in front of a white terraced house. There were small cast-iron balconies outside each long window at first-floor level, and railing along the front bordering the pavement.

Lord Lynwood helped his mother from the carriage and then he led Adelina up the steps to the round-arched doorway. Inside, the comparative plainness of the exterior of the house gave way to opulence and luxury. The carpeted staircase, with white cast-iron balusters, arose from the centre of the hall and then divided into two separate flights from the first floor to the other floors.

Lord Lynwood led Adelina into the spacious drawing-room with its high arched ceiling. The decorations were in white but this austerity was offset by the vividly coloured carpet and rich, wine-coloured velvet drapes at the huge bay window. Brightly patterned silk covered the gilt sofas and chairs, and elegant spindly-legged tables and sideboards were set here and there. In one corner there was a harp, and a Chinese screen stood behind one of the sofas. Above her head hung two crystal chandeliers.

Lady Lynwood took complete charge and soon her household staff had made ready a room for her guest. It said much for her generous spirit that Lady Lynwood had demanded no explanations for the sudden arrival of Adelina – dishevelled, weeping and homeless – upon her doorstep.

Adelina was taken upstairs to a sumptuous bedroom. All the furnishings were in the Chinese style, from the carpet and wallpaper to the small table and chairs which were bamboo. Even the bed coverlet was richly patterned with oriental motifs. The whole effect was unusual and delicate. Hardly noticing her surroundings, Adelina fell into bed and closed her eyes, completely exhausted and wishing she might never wake up!

For three days Adelina kept to her room, listlessly picking at the dainty trays of food set before her, or idly lying in bed just staring at the ceiling. She neither washed her face nor brushed her hair, nor even looked into the mirror.

On the fourth day, Lady Lynwood entered the bedroom, her stick tapping determinedly on the floor. She stood at the end of the bed and regarded Adelina for several moments.

"Well, you do look a poor creature," she said briskly, not allowing even a hint of the sympathy she felt for the girl to show in her tone. "I don't know what happened in Abbeyford – and I don't want to," she added swiftly. "But, whatever it was, it doesn't warrant you moping your young life away. Now, come along, my girl. Out of that bed!"

Adelina made no move.

Smartly Lady Lynwood rapped her stick upon the end of the bed. The sudden and unexpected noise made Adelina jump and she sat up, her green eyes flashing, her auburn hair tumbling in a tousled mass about her shoulders.

"Ah – that's better," the old lady laughed her cackling laugh. "Some response at last!"

"Go away!" Adelina muttered. "Just leave me alone."

"Don't give me orders in my own house, my girl," Lady Lynwood snapped, and inwardly congratulated herself to see a spark of anger flash again in Adelina's green eyes.

"Come along, get up. I'm taking you shopping." Lady Lynwood eyed the torn, stained riding-habit, the only garment Adelina now possessed. "You have need of some new gowns, I believe," she added wryly, and turned to leave, her cackling laughter ringing in Adelina's ears.

Within three weeks Lord Lynwood had established the unresisting Adelina in an apartment of her own – only a short distance from his own London home – and had provided her with a staff to run it, including her own personal maid. With Lady Lynwood's help, Adelina now possessed a wardrobe of fashionable gowns and accessories.

Slowly, life began to flood back into Adelina's frozen veins and the nightmare of Abbeyford receded a little – but never, ever, could it be obliterated.

A few weeks passed before Adelina began to regain her vitality and her beauty, for so deep were the emotional scars inflicted upon her. During this time Lynwood was kind and solicitous, taking her to small, select supper-parties where she did not have to meet too many people at once. But as winter gave way to spring and spring to early summer and the London Season began, Adelina was fully recovered.

Her new life in London began to intrigue and excite her.

"Well, Adelina my love," Lynwood smiled. "I think it is time I introduced you to the high life of Society. I shall take you to visit the Vauxhall Pleasure Gardens."

Her excitement mounted as she dressed. From among her new gowns Adelina chose one of emerald green silk, its neckline daringly low. Diamonds clustered about her snowy throat and shone in her hair, dimmed only by the sparkle in her shining eyes. Jane, her maid, dressed Adelina's hair high upon her head with a profusion of curls framing her face.

It was masquerade night and the gardens were illuminated with hundreds of lamps. Adelina, on Lord Lynwood's arm, strolled down the long avenues lined with trees. To her eyes, all of Society seemed to be here this night. Laughter rang through the still, early summer evening air. Adelina took a deep breath, savouring the scent of the trees, marvelling at the sweet air.

"It scarcely seems credible," she remarked to the Earl, "that we are in the heart of the city of London."

Lord Lynwood's eyes were upon her, admiring her beauty, trying desperately to blot out the memory of that other face so like Adelina's. She did not seem to notice, for she was still eagerly drinking in the scene around her, her lips slightly apart, her lovely face vibrantly alive. Almost against his will Lord Lynwood felt his pulses quicken and he put his hand over hers where it rested, lightly, on his arm.

At his touch she looked up at him. "Oh, my lord, this is so wonderful. I've never – ever – seen anything like this?" she murmured, entranced. Her hand tightened on his arm in a gesture of gratitude. "Thank you for bringing me, for making it all possible. I ..." She stopped in mid-sentence and put her head slightly on one side, listening intently. "Is that music I hear?"

"Most probably."

"Oh, do let's find it."

Smiling indulgently at her sudden childlike enthusiasm,

Lord Lynwood led the way to the orchestra pavilion. He found that Adelina's lack of sophistication, such a contrast to her mother, helped to erase some of the memories.

They found quite a crowd mingling around the pavilion, listening to the musicians or merely engaging in conversation in select little groups.

"I say, Lynwood!" a voice greeted him out of the shadows. Adelina turned to see an elegantly dressed young man approaching.

"Eversleigh!" Lord Lynwood greeted him with genuine delight. He turned to Adelina. "This is my good friend, Lord Peter Eversleigh." Lynwood laid his hand upon the shoulder of the young man as he made the introductions. Lord Eversleigh bowed over Adelina's hand.

"The pleasure is all mine, ma'am."

He was very tall, lanky rather, for he was a little too thin for his height so that he appeared to stoop slightly. He was dressed fashionably. His hair was black and curled crisply. His skin was dark and his eyes a deep azure blue. His tailed coat and trousers were of the finest material and the silk waistcoat was cut low to show a frilled shirt. He was aristocratic and elegant.

"Look, will you join me for supper?" He turned towards Lynwood.

"Well ..." Lynwood hesitated.

"Oh, come on, Lynwood. Don't keep this lovely lady all to yourself."

For an instant a shadow crossed Lynwood's face, but resolutely he smiled and allowed his friend to lead them to one of the small supper-boxes arranged amongst the trees. Gallantly, Lord Eversleigh helped Adelina to seat herself comfortably.

"Now don't run away, Miss Cole, I beg you," and so saying he hurried away again and was soon lost amongst the throng.

"Where has he gone?"

Lynwood sat down beside her. "To find refreshment for us, I suspect."

They sat in companionable silence, watching the young dandies strolling by with languid elegance and the young ladies flirting outrageously.

Lord Eversleigh returned with a manservant carrying a tray of glasses of punch and dishes of sillabub laced with wine.

"Oh, this is heavenly," Adelina enthused as she tasted the sweet concoction.

"Indeed it is, ma'am," Lord Eversleigh concurred, his eyes upon her face with open admiration, as if he would agree with anything and everything she said.

"Careful, my friend," Lynwood murmured. "You're in danger of poaching upon my preserves."

Lord Eversleigh laughed good-naturedly.

"Oh, *there* you are, my lord!"

Adelina looked up sharply to see who had spoken. Standing close by their table was a young woman, pretty but in an overdressed, vulgar way. Her gown was revealingly low and so tight that her ample bosoms were pushed unnaturally high. Her face was heavily powdered and rouged, and her throat, arms and hair seemed covered with cheap jewellery.

"Ah, yes – Harriet. Here I am." Lord Eversleigh rose to his feet – reluctantly, Adelina thought – and invited the girl to sit down.

"I ran into my old friend Lynwood here."

"And decided to desert me in favour of them?" the girl snapped, her eyes smouldering. Adelina sipped her glass of punch and regarded the girl with amusement.

Colour crept slowly up Eversleigh's neck and he shuffled his feet in embarrassment. "No – no. Of course not. I was but spending a few moments with my friends and then I was coming back to you. I thought you were happily enjoying the music."

"I was," the girl countered swiftly, "until I found you were no longer at my side."

There was an awkward silence in which Harriet transferred her resentful gaze from Lord Eversleigh to Adelina. The two girls eyed each other speculatively.

"Well," Harriet said petulantly, "aren't you going to make the introductions?"

A small sigh escaped Lord Eversleigh's lips, and he said swiftly and without courtesy.

"Miss Cole – this is Harriet. Miss Adelina Cole, from America."

"America? Heavens!" The girl had the grace to look impressed. "I thought I hadn't seen you before and I know everyone there is to know," she added smugly.

"I guess you do," Adelina drawled, her left eyebrow raised fractionally, her eyes never leaving Harriet's face. She recognised her at once for what she was. There had been plenty of girls like Harriet in the waterfront taverns, but despite their desperate straits, Adelina had refused to become one of them.

Obviously, Harriet was Lord Eversleigh's mistress.

Adelina was motionless, the colour suddenly creeping up her neck and over her face. She swallowed and laced her fingers together tightly in an effort to still their shaking.

That is what everyone here would think of her! That she, Adelina Cole, was Lord Lynwood's mistress. The realisation hit her with such force, left her feeling as if she stood – helpless – at the edge of a precipice, unable to take the step back to safety.

Unaware of her anguish, Lynwood watched the crowd passing back and forth before them, lost in his own brooding thoughts.

The following evening they were to attend a grand ball and Adelina dressed with supreme care. She chose an evening gown of pale blue crape over a slip of white satin. The neckline was cut square and very low. The hemline was heavily decorated with crape bows and frills.

Lord Lynwood called for her at her apartment.

"You are enchanting, ma'am," he said and bowed deeply as she curtsied playfully to him.

Lynwood himself handed her into his carriage and they bowled through the fashionable streets of London.

They drew up outside a grand terraced house with pillars on either side of a huge oak front door. More carriages lined the road and the night air was filled with the sound of laughter and excited chatter.

"Well," Lord Lynwood smiled down at her as he escorted her up the steps and into the house. "Are you ready to rock London Society?"

Adelina laughed. "I hope so."

As they entered, their names were announced and Adelina was aware of the heads turning, of the sudden stillness in the room, swiftly broken by the babble of speculation which swept through the vast room. The young men soon gravitated towards her and before long she was dancing every dance and never twice with the same partner – except for Lynwood, who demanded four. He watched as she danced with other men, his eyes following her swaying body, her parted lips, her shining eyes. She was easily the most beautiful girl in the room and a new face amongst the familiar ones of this particular set was bound to create excitement amongst the gentlemen and jealousy amongst the ladies.

Breathless and laughing, Adelina returned to Lord Lynwood. For the first time Abbeyford and all its unhappy memories seemed a hundred years away.

"Oh, Francis, this is wonderful. Oh look, there's Lord Eversleigh!" The use of Lynwood's Christian name sprang naturally to her lips. Now she felt his equal as his friends and contemporaries laughed and flirted with her.

But Adelina's growing confidence was like a knife in Lynwood's heart – now she was even more like her mother!

Gaily she waved her ivory fan at Lord Eversleigh across the room. Immediately he threaded his way through the people to reach her.

"Miss Cole – Lynwood. 'Tis good to see you here." His words were intended to include them both, but his eyes rested solely upon Adelina. But her restless gaze was wandering about the room, drinking in the elegance, the atmosphere of frivolity and enjoyment. She had never known anything like it in her life. She had not known such a world even existed.

Suddenly she saw the smile fade from Lord Eversleigh's face. "I say, Lynwood," he said in a low, urgent tone and nodded his head towards the door.

Lynwood turned and Adelina's eyes followed the direction of his gaze. Standing at the top of the stairs, framed in the doorway, stood a beautiful woman. Adelina eyed her critically ... Whoever she was, she was certainly lovely. Her skin was creamy white and her black hair shone and glinted in the light. Her low-cut gown was of transparent pink net over a deeper shade of pink.

"Who is she?" Adelina asked. She saw Lord Lynwood and his friend exchange a glance.

"That," remarked the Earl of Lynwood drily, "is Helene Lyon."

"Do you know her?" Adelina asked innocently.

Lynwood coughed and Lord Eversleigh seemed to stifle his laughter.

"Slightly," Lynwood replied, but there was sarcasm in his tone.

Helene Lyon floated elegantly down the steps, graciously acknowledging greetings on every side. She smiled and fluttered her fan, but all the while she was making her way directly across the room towards Lord Lynwood.

"Francis! How wonderful you're back in London," she cried, stretching out her hands towards him. "I couldn't imagine *you*, of all people, vegetating in the dreary countryside." Helene's voice was low and seductively husky. Her eyes flirted openly with him.

"Helene." Lynwood kissed her hand and then turned towards Adelina.

"I must introduce you to Miss Adelina Cole from America." Now that she was close, Adelina could see that Helene Lyon's face was perfectly proportioned, with pale blue eyes, finely arched brows and full, well-shaped lips.

"How do you do?" The expression in Helene's eyes belied her friendly greeting. Her scathing glance raked Adelina from head to toe and her lip curled disdainfully. "Are you staying in London long, Miss Cole?"

Adelina glanced at Lynwood. "I'm not sure. I hope so, but the decision rests with Lord Lynwood."

Adelina heard Helene's swift intake of breath and saw the anger spark within her eyes. Helene turned to face Lynwood and her eyes narrowed.

"So – that's the way it is!" She gave a snort of contempt and turned away abruptly, her skirts swirling angrily.

"Methinks you have offended the lady," Eversleigh murmured.

"It would appear so," Lynwood remarked in an offhand manner. He held out his arm to Adelina, "Come, Adelina, 'tis time you danced with *me* again."

Watching her dance with other men had caused Lynwood to feel acute jealousy. Seeing her admired had at last made him acknowledge his own deepening passion for her.

As they joined three other couples in a quadrille, Adelina was aware, all the time, of Miss Lyon's hostile gaze following their every movement.

Adelina found herself dancing opposite a tall, thin, young dandy, whose admiration for her was plain to see.

As the dance came to an end he demanded to be introduced to her. Lynwood performed the introductions with bad grace. It was the first time Adelina had seen him openly discourteous towards someone. His lips were a thin, hard line and anger glittered in his blue eyes making them seem suddenly cold.

"Mr Thomas de Courtney – Miss Adelina Cole."

"Madam – I am charmed. You are like a breath of spring amongst our dull company. May I pray beseech the pleasure of the next dance?"

"Of course ..."

But Adelina's words were interrupted by Lynwood saying sharply, "It's time we were leaving, Adelina."

"Oh, no, Francis," she spoke without thinking. "I'm having such a wonderful time. I don't want to go yet."

"Madam," Lynwood said warningly, "you will oblige me by leaving when *I* say."

For a moment the fire of challenge was between them, their determined, wilful spirits clashing. Then colour flooded Adelina's face as she remembered that she was only here by Lynwood's kindness. She had allowed the flattery of all the young men here to turn her head for a moment. Submissively, she put her hand on his arm. "Of course. I'm sorry, my lord."

His anger melted at once and Lynwood caressed her

cheek with the tips of his fingers. The scene did not go unnoticed by those nearby. As Lynwood led Adelina from the room it was not only Helene Lyon's eyes which followed them.

"My Lord Lynwood seems to be smitten somewhat," remarked one of Thomas de Courtney's friends.

"Egad, but she's a fine filly. From the New World, ain't she?" murmured de Courtney. "I'd like to try my hand at prising her away from Lynwood."

"Why don't you, then?"

"I might at that," he remarked casually.

"Damned fool if you do, de Courtney. He'll call you out for sure and he's reputed to be the best swordsman this side of the Channel."

De Courtney shrugged and his eyes followed Adelina until she left the room and disappeared from view.

"It might even be worth it if I'd had that little filly first!"

His fellow companions guffawed loudly.

In the carriage Lynwood and Adelina did not speak to each other, but each was acutely aware of the tension between them.

Lynwood, his desire, his love and all the bitter memories he'd tried so hard to crush had come crowding to the surface as he had watched Adelina dancing with other men.

He followed her into her apartment and slammed the door behind them. Adelina gasped and whirled to face him, her eyes wide, her lips apart. At the look on his face, she backed away and put her hand out as if to fend him off. "No, my lord, please. I ..."

"Adelina!" he whispered hoarsely and reached out towards her. "Don't be afraid. I won't – hurt you." He grasped her shoulders and drew her into his embrace. His mouth found hers, demanding, searching, pleading for love, so that she found herself, unwilling at first, responding to his desperate need for her. His hands stroked her hair, his mouth was against her neck, his lips seeming to burn her skin. Then he picked her up and carried her towards the bedroom, kicking shut the door behind them.

He lay beside her, his arms about her. For a moment his lips were gentle, his caresses tender and worshipping, but as his passion grew, a swift change of mood overwhelmed him and he took her swiftly, using her for his own selfish gratification, punishing her for something she could not understand.

His passion spent, he still lay heavily across her, his face buried against her neck, great shuddering sobs shaking his whole being. She could feel the wetness of his tears against her skin.

Suddenly he raised himself from her and, keeping his face averted, rolled off the bed and stumbled towards the door.

As the door shut behind him, Adelina curled her lovely body into a ball as if to protect herself from further misuse.

Was there no love in this world? Were all men as cruel as this? She covered her face with her arms and sobbed and sobbed.

Eventually she fell into a deep, troubled sleep where Evan Smithson's twisted features became Lynwood's tortured face!

The following day, there was no word from Lynwood, nor on the next, but on the third day Adelina was surprised to receive a visit from Lord Eversleigh during the morning. As she bade him sit down, she noticed he seemed ill at ease.

"Er – Lynwood is – er – staying with me."

Adelina raised her left eyebrow fractionally. "Really?"

"He – er – asked me to come and – well – see if you were still here."

The silence grew between them and then Lord Eversleigh's eyes met Adelina's steady gaze.

"Yes," she said quietly. "I am still here."

"And – and are you going to stay?"

Slowly she inclined her head. "Yes."

Relief flooded through his face. "Lynwood will be glad. He's very fond of you, you know, Miss Cole."

"Did he tell you to say that?"

"No – no – but I know he is. I can tell." Eversleigh stood up. "He'll be back this evening, then."

"Tell him …" Adelina paused.

"Yes?" Eversleigh queried eagerly.

"Tell him – I look forward to seeing him."

Eversleigh smiled. "I will."

After Lord Eversleigh had left, Adelina decided she would not remain closeted within her rooms any longer. She would go driving in Hyde Park that afternoon.

So, at five o'clock, the fashionable time when all the Society people appeared to drive or ride in the Park, she sent word that she required Lord Lynwood's carriage. Her arrival there caused a stir amongst those who went there regularly. Adelina recognised one or two faces from her attendance at the ball and, before many minutes had passed, she found that several of the young men on horseback were keeping pace with her carriage. One seemed determined to get close to her.

"Why, it's Mr de Courtney, is it not?"

"It is, ma'am, and I am mighty flattered that you should have remembered my name. I, of course, could not forget yours if I had tried. Indeed, Miss Cole, my *dear* Miss Cole, you have been scarcely out of my thoughts since I laid eyes on you the other evening."

"Really, Mr de Courtney?" Adelina knew his words to

be outrageous flattery. "Aren't you going to introduce me to some of your companions?" she nodded towards the other riders beside her carriage.

"What? And have them usurp my place beside you, Miss Cole? Indeed I am not!"

Her carriage had slowed to a snail's pace so that she might carry on a conversation with Thomas de Courtney. Several other carriages rattled past.

"Why, there's Miss Lyon!" Adelina waved her gloved hand in greeting, but Helene Lyon appeared not to have noticed, for, although she seemed to be looking in Adelina's direction, her eyes wore a steely, glazed expression.

"Why," Adelina cried with a spurt of anger. "She cut me!"

Thomas de Courtney guffawed loudly. "Are you surprised?"

Adelina's eyes widened as she looked at him. "I don't understand you."

"You can hardly expect her to show friendliness towards the lady who has taken her place, can you?"

Adelina looked puzzled and shook her head slightly. Brutally, Thomas de Courtney took great pleasure in informing her, "Helene Lyon was Lynwood's mistress. That is until you arrived on the scene."

"What makes you think I am his mistress?" Adelina snapped defiantly.

"Oh, come now, Miss Cole," Mr de Courtney waved his hand towards the numerous ladies in their carriages, most of whom seemed to be engaged in conversation with some gentleman. "There isn't one of these lovely ladies here who hasn't a string of lovers to her name. It's the occupational pastime of the idle rich, my dear."

Adelina opened her parasol. "Well, Mr de Courtney. I

am not a Britisher – so pray don't judge *me* by your own standards!"

"Brave words, Miss Cole, but I wonder just how long you'll be able to live up to such a high moral code if you plan to become part of our decadent Society?"

Adelina declined to answer. "Drive on," she instructed her coachman sharply. "Goodday, Mr de Courtney."

"Goodday, Miss Cole. We shall meet again."

Adelina was in a fine temper when she arrived home, partly because she had found Thomas de Courtney's arrogance disturbing but more so because he, and most likely everyone else, had recognised her for just what she had become – the mistress of Lord Francis Lynwood.

Jane was waiting for her. "His lordship has sent word he is taking you to dine tonight, madam, and afterwards to the Opera."

"The Opera!"

Adelina's ill-humour was dispelled in an instant. "How wonderful! I've heard such a lot about it, but I've never been. Oh, Jane, what shall I wear? How shall I dress my hair?"

When Lynwood greeted her that evening it was as if the unhappy incident between them had never occurred. He bowed to her. "You look exquisite, my love. I shall be the envy of all the young men present."

Taking her cue from him, Adelina smiled. "And I shall be the envy of all the fine ladies with the handsome Lord Lynwood as my – escort." She hesitated fractionally over the last word, for she had been about to say 'lover', but had thought better of it. She did not want to quarrel with Francis, though she longed to challenge him about Helene Lyon.

"I hope you don't mind," Lynwood told her as they sat side by side in the carriage. "I have invited Eversleigh and his wife to dine with us."

So, Eversleigh was married, yet kept a mistress too!

"His wife?" Adelina asked with sarcasm. "Not – Harriet?"

In the darkness of the carriage, she heard Lynwood laugh wryly. "No – not on this occasion, though no doubt Eversleigh would have preferred her."

Adelina was puzzled by the remark until she saw Lady Madeleine Eversleigh for herself. The poor woman was cursed with a face which could only be described as plain – and then if one were being very kind. She had a long, oblong-shaped face, with a hooked nose and eyes set too close together and a row of huge teeth which protruded alarmingly. Her teeth seemed to fill her whole mouth! Despite the disadvantage of her looks, Lady Eversleigh seemed a kindly creature whose desire to be friendly and to please was almost pathetic. It was also obvious to Adelina's shrewd eye that the poor woman was deeply in love with her handsome husband and equally obvious that he did not return her devotion.

The dinner was sumptuous. Everything was served on silver plates and dishes. Hot soups and salmon, a saddle of mutton and a selection of cold meat dishes too. Iced champagne was served and then bowls of peaches, grapes, pineapples and all manner of fruit were placed within easy reach.

Afterwards they went to the Opera House. During the interval after the First Act, Adelina looked about her again. She was intrigued by the finery of the ladies and the dandies. She leant forward to look down into the pit, fascinated to see the fops strolling about showing off the fine cut of their new clothes, elegantly taking snuff from jewelled snuff-boxes and chattering noisily, even throughout the performance.

Adelina's eyes took in every detail of the rich and ornate surroundings, scanning the gallery and the boxes, admiring all the fine gowns of the ladies. This was the world to which her mother had belonged – and now Adelina was part of it too.

As they drove home in the darkness of the carriage, she was surprised to feel Francis search for her hand and clasp it, holding it tenderly. It was as if he was trying to communicate an apology to her. She was touched by his concern, by his desire to rectify matters between them. She blinked back the tears, smiled tremulously and squeezed his hand in return.

That night when Lynwood stayed with her once more, Adelina learnt that there could indeed be a different kind of lovemaking to the brutal ways she had hitherto experienced. Lynwood was gentle, seeming to give rather than to take, so that she found her fears falling away and her natural sensuality responding to his caresses.

But even at the height of their passion she was acutely aware that there was a bitterness in Lynwood's heart.

So many shadows lay between them.

Thomas de Courtney had been quite correct when he said they would meet again, for some weeks later Lynwood took her to a private party where card-playing and gambling were to take place. The weeks since her arrival in London had been filled with balls, suppers, routs and sightseeing, but this was the first party she had attended where the main interest was to be gambling.

The moment she entered the room Adelina was dismayed to see Mr de Courtney and Helene Lyon deep in conversation on the far side of the room. Adelina put her hand on Lynwood's arm possessively. He smiled down at her and, out of the corner of her eye, she saw Miss Lyon's face grow dark with anger. Adelina smiled and nodded to those who greeted her. Her confidence had grown and she moved with ease now in Lord Lynwood's world. He led her about the room, introducing her to those she had not met before and greeting those she already knew. Eventually they stood in front of Mr de Courtney and Miss Lyon.

"So, we meet again, Miss Cole." Mr de Courtney gave an elegant but exaggerated bow.

"So it seems," Adelina replied tartly, all the while watching Miss Lyon's face as she smiled and fluttered her eyelashes at Lord Lynwood.

"Why, Francis," Helen Lyon purred in her husky voice. "It seems an age since I saw you. Now, let me see, whenever was it – ah, I remember. When you were staying with Lord Eversleigh for a night or two." Her glance slanted meaningly towards Adelina.

Adelina stiffened and almost a gasp of surprise escaped her lips, but with supreme control she managed to keep her features composed, for she knew the woman was merely trying to goad her. So, she thought, seething inwardly, Francis had found comfort in Miss Lyon's arms, had he? And, not only that, the whole of Society must know that he and she had quarrelled and that he had found refuge with Eversleigh – and with Helene Lyon!

Once out of earshot of Miss Lyon and away from her scheming eyes, Adelina snatched her hand away from Lynwood's arm. She heard him sigh softly.

"Adelina, Eversleigh and I went to a private card party and Helene – Miss Lyon – happened to be there."

Adelina was surprised and shaken to find how the thought of Helene Lyon in Lynwood's arms hurt her desperately. But she would not let him know that. Proudly she said, "I'm sure it's of no consequence where you were – or whom you were with," she added pointedly. Then she turned swiftly to face him. "But pray credit me with a little intelligence in such matters, Francis. I know of your liaison with – *her*!"

"I'll not deny it, my love. But that was before I even met you. I have not visited her since then." He seemed almost surprised himself at the fact.

Adelina searched his face but from his expression he gave every appearance of telling the truth.

There was a stir of excitement in the room as the gaming-tables were set up and the serious business of the evening began.

As the night wore on, one or two of the men, befuddled by drink, began to lose money consistently and heavily. To Adelina the huge sums of money the dandies wagered were ridiculously large. Despite their obvious wealth she could not imagine how their finances could stand such depletion. She was not enjoying the evening, for the gambling reminded her of her father and the unhappiness it had caused them both.

Lynwood and Eversleigh were playing at a table with Thomas de Courtney and another young dandy, Geoffrey Dalton, a fair-haired, pale-skinned and somewhat effeminate man. Mr de Courtney had become decidedly tipsy from the numerous glasses of wine he had consumed. He seemed to lose all sense of caution, betting wildly on his cards when experience should have told him he had no chance of winning with such a hand. Adelina stood quietly behind Lynwood's chair, watching. She knew that both he and Eversleigh were finding the game an embarrassment now rather than a pleasure.

"Well, I think I'll call it a day," Eversleigh said, attempting to break up the game.

"What?" De Courtney gripped Eversleigh's arm drunkenly. "Tha's right, try to walk away with all the winnings without giving a fellow time to redeem himself. Call yourself a gen-," he hiccupped loudly, "gentleman?"

"You're drunk, de Courtney," Lynwood said bluntly. "You'd do better to leave the table now before you lose even more of your inheritance than you've lost already."

"No damn business of yours, Lynwood, if I lose the lot!" He banged his fist down on the table, making the cards jump and the money rattle.

Lynwood shrugged. "Have it your own way, then."

"Tell you what, Lynwood," de Courtney leant towards him, but his glance leered up at Adelina standing behind Lord Lynwood's chair. "I'll play you one hand for the greatest prize of all! My entire inheritance against your whore!"

There was a moment's stunned silence about the table and then startled gasps and shocked murmurings.

Lynwood leapt to his feet, overturning the table, scattering cards and money in all directions and even knocking poor Lord Eversleigh on to the floor.

Lynwood's face was a picture of terrifying and revengeful rage. He grasped de Courtney by the lapels of his jacket and hauled him to his feet. Then his strong fingers gripped de Courtney's throat, choking him so that his face grew purple and his eyes bulged. Eversleigh pulled at Lynwood's arm.

"Lynwood – for God's sake. You'll throttle him."

Other hands began to reach forward to separate Lynwood's murderous grasp from de Courtney's neck.

Adelina tried to swallow the fear rising in her throat. There was maniacal revenge in Lynwood's eyes. It was not only de Courtney beneath those fingers but Evan Smithson and Thomas Cole too! Time after time, it seemed to

Lynwood, other men came between him and the girl he loved. Now here was a conceited dandy calling Adelina the most insulting name he could think of, and yet wanting her for himself.

"Lynwood! *Lynwood*!" The fear in Eversleigh's voice penetrated Lynwood's mind and slowly he relaxed his hold.

De Courtney slipped to the floor – unconscious. Lynwood stood over him, swaying slightly, breathing hard, his arms hanging loosely at his sides. Several ladies screamed and decided they should faint, but since all attention seemed to be on the prostrate de Courtney, they thought better of it and contented themselves with fanning their hot faces vigorously.

Geoffrey Dalton, de Courtney's foppish young friend, gasped, "You've killed him – you've killed him."

"Nonsense," Eversleigh declared stoutly, but Adelina could see the worry in his eyes. "Lynwood, come, man, sit down." He turned his dazed friend around and led him to a couch. The others closed around de Courtney still lying on the floor.

Adelina ran to Lynwood, sat beside him and slipped her hand into his. His fingers gripped hers, clinging to her and together they watched until the circle around de Courtney parted and they saw him sitting up on the floor, holding his throat and coughing.

"Oh, Francis – he's alive. He's — he's all right."

Geoffrey Dalton stood before Lynwood and Eversleigh rose and faced him.

"De Courtney will demand satisfaction," he sneered. "When he's sufficiently recovered from your cowardly attack to meet you in a fair duel!"

Lynwood stood up, in complete control of his emotions now, his coolness belying the blind rage of only minutes ago.

"Any time, Dalton!"

And with that he strode from the room, Adelina and Eversleigh hurrying after him. She plucked at Lynwood's arm.

"Francis – I don't want you to fight on my account. Please don't. Lord Eversleigh," she appealed to their friend. "Please stop him."

There was a moment's silence before Eversleigh said quietly, "We can't back out now, Miss Cole, it would seem like cowardice to withdraw from such a challenge."

"But – but what is going to happen?"

Neither answered her, but she saw them glance at each other, their faces grim and serious.

SEVEN

The duel – when all the arrangements had been made between the contestants' seconds, Lord Eversleigh acting for Lynwood and Geoffrey Dalton for de Courtney – was scheduled to take place four days after the challenge had been made, on the Heath at dawn.

In the long hours of darkness Adelina felt physically sick with fear at the thought of what might happen to Lynwood. As she tossed and turned, unable to sleep, slowly the realisation came to her. She loved him! Adelina had fallen in love with Lord Lynwood, so deeply that the thought of losing him, even the thought of him being wounded, filled her with a kind of panic she had never before experienced. Even the death of her father, sudden and shocking though it had been, had not caused her such nightmarish anguish. Now she knew why she had stayed with him, had become his mistress. Even then, without knowing it, she must have loved him.

Early on the morning of the duel, when it was still dark, she slipped from her warm bed and, shivering, for the maid had not yet lit a fire in her bedroom so early was the hour, she began to dress herself. Lynwood had forbade her to attend the scene of the duel, but· Adelina could not keep away. She was so afraid that Francis would be hurt, perhaps even killed, that she could not sit at home, waiting for the dreadful news. She just had to be there. She pulled the hood of her black velvet cloak well down over her face and left her apartment. She hurried along the deserted streets until she came to Lynwood's house. Slipping down the stairs to the servants' entrance, she rapped on the kitchen door. It must be five o'clock already and she knew Francis would have left. The servants were already about their early morning tasks, so she was soon able to despatch a young footman to have Lynwood's phaeton brought immediately to the front door. Adelina paced the pavement in a ferment of anxiety. She planned to drive herself and yet she was not quite sure how she should get to the Heath. As the young footman assisted her into the phaeton, she grabbed him by the arm.

"You'll have to come with me to show me the way. If I get lost, I'll never find my way through this maze of streets, and I'll miss the whole thing."

"But, madam," stammered the unfortunate young man, "my duties – I have work to do – I can't come ..."

"You can and you will. I'll explain later," she replied hastily, almost pulling him into the phaeton.

Eventually they arrived on the Heath just as the first pale fingers of dawn stretched their way over the grass. The Heath, partially shrouded in morning mist, appeared to be deserted.

"Are you sure this is the right place?" Adelina asked worriedly.

"Yes, ma'am. This is where they normally hold the duels."

Adelina shuddered. "You make it sound like a regular occurrence?"

The young footman shrugged. "It seems to be, madam, amongst the dandies who have naught better to do."

Adelina cast him a severe, disapproving glance and the man apologised hastily. "I beg your pardon, ma'am."

She nodded. "I should think so, too. It's not for you to judge your master." Then she added, "Look, we're right out in the open here. Isn't there somewhere we can conceal ourselves? I don't want to be seen if I can avoid it."

The footman pointed. "Over there, there's a clump of bushes. They'll just about hide the phaeton."

"Fine." Adelina manoeuvred the horses until the vehicle was standing behind the bushes, hidden, she hoped, from view from the duelling place. She alighted and found a place amongst the bushes where she was concealed from view and yet she had a good view of the scene.

Scarcely had she settled herself before she saw a carriage and pair loom out of the mist and come to a halt some distance away. Though she strained her eyes to see through the mist, she could only see two figures light from the vehicle and stand talking together. A second, smaller carriage appeared, but only one person got down, and he too, remained near his vehicle and made no move to speak to the other two.

The footman, who had come to crouch amongst the bushes beside her, whispered, "That fellow on his own, that'll be the surgeon."

"Surgeon!" Adelina squeaked and then clapped her hand to her mouth, fearful that her voice would be heard and she would be discovered and sent away. She lowered her voice to an urgent whisper. "What do you mean – surgeon? Do you mean someone *always* gets hurt?"

"Or killed," the young footman replied nonchalantly.

Adelina bit her lip hard. At that moment yet another carriage drew up not many paces from her hiding-place. She drew breath sharply as she recognised the vehicle and saw, a moment later, Lynwood and Lord Eversleigh step from its interior. They were so near she could hear their conversation plainly.

"This is a fool's errand you're on, Lynwood," Eversleigh said. "He's reputedly an expert with an épée."

Lynwood remained grimly silent.

The minutes ticked by and Adelina began to wish they would get on with the wretched duel if there was to be one. She was becoming very cramped, squatting in this undignified position in the bushes. The dank morning was seeping through her cloak and making her shiver and the mist had dampened her hair, plastering tiny curls around her face.

At that moment the surgeon moved out to the centre of the field and the protagonists' two seconds stepped forward, to converse with him.

"He's acting as referee," whispered the footman in Adelina's ear. "He's asking them to settle the matter without bloodshed. It's only a formality of course, no one ever does when it's got to this stage."

In confirmation of his words, she saw Lord Eversleigh and Mr Dalton shake their heads.

Moments later the two duellists stepped forward and faced each other. The thin blades glittered and shivered as, on guard, they circled each other warily. De Courtney lunged but Lynwood parried by dropping the point of his épée down sharply and holding off his opponent's weapon. Again on guard they circled. Each lunged and parried alternately, and this gamesmanship seemed to Adelina to go in interminably.

"I think they're enjoying it!" she muttered, impatiently.

She shivered and blew on to her frozen fingers in an effort to warm them.

Suddenly Adelina saw Francis lunge and the point of his rapier disappeared into de Courtney's chest. The latter gave a cry of pain which rent the still morning and startled the onlookers, even though they were half expecting it.

Thomas de Courtney sank to the ground, Lynwood's rapier still embedded in his body. The surgeon rushed forward and immediately took hold of Lynwood's weapon. Gently he eased the blade from de Courtney's chest and threw it to one side. Then he dropped to his knees beside the still form. Eversleigh and Geoffrey Dalton ran forward, one to stand at Lynwood's side while Dalton fell to his knees beside his friend.

From her position, Adelina could not hear what was said, merely a low murmuring of voices.

"We should go now, madam," whispered the footman. "'Tis over and his lordship is unharmed."

"No – they'll hear us – I don't want Lord Lynwood to know I was even here – you understand?" She pressed his arm warningly.

"Of course, madam."

They remained hidden until Lynwood and Eversleigh had crossed the grass towards their carriage. Their faces were grim and neither of them spoke to each other. They climbed into the vehicle, which, seconds later, moved away. The prostrate form of Thomas de Courtney had not moved, and both the surgeon and Mr Dalton were still bending over him.

"Oh God," Adelina whispered. "I think he really has killed him this time." She stood up, easing her aching limbs, and pulled her cloak closer around her. Her teeth were chattering with cold. "Come on, let's get away from here before we're discovered!"

She had not expected Lynwood would visit her apartment immediately, but she had only managed to take off her damp cloak and rough dry her long hair with a towel when she heard the sound of a carriage in the street below, his footsteps pounding up the stairs and the door of her apartment flung wide open.

Lynwood strode into her bedroom and then stopped in surprise. "Awake already, my love?" Though his tone was bantering, Adelina could detect the tension beneath the surface. She seated herself before the mirror and began to brush her long, shining hair. They each seemed to be waiting for the other to speak.

"So," Adelina remarked with apparent indifference, even though her heart was thudding and her hands were wet with sweat, "you managed not to get yourself killed this morning."

Lynwood came to stand behind her, watching her through the mirror. "You don't seem very concerned, madam?" The cynical smile twisted his mouth.

"Well – you're here, aren't you?" she raised an eyebrow.

"Don't you want to know what happened to de Courtney?"

"Did you – kill him?"

"To be honest – I don't know. He was still breathing when I left the field, but the injury was – severe. In any case," Lynwood bent down, putting his face close to hers, though they still looked at each other through the looking-glass, "it would be better if I were away from town until the scandal has died down a little. We shall be leaving tonight for Lynwood Hall. My mother, too, since, this time, you will have to stay at the Hall."

Adelina's mouth fell open and her eyes widened with horror at his statement. "Oh, no, Francis, I can't go back there. It's too near Abbeyford. Don't ask me to!"

"Well," Lynwood muttered, "we have no choice!"

The last thing in the world Adelina wanted was to return to the vicinity of Abbeyford and all its bitter memories. She cringed at the thought and closed her eyes and groaned.

"You promise we'll come back to London once the scandal of the duel is all over?" she begged him.

"Yes, yes," was his impatient reply, anxious to put distance between himself and his victim's family and friends, who, he knew, would shortly be howling for his blood in revenge for the injury he had inflicted upon de Courtney.

Lynwood Hall was every bit as beautiful as Adelina remembered it. But now, having tasted the exhilarating, busy life of Society London, she soon found her life at Lynwood Hall, though comfortable, was dull and tedious.

Lynwood was withdrawn and moody. He went out most days on his own, shooting on his estate, leaving Adelina with only Lady Lynwood, his mother, for company.

"So, Miss Cole, I suppose you think you have progressed in the world since you were last here?" Lady Lynwood gave a short cackle of laughter, her bright eyes sharp and perceptive. Adelina raised her left eyebrow. She enjoyed the verbal sparring with Lady Lynwood, for beneath the surface there was a good deal of respect for each other's strength of character.

"That's a matter of opinion. Mrs Langley would not agree with you." Nor Adelina thought sadly to herself, would her grandfather.

Lady Lynwood's piercing eyes scanned Adelina's face. "Have you any regrets about becoming a courtesan, miss?"

Adelina winced, startled by Lady Lynwood's bluntness. "I'm not exactly that," she bridled, "though I'll not deny being your son's mistress."

"Is he – kind to you?" The sharp, all-knowing eyes were boring into her very soul. Adelina felt the colour creeping up her neck.

"Yes," she said, determinedly shutting her mind to the times when Lynwood's dark, brooding moods over-shadowed both their lives. "Yes – of course he is!"

Lady Lynwood eyed her, shrewdly disbelieving. "Poor Francis," she murmured. "I wonder if he can ever hope to find real happiness? He was badly hurt by – a woman a long time ago."

"Who?"

"Oh, I can't tell you that," Lady Lynwood said. "He was only a boy. A boy's first love. It can be very painful, you know." The old eyes, still bright and vital, regarded Adelina.

"I – guess so," the young girl said. Then with sudden understanding, "And you mean it – it still hurts him now?"

Lady Lynwood nodded. "I mean that it has affected his whole attitude towards women and – love."

"I – see," Adelina murmured. "Perhaps I can help him to forget her."

"I doubt it. I think it most likely you are a constant reminder."

But Adelina, deep in her own thoughts of Lynwood, of her love for him, remembering his many kindnesses to her, the many times when his lovemaking had been tender and joyful, failed to question the full meaning behind Lady Lynwood's words.

Lord Lynwood arranged a Meet of the local Amberly and Abbeyford Hunt as a little diversion for Adelina.

"I am Joint Master with Wallis Trent," he told Adelina, "but he declined to join us this time."

She felt Lynwood's eyes upon her, watching her face for any sign of emotion at the mention of Wallis Trent's name. Still the memory of her meeting Wallis Trent on the hillside above Abbeyford haunted him, fusing in his mind with that other meeting of so long ago.

The Hunt met at Lynwood Hall. Adelina was the only woman to ride with them, though there were several ladies in their carriages from neighbouring estates who came to watch the Hunt, following as best they could along the narrow lanes and rough cart-tracks.

The morning was bright and cold and Adelina was ready early, determined to enjoy the new experience despite Lynwood's black mood. She wore a new emerald green riding-habit which she knew suited her to perfection, contrasting as it did with her rich auburn hair and making her eyes a brighter green than ever. The long skirt billowed out as she rode, the tight-fitting jacket accentuating her tiny waist.

Lynwood looked extremely handsome in his Master's coat. He greeted Adelina with his half-mocking smile, yet she could see the desire leap in his eyes. "That habit becomes you, my love."

"Thank you, kind sir," she laughed and was surprised to find how much his casual compliment meant to her.

The horses and hounds moved off and, gathering speed, they pounded across the countryside. Suddenly a fox broke covert, and the hounds, barking shrilly, were in pursuit, the huntsmen hotfoot after them. Adelina felt the thrill of the chase. The fox was well ahead, running across Lord Lynwood's estate and on to the Trents' lands, through the woodland across the brow of the hill and past the abbey ruins and on yet farther. Then the hounds were gaining ground as the poor, harried creature began to tire.

The huntsmen's blood-thirsty cries echoed across the valley. Then the hounds were upon the fox, brutally ravaging, their sharp teeth tearing the animal limb from limb. Adelina reined in and sat upon her horse watching in horrified silence. She had not imagined the kill would be so nauseating.

Beside her she heard one of Lynwood's neighbouring landowners remark languidly, "Lynwood – don't forget we have a new member of the Hunt with us. I think she should be bloodied."

Cries of assent arose from the other men.

Lynwood laughed. "Not satisfied with the day's sport, gentlemen?" he said with sarcasm. "Very well."

He dismounted and with another huntsman went amongst the hounds to return a few moments later with the decapitated head of the fox in his hand, the red blood dripping through his fingers.

He stood beside Adelina's horse. For a moment Lynwood hesitated. He was remembering that other time, the occasion of his own initiation. Then Caroline had been watching, smiling with congratulation.

"You'll have to dismount, my dear," he said now to Adelina.

"What are you going to do?"

"You'll see."

Reluctantly, Adelina dismounted and stood before him. Holding her arm firmly with his free hand so that she could not draw back, Lynwood raised his hand and pressed the raw and bleeding head upon Adelina's face, moving it across her forehead and once down each cheek, accompanied by cheers of encouragement from the watchers.

Adelina screamed!

In that moment she saw Lord Lynwood's face change from amusement to anger. He put his face close to hers. "How dare you make a sound? It's a disgrace to be cowardly at this ceremony. And you have humiliated me by being so!"

Swiftly he turned his back upon her and strode back to his horse. The onlookers were quiet now, watching her with silent disapproval. Without a backward glance at her,

Lynwood rode away and, one by one, the huntsmen followed, until she was left alone.

Adelina rubbed at the blood, drying now, on her face and spattered down the bodice of her lovely riding-habit.

"What a barbaric custom," she exploded angrily, but there was no one to hear her. "And to think the British have the audacity to think us Yankees wild and uncivilised. Oh!" she cried and stamped her foot in rage. She remounted and spurred her horse to a gallop back towards Lynwood Hall where, she went straight away to her room to change and clean the blood from her face.

Jane's cry of indignation was fuel to Adelina's own anger and disgust. "Oh, madam, your face and your beautiful habit. It's a disgrace and no mistake!"

Gently, Adelina sponged the blood from her face, wincing slightly as she did so. Once clean again she stared at herself in the mirror. There, for all to see, was the reason for her screams. Across her forehead and down each cheek were two scratch marks, one quite deep so that even now it oozed blood – her own. The other, fainter scratches, merely marking the surface of the skin.

'Just wait till his lordship sees *that*!' Adelina thought, and said aloud, "Jane, go and find out what is happening downstairs."

After a few moments her maid arrived back a little breathless. "His lordship is in the library, madam, with all his guests – the gentlemen, that is. The ladies are in the drawing-room."

Adelina nodded, her eyes gleaming with satisfaction. Regally, she descended the stairs and went towards the library. A footman opened the door for her and she stood, just inside the doorway, watching the assembled company.

One of Lynwood's guests was the first to notice her

standing there. His mouth dropped open at the sight of her lovely face marked by the ugly scratches. He nudged Lynwood, who turned and then, gradually, every gentleman in the room had seen her and everyone fell silent.

Adelina saw the last traces of anger, which still lingered in Lynwood's expression, disappear at the sight of her.

She saw his lips form her name in a soft whisper, saw the mute apology in his eyes. He made a step towards her, but Adelina, satisfied to have proved her point not only to Lynwood but to all his aristocratic friends as well, turned on her heel and walked sedately through the hall and into the drawing-room.

Later, when all his guests had departed, Lynwood sought her out.

"Adelina – my love," his voice was hoarse. "I apologise most humbly. I had no idea. It must have been a sharp piece of bone sticking out."

He held out his arms to her and, with a little sob, Adelina turned to him and was enfolded in his embrace. He held her close, murmuring endearments, whilst she wound her arms about him and hugged him.

That night their lovemaking was the joyous, tender union of two people who loved each other – yet still neither could speak aloud the very words the other so longed to hear.

Still the shadows were between them!

The weeks and months passed and still no word came that they could return to London. Adelina, when Lynwood left her alone, took long, solitary rides on horseback to try to alleviate the boredom.

So far, she had kept away from Abbeyford, but one afternoon she found herself, almost against her will, taking the road through Amberly and towards Abbeyford. She felt an overwhelming desire to hear news of her grandfather. There had never been a day pass – even during the time she had spent in London – when she had not thought of him. A shadowy figure built in her imagination from the faded miniature in her locket. If only she could meet him – just once – so that she could carry a true likeness of him in her mind.

There was a need to see him, a need to feel close, for over the past two weeks there had been a secret fear in her mind, a fear she had not even confided to Lord Lynwood. But if it were to be true – then she had more need than ever of her family.

Though it was still March and the air sharp, the sun was bright.

As she passed through the village of Amberly, a crowd of ragamuffin, barefoot children gaped at the fine lady on horseback. Then one boy, older than the rest, recognised her.

"Why, it's 'er as went an' ran off to London wi' Lord Lynwood. Ha-ha – you know what *she* is? She's 'is whore!'"

Suddenly something hit her horse's flanks, making the animal rear and snort and then bolt, with the sound of the children's laughter ringing in her ears. Adelina, though startled, managed to keep her seat and soon brought the animal under control once more. The boy had thrown a stone at her! Adelina was outraged. She turned her horse round to ride back and give the boy a box on the ears. As she did so she saw that now the crowd of children were ranged across the road and all were armed with missiles. A shower of stones and sticks came towards her and, though she was too far away to be in danger of being hit this time, the children's actions and their cries of derision unsettled her horse again. Adelina noticed that several of the women had now appeared in the doorways of their cottages, but far from chastising their children, they appeared to be encouraging them.

Adelina turned her horse about again and spurred him into a gallop. When at last she slowed to a trot again, she herself was breathless, her cheeks aflame, her eyes bright and sparkling with anger, her auburn hair flowing loose and free.

And this was how Wallis Trent saw her again.

He was on his way, riding his black stallion, Jupiter, to Amberly village when, cresting the hill, he saw Adelina riding towards him. He reined in and sat upon his horse, watching her. Still thinking of the insults of the village children, Adelina did not see him until she was upon him. She pulled on the reins and her horse stopped.

Wallis's face was expressionless.

"Mr Trent," Adelina greeted him cautiously.

At last he spoke. "So, Miss Cole, you have dared to return. I doubt you'll find much of a welcome in this vicinity."

"I did not expect one, Mr Trent," she replied tersely. "I merely wish to – to enquire after my grandfather. Is he well?"

Wallis Trent smiled, a small quirk of his lips, but there was no pleasantness. "Your determination surprises me, Miss Cole. Are you *still* harbouring hopes of reconciliation?" He laughed sarcastically. "You're wasting your time."

"Is he well?" Adelina persisted, determined to have him answer her.

"Yes, he's well." Wallis Trent leaned forward, his eyes hard and cold, boring into her. "Happily anticipating the arrival of my son. He's already made a generous settlement upon the child – even before its birth!"

Adelina gasped. So Wallis Trent and Emily were married and she was to have a child. A child who would eventually inherit Lord Royston's entire estate.

Adelina did not care about the inheritance, but the news did make her feel even more excluded from the family to which she rightfully belonged. Lord Royston's affection was to be lavished upon Emily's child – instead of upon his own granddaughter. She swallowed the lump in her throat and raised her head in proud defiance. She would not let Wallis Trent see how the news upset her, but she could not bring herself to speak the words of congratulation.

"So your inheritance slips a little farther out of reach, my dear."

"I care not for any inheritance – I've told you that!"

But how could she expect an avaricious man like Wallis Trent to understand her longing to be loved, her need to belong?

"Wallis," Adelina asked suddenly. "What – what happened to Evan?"

Wallis shrugged. "He disappeared from the village the same night as you. For a time it was thought that you and he ..." His eyes glinted. "Then we heard you were with Lynwood." His lips curled disdainfully.

Embarrassment coloured her face at the innuendo in his tone. And then fear crept into her heart. That night – had Lynwood killed Evan? She swallowed, torn between the desire to know the truth and the need to protect Lynwood. He was in enough trouble already over de Courtney. Then Wallis said, "Shortly afterwards Lucy Walters disappeared from the village too, so I rather think she went with him, away from Abbeyford. All I hope is that they *stay* away!"

Adelina felt relief flood through her for Lynwood's sake.

At that moment three riders appeared out of the wood and rode across the open fields a short distance away. One horseman slowed down and drew apart from the others. He stopped and looked towards Adelina and Wallis Trent, their horses close together as they talked. He watched them for a few moments then spurred his horse, and, with the wild abandon of jealous rage, galloped madly away.

"Oh no!" Adelina whispered. "That was Francis. Oh *no*!"

On her return to Lynwood Hall Adelina tried to seek out Lynwood, but he had shut himself in the library and posted a footman at the door with the strictest order – on pain of dismissal – that he was available to no one.

He did not appear at dinner, nor did he visit her room that night. Adelina sent a note to him, begging '*please let me explain*', but there was no response.

The following morning Adelina found that Lord Lynwood had left early for London – without her!

Adelina hurried to Lady Lynwood's apartments. Without pausing to knock, she burst into the small room Lady Lynwood called her boudoir.

"How dare he go back to London without me? How dare he leave me stranded here?"

The old lady showed no surprise at Adelina's sudden, unheralded appearance, nor at her anger. An amused smile played upon her lips. "It seems you haven't yet tethered him as securely as you thought, miss."

The fire of Adelina's rage died and she sank miserably into a chair. "What shall I do – what am I to do? He can't leave me – not *now*!" It was a cry of anguish from the heart.

Lady Lynwood eyed her shrewdly, seeming to be able to look deep into Adelina's mind and read even her most secret fears. She nodded thoughtfully, then, appearing to come to a decision she said quietly, "Then go after him, my dear."

Adelina raised her head slowly. "Go — after him?" she repeated dazedly.

"If I'm not much mistaken," the Countess said briskly, "you're in love with him, and — I think you have an even greater need of him now than ever before. Am I right?"

Adelina gasped and the colour flooded her face. "How — did you know? How could you?"

"Women know these things, Adelina," she nodded wisely, then she added with a snort of derision, "but you cannot expect a *man* to guess. You'll have to tell him — then see what he'll do about it."

"Yes, yes, I must tell him."

"Come along then, girl, go and pack your belongings. We'll leave the day after tomorrow."

The coach bumped and rattled over the rough roads until Adelina felt herself shaken limb from limb. So, as they reached the outskirts of the great sprawling city, Adelina was irritable and weary, though Lady Lynwood seemed unruffled.

Towards evening the vehicle drew up outside Adelina's apartment. Tired and hungry and feeling dusty from so much travelling, what she most wanted was to fall into bed and sleep and sleep. But determination drove her on.

Lady Lynwood peered out of the coach as Adelina alighted. "No doubt I shall be seeing you again shortly?"

"I guess you will, my lady," Adelina said and, as she hurried up the steps to her apartment, she heard Lady Lynwood's laughter before the carriage rattled away over the cobblestones to her own home.

Some two hours later Adelina descended the staircase and entered a hired cab which she instructed to drive to Lynwood's Mayfair house.

The windows were ablaze with light and the sound of music met her as she alighted. Obviously Lynwood was entertaining and in great style.

When she entered the ballroom, there was, for a few seconds a stunned silence, swiftly followed by a babble of voices as everyone tried to appear disinterested.

Adelina's eyes scanned the dancing couples until she saw Lynwood. He was dancing with Helene Lyon! So, Adelina thought grimly, it had not taken him many hours to seek out his former mistress.

Lord Eversleigh and his wife, Madeleine, soon found their way to Adelina's side through the throng of people.

"Adelina, my dear," Madeleine smiled revealing her ugly teeth. "How good it is to see you again."

"Well, my lord, are you going to dance with me?" she asked Eversleigh. His eyes met hers and he smiled. "Delighted, madam," he quipped and raised her hand gallantly to his lips. Adelina refused to see the hurt in Madeleine's eyes, her only thought was to make Lynwood jealous.

Adelina danced the whole night away, determined to captivate, to flirt, even to break a few hearts, but every moment she was aware of the time Lynwood spent with Helene Lyon.

Not until dawn did the guests begin to depart in their carriages. Adelina was exhausted. The long, wearisome journey followed by a night of merrymaking had taken their toll. Her aching limbs felt like lead and she could scarcely force her eyelids to stay open. But, doggedly, she refused to leave until she had spoken to Lynwood – and alone!

Breakfast was being served for those guests who still lingered. Adelina found a cold colation laid out in the dining-room and the guests were helping themselves in a casual and informal manner. There was much laughter and banter and a few malicious whisperings of the way Adelina and Helene had, by mutual silent consent, tried to ignore each other for the most part, and, when obliged to come face to face, had been icily polite.

Adelina sighed as she ate. They were still too many people about for her to speak to Francis in private and yet she could not leave the matter unresolved much longer.

Helene Lyon seemed to be making no preparations for her departure. It was as if each one were weighing up the odds, pitting her hold on Lynwood against the other.

Meanwhile, Lynwood seemed unconcerned. He sauntered amongst his guests, laughing and talking and when his glance rested upon either Adelina or Helene, there was the cynical half smile upon his lips.

At last Adelina could bear it no longer. Touching Lynwood lightly on the arm she said meekly, "My lord, may I speak with you?"

"Of course, my dear," Lynwood's eyes challenged hers, then lazily he scanned the whole of her body as if, mentally, he were seeing her in all her naked loveliness.

"What is it you want to say to me?"

"May we speak – in private?"

His eyes mocked her. "Are you propositioning me, madam, before all my guests?" He laughed, and those nearby who had overheard the interchange of conversation, joined in the laughter.

Adelina felt her temper rising, but with a superb effort she willed herself to smile brightly and say, "I think you will agree that what I have to say is best said in privacy, my lord."

The laughter changed from mere amusement to ribald guffaws. "Oho, Francis, what have you been about?"

"You'll have to choose now, Francis. I'll put my money on the red-haired filly against the black-haired mare!"

More shouts of laughter followed: "I'll wager twenty to one on the mare."

At once the room was a babble of noisy bantering. Adelina felt the colour rise in her cheeks. She felt insulted.

"Come, Adelina, let them have their fun at our expense. They mean no harm." He took her arm and gently steered her through the throng to his study.

It was still quite dark and the room was only dimly lit by a candelabrum suspended from the ceiling. In the grate a cheerful log fire crackled, the flames leaping and dancing. It was a cosy, quiet room away from the noise and laughter. Lord Lynwood stood with his back to the fire, his feet set wide apart. His eyes were upon Adelina mockingly. "Well, my dear, what is it you have to say to me which is of such importance that I must be dragged away from my guests?"

Suddenly, Adelina felt nervous. She had been so sure that her news would win him over to her, away from Helene Lyon again. Now that the moment of truth was here, she was not so certain. He seemed so remote from her somehow. She decided that a gentle, feminine humility was the best attitude to adopt. She would try to appeal to his protective instincts once more, for wasn't that how their relationship had begun? Even though now, for her part at least, it had grown to love.

She moved across the room and stood close to him, looking up into his face, a tremulous smile upon her lips, her eyes brimming with unshed tears. "Francis," she said in a husky whisper. "I am with child. Your child."

She waited, watching the expression upon his face change from cynical amusement to shock and then there was that strange look of torment so often in his eyes and his mouth twisted cruelly.

"*My* child, madam? How can I be sure of that? How do I know it isn't Trent's brat?"

If he had struck her across the face with all his might it would not have hurt as much as his savage words did. Adelina gasped and her eyes were wide. "Francis – I swear to you it's your child. You must believe me."

"Must, madam? There's no *must* about it. I saw you talking to him that day. How do I know you haven't been meeting him in secret all the time we were at Lynwood Hall?"

Anger flashed in her green eyes and pride came to her rescue. "How dare you even *think* that of me, Francis?" She whirled around and made for the door, but Lynwood caught hold of her. They stared at each other, so many emotions between them, pride, anger, love and passion – and even a little hatred!

Suddenly Lynwood's shoulders slumped. "Oh, Adelina! Adelina!" he passed his hand wearily over his forehead. He put his arms about her and laid his cheek against her hair.

"Don't go, Adelina! It'll be – all right – I promise."

Adelina sighed. His promise held no note of conviction. It seemed they could not find happiness together. And yet to be apart would bring them even greater torment!

EIGHT

So their life slipped back into what it had been before Lord Lynwood's unfortunate duel with Thomas de Courtney. Society had taken both of them into its bosom again, for Adelina was to meet Mr de Courtney frequently at social gatherings and the onlookers – ignorant of previous events – would not have been aware that anything had ever been amiss.

Lynwood, despite his promise, continued to treat Adelina at times with love, at times with a calculated indifference and sometimes with almost hatred!

Adelina, confused by his weather-vane moods and in the final, emotional stages of pregnancy, for the first time in her life felt vulnerable and so alone.

More than ever she yearned for the security of her grandfather's love.

About two months before the expected date of her confinement, Lord Lynwood entered her boudoir shortly after breakfast. He held a letter in his hand.

"Adelina my dear. I have some bad news from Abbeyford."

Her face turned pale and her hands fluttered nervously to her throat. "Not – not my grandfather?"

"No – no. Emily. She – she died shortly after the birth of her son."

"Oh I'm sorry. So very sorry. Poor Emily."

"The child will live. He is to be called James."

Lynwood stood watching her, as she turned her green eyes brimming with unshed tears towards him. "Oh, Francis, is it so – dangerous to give birth? My mother and now Emily."

He knelt beside her and put his own hand over hers in a gesture of tenderness. "No – no, my dear. Don't fear. I shall see you have the best care. I promise."

One evening towards the middle of October, Adelina felt the first twinge of labour pains. Lynwood was away from home so it was left to Jane to make all the arrangements for Adelina's confinement. Adelina was well advanced in labour when Lynwood returned home in the early hours of the following morning and was informed of the news by his butler. By the time he arrived at her apartment to see Adelina, all her conscious thought was so filled with pain that she was scarcely aware of his presence. The room was so hot and stifling. Faces wafted about her in a pain-ridden haze, voices shouted commands at her that she had no idea how to obey. The world was suddenly a hostile and frightening place. It was a nightmare of darkness, of a throbbing in her ears, of being tossed about in a violent storm. Strange, horrific pictures came before her eyes. The suffocating blackness, then, unbidden, Evan's face, cruelly twisted with passion and revenge.

"No – no," her parched, cracked lips parted.

Then Lynwood's face, haggard and white with worry, was before her. Through her delirium she tried to reach out with trembling fingers to touch his face. But the mists closed in and his face faded from her sight.

Then there was pain again and a pulling and pushing and she felt as if her insides were being pulled from her. She screamed but once and then it was over. Somewhere, as if from a long way off, she heard the sound of a new-born baby yelling lustily. Faces came close to hers, mouthing words she heard but could not understand. Still they were pummelling her body as if, even yet, it was not all done. Finally, they left her in peace, washed and wrapped in clean linen. Exhausted, she slept.

It was not until much later that she awoke and realised that, except for a soreness, all the pain was gone. She moved her hands and felt the flatness of her stomach. She sighed. Then it was over. She turned her head and found herself looking into Francis's eyes. For a long moment they regarded each other solemnly. He saw a woman with her fine auburn hair strewn across the pillow, her face pale and her eyes with deep smudges of blue beneath them, telling of her suffering, and yet she was still beautiful, and damn it, he thought irritated with himself, still desirable!

Adelina observed Francis. He was unshaven, with a shadow of stubble upon his face, his eyes were weary, his hair ruffled, his shirt open at the neck. She guessed he had been sitting beside her bed, dozing and waking and watching over her. But there was still a remoteness about him, a bitter twist to his mouth and a hurt look deep in his blue eyes.

She smiled tremulously, but he did not return her smile. A new fear struck her. Perhaps there was something amiss – something wrong with the baby, or even with her! Perhaps she, too, like her mother and Emily, was going to die!

"Francis?" she whispered. "The baby?"

He leaned forward and after a moment's hesitation he said, "You have a daughter, Adelina."

"She – is she – healthy?"

"She is healthy, though not particularly beautiful. But, then, what newborn babes are?" His tone was bitter with disappointment. Hours earlier he had looked upon the baby, eagerly searching for some likeness to himself. But the child's hair was black and her skin dark, whereas Lynwood's hair and skin were fair!

Sick at heart he had turned away. Wallis Trent had black hair and a swarthy skin. The picture of Adelina and Wallis Trent talking together merged with that other image of his adored Caroline running into the arms of Thomas Cole.

"And me? What about me?" Adelina was saying.

"You?" There was a harsh note in his voice, a cruel tone. "You, madam, are in excellent health. The doctor said he rarely saw an easier birth."

Adelina smiled with wry amusement. "Perhaps it was — from where he was standing!" She twisted her head upon the pillow and looked into Lynwood's face. "Why did you say 'you have a daughter'? She's your daughter as well."

"Is she?" Still the doubt was there.

Adelina tried to raise herself on one elbow but found the effort too painful. "Why don't you believe me? I wouldn't lie to you over a thing like that?"

But the painful memories, seen through the uncomprehending eyes of boyhood, had warped the emotions he had carried forward into manhood. He could not allow himself to trust Caroline's daughter!

If they stayed together, Lynwood thought, if he married her even, there was no hope of happiness and contentment for them while this jealousy and distrust ate at him like a canker. Yet, if he sent her away, his life would be empty and a lonely misery.

She was looking at him now, her green eyes beseeching him, but he hardened his heart against her silent plea.

"Well, madam," he stood up and walked to the end of the bed. "I am glad you are safely delivered of your child and that both of you are healthy, but I must make it clear that I have no intention of marrying you – not now or ever!''

Adelina trembled. "Oh, Francis. You can't mean to allow your daughter to go through life with the stigma of being a bastard? You could not be so cruel to an innocent child?"

Lynwood flinched, but he set his jaw in a hard, unyielding line and said slowly and deliberately, "I will not marry you, Adelina. I – cannot!" He came close to the bed and, looking down at her he said through clenched teeth, "If you had been a virgin when you came to me, or if your child had been a boy, then I might – I just might – have married you!"

It took some seconds for the full impact of his words to strike her. Then her hopes crumpled. Never had she loved him as much as she did at this moment, when he turned his back resolutely upon her and walked out of the room – and out of her life!

Some while later Jane came into the room.

"Oh, madam, what is it?" she asked sympathetically, putting her arm around Adelina's shaking shoulders. "Don't fret so. The baby's fine. She's a beauty. Nurse will be bringing her along to see you soon."

"Nurse?"

"Why yes, didn't his lordship tell you? He's engaged one of the best dry-nurses in London. Rumour has it she's been nurse to a duke's children. She's a bit old and very strict with all of us, but she's as gentle as a lamb when she holds the baby. Then, of course there's the wet-nurse."

"Well, you can send *her* away. No one but me is going to suckle my child," Adelina declared.

Jane's mouth dropped open in surprise, but she made no

comment. After a few moments she said, "By the way, madam, what are you going to call the dear little thing?"

Adelina dried her eyes and blew her nose. Anger made her stop weeping. "I don't know." She paused then asked, "What's the equivalent of Francis for a girl?"

"Well, there's Frances, but I think it's spelt differently, but I'm not right good at spelling, ma'am."

Adelina nodded. "Yes, with an 'e' instead of an 'i'. Can you think of any more?"

Jane wrinkled her brow and thought. "The only other one I can think of, ma'am, is Francesca."

"Francesca," Adelina repeated the name and thought for a moment and then nodded. "Yes, I like it. I'll call her Francesca Caroline. My mother's name was Caroline."

She did not see Lynwood again, but he made lavish and generous arrangements for the care of the baby – whether or not he really believed the child to be his. As soon as she felt well enough, Adelina made preparations to leave London.

And there was only one place she could go.

Adelina was returning to Abbeyford.

She travelled by stage-coach, taking only Jane with her to care for the child. The nurse, engaged by Lynwood, was dismissed.

The journey was a nightmare. The baby, Francesca, became sick. The horses were old and tired and travelled at only five miles or so an hour. The journey seemed endless and took three days instead of two. The cold seeped into their bones and once all the passengers were obliged to alight from the coach at a particularly steep hill, for the horses could not pull the loaded coach up the hill.

"I hope we don't have an accident, ma'am," Jane said, panting along at the side of Adelina who carried the baby.

"I reckon this coachman's not to be trusted. Strikes me he's overloaded the coach."

Adelina said nothing, but bit down hard upon her lower lip and held the child closer to her against the winter wind.

After what seemed weeks instead of days, bruised and battered through being tossed about in the rattling coach, they arrived near Amberly. Hiring a local cab, Adelina took a bold step. "Lynwood Hall, please, driver," she instructed him.

Jane gasped and looked at Adelina with wide eyes. "Oh ma'am. Ought we to?"

"Just for the present, Jane, until I've had time to look around."

Adelina did not take her maidservant into her confidence, but she intended to stay at Lynwood Hall just long enough to find out, once and for all, whether she could be reconciled with her grandfather. If not, then she would return to America.

Their arrival at Lynwood Hall caused little stir. Lady Lynwood, who had seen no reason to remain in London during Adelina's necessary absence from Society, had returned earlier to her country home. Now, as she greeted Adelina, she seemed amused by the situation. Her laughter cackled readily. "Well, miss, you didn't manage to lead him to the altar, then? Hmm – I'm surprised. I thought he loved you." Her sharp eyes scanned Adelina's face. "And you him."

Adelina remained silent.

"Have you had news of your relatives while you've been in London?" Lady Lynwood asked suddenly.

"Only – only about Emily."

"Martha Langley has been very ill. Just after Emily's death. She is partially paralysed. Her husband's at his wit's end to know how to cope with her." Her beady eyes looked straight at Adelina. "Shall you go and see them?"

Adelina shrugged. "I doubt if I'd be welcomed."

"I think in their present pitiable state, they'd welcome the Devil himself, if he offered help."

"Well," Adelina hesitated. "I'll have to think about it."

Two days later, however, when her small daughter had recovered from the harassing journey and was once again a happy, gurgling infant, Adelina, driving herself and dressed warmly, took the gig from Lord Lynwood's stables and set out towards Abbeyford.

It was early January 1818, and her heart lifted as she drove along the narrow lanes. She found the frosty, country air invigorating after city life. As she drove through Amberly, Adelina scarcely glanced at the villagers, remembering their previous hostility. Children scuttled out of the way of her horse's flying hooves and mothers scooped up their toddlers to safety. Just as she left the village she passed by a small cottage set a little apart from the other dwellings and standing some distance back from the road. A barefoot toddler, with a dirty face, bright red curls and a ragged shirt, tottered down the path, and briefly she saw a man emerging from the cottage doorway. She was past so quickly and he was some way from her that she could not really recognise him, yet there was something vaguely familiar about the stocky build and broad shoulders. But she knew no one in Amberly, she told herself. For some inexplicable reason the sight of the shadowy figure had awakened in her a feeling of unease. Then she whipped up the horse towards Abbeyford and forgot all about the man and his red-haired child.

As she emerged from the trees she pulled on the reins and drew the horse to a halt. She sat for a moment, drinking in the scene before her. Immediately below her was Abbeyford

Manor, then farther down the valley she followed the twisting lane with her eyes, catching sight of the ford and the tiny footbridge and then the village itself with the church in its midst and, close by, the Vicarage and, far beyond on the opposite hill, was Abbeyford Grange where her grandfather lived in self-imposed loneliness. To her right were the abbey ruins and all around lay the farmlands belonging to Lord Royston.

Adelina slapped the reins and her horse trotted on obediently. She took the narrow lane towards Abbeyford village and was soon turning in the Vicarage gates.

The story Lady Lynwood had told Adelina about Mrs Langley proved to be true. She was in a pitiable state and Mr Langley was thin and ill with worry and the burden of caring for his truculent wife.

The door was opened to Adelina by the maid and when she was shown into the Vicar's study, Adelina gasped to see the change in him. His hair was now completely snow-white but ruffled and unkempt. He had always stooped slightly, but now his shoulders were hunched more than ever. His face was gaunt and his eyes ringed with dark shadows from lack of sleep. His yellowy skin was loose and pouchy as if he had suddenly lost weight. His clothes, hanging untidily on him, were blotched with stains.

His eyes widened as he realised who his visitor was. "Adelina my dear. How glad I am to see you." The tears welled in his eyes, and Adelina was moved to bend and kiss his forehead. As she followed the Vicar's shambling steps into the drawing-room, Adelina noticed the thick film of dust everywhere.

She stepped into the room. Sitting in a chair near the fire was Mrs Langley – a mere shadow of the formidable woman Adelina remembered. She seemed shrunken and wasted away. Her hands, lying uselessly in her lap, twitched from time to time. She breathed noisily through her mouth, which hung open. Her eyes turned towards Adelina and there was a flash of recognition in them. There was bitterness and venom in her eyes, but, though she worked her mouth, Martha Langley could no longer give vent to her feelings with her tongue.

For all her dislike of this woman, Adelina felt sorry for her. She sat down opposite her and forced herself to smile at Mrs Langley.

"She knows you, Adelina, and she understands what we say to her. Her comprehension is quite unimpaired," Mr Langley explained. "It's purely – physical."

Adelina nodded. "I'm truly sorry to see you like this, ma'am, believe me."

Mrs Langley gave a loud sniff and Adelina almost laughed aloud. She hadn't forgotten how to give that famous sniff which in itself could speak volumes!

Swiftly, Adelina made up her mind. "Mrs Langley – you need help, don't you? And I need somewhere to stay – just for a few weeks."

Mrs Langley made some weird noises and her head rocked from side to side.

"No – no, I know you don't like me – never have, and I know what you must think of me now. But for once you're going to have to forget your pride for your husband's sake. Just look at him. He'll be ill next if he goes on much longer the way he is."

Mrs Langley's eyes swivelled to look at him, then, giving a peculiar sort of strangulated groan, she closed her eyes and rocked her whole being to and fro.

"That's settled then," Adelina said, standing up. "We'll be moving in within the next few days."

"We?" Mr Langley questioned.

"Er – yes. Myself, my maid and – er – the baby."

"Baby!" He was obviously startled, and Mrs Langley began to make a gurgling noise, which Adelina ignored.

"Yes," she said, as casually as she could manage. "Didn't you know I have a baby daughter. She's three months old."

"Adelina!" There was a world of sadness and disappointment in his tone. "Oh, Adelina – how could you?"

He paused and then said slowly, as if battling with himself. "Well – I don't know what to say about that, I'm sure. I mean ..."

"Look, you need help – desperately. And now poor Emily's gone ..." She saw him flinch at the mention of his daughter, but Adelina continued with a little of the ruthlessness that had been her mother's nature. "There's only me left to come and help out a while. Now don't let pride stand in your way. By the look of both of you, you could sure use a little help right now."

She paused while he appeared to be struggling with his conscience. Quietly, she said, "I really don't think you have any choice, have you?"

He sighed. "I suppose not."

Within a few days Adelina had packed her trunks once more and taken leave of Lynwood Hall.

"So," Lady Lynwood had remarked drily, "you're going to play nursemaid for a while, are you, miss?" She laughed. "You'll soon tire of that I don't doubt and be back knocking on our door."

"No," Adelina said quietly with infinite sadness. "I can never ask another favour of Lord Lynwood."

"Really?" The old lady raised her eyebrows sceptically. "Mmm – well, we'll see."

"If I have to leave Abbeyford again, I shall go back to America."

Lady Lynwood showed surprise at Adelina's remark. Adelina turned her clear green eyes upon the old lady, whom she had come to regard with affection. "There's only one thing I want now other than ..." she stopped, unable to speak Lynwood's name. "Only one thing – to meet my grandfather. If – if that is not possible, then – then there is nothing else I can do."

"Don't waste your life waiting for a stupid old man to overcome his hurt pride – or for that matter," she added, referring to her own son, "a stupid *young* one!"

Surprisingly, Adelina's way of life back at the Vicarage bore little resemblance to the previous time. Mr Langley, worn out by the unaccustomed domestic burden, was only too thankful to relinquish the reins to Adelina, who soon had the servants performing their duties properly instead of idly taking advantage of the elderly, mild-tempered Vicar. Mrs Langley was completely helpless physically, nor could she voice her disapproval. Only her eyes showed the resentment she still felt towards Adelina.

"It won't be for long," Adelina comforted herself.

When the house had been restored to some sort of order and Mr Langley sufficiently recovered to take up his parish duties once more, and Francesca had settled to a routine and began to thrive in the country air, Adelina decided it was time she visited Abbeyford Grange.

One particularly warm and spring-like day in early March Adelina left the Vicarage and the village and took the footpath through the open fields until she came to the small footbridge crossing the stream. She stood on the bridge, her hand resting on the rail and looked up at

Abbeyford Grange. Her heart began to beat faster as she walked up the slope towards the high wall surrounding the house and garden. Reaching the wall she found a door and, twisting the heavy ring, she pushed it open and stepped into the sunken garden. Her gaze was drawn to the house – the house which had been her mother's home. It looked empty, deserted almost, although she knew Lord Royston still lived here, no doubt with several servants. But the house had a desolate air, an atmosphere of decay and neglect.

Without realising she had moved, she found herself in a square in the centre of the rose garden and when a voice spoke close by, Adelina jumped violently.

"No need to ask who *you* are."

Adelina turned to see an old man sitting on a garden seat, a rug wrapped warmly over his knees. His face was wrinkled and his bushy white eyebrows almost met in the centre of his forehead as he frowned. His head was bald, except for a white tuft of hair over each ear. His hand held a walking-stick, the gnarled knuckles showing white as he gripped the stick and from time to time he struck the ground with it.

This was Lord Royston – her grandfather!

"No tongue in your head?" he growled, as Adelina continued to stare at him. His reprimand made her hold her head higher – proud and defiant.

"Goodday, my lord."

"Oh, sit down, sit down, now you're here," he said irritably.

Obediently, she sat beside him on the seat, half turned towards him.

"Well – am I what you expected?" The eyebrows rose and fell.

Adelina laughed. "Not really."

"Hmm," he grunted.

"How do you know who I am?" she asked.

"Because you're the image of your mother," he muttered and thumped his stick on the ground.

"Oh – I'm sorry."

"Sorry? Why be sorry? She was a lovely girl – a lovely girl."

"I'm sorry because I must bring back painful memories for you."

"Why did she do it? Why – why?" Again the stick thumped the ground as he voiced aloud the question which had haunted him for over twenty years.

"I can't remember things clearly because I was only nine when she died."

"So long ago and I didn't even know she was dead until you first came to Abbeyford," the old man murmured and he seemed to shrink a little more.

"But I can recall little things," Adelina went on. "I can remember the happiness in our house when I was little, the warmth and the love. I believe she and my father were devoted to each other."

"Was he good to her?"

"Yes – yes, I think he was. After she died – he – well – he ceased to care, even for me. He took to drinking and gambling. He lost his job, we lost our home. Not immediately, of course, but over the years we lost everything until we had to move from the plantation in South Carolina to New York, to the poorest, roughest neighbourhood." Why, she thought, am I blurting all this out within moments of meeting him?

"You say your father ceased to care for you. Did – did he ill-treat you?"

"No," Adelina shrugged and smiled sadly, remembering. "But the roles were reversed. I looked after him. I became the strong one. I had to be, to survive. That's why I'm so sure he loved my mother. When she died, he just stopped living too."

There was silence between them while the embittered old man struggled to understand. At last he sighed. "Ah, well, I suppose none of it is your fault anyway. Perhaps I was not entirely blameless. I was trying to arrange a marriage for her to a man she obviously did not love. That locket round your neck ...?" he asked suddenly.

"It was my mother's — she always wore it and I have worn it ever since I was – given it."

"Open it," he commanded. As she did so, he leant forward to look at the two tiny likenesses enclosed within. Slowly, he nodded. "Yes – that's the locket I gave her on the very same day she ran away. And she wore it all the time?"

Adelina nodded. "Yes. She loved you dearly, but she loved my father too and couldn't bear to spend her life without him, even though he wasn't your choice. I'm sure she didn't mean to hurt you so. I think she really thought that, once they were married and I was born, you would forgive them."

"It seems – I left it too late. But I could," the old man added with surprising briskness, "make it up to you. Would you care to come up to the house?"

Adelina's lips parted as she drew breath sharply and her green eyes shone with happiness. Then her delight faded.

"Grandfather – there's something you should know. I – I have a child."

"So – I have a great-grandchild, have I?" The old man began to smile.

"But," she blurted out. "I'm not married. My child is – illegitimate."

Lord Royston was still, his face immobile. "I see," he said flatly. "I wonder I hadn't heard."

"Your servants would know, but I guess none of them dared to tell you."

"And the father?"

Adelina hesitated then said bluntly. "Francis – Lord Lynwood."

"Lynwood! My God!" For a moment his face was contorted with disbelief, then he sighed heavily. "Lynwood!" He repeated incredulously. "Of all people – Lynwood!"

He recovered himself a little and turned his sharp eyes upon her. "And he won't marry you?"

Sadly Adelina shook her head. "No."

"But you love him?"

"Yes," Adelina whispered. "Yes, I do. And I thought he – he cared for me but – but ..." the unfinished sentence lay between them. There was some reason why Lynwood would not marry her, some reason she could not understand.

"You're too like your mother!" Lord Royston said bluntly.

Adelina gasped. "I don't understand. What has that to do with it?"

"Don't you know?"

Slowly Adelina shook her head.

"As a boy, Francis idolised your mother, followed her about his eyes always on her. Then suddenly, I remember, he held himself aloof, remote from her. He seemed to pass from boyhood to manhood in the space of a day. Very soon afterwards she ran away with Thomas Cole and I believe – though I never had any proof – that Francis learnt of her – her affair – perhaps even saw them together and was hurt – deeply."

He turned to look straight into Adelina's eyes. "I realise you cannot be expected to understand, but what your mother did was a shocking thing. She deceived me, she risked her reputation and she married beneath her – good and honourable though Thomas Cole may have been," he added swiftly, as Adelina opened her mouth to defend her father. "They came from such different worlds – it could never have worked."

"But it *did* work. They were happy – I know they were, until she died."

Lord Royston smiled sadly. "You have your mother's spirit, I see. But Caroline was too spoilt, too selfish. Eventually life with Thomas Cole would not have been enough for her."

"I suppose we can never know that really, can we?" Adelina said.

"No, my dear, not now." He patted her hand. "At least, if she was happy for a while, that's something. And, knowing my wilful daughter, she would never, ever, have admitted she'd been wrong anyway." Suddenly his eyes twinkled with a merriment long buried. "Any more than *I'm* likely to admit I could have been wrong. You've a stubborn old man for a grandfather, my dear."

She smiled at him. "So I see," she said impishly, the happiness flooding through her. He was not going to turn her away.

At last, Adelina had come home.

Together they rose and she put her arm through his and slowly they walked towards the house.

Unobserved by either of them, a man on a jet black horse stood beneath the shadow of a huge elm tree at the main gate, watching the slow progress of the old man and the young woman, arm in arm, their heads bent close to each other.

Stealthily, Wallis Trent turned his horse away and cantered down the hill.

NINE

So one of Adelina's dearest wishes had come true – she had found her grandfather and their mutual joy in each other helped to ease her sense of loss over Lynwood.

She asked nothing of Lord Royston and he offered nothing, but each was happy in their closeness. He even accepted her child and the sight of the old man with the baby on his knee made Adelina's heart fill with love.

One afternoon, driving the small gig her grandfather had insisted she borrow from his stables whenever she wished, Adelina took a drive along the narrow lanes. Returning to the Grange, she rounded a corner and almost collided with Wallis Trent on his huge black stallion. Wallis pulled on his reins so hard that Jupiter reared and Adelina pulled hard to the right and her horse and gig ran into the steep bank bordering the lane. The small vehicle tipped sideways and Adelina screamed as she fell to the ground. For a moment the gig hung suspended and then slowly it topped right over. Adelina screamed again, a piercing shriek of pain as the gig fell upon her legs.

Wallis was already down from his horse and running towards her as it fell, but too late to prevent it. The weight was only heavy on her for a few seconds, for he immediately grasped the gig and with his great strength lifted it clear of her.

"Can you pull yourself free, Adelina?" Wallis asked.

"I think so," she gasped and dragged herself along the grass until she was clear. Wallis, grunting with exertion, heaved and pushed until the gig was almost upright then he shouted a command to the horse, which had been brought down when the vehicle toppled over. "Up, boy, come on," and he clicked encouragingly. The horse struggled valiantly to get to its feet and at the same time Wallis righted the gig. Then he turned swiftly to Adelina.

"Adelina – are you hurt?" He knelt beside her, concern on his handsome face.

"It's my right leg."

"Keep still," he commanded and placed gentle fingers upon her leg, searching to see if a bone might be broken.

"Ouch!" Adelina cried in pain as he touched a tender spot just below her knee.

"I don't think there's anything broken, my dear," Wallis said, "but your leg's no doubt badly bruised. Whatever were you doing driving so recklessly along a narrow lane?" His tone took on a note of severity. "You are lucky to escape with slight injury!"

"If it comes to that," Adelina said crossly, rubbing her leg, "what were you doing galloping along the lane? You were going every bit as fast as me!"

Wallis frowned. "Well – perhaps I was." He stood up. "See if you can stand, Adelina. Here, take my hand."

Carefully, she stood up. Though she could feel her leg was badly bruised and she was feeling very shaken from the incident, there were certainly no bones broken.

"I'm quite all right, thank you," Adelina said stiffly, and tried to pull her hand away from his, but he held her fast. Surprised, she looked up into his face. He was looking down at her now with an expression which she had never expected to see in Wallis Trent's cold eyes.

"My dear Adelina," his deep voice was soft. "I can't tell

you how glad I am to see you again."

Adelina almost laughed aloud at the contrast between this greeting and the last occasion, but she held herself in check and merely allowed herself a small smile.

"Are you well, Mr Trent?"

"I am – and I'm thankful to see you're not hurt. Let me help you into the gig. I'll tether Jupiter to the rear and drive you home."

"Oh, that won't be necessary. I am quite able to drive myself ..."

"Nonsense, I won't hear of it," Wallis said with authority.

Minutes later the gig was moving through the country lanes once more, this time with Wallis Trent at the reins and Adelina close beside him on the narrow seat.

As they passed by a group of workmen, going home at the end of their day's work, Adelina caught a fleeting glimpse of the grim, resentful expressions upon their faces. Where recently she had begun to be greeted with courtesy and friendliness by the villagers, now their hostility was plain to see.

She glanced thoughtfully at the man beside her. It was not she herself they resented, but the man in whose company they saw her!

Wallis Trent was a hated man!

He drove through the village and took the lane back to the Grange. "I was delighted to learn of your reconciliation with your grandfather, my dear."

"Oh, so you've heard?" Immediately she knew the reason for the swift change in his attitude towards her, for his sudden friendliness.

"News of any sort always travels fast in a small community but, of course, on this occasion," he added loftily, "I heard it from Lord Royston himself."

"Really?" Adelina frowned slightly. She was not aware that Wallis Trent had seen her grandfather recently. She wondered if he was telling the truth.

"I'll just pay my respects to Lord Royston," he was saying as he helped her from the gig. But it seemed that her grandfather was not as pleased to see him as Wallis Trent would have her believe.

"What are you doing here, Trent? Not your day to come for another week."

Wallis explained their accidental meeting.

"Hmm," the old man growled. "Well – now you're here, sit down, sit down."

His old eyes searched for Adelina and softened at the sight of her as she moved forward to kiss his cheek. His knarled hand clasped hers and he looked up into her face.

Thoughtfully, Wallis Trent watched the affectionate scene.

Wallis Trent became a frequent visitor to the Vicarage, where Adelina and her daughter still lived. He insisted he should accompany Adelina whenever she took a drive or a walk. He brought small gifts for the baby and saw to it that whatever was needed at the Vicarage was provided immediately. As the summer passed, he became more and more attentive.

Adelina had no doubt as to the reason behind Wallis Trent's sudden friendship, almost courtship. Since her reconciliation with Lord Royston, she knew Wallis would believe the old man had now made Adelina his heiress. But she did not think that even Wallis Trent had the gall to admit this fact openly. She was to be proved wrong!

One evening he came to the Vicarage and asked Adelina if they might talk privately. She took him into the drawing-room, seated herself before the fire and waited for him to speak. Wallis stood in front of the fireplace and looked down at her.

"Adelina – during the past few weeks and months we have spent a deal of time in each other's company and we seem compatible. I – in my position in the county and with a young son – have need of a wife. You ..." he paused momentarily as if the subject which he must touch upon was abhorrent to him. "Have need of a husband and a father for your daughter."

Adelina remained silent, but her fingers were laced tightly together until the knuckles showed white.

"I must presume that Lynwood has not offered you marriage, or you would not have arrived back in Abbeyford."

Adelina swallowed hard and fought back the tears which threatened as Wallis's words brought back vividly her memories of Lynwood.

With her new-found joy in her closeness with her grandfather, Adelina had resolutely told herself she was happy, that she now had what she had most wanted. But at this moment – in the midst of what was obviously a proposal of marriage from Wallis Trent – desolation and longing for Lynwood swept over her. The sight of his face, the feel of his arms about her. Her sense of loss was a physical ache.

"And so, my dear," Wallis was saying, "I am asking you to become my wife. I think you will agree that the arrangement would be of advantage to us both. It would also solve any dilemma Lord Royston may now feel."

"Lord Royston?" Adelina pretended deliberately not to understand, wanting to force the words from Wallis's own lips.

"Well, my dear," Wallis Trent straightened his back and thrust out his chest. "You know that my wife, Emily, was Lord Royston's heiress?"

"Yes."

"Since her death his lordship has entailed his estate to our son, Jamie. Now," he shrugged and laughed and spread his hands expansively, "you must see that with your recent reconciliation the old man must feel – well – torn between his obligation to keep his promise to my son and his – quite natural – new-found affection for you."

With difficulty Adelina kept her face straight. Without the least desire for material gain, she found the whole absurd situation vastly amusing.

"And you think our marriage would safely ensure that the estate still comes to your son?"

Swiftly, he reassured her but his words lacked sincerity. "My dear, I wouldn't want you to think that that was the sole purpose behind my proposal. Dear me, no! But, nevertheless, it is a consideration, a quite usual consideration among marriages in our Society. Though as an American you may not fully understand."

"Oh, I think I do," Adelina said wryly.

"Well, then, my dear, what is your answer?"

"Wallis – I, too, will be utterly frank. I do not love you, but I do love my daughter dearly and for her sake, and her sake alone, I will agree to become your wife."

Resolutely, Adelina banished all thought of Lynwood's beloved face from her mind. For the sake of her baby daughter she ought to marry and, since there was no chance of Lynwood ever proposing to her, then she must accept Wallis Trent, even though she shuddered at the mere thought of being tied to this cold, ambitious man. Adelina loved her baby daughter ferociously and she would sacrifice all her own hopes of happiness to ensure her child's future and the security of a kind of legitimacy.

So Adelina agreed to marry Wallis Trent and the date of their marriage was set for New Year's Day.

On Christmas Day, a carriage drew into the Vicarage drive. A fine carriage bearing the Lynwood crest.

Lord Lynwood stepped down from it and stood looking at the house for a moment, as if still considering whether he should approach the door, or get back into his carriage and drive away.

At last, he climbed the steps slowly and pulled on the bell-chord.

Adelina, who had seen his arrival, greeted him herself. It had taken a few moments for her to compose herself before opening the door, and although she managed to meet his eyes calmly, inside herself she was quivering with joy and fear and longing at the sight of him. She could see the sadness in his eyes as he gazed at her. He had struggled for days against coming, for to his mind it would show weakness on his part. It would appear as if he could not live without sight of her. And Francis, Earl of Lynwood, was not a man who liked to appear weak.

But the anguish in his heart had at last overcome his pride. He had found that, since Adelina had left him, he was obsessed by memories of her. Now, as he stood before her, still he could not say all the tender endearments which were in his heart. He merely said brusquely. "I've come to bring the child some presents." He could not even say 'my daughter'.

Adelina smiled, though still a little uncertainly. "It's good to see you, Francis. And very kind of you to think of Francesca. Please come in."

She led the way into the morning room. Francis paused in the doorway as his glance fell upon the child playing on the rug. The infant raised her brilliant blue eyes to look at the stranger, then her face broke into a cherubic beam and she gurgled at him, holding out her chubby arms invitingly. Completely bemused, Lord Lynwood knelt before the child.

Wonderingly, he reached out his fingers to touch her golden curls and gazed into her blue eyes so like his own. "But – but she – her hair was – *black*!" he murmured.

"At first – yes. But a new-born baby's hair can change colour," Adelina laughed, completely unaware of Lynwood's inner conflict. "That black fuzz soon rubbed off. She was almost bald for a time and then her hair grew fair – and curly."

Francesca reached out and grasped Lynwood's finger, pulling it towards her mouth.

"Mind," Adelina warned. "She's cutting teeth – she'll give you a nip."

Francis said softly. "Oh, we can stand that, my little love, can't we?"

The baby chuckled and chewed happily upon his finger. Never taking his eyes from the child, Francis said, "Ask my coachman to bring in the parcels, will you please, Adelina?"

"Parcels?"

"Yes. Christmas gifts. Didn't you know, it's all the rage in London? The Duchess of York started it. She decorates her dining-room and piles it high with presents and invites not only her family and friends in but all her servants and many local children, and each one receives a gift."

A few moments later the sofa-table was piled high with boxes of various shapes. With a smile of genuine pleasure, Lynwood reached for some of the parcels and placed them on the rug near Francesca. The baby's eyes grew round with wonder and her fingers touched the boxes.

"I think you'll have to help her open them," Adelina said.

"There are some for you too," Lynwood murmured, his attention still wholly upon the child.

Some little time later the room was littered with

discarded wrappings and Francesca surrounded by numerous toys.

There was a rocking-horse with baby foot-rests: a doll's house complete with intricately made furniture and three tiny dolls, father, mother and baby each dressed in the fashion of the day. There were two bigger dolls, one a rag doll and one with a wax, painted face attached to a stuffed body. There was a jumping-jack, a ball, a drum and a rattle.

Adelina was still exclaiming with delight over her gifts from Lynwood. Impulsively, she threw her arms around his neck and kissed him on the mouth. "Oh, thank you, Francis, you are generous."

He slipped his arm around her waist. "It's good to see you happy, my dear. Adelina ..." He seemed about to say more, but at that moment the door opened and Wallis entered the room.

He stopped short as the picture of Adelina and Lord Lynwood in each other's arms met his eyes and Adelina's joy died instantly. In her happiness at seeing Lynwood again she had completely forgotten Wallis Trent!

"Francis has brought some wonderful gifts for Francesca, isn't it kind of him?" she explained. "He says it's all the rage in London now."

The two men eyed each other warily, dark anger upon Wallis Trent's face, while the bitterness and jealousy once more flooded through Lynwood's heart.

"You must know, my lord," Wallis said tersely, "that I cannot allow Adelina to accept your gifts."

Now anger flared in Lynwood's handsome face too. "I beg your pardon ...?"

"You will allow me to be the judge of that, Wallis," Adelina said boldly. Wallis turned his scowling face upon her.

"Adelina – you have agreed to become my wife in a week's time. You will oblige me by obeying my wishes."

Defiantly, Adelina raised her head higher and met Wallis's cold, hard eyes, at the same time she was acutely aware of the misery on Lynwood's face.

"When I become your wife – I will obey you. But this once, at least, you must allow Lord Lynwood to give the child his gifts. After all – *she is his daughter!*"

"Madam, by next week, legally, she will be my daughter, and he will have no claim upon her."

"Married?" Lynwood said softly, turning towards Adelina. "You are to marry Trent?"

Adelina closed her eyes in momentary overwhelming anguish. When she opened them again, Lynwood's face was a closed mask of indifference. "Then it is as I thought – all the time," he said bitterly, "and to think I came here today hoping ... Ahh!" he let out a groan of utter rejection and dismissal.

As he turned to leave, Adelina stretched out her hands towards him. "Francis!" she cried from the very depths of her being. "*Francis!*"

But Wallis caught hold of her and prevented her from following Lynwood. She heard the front door slam, heard the carriage move away, the sounds of its wheels growing fainter and knew that this time Lynwood would never return.

Adelina tore herself from Wallis's grasp and ran from the room, upstairs, to throw herself on her bed and give way to a paroxysm of weeping.

The marriage of Wallis Trent and Adelina Cole took place at eight-thirty on the morning of the first of January 1819. The only people present were Mr Langley, as officiating clergyman, Squire Guy Trent and his wife, and one or two of the Trents' employees.

There was to be no honeymoon, and Adelina, her child and her maid moved their belongings to Abbeyford Manor that same afternoon. Francesca was taken to the nursery wing to be cared for, along with Jamie Trent, Wallis's son, by the nanny and the nursery maid. Jane was retained as Adelina's personal maid.

At the Vicarage, Adelina had dismissed the indolent servants who had been of little help to Mr Langley in his wife's illness and had persuaded Sarah Smithson to come back, this time as housekeeper. Adelina was sorry for the desperately unhappy, work-worn woman, who had lived her life sorrowing for a love that could not be, living with a man whose bitterness and resentment festered and grew over the years and was carried on by his stepson who had sworn revenge upon the Trents.

Adelina could not help but see that she was perhaps following the very same path as Sarah Smithson, for was not she marrying one man in order to give her illegitimate child a name, while still loving the father of her child? Just as Sarah Smithson had been obliged to do.

So a routine was established at Abbeyford Manor, but it was an existence without purpose for Adelina, a life which held little hope for the future. She found solace in her love for her daughter and her grandfather, but between herself and her husband there was a coldness, a remoteness. They had separate bedrooms and, though he visited her at night occasionally, his lovemaking was accomplished as if it were an act of duty, or a physical need which must be satisfied. No word of love or affection ever passed his lips. There was no tender wooing, no moments of joy and intimate laughter between them.

Lynwood, for all that his jealousy and distrust had overshadowed their complete happiness, at least he had cared for her. Only now, living with the selfish, arrogant Wallis

Trent, did Adelina realise how great her loss of Lynwood had been!

Adelina found that there was little, for her to do in her new role at the Manor for Louisa Trent was still the mistress. Wallis entertained occasionally, but not often. From time to time she would accompany him as he rode around the estate, but she found the sullen, hostile stares of the workmen unnerving. Where before she could have been sure of a smile from the village folk, now all sign of friendliness from them was gone, because she had married the man they feared and disliked.

Strangely, her one adult companion at Abbeyford Manor proved to be Squire Guy Trent. Between the lonely man and the young bride of a marriage of convenience there grew an affinity, an understanding born of a mutual loss and loneliness.

"There's a horse-dealer coming this afternoon," Squire Trent told her one morning. "Get Wallis to buy you a horse – then we could go for rides together."

"Oh – I don't know," Adelina hesitated. "I don't like to ask …"

"Then it's time you did." His bleary eyes were upon her face. "You're a lovely girl, Adelina. My son doesn't realise how fortunate he is."

Adelina smiled. "I'll come and see the horses – I promise."

That afternoon she found her way to the Squire's study, knocked sharply and then opened the door. A cloud of cigar smoke and the smell of whisky met her. She blinked as the smoke stung her eyes. Two men sat at the huge desk, the Squire and a stranger – a thin, shrewish little man with hollowed cheeks and shifty eyes.

Of Wallis there was no sign.

For a moment the two men stared at her, surprised by

the vision of loveliness which had suddenly burst in upon their male domain.

"Ah, there you are, my dear," Squire Trent, struggling to his feet, held out his hand towards her. "Now *this*, Trotter, is my new daughter-in-law."

The thin man smirked, but the smile never reached his eyes. Squire Trent, swaying slightly, crossed the short space between them and put his arm clumsily about her waist and drew her into the room. He kicked the door shut. "This is Mr Trotter, the horse-dealer I was telling you about."

"I'm honoured to meet you, ma'am." Mr Trotter rose and bowed. He was very tall, but so thin that he seemed like a reed wavering in the wind. He was a man of middle age, untidily dressed.

"Shall we go and look at the horses?" the Squire suggested.

"Shouldn't we wait for Wallis?" Adelina said.

"No – no. Come along. Trotter says he has the very horse for you, a lovely stallion ..."

At that moment the door opened and Wallis strode in. He stopped short, surprised to find Adelina there. His glance took in his father's arm about her waist and the expression in his eyes hardened and his mouth tightened.

"Ar – hum," Guy Trent grunted and let his arm fall away. He sat down heavily in his chair, picked up his tumbler of whisky and drained it, his enthusiasm gone with the arrival of his son!

Wallis said brusquely, "Come along, then, Trotter, I haven't got all day."

"Very good, Mr Trent." Obediently, Trotter grabbed his hat and followed the long, angry strides of Wallis Trent. Thoughtfully, Adelina followed, leaving Squire Guy alone with his whisky bottle.

A young boy was standing holding the reins of the two
horses Trotter had brought for Wallis's inspection. Adelina
ran a speculative eye over them both.

"Now this would suit the lady fine," Trotter said, patting
a small brown mare on the neck. "She's gentle and docile
but strong, ma'am. She'd cause a fine lady like yourself not
a bit of trouble."

Adelina raised her left eyebrow but said nothing. Now
that she had gained confidence on horseback she wanted an
animal with a little more spirit than Stardust, who was
getting old now. Her glance ran over the other horse. It was
a white stallion and, except for its colour, the animal could
have been the twin of Wallis's horse, Jupiter. Adelina's
green eyes were afire with excitement. She moved towards
the horse's head and stroked his nose. The proud beast
tossed his head and pawed the ground. Wallis was
examining the animal in great detail.

"Isn't he a fine animal, Mr Trent, sir? Now he'd be a
valuable addition to your stables, wouldn't he now?"

"He would indeed, but I don't think I have need of
another hunter. I'm really looking for work-horses. Have
you no shires?"

"Not today, sir, but ..."

"Then I'll bid you goodday." Wallis was turning away as
Adelina spoke.

"Wallis, would you object to me buying the white
stallion?"

He turned abruptly. "You, my dear? I think you'd find
him too robust for you to handle. Besides, I cannot spend
large sums of money on a horse we do not really need."

"I – I could buy him myself."

Wallis's face darkened, his jaw clenched. "Really?"
Sarcasm lined his tone. Adelina knew he must realise that
any money she possessed of her own must have come from

Lynwood or from her grandfather and, either way, the knowledge angered him. But she was determined not to be intimidated. She felt the time was now when – even in this strange marriage – she must assert some individuality. She would not become a downtrodden, pathetic creature. He had married her and had given her daughter his name – and for that she was grateful – but she would not allow him to possess her mind, for her heart he could never hold.

"I am thinking of your safety, Adelina. I wouldn't be happy knowing you were riding this animal. He's too strong for any woman, however competent a horsewoman she may be."

"I am sure I could handle him, Wallis."

Wallis shrugged. "Very well, then," he said. "But mind," he wagged his finger at Trotter, "the price is fair. I don't want to see my wife cheated."

Mr Trotter's expression was pained. "As if I would take advantage of a lady, sir!"

"You would, Trotter, you would," Wallis remarked and began to walk towards the house. Trotter called after him, "But what about the mare, sir? Aren't you interested in the mare?"

Wallis paused and half turned to call over his shoulder, "Hardly, Trotter, hardly," and turned away again and moved on.

Trotter shrugged philosophically. "Ah well, one sale is better than none at all."

"What is the price?" Adelina asked.

"One hundred guineas, ma'am."

"That's too much," Adelina retorted sharply. "I'll give you eighty."

Trotter spread his hands, palms upwards. "I'd lose on a price like that, madam. My lowest would be ninety-five."

"Oh, come now," Adelina purred, flashing him her most

winning smile. "I'm sure you make a handsome profit. Eighty-five."

Trotter shook his head slowly.

Adelina sighed in mock regret and turned away. "Well, I'm sorry, I don't believe the horse worth that much." She began to walk away, though her heart was pounding in case Trotter was tougher than she had imagined and would not yield.

But she had not misjudged his kind. "Hey, wait a minute. All right – ninety – and that's my very last offer."

Adelina whirled round. "It's a deal!" she cried.

"Where do you want the horse taking?"

"To the stables. You know where they are."

"Yes, ma'am."

Mrs Wallis Trent on her white stallion soon became a familiar figure in the countryside surrounding Abbeyford. The stallion – which she named Zeus – was wild and unmanageable with anyone else, but with Adelina the animal behaved perfectly. He was her horse and hers alone. She joined the Hunt whenever it rode to hounds, and almost daily she went riding, sometimes alone, sometimes with Squire Trent and occasionally – very occasionally – with her husband.

There were two places Adelina never ventured – the abbey ruins and Lynwood Hall. Though in her heart she longed to see Lynwood again, she knew there was no turning back. He did not want her – he had made that clear. Now she was Wallis's wife and Lynwood thought all his jealous beliefs had been true.

Her greatest joy was to take her daughter and her stepson to visit Lord Royston. Here, in the disused nursery, she found a happiness and contentment she had only known in her early childhood – dim and distant memories

brought to life again by two small children. And for Lord
Royston, too, his days were filled with love and companion-
ship once more.

Adelina visited the Vicarage often and, ironically, there
grew between her and Sarah Smithson an uneasy friendship. It seemed as if Adelina was a tangible link between
the two people who had loved each other so many years
ago, who had been forced to live out their lives so close to
each other and yet worlds apart.

One morning, when Adelina found herself alone with
Sarah in the kitchen at the Vicarage, she said, "Squire
Trent was asking after you yesterday, Sarah."

Sarah dropped the cup she was holding, the crash of
shattering china resounding in the silent kitchen. For the
first time since she had known her Adelina could see a
spark in the woman's weary eyes.

"Guy? He – asked after – me?" she whispered, the words
almost like a prayer of thankfulness.

Adelina felt a lump in her throat and could not stop her
thoughts straying to her own lost love – Lynwood. "Yes –
yes, he wanted to know how you were and if you like being
here, at the Vicarage."

Sarah sat down at the bare, scrubbed table and folded
her hands together, her eyes gazing ahead, as if instead of
the kitchen about her she was seeing pictures from the past.
A rare, faint smile curved her mouth. Adelina watched her,
then she sat down opposite her at the table.

"Maybe I was wrong – all those years ago," Sarah
began, almost more to herself than to Adelina. "Maybe he
did love me enough. I thought, you see, that I was just
another village girl to him. And then – when I – found I was
with child my family were so angry – so angry. They
wouldna let me even see Guy again. We weren't allowed to
sort things out for oursel's. I was weak, I know, and I

disappointed him. Oh, I believe he'd have stood up to his parents if I'd been strong too. But I thought – that, in years to come, he'd blame me. I thought it better that we married our own kind. And then," her eyes clouded and her fingers twisted nervously. "Then someone attacked Guy – in the wood – left him for dead."

Adelina gasped but said nothing and waited for Sarah to continue. "Sir Matthew – Guy's father – arrested my pa and sent him to gaol. He died there of gaol fever," she finished flatly.

"However could he do that?"

"He was magistrate for this district," she said, and the way in which she said it told Adelina that the ordinary peasant folk had been powerless under his tyranny.

"By the time – Guy recovered, I was married to Henry Smithson," Sarah was saying. "He's carried his bitterness agen Guy all these years and reared Evan to hate his own father." Sarah shook her head sadly and her shoulders sagged even more as if she carried the whole burden of guilt. "He'll not rest till he's brought trouble to the Trents."

"Did Guy Trent manage the estate before Wallis?" Adelina asked gently.

"Not really. His father, Sir Matthew, lived to be quite an old man and was active up to the last. Wallis was almost a young man when his grandfather died and he seemed to take over straight away. Guy never really held the reins at all. Perhaps it would have been better if he had."

"How do you mean?"

Sarah looked directly at Adelina. "Maybe I shouldna be saying such things to you, ma'am, but you've been kind to me, and I'm grateful and – and I think you like Guy."

Adelina nodded. "I'm very fond of him – yes."

"And your husband, ma'am?" Sarah asked quietly.

"I can't understand him, Sarah." Adelina raised her shoulders slightly. "He seems so ..." She paused searching for the right word, but Sarah supplied it. "Cold, hard, ruthless?"

Adelina sighed. "I'm afraid so."

Sarah nodded. "The resentment against him in the village is growing, ma'am, and I canna do anything to prevent it."

"Why do they dislike him so?"

"He's a hard man. The wages he pays us are poor. He never repairs the cottages he owns. An' then there's this Corn Law. Oh, I don't understand it all – it all has to do wi' politics. All I know is, the workers are worse off for't."

"May I come and see the cottages for myself?" Adelina asked.

There was fear immediately in Sarah's eyes. "I don't know about that, ma'am. If Henry knew I was even talkin' to you like this, he'd – he'd half kill me!"

"Some time when he's not there, then?"

"Well ..." Sarah was still reluctant, but a week later Adelina visited Sarah's tiny cottage.

As she entered she felt immediately closed in by the smallness, the darkness and the overpowering dankness. The hard beaten-earth floor, covered with rush mats, was cold and damp, the walls were rough and cracked. Two window panes were broken.

"What's that rustling in the roof?" Adelina asked.

"Rats!"

Adelina's mouth compressed. It was not that she had never seen such conditions before – indeed, on occasions when her father's debts had plunged them into abject poverty, she had had to suffer such hardship herself. But that she should find it here, in a village where the workmen should have been cared for by their employer, shocked and angered her.

"Sarah," Adelina faced her, "I don't blame the villagers for how they feel, in fact – I can't promise anything, but ..."

At that moment the low door creaked open and Henry Smithson stood there. Adelina heard Sarah's gasp and could feel the woman's fear.

"Good afternoon, Mr Smithson," Adelina said swiftly. "I ..."

"What are you doin' here?"

"I came to bring your wife her wages." Adelina opened her reticule, thankful that she had had the foresight to have an excuse ready. She placed the coins on the rough table. She smiled at the glowering man. "I am sorry to intrude upon you, but I missed Mrs Smithson at the Vicarage earlier."

"Oh. I see." He looked as if he did not believe her, but there was nothing he could do.

Adelina turned to Sarah. "Thank you, Mrs Smithson, for all you're doing for my relatives. I do appreciate it and I'll see you are rewarded."

As she left the cottage she heard Henry Smithson's voice rise. "Rewarded, is it? Pah! We know what their promises are, don't we? Looked after you, didn't they? Left me to bring up their bastard ..."

Adelina walked away, sorry to have brought his wrath upon Sarah's head, but she guessed that the poor woman was used to it anyway.

As Adelina left the village and walked up the lane towards the Manor, she heard hoofbeats behind her, and turned to see Wallis approaching. He reined in close beside her, causing her to step back to avoid Jupiter's restive hooves.

"Where the devil have you been?" Wallis shouted, glaring down at her.

"To the village," Adelina replied, calmly determined not to be intimidated by him.

"You have no business there. I saw you coming out of one of the cottages. What were you doing?"

"I've been to pay Sarah Smithson her wages, that's all," she lied glibly, using the same excuse she'd given Sarah's husband.

Wallis leaned down towards her. "You'll keep away from the village folk. Do you hear me?"

Adelina gasped at his arrogance. Defiantly, she remained silent.

"Do you hear me, Adelina?" he shouted.

"I hear you, Wallis," Adelina replied quietly. "But by what right do you order me as to whom I may visit?"

"As your *husband*!"

They glared at each other, for the first time since their strange marriage had begun, openly hostile.

"I don't think much of the way you treat your employees. They are living in squalor."

"Keep out of my affairs," Wallis warned her.

"It is my affair. They're my grandfather's lands."

"At the moment, maybe. But not for ever, my dear, not for ever. One way or another, they will be mine one day!"

He kicked his heels and Jupiter leapt forward, the horse's hooves narrowly missing Adelina.

She gazed after Wallis as he galloped away.

"How could I have been so foolish – even for Francesca's sake?" she murmured to herself and a picture of herself in twenty or thirty years' time – remarkably like Sarah Smithson – flashed before her mind's eye.

Adelina shuddered, pulled her cloak around her and hurried home to see the children.

TEN

It was just over two months after their marriage that the villagers' open hostility towards Wallis Trent became more ominous.

A wild dog, or, as Wallis thought, probably two, got in among the in-lamb ewes, causing havoc. The dog, or dogs, ravaged and killed several sheep and chased others or frightened them so that quite a few aborted stillborn lambs. The slaughter was terrible to see. Adelina rode out on Zeus to the fields beyond the abbey ruins where the incident had occurred. There were six ewes dead, their bodies mutilated, their thick wool drenched with their own blood. Tiny lambs, which had never had time to draw breath, lay upon the ground, mere bundles of bones. Several other ewes were obviously very sick and did not look as though they would survive.

Adelina, unseen by him, watched Wallis sitting astride Jupiter, motionless as a stone statue, looking upon the carnage with a grim face. Beneath his arm he carried a shotgun.

Adelina urged Zeus closer until she stood beside him. "What has caused this, Wallis? Foxes?"

"I suppose it could be – but I rather think it's a wild dog or – more likely – two. They roam and hunt in pairs."

"Have you seen the dogs?"

"No, but I intend to find them. Now you're here perhaps you'd better come too. Just to see what lengths your village friends will go to!"

He turned his horse away from the awful scene and Adelina followed him. She wanted to learn the truth as much as he did, though for a different reason. At walking pace, they rode side by side so that they might talk.

"The men look even more sullen than usual, Wallis. Are they upset by what has happened?"

"I doubt it," he said shortly. "Not one of them seems shocked by what has occurred. It was as if they'd known it was going to happen."

Adelina gasped. "You don't mean – you can't mean they've planned it? That they've done it on purpose?"

Wallis nodded, his expression hard. "They'll rue the day they tried to tangle with me," he muttered, harshly, more to himself than to her. His eyes, as he watched his workmen clearing away the carcasses, were bright with malice. That anyone – particularly anyone he considered his inferior – should dare to raise his hand against his master was beyond Wallis Trent's arrogant understanding.

His words brought a chill to her heart.

Adelina said nothing but rode in thoughtful silence.

At a steady canter they rode northwards away from Abbeyford. Behind them lay the Royston farmlands, in front, rolling countryside with scarcely a farm or a cottage in sight.

"Do you farm all these fields, Wallis?"

He pointed with his riding crop. "These directly north and east are your grandfather's lands. Over the hill to the west are Lynwood's."

They rode on, still going northwards. The ground was frozen hard, but there had been no snow as yet. The day was bright but bitterly cold and though Adelina was warmly dressed, she still shivered.

"Wallis, I'm cold. Let's gallop to warm ourselves." She spurred Zeus and he leapt forward, his restless energy responding eagerly. Jupiter, not to be outdone, thundered alongside. The sharp air stung her face, but Adelina found the ride exhilarating. Across the meadows they galloped, jumping low stone walls, steadying to a canter to thread their way through a copse, rustling through the dead leaves of autumn, then out into the open fields again, with flying hooves.

At last Adelina pulled her white stallion to a steady trot. Her cheeks were rosy, her eyes bright, but Wallis did not notice.

Still frowning, he said, "There's no sign of any dogs here. We'd better turn back now."

They rode back towards Abbeyford in silence. As they crested the hill overlooking the village, they reined in and stood surveying the valley below them. The dead sheep had been removed, but there were still visible signs of the slaughter. Tufts of bloodstained wool and pieces of flesh littered the field.

Adelina said, "Where would wild dogs go in the daytime? Where would they hide out?" She watched Wallis as his eyes roamed over the valley, the fields and the hillsides. She saw his gaze come to rest upon the abbey ruins. Without another word needing to be spoken between them, they both turned their horses towards the abbey.

It was wild and lonely near the crumbling, desolate ruins. The wind whipped through the broken-down building, howling mournfully. It was eerie and forbidding. Adelina shuddered.

"Stay here, Adelina. I'll take a look." Wallis dismounted and stood a moment to load his shotgun. He did not go inside the ruins but climbed up on to a low wall. Then she noticed that he was beckoning her to join him. Swallowing the fear which rose in her throat at being so close once more to the ruins which evoked such horrific memories, Adelina dismounted and moved towards him. Without speaking, he gave her his hand to help her climb the low wall to stand beside him. Clinging to his arm she stood on the precarious, crumbling stonework and looked into the ruins. Wallis pointed and in the farthest, darkest corner she saw something move. She narrowed her eyes and gasped as, all at once, she realised there were two mangy, wild-eyed dogs in the corner – though to Adelina they looked more like wolves.

"They are *tethered*!" Wallis said in a low voice. "Can you see the rope tying them to that ring in the wall?"

"*Tethered*!" Adelina repeated in a shocked whisper. Then, as she realised the full implication, horror-struck, she added, "You mean – someone had them and – and – let them loose on your sheep?"

Wallis nodded grimly. "It looks very much like it. It's what I expected. Stand down now, Adelina."

"What are you going to do?"

"Shoot them," he replied bluntly.

Adelina climbed down from the wall and stood watching him as he raised the shotgun to his shoulder. There was a loud report which echoed through the ruins and one of the dogs fell dead. The other immediately began barking frenziedly, straining at its leash in wild terror. Seconds later, Wallis steadied his gun again. A second shot rang out and the dog ceased its barking, swayed and fell.

Slowly Wallis lowered his gun. Then he stood looking at the dogs for a moment. He turned and jumped down from the wall. Together they walked into the ruins. They stood over the dogs. They were indeed the ones which had savaged the sheep, for their rough hair coats were matted with blood and scraps of sheep's wool clung to their jaws.

There were also a few tell-tale bones scattered nearby as if they had carried off a lamb or two to their hiding-place.

Adelina turned away, sick at heart, and went back to their horses. She watched Wallis anxiously as he walked towards her. His face was twisted with fury. His shoulders were rigid and his hands clenched. "The dogs were obviously unleashed amongst my sheep on purpose." He spat out the words. "It was planned – all planned!"

"Unless someone has caught them since and tied them up here for safety," Adelina suggested, clinging desperately to the hope that it had not been a deliberate act of vengeance.

He shook his head. "No, it was deliberate."

Adelina was forced to agree that he was right.

The slaughter of the sheep was the beginning of a campaign of hatred against Wallis Trent. His enemies were unseen and unknown. Whoever they were they came stealthily in the dead of night. There was a tense atmosphere of distrust throughout the village. Each villager suspected his neighbour, whilst Wallis believed that the whole village was involved in this war against him as an employer, but, above all, as a member of the hated Trent family, for no hand was laid against Abbeyford Grange and Lord Royston. The trouble was confined to Abbeyford; there was no sign of unrest at Amberly or at any of the other adjoining estates.

The vendetta went on for weeks and then months, right through the summer, and the tension mounted. Abbeyford was a village of unhappy, frightened people. Adelina mentally listed the damage caused and felt helpless to do anything. Fences were smashed and hedges torn up so that cattle escaped and wandered away. Wheels would come off farm-wagons without reason, causing a deal of damage to Wallis's vehicles. Jupiter went suddenly lame. And poaching reached frightening proportions.

One afternoon in early September, Adelina was riding Zeus through the wood behind the Manor when she heard a horse's thudding hooves behind her. Startled, she turned to see Squire Trent galloping towards her through the trees. He pulled hard on the reins and his horse halted abruptly beside her. It tossed its head and stamped angrily at its rider's rough treatment of it. Zeus, too, became restive.

"Whoa there, boy," Guy shouted and grinned broadly at Adelina.

Adelina smiled warmly at him. "Shall we ride a little way together?" she offered.

"I'd be honoured, my dear. If you'll permit me, I'll show you something worth your while. You like a bit of sport, eh?" His eyes were feverishly bright. Adelina hesitated.

"Come on," he said and spurred his horse forward. Adelina followed, a little reluctantly.

As they reached the edge of the wood, Guy Trent said, "We'd best leave the horses here, Adelina."

"Why?"

"It's all right. You're safe with me. But we must go quietly, we don't want to be seen."

"I don't understand you. Where are you taking me?"

"To the abbey ruins."

"No!" Adelina cried out. "I won't come."

"It's all right, my dear," he said again. "I just want you to see a sport the village menfolk enjoy." He pointed. "Look, several are making their way there now. Only we mustn't be seen. We must stay here in the trees until all the men are inside and then we'll creep up and watch from a place I know where they can't see us. Don't worry – I often come, but I always take care they don't know I'm there."

"But what is it?"

"You'll see. I want it to be a surprise."

They waited some time, watching from the shelter of the trees as men from the village arrived in twos and threes and slipped into the abbey ruins.

"There – I can't see anyone else coming. Come on. Follow me and don't make a noise whatever you do."

Adelina, still wary, followed Squire Trent. He skirted the ruins and went round to the opposite side from that overlooking the valley. They climbed a small bank at the top of which were some bushes growing against a wall which was not so badly broken down as some of the others. Guy pushed his way through, holding the branches aside for Adelina. They came up against the wall.

"Here, over here," he whispered, and Adelina saw him crouching down to peer through a peephole in the wall. Curiosity overcame her doubts and she crouched down beside him. Below them in the abbey, in what had once been one of the larger rooms, about twenty-five to thirty men were gathered. The rubble had been cleared away from the ground and they were all standing in a circle with a clear space in the centre.

At first Adelina could not think what it was they were going to do. Then on either side of the ring she saw two men each holding a fine cockerel. On the cocks' feet were fitted metal spurs. The birds were struggling to free themselves, but the men held them fast, whilst a third man went round the others taking money from them.

Adelina put her mouth close to the squire's ear and whispered, "What are they doing?"

In turn he whispered to her. "Cock-fighting. The man in the middle taking money is taking bets on which will be the victor. I fancy the one on the left. Look at those legs! He'll tear the other one to pieces."

Adelina was not quite sure what he meant or exactly

what was going to happen until she saw the fight begin. The man in the centre of the ring completed his bet-collecting and then the two cockerels were released. In a wild flurry of beating wings, necks outstretched, the cocks flew at each other. Their sharp, pointed beaks pecked viciously at each other's head and neck. Then, one backed off a little and then surged forward. His wings flapping and both feet clear of the ground, he aimed the metal spurs straight at his opponent's chest. The wounded cock staggered. Adelina clapped her hand to her mouth to still a horrified scream which threatened to escape her lips. It was not that she was squeamish, but the bloodthirsty attack was so unexpected.

"Come on, come on," Guy urged in a whisper, for the wounded cock was the one which he had thought would win. Adelina glanced at him. His eyes were bright with excitement. He ran his tongue over his dry lips.

The noise from the watching men below was deafening. They were shouting or cursing whichever cock they had backed. Again the first cock made another lunge towards the already bleeding one, but he dodged away at the last moment, so that the assailant fell on to the ground instead, momentarily losing his balance. Taking swift advantage, the other cock flew at him from behind and mounted his back, digging in his spurs. The shouts increased as the fight swung this way and that, with first one bird seeming the strongest, then the other. All the time the watchers – all except the two hidden in the bushes – shouted encouragement.

At last the fight was over when one of the cocks lay, a bleeding mass of feathers, upon the ground. The other could hardly be said to strut proudly, for it staggered around hardly able to stand either.

Squire Trent nodded with satisfaction. "There, I told you that one would win. Wish I'd had a sovereign on it. Good fight, wasn't it?"

Adelina shuddered. "I suppose so, if you like that sort of thing."

He looked at her in surprise. "I thought you liked a bit of sport. You joined the Hunt."

She grimaced. "I joined the Hunt for the riding and the social gathering. I can't say I relish the kill very much."

"Oh, well, I'm sorry I brought you then," he said huffily.

"I'm glad to have seen it," Adelina tried to placate him. "Thank you for bringing me. I heard tell George Washington used to enjoy the sport."

"Really?" the squire said, somewhat mollified.

"What do we do now?"

"Wait until they've all gone before we leave or we'll risk being seen."

But the village men showed no sign of dispersing. In fact, the atmosphere became quieter, more serious, as if, the sport over for the day, they now had business to discuss. They talked amongst themselves for some five minutes whilst Squire Trent grumbled. "Whatever are they playing at? Why don't they get off home? They don't usually dally once the fight's done. Can't understand it ..."

At that moment his whispered mutterings were cut short by the arrival through the broken, stone archway of another man. Squire Trent's mouth dropped open and his eyes bulged in surprise. Adelina, tired of watching through the peephole, was now sitting with her back against the wall just waiting until her companion should give the word that all was clear for them to leave. She saw the strange expression upon his face and sat upright again.

"What is it?" she hissed.

He put his forefinger to his lips and Adelina was

surprised to see that his hand trembled. Mystified and intrigued she twisted round to see the cause. She almost cried out as she recognised the man who had just come into the ruins and now stood on a low wall some three feet high so that he could address the other men and be clearly seen and heard by them.

"Evan," Adelina whispered hoarsely. "It's Evan Smithson!"

Squire Trent nodded soberly. "I wonder where the devil he's sprung from again?"

A shadowy incident, just out of reach of her conscious mind, seemed to flicker across Adelina's memory, as if she ought to know and yet she could just not remember …

Evan was speaking now. Squire Trent and Adelina bent forward, their faces close together, to listen. There was something ominous about this meeting of the village men, and both were anxious to learn what it was.

"My friends," Evan was shouting, spreading his arms wide in a gesture of grand eloquence. "I have come here today to show you that I am alive. I left Abbeyford – vowing never to return. But, my friends, I kept thinking of you all under the whip of that tyrant, Wallis Trent. So I came back." He grinned. "I have been back several months!" And Adelina knew instinctively that Evan Smithson had been behind the mysterious happenings against the Trents. "You all know I have reason enough to hate him and his kind," he was saying. "And so have you, if you think on't."

He prodded his forefinger towards the men. A low murmuring ran amongst them. "He doesn't care if you work yourselves into an early grave, or if you've a roof over your head or enough food in your bellies, or whether your children run barefoot and shiver in winter and die of starvation."

The murmurings grew louder.

"Does he put more money in your pocket, my friends? He's lining his own whilst you starve. Does *his* family live on a diet of rye bread, potatoes and skim-milk? No, his son will eat meat every day, if he wants. When did your children last eat *meat*?"

"We share a pig now and again," someone muttered, but Evan, if he heard, ignored the remark.

"And so, my fellow peasants, I say it is time for revolution. It is time we stood up for our rights as human beings instead of being slaves to the gentry. The whole country wants Parliamentary reform. We want the Corn Law abolished."

The cries of assent rang through the crumbling walls, and Adelina and Guy Trent exchanged a look of deep anxiety. Only one voice tried to bring a note of sanity. "Aye, but Trents is cattle-farmers. This 'ere Corn Law won't mek no difference to us." But he was quickly silenced.

Evan's tirade was relentless. "Last week I went to a meeting near Manchester – at Peterloo – only about twenty miles from here. A peaceful meeting it was, of farm labourers from hereabouts and men from the cotton mills too. It wasn't intended to be a riot or a rebellion. Men took their families, their wives and little children – even babes in arms. But what did the magistrates do? They called out the yeomanry, who charged amongst the people, killin' and maiming. I tell you, my friends, if you could 'ave seen the sight afterwards – the field was littered like a battlefield. Men wounded and dying, women trampled by the horses, children orphaned in the space of a few seconds, crying pitifully. It was a massacre, a bloody massacre!"

The angry resentment and hatred was now written upon every face. The murmurings grew to a cry for revenge.

Evan held up his hand and the noise abated. In a lower,

more conspiratorial voice, he said, "But *our* grievances are closer to home than with Parliament, aren't they, my friends? We will meet on the village green on Saturday next and go to the Manor to ask for, no, to demand a better wage and better conditions. The Trents sit up there in their grand Manor living off the fruits of your labours whilst you live out your dismal lives with scarcely enough to eat in your tumble-down cottages – which he owns."

"What if he wun't do aught?"

"Then we'll have to get a little nasty, wun't us?" Evan's face twisted into such an expression of bitter hatred that Adelina shuddered, remembering all too clearly how, once, she had seen that same expression on Evan's face – at very close proximity!

"What d'you mean?"

Evan shrugged. "We'll burn his stacks, his barn, even his fine house, an' see how *he* likes being poor!"

"No, no, it's too much."

"No – we munna do harm."

"He deserves it – he dunna care for us."

"Evan's right. After all – he should know."

The remarks flew furiously amongst the men, only a few rising clearly to Adelina's ears above the general babble.

Evan caught and held on to the last remark.

"Yes, I should know. For am I not a Trent by birth? But you all know what that drunken old sot did? Left an innocent village girl to live a life of shame just because he had to marry one of his own class. An' the older ones among you will remember me grandpa – how he was sent to gaol for summat he didna do, an' how he died there!"

Adelina saw Squire Trent's face turn a deathly grey colour and a soft moan escaped his lips. "Oh, Sarah, Sarah! What have we done? Is it not enough how we have suffered all these years apart?"

Adelina was moved to take his hand and hold it comfortingly. She was hearing proof from his own lips that Squire Trent had really loved Sarah. What pain Evan's actions must be causing him, for, after all, he was his son!

At last the meeting broke up and the men sneaked away out of the ruins back towards Abbeyford. Evan Smithson disappeared in the opposite direction. Not until everyone had been gone for some minutes did Guy Trent and Adelina dare to move their cramped limbs and leave their hiding-place.

The hillside was deserted as they hurried across the open space to the wood.

"Whatever shall we do?" Adelina panted as she took little running steps in her haste to escape from the scene she had just witnessed. The horrors of the cock-fight were completely obliterated by the mutinous meeting which had followed.

"We – must tell Wallis."

"Yes, yes, of course, we must tell Wallis," she agreed, but added, "but what will *he* do?"

"What are you going to do?" Adelina repeated her question to Wallis some time later as she and Squire Trent stood facing him across the smooth leather-top of the desk in his study. They had recounted the full story of the scene they had witnessed. Between them they were able to repeat what had been said almost word for word. She bit her lip, waiting apprehensively for his reply.

"I shall follow the good example of the Manchester magistrates and call out the yeomanry."

"Oh, no, Wallis. You can't possibly do that – not against your own people."

Wallis, a fearsome frown upon his face, leaned towards her threateningly. "My people? You dare to call them *my people* after what they have done to me these last months. It started with the sheep and, every week since something has been destroyed or stolen, or animals injured. *My people!* Pah!" He thumped one fist against the palm of his other hand. "Adelina, you will not interfere. You hear me?"

Adelina stared at him in disbelief. Was she really married to this cold, heartless man who would call out the soldiers against his own workers?

She turned away sick at heart.

For two days Adelina worried and fretted over what she could do to prevent the tragedy which was sure to occur.

There was a stillness in the air, an oppressiveness, as if everyone and everything were waiting — waiting for the storm of hatred and revenge and arrogance to unleash itself. She feared for the safety of the children. Jamie Trent and her own daughter. If the rioters meant what they said — then the whole Trent family was in danger.

On the Friday, Adelina could bear the suspense no longer. When she knew Wallis was out, she gave orders for the carriage to be made ready and brought to the side entrance. Hastily she thrust some garments for the children and herself into a portmanteau and instructed Jane to do likewise. "You'll be staying at Abbeyford Grange for a few nights. I'm sure Lord Royston won't mind."

"Aren't you coming, ma'am?"

"I'm taking you there, but — I don't know yet."

Once the children were safe, Adelina told herself, perhaps she would be able to think more rationally.

She did not tell anyone else in the household what she was doing — Wallis would be angry enough when he found out.

As the carriage passed through the village, the strangely silent street made Adelina's nerves tremble with dread. When they arrived at Abbeyford Grange, Adelina sent Jane with the children to find the housekeeper while she went in search of Lord Royston.

She flew through the hallway and into the drawing-room.

"Grandfather," she cried, "Grandfather ..." Then she stopped in surprise as she saw that her grandfather had a visitor.

The world seemed to rock beneath her feet as she breathed his name. "Francis! Oh, Francis!"

ELEVEN

The Earl of Lynwood had turned at the sound of her voice. For a moment, across the room, their eyes met and held. She read the longing in his gaze and for a moment all the love in her heart was in her eyes for him to see. There was a flash of exultation, of love, in his. She stood before him, a woman, beautiful, yet with the maturity and serenity and kindliness that Life's harsh experiences had taught her. In her lovely face was the strength of a fine character.

How could he have ever thought she was like Caroline, who, though equally lovely, had been selfish and ruthless?

The pain of his final loss of Adelina on her marriage to Wallis Trent and the realisation that it had been his own blind stupidity which had forced her to take such a disastrous step, had finally – once and for all – obliterated his boyish memories.

Ironically, when at last Lynwood realised that it was Adelina he loved for herself alone, it was too late for she was the wife of Wallis Trent!

Lord Royston broke the spell. "What ever is the matter, my child?"

"Oh – I – yes. Grandfather – it's Wallis. He's going to – to call out the yeomanry. The villagers – they're planning to march to the Manor and he – he intends to quell what he thinks will be a riot with the use of soldiers."

Lord Royston and Lynwood exchanged anxious glances.

"This is serious, my lord," Lynwood said earnestly.

Lord Royston nodded, his old eyes full of concern. He thumped his stick on the floor. "The stupid, arrogant fool! What does he think he's playing at? And how's he managed to call them out? He's not a magistrate, is he?"

"No," Lynwood answered soberly. "But you are!"

"Well, I haven't given any such order."

"No, I realise that. But Trent wields power and influence, often in your name."

"Does he indeed? The scoundrel!"

Lynwood glanced at Adelina as if to see what effect her grandfather's words had upon her. She moved forward and said softly, "Grandfather, it's the villagers I'm afraid for. They're angry and bitter and resentful, roused by Evan Smithson."

"Who?"

"Evan Smithson. Guy Trent's – illegitimate son."

Adelina glanced at Lynwood. They were both remembering Evan, the abbey ruins and Lynwood's fight with him – and the reason for it.

"Good lord! So he's at the bottom of this, is he?" Lord Royston murmured, knowing nothing of their memories.

Swiftly, Adelina told them of the scene Squire Trent and she had witnessed at the abbey ruins. "We told Wallis, thinking he'd be able to handle the situation, but instead all he would say is that they deserve all they get and he'll put an end to it once and for all."

She sat down heavily and dropped her head into her hands. "There will be such bloodshed and suffering. I don't know how he can be so – so cruel. I can't bear it!"

She felt Lynwood's hand upon her shoulder. "I'll see what I can do. But it's late now, I doubt I'll be in time."

Adelina lifted her tear-streaked face and covered his

hand with her own. "Oh, Francis, thank you."

Swiftly he bent and kissed her, their lips clinging desperately, hungrily, for a moment and then he turned and hurried from the room.

Adelina and her grandfather looked at each other sadly. "Oh, Grandfather – what have I done?" she said heavily, not expecting him to answer. Then briskly she roused herself. She could not let herself wallow in the self-pity the sight of Francis had aroused in her. There was no time now for indulging in thoughts of what might have been.

"I hope you don't mind – I've brought the children here to stay for a few days."

"Of course not, my dear. And you must stay here too."

"No," Adelina said quietly. "I must go back. There may be something I can do, even now, to prevent it."

"I wish you wouldn't go," Lord Royston said, then he sighed. "But in some ways you're too much like your mother to take notice of me – but not in every way, my dear, dear girl."

Adelina bent and kissed his bald head. "Dear Grandfather," she murmured and then hurried away.

She mounted Zeus, which she had brought for her return, and left Abbeyford Grange.

As she entered the hall at the Manor, Wallis was waiting for her. He grasped her arm in a vice-like grip, and half dragged her into his study. Slamming the door behind him, he turned upon her. "Where is my son? What have you done with him?"

Courageously, Adelina squared her shoulders and faced him. "I have taken both children, and Jane, to Abbeyford Grange. They will be safe there."

"Then you will fetch them back at once," he said, his teeth clenched, his eyes bright with anger.

"Not until the danger is over."

Menacingly, he said. "Do you think, madam, that I cannot protect my own son? You will fetch him back – *now*!"

"I – will – not," Adelina said meeting his almost maniacal wrath with an outward show of fearlessness.

Wallis raised his right arm and with the back of his hand dealt her a stinging blow across the face. She fell against a chair, knocking it over as she tumbled to the floor. He stood over her, powerful, arrogant and utterly ruthless. Roughly, he grasped her arm and pulled her to her feet, almost dislocating her shoulder. Adelina cried out in pain.

At that moment the door opened and his father came in. He stopped in amazement. "What the devil ...? Wallis, have you taken leave of your senses?"

"Get out," Wallis snarled. But as he turned momentarily towards his father he relaxed his grip upon Adelina. All her instincts for survival, which had saved her so often in the waterfront taverns, rose to the surface. Twisting away, she pushed past Squire Trent and ran through the hall. She heard Wallis shout, was dimly aware of a scuffle as the older man attempted to stop Wallis following her. Out of the front door and down the steps. Zeus was being led away by a stable-boy.

"Wait, wait!" Adelina cried, desperately afraid her shaking legs would not carry her. Wallis was at the door as she reached her horse. The boy took one look at his angry master, bent quickly and cupped his hands.

"Here, missus, quick!"

Gratefully, Adelina put her foot into his hands and hoisted herself on to the horse. She grasped the reins and as Wallis ran towards them, she kicked at Zeus. As she galloped away out of reach she turned back to see Wallis attacking the stable-lad, venting his frustration on the innocent boy.

Adelina galloped down the lane, through the village and up to Abbeyford Grange.

It was only when she knew she was safe, that the fear and terror overwhelmed her. "I can never go back to him," she whispered to herself. "Never!"

Saturday dawned, and, as if to match the ominous situation, the weather was sultry. Black clouds hung over the village and yet there was no rain. Thunder rumbled in the far distance and the air was breathless.

Adelina worried the hours away, watching from the long windows in the library at the Grange. As it began to grow dusk, she could see, far below, lighted torches moving towards the village green, until there seemed to be a pool of flickering light in the centre of the village.

There had been no word from Lynwood. Adelina did not know whether he had prevented the yeomanry from being called out or not.

"I must warn them," she whispered. "I cannot let this foolishness go any further."

She hurried upstairs to dress herself. With shaking fingers she put on her dark riding-habit and black cloak. Pulling the hood well down over her face, she let herself quietly out of the side door and out on to the terrace. She hurried down the steps and through the rose garden and out of the door in the wall. Slipping and stumbling, Adelina ran down the sloping field towards the village.

As she neared the green, she heard on the still air the sound of many voices and saw the gathering of men, several holding flaming torches. She watched them assemble, form into ranks and begin to march in reasonably orderly fashion out of the village and up the lane towards Abbeyford Manor. Evan Smithson, his torch held high like a banner, led them.

She began to run after them. "Evan, Evan! Wait! I must tell you ..."

The men faltered and several stopped at the sound of her voice to look around. She moved into the light from their torches and stood facing Evan. Close behind him she could see Henry Smithson, his face grim.

"Why, if it ain't the Lady of the Manor hersel'!" Evan said. "And what might you be doin' out on a dangerous night like this'n? Your dear husband should take better care of you, my lovely Adelina."

"Evan – all of you," she cried, "you must listen to me. Wallis has called out the yeomanry to put down your riot."

For a moment there was silence, then Evan laughed. "Tekin' a tip from the Peterloo magistrates, is he?" He paused a moment as if thinking rapidly. "I don't believe you. He hasn't the power. Only your grandfather has that power. Has *he* ...?"

"No – no, he wouldn't do such a thing. But we think Wallis may have – may have used Lord Royston's name to influence those concerned. Lord Lynwood has tried to stop it, but – but I – we haven't heard from him."

"Huh, expect us to believe any of *his* sort would try to stop it?" Henry Smithson growled. "Tek no notice of her."

"Lord Lynwood is a good man," Adelina said quietly.

"What about Trent – your husband? Is he 'a good man'?" Evan asked.

"I ..." Adelina could not speak. She was torn apart. Her shoulders slumped and weariness swept over her. "I came to warn you. I don't want there to be bloodshed."

Evan moved closer. In the light from his torch she saw again the face of the man who had caused her so much unhappiness. And yet she had been moved to try to save him and his friends. Whatever heartache Evan Smithson had caused her, she could not allow him to walk towards the destruction his own half-brother planned.

"I think *he's* sent you. He's only using you to save himself. I don't believe he could call out the yeomanry, though I know he would. So," he grasped hold of her arm, giving it a vicious wrench and twisting it behind her so that she was obliged to walk in front of him. "We'll take you with us, my lovely. Perhaps with you as hostage, he'll listen more readily to what we have to say."

Adelina sobbed with fear and frustration, panting for breath as Evan pushed her in front of him. Every limb in her body was trembling and her heart was thudding painfully.

With Evan once more leading them but now with Adelina in the very front, the men resumed their march towards the Manor.

Without warning there came through the night the sound of thudding hooves – but the sound did not come from the Manor stables. It was the noise of many horses being ridden hard. Then Adelina saw them – dark, swiftly-moving shadows emerging from the trees at the top of the hill, swooping, recklessly, down the hillside towards the band of village men carrying torches. For a moment time seemed to stand still. The village men stopped and with one accord looked up at the brigade of yeomanry charging down upon them.

"My God! He *has* done it!" Evan muttered.

The horses came nearer and nearer and the village men, the mesmerism broken, gave wild cries of terror and began to flee in all directions. Torches were thrown aside and the reason for their march upon the Manor forgotten as they fled to save their own lives. Adelina stood quite still, so filled with terror that she could not move. She faced certain death, brought about by her own husband!

Then she felt herself grasped round the waist by Evan

and thrown bodily over a stone wall. He jumped over after her and crouched down for protection. She lay where she had fallen the breath knocked from her body. The horsemen were upon the men, chasing and harassing like huntsmen after a fox. Screams of fear and pain filled the night air as some of the men were trampled upon by the horses or caught by the flashing sabres of the yeomen. The carnage, the screaming, the horses trampling and rearing, seemed to go on for ever. Only Adelina, saved by Evan, and Evan himself, were safe behind the stone wall.

Then suddenly it was over. The cavalry re-formed and rode back the way they had come, leaving a scene of devastation.

Evan rose and stood looking at the scene. Adelina, too, pulled herself up. In the moonlight she could see the dark shapes of men lying on the ground, hear their groans and the cries of those badly injured.

"My God!" whispered Evan.

Adelina moaned aloud. "How could he do it? How *could* he?"

Grimly, Evan picked up one of the torches still alight, its flame licking the grass. He looked down at her, and now there was no hatred towards her. "I'm sorry. I should have believed you. Stay here and you won't be hurt ..."

"Where are you going?" Panic rose again. "What are you going to do?"

"Never mind. Just stay here." There was a lust for revenge on his face as he turned away.

"Evan – no – you mustn't." She scrambled after him, but he was running now, too fast for her, towards the Manor.

"Evan – no!"

Adelina stumbled and fell against a prickly bush, which tore at her hands and face and wrenched at her clothes. Weeping and sobbing with frustration, she struggled to free herself. Then as she stumbled on, she saw the first flames leaping from the stack-yard at the side of the Manor.

"Oh, no!" she breathed. "Evan's setting fire to the Manor. My God!"

She ran, fear giving her added strength. By the time she reached the yard, she saw Evan silhouetted against the orange glow moving towards the stables.

"No – Evan – not the horses." Then she saw Wallis's tall figure, saw Evan turn to face him, saw them pause, stare at each other. Evan turned and threw his lighted torch upon the stable roof as Wallis leapt upon him, too late to prevent his action.

They crashed to the ground and rolled over and over. Burning wisps of straw floated everywhere and the air was filled with acrid fumes. The stable roof began to burn, unnoticed by the two grappling men.

"Wallis, Wallis, the horses," Adelina cried desperately.

Then she heard the sound of horse's hooves and turned to see Lynwood galloping towards her. He threw himself from his horse and ran to her. "Adelina – my darling. You're safe – thank God."

Oblivious to the fact that her husband was close by, Lynwood folded her into his embrace, burying his face against her hair, murmuring, "Adelina – oh, Adelina."

For one blissful moment she clung to him, suspended in time, one moment from all eternity when they were locked together in pure, overflowing love for each other; the world forgotten save their own two selves.

Then brutal reality awoke them, as a roof timber of the stable crashed to the ground, and the horses in the burning building kicked and fought to release themselves from their stalls, the sound they made like screams of terror.

"The horses!" Adelina made to pull herself away, but Lynwood held her fast.

"No, Adelina. You cannot help them. You'd be killed."

Wallis seemed suddenly to realise what was happening, and pushing Evan Smithson from him he ran towards the burning stable.

"Trent – don't be a fool!" Lynwood shouted, but Adelina could utter no word. She could only stand and watch as the tall, broad figure of her husband rushed headlong into the flames towards the stall holding his horse, Jupiter.

Evan Smithson fled and Lynwood, seeing him go, made a lunge forward to prevent him, but it was Adelina's turn now to restrain him. "No, Francis. Let him go."

Lynwood looked down at her in amazement. "Let him – go?"

Adelina nodded. "He saved my life – back there. When the yeomanry charged the men, I was with them – in the very front. Evan saved my life."

Lynwood held her face cupped in his hands and kissed her lips gently. "Then – for that alone – he deserves to go free," he murmured. "Adelina – there's so much I want to say...." But at that moment Wallis appeared once more, trying to lead out his stallion from the burning stable. The animal was hurt and wild with terror. It reared and plunged and kicked. For a moment Wallis seemed about to master Jupiter, then, as another roof timber crashed down behind the animal and the flames roared with renewed force, the horse reared, standing on its hind legs, a colossal black shape, its hooves flailing, to come crashing down – its full weight upon Wallis.

Adelina screamed and Lynwood leapt forward as Jupiter, free now, galloped away.

Wallis lay quite still, his head at a peculiar angle, blood pouring from his head, his eyes open, staring, his mouth gaping.

Gently, Lynwood felt for his pulse, then his heart. "I think he's dead, Adelina."

"Dead?" she repeated stupidly.

Then, quietly and without warning, she fainted.

Adelina awoke in a strange room – a bedroom at Abbeyford Grange. She became aware of Jane sitting close by.

"Oh, madam, you're awake."

"The children?" was Adelina's first question.

"Quite safe."

"And – and," Adelina raised herself on one elbow. "Lord Lynwood?"

"He's safe. He's downstairs, ma'am, pacing up and down like a caged lion, waiting for you to wake up, but – but …"

"Yes?" Panic caught at her again.

"Mr Wallis, ma'am. He – he's dead."

The panic faded. She lay back and sighed deeply. "I know. I remember," she said heavily. "Was anyone else killed?"

"Three from the village, ma'am, and several badly injured. Henry Smithson – he may not live, but, if he does, he'll never walk again. Crippled for life, he'll be."

Adelina groaned. "What about Evan?"

"Oh, he's gone again, ma'am, as quick as he come. Mind you, they reckon he's been living in Amberly for quite some time. Married he is, they say, with children. Not that I know him, ma'am, but I've heard all the gossip up at the Manor." She glanced at Adelina. "He's been planning all this for a long time. He's used the unrest of the times for his own purpose. To bring revenge on the Trents."

"Yes, yes," Adelina said heavily. She frowned. "And now I remember. I think I saw him once – in Amberly. I saw this man in the shadows and he seemed familiar. But I never thought, never dreamt, it was Evan. I hope this time he's gone for good!"

She lay back and closed her eyes and, as the heartache began to recede, the warm and comforting knowledge enveloped her.

Downstairs Lynwood was waiting ...

ABBEYFORD REMEMBERED

ONE

Abbeyford, England, 1841

"What's this place called, then?"

Carrie Smithson stood at the top of the hill, looking down upon the village nestling in the valley below. The breeze blew her long black hair into a tangle of curls. Her arms akimbo, she stood with her feet, in their wooden clogs, planted slightly apart. Her thin blouse and coarse-woven skirt were flattened by the breeze against her young, firm body. She was slim, almost to the point of thinness, and yet there was a wiry strength about her and a determination about the set of her chin and in her eyes. It was her eyes which were her most striking feature. They were a most unusual colour – a deep violet.

She glanced towards her father standing beside her. His arms were folded across his broad chest. His eyes, as he gazed down into the valley, seemed far away, hazy with memories. He was small and stocky, yet immensely strong. He was dressed in a shirt with the sleeves rolled up above his elbows, a spotted neckcloth knotted carelessly about his throat. His feet were encased in boots with leather leggings buttoned each side as far as the knee. He wore breeches, worn and faded.

"I said, 'What's this place called', Pa?" Carrie prompted.

"Abbeyford."

"Are we going down?"

"I suppose so," he murmured.

"Why have we come here?"

"I've someone to see."

"Who? Someone you know? Have you been here before?"

"Aye. Twenty years ago 'n more, I lived here."

"Lived here?"

"I was born here."

"Really?" Eagerly her eyes scanned the valley. "Where? Which house?" She glanced at him and saw his gaze upon a square house just below them, standing halfway up the western hillside of the valley.

Innocently she asked, "Is that the house you were born in?"

Evan Smithson's laugh was more bitter than humorous. "Nay, child. The likes of us aren't born into Manor Houses. No," his eyes swivelled and dropped to the cottages nestling in the bottom of the valley. "*We're* born into hovels!"

"What about your parents? Are they still here?"

His eyes were on her, angry and resentful. Inwardly Carrie shrank a little but she gave no outward sign of fear and faced her father squarely.

"How the devil should I know?" he muttered. Carrie was shocked, but her questions ran on.

"Would you ever have come back, if it hadn't been for the railway coming this way?"

Carrie had never known any way of life other than the one they lived now. Her father – as far as she knew – had always been a ganger, the man in charge of the gangs of navvies building the new railways, his family moving after him wherever his work took him. As the railway lines extended slowly forward throughout the countryside, the Smithson family shifted once more, always moving a few miles in front of the line, living there until the line caught up with them and passed them by and then moving on once more. Home was a derelict cottage, a shack or even a farmer's barn. Sometimes their shelter was a mere tent of boughs and a tarpaulin, or a hastily constructed hut of stone and turf. Their possessions were few and loaded with monotonous regularity on to the pony and trap – their one means of removal.

"Aye, I'd have come back, some time, some day. I've unfinished business hereabouts."

"What?"

"You ask too many questions, girl," Evan growled and began to walk briskly down the hill towards the village. As she followed him Carrie's eyes still took in the scene before her. She pointed to the house she had imagined might have been her father's home. It was a square, solid house, with stables to one side and farm buildings to the rear.

"What's that place called, then?" Carrie asked, refusing to be cowed by his sharpness.

"Abbeyford Manor."

"Who lives there?"

"How should I know?" he replied testily, but she had the distinct feeling that he knew very well. That house had drawn his gaze and there had been a glint of bitterness in his eyes as he remembered – memories he had no intention of sharing with his daughter.

"What are those ruins? Right on top of the hill – above the Manor?"

"The abbey ruins. That's how the village gets its name. We're coming to the ford now."

The stream ran right across the lane down which they

were walking towards the village. They crossed over by means of a small footbridge.

Carrie's restless eyes now turned to the eastern slope of the valley, where a half-timbered mansion – far grander than the Manor – stood just below the brow of the hill.

"What about that 'un? Who lives there?" Carrie's ceaseless curiosity continued.

"Abbeyford Grange. Used to be a Lord Royston live there. I 'spect he's dead now."

They were walking along the winding village street now. They passed the church in the centre of the village with the Vicarage close beside it and crossed the village green. Skirting the duck pond, they approached the line of small, squat cottages huddled around the green.

Carrie's sharp eyes darted about her. How quiet it seemed. How deserted almost. Many of the cottages were dilapidated. Broken windows were stuffed with sackcloth to keep out the cold and yet she could see that people still lived in them. Smoke curled from one or two chimneys and a scrawny black cat sprawled on a stone step, idly washing its face.

Evan stopped in front of one of the cottages facing the green and paused before reaching the door. This dwelling seemed in a better state of repair than the others. Bright flowers grew in the garden and pretty curtains blew at the windows. Carrie glanced back towards the next door cottage. Their window pane was broken, the remaining glass dirty and no curtains hung at the window. The garden was neglected and overgrown.

Evan knocked upon the door and Carrie stood on tiptoe, peering over his shoulder to see who would answer the door. When it opened, an old woman stood there, her eyes watering as she squinted up at them. Her hair was white and she stooped, her shoulders hunched, her thin, claw-like hand clasping her shawl about her.

"Who is it?" she asked in a quavering voice. "I can't see so well."

"Don't you know your own son, Mother?"

Carrie gasped to hear her father's tone of voice. There was no affection but a kind of belligerence in his words of greeting. The old woman's toothless mouth sagged open and she swayed slightly. Shading her eyes, she peered closely at him. "Evan? Is it – Evan?"

"Who else might it be? You have no other son, have you?"

A peculiar kind of choking sound escaped her thin lips. Again she seemed about to topple over. Carrie darted forward and caught hold of the woman's arm.

"Here, Grandmother, let me help you." She led the old lady back into the cottage and helped her to sit beside a blazing log fire. "There. We've given you a shock, coming unexpectedly like this."

She turned her brilliant eyes upon her father. "How can you be so unfeeling," she hissed at him, but Evan Smithson merely shrugged his shoulders and glanced about the cottage. "Been some changes here, I see."

Carrie, too, glanced around and then she jumped as she realised there was someone else in the tiny room. In a corner by the fire, sitting huddled in a chair, a rug over his knees was an old man. His eyes glowered towards Evan and his thin hands, lined with purple veins, plucked restlessly at the rug on his knee.

"Well, well, well," Evan, too, had seen him and moved towards the old man. "You're still here then?"

"No thanks to you if I am. Crippled, I am, because of what you did ..."

"Hush, Henry," the old woman murmured worriedly.

"... Crippled ever since that night you led the whole village against the Trents, just because ..."

"No, Henry," her voice rose, shrill with fear, and his faded away to incoherent mutterings, and though Carrie strained to hear his words she could learn no more.

Evan's glance was still roving about the small room – the singing kettle on the hob, a rug covering the floor, two comfortable chairs and a blazing fire.

"Very cosy! Very comfortable!" Sarcasm lined his tone. "Put his hand in his pocket at last, did he?"

The old woman glanced at her son, her eyes pleading, her shrivelled mouth working but she uttered no sound. Evan's eyes, full of resentment, were upon his mother.

Intuitively, Carrie knew her father was not referring to Henry Smithson, huddled in the corner, a broken, pitiful figure. There was some mystery surrounding this household, events from the past which overshadowed the present and perhaps all their lives. She shuddered, and then to try to relieve the tense atmosphere, she said brightly, "I'm so happy to meet you, Grandma – and Grandpa, of course," she added hastily.

The old man's frown deepened and beneath his breath he still muttered darkly. Sarah Smithson tried, valiantly, to smile, but all the while her eyes, anxious and watchful, were upon her son.

"He's still alive, then?" Evan said.

Before his mother could answer, Henry Smithson's voice rose, more strongly, from the corner. "Aye, God rot his soul! Still up to his wicked ways – gambling and drunk most o' the time. Keeps selling land off to pay his debts."

Evan's interest sharpened visibly. He moved closer to the

old man. "What d'you say? Selling land? How can he – he dunna own it?"

Henry Smithson sniggered. "A lot's happened since you left. That night – when you led the village men against the Trents – caused a lot of trouble and we've had to live with it ever since."

Evan brought his fist down upon the table with a thump. "We had every reason to rebel – the whole country was up in arms against the Corn Law. Remember Peterloo? How the magistrates called out the yeomanry to charge upon a peaceful meeting, killing and maiming innocent men, women and children?"

"Aye an' Wallis Trent did the same, didn't he? Called out the yeomanry against his own employees. Killed three and injured several – including me," Henry Smithson said bitterly. "I nearly died – wish to God I had. But I didn't, I've had to sit here the last twenty years – useless – and curse your name!"

Carrie gasped, shocked by the venom in the old man's tone. There was positive hatred in his attitude towards Evan, who, she believed, was his own son.

"Evan," Sarah's voice was hesitant, "did you know – Wallis Trent was killed that night?"

Evan turned sharply to look at his mother, surprise on his face. "No – no, I didn't. How? In the fire?"

"No – well, not exactly. He tried to rescue his horse from the burning stable," Sarah's eyes were downcast. "But the animal was wild with fear, reared and came down upon him, breaking his neck."

There was silence in the room whilst Carrie's eyes darted from one to another, trying to piece together the snippets of information she was hearing. She longed to ask for explanations but bit her lip to keep the ready questions in check.

Now was not the time.

"Adelina – what happened to his wife, Adelina?"

"She married Lord Lynwood."

Evan grinned suddenly. "Adelina – Lady Lynwood! Aye, an' it'll suit her, too."

Carrie's eyes widened. All these people her father seemed to know so well, she'd never heard of them, never heard him even speak of them. But then, she thought she had not even known before today that his own mother and father were still alive. She sat down on a low stool, resting her chin on her hands, her elbows on her knees and listened to their conversation, her sharp ears missing nothing, her violet eyes darting from one to another, but, for once, her tongue was still.

"What's this about *him* selling land?" her father was asking again.

"Lord Royston died and split his estate between Francesca, Adelina's daughter, and Jamie Trent. He left Abbeyford Grange and land to the north to her and the Manor and about five hundred acres to Jamie Trent," Henry explained.

"That was Wallis Trent's boy," Evan murmured.

"Squire Trent," Sarah spoke softly, "has control until Jamie reaches the age of twenty-five."

"And in the meantime," Henry added with malicious delight, "the old man has sold more than half of it off already!"

"Has he, b'God?" There was satisfaction in Evan's tone.

Within minutes Evan had taken his leave of his parents and hustled Carrie out of the door, scarcely giving her time to make her polite farewells. It was as if the sole purpose of his visit had been to find out about the Trents and having done so, he left.

He was striding up the village street towards the hill with Carrie taking little running steps to keep pace with him.

He seemed, now, a man with a purpose, as if the information he had learned had injected new life into his blood.

"Pa – Pa – what was all that about? What happened here? What was that about you and the villagers and the Trents? Pa ...?"

"Hold your tongue, girl. 'Tis none of your business."

Carrie fell silent, pouting her lips and wrinkling her nose moodily, but she knew better than to push her father or she would feel the weight of his hand.

Halfway up the hill, a horseman came galloping towards them. Drawing level, he reined in beside them. Carrie gazed up at the man on horseback towering above them. He was a young man of twenty or so, very tall and already broad-shouldered. His hair was dark brown with reddish highlights glinting in the sun. His face tanned and his eyes a deep brown, his chin was firm and resolute and his mouth set in a hard line. "Good-day."

Evan folded his arms across his chest and stood looking up at the young man. "Good-day – *sir*!" There was an unnecessary accent upon the salutation.

Carrie felt her pulses quicken as the young man's eyes strayed towards her. A slow smile touched his lips, softening their hardness, and his sombre expression lightened. "How do you do, Miss – er ...?"

"Smithson. Carrie Smithson," she replied and smiled in return.

"I'm happy to meet you. My name is Jamie Trent."

Carrie's eyes widened and her lips parted in a gasp. She

glanced swiftly at her father and saw that his eyes had narrowed calculatingly.

"I don't think I have seen you hereabouts before," Jamie Trent was saying, his eyes still upon Carrie's face. "Are you visiting?"

"My father is the ..." Carrie had been about to say that her father was the ganger on the new railway, but Evan interrupted her. "We are visiting relatives, Mr Trent. Come, Carrie, it's time we were on our way."

His manner was curt, almost rude, and Carrie saw Jamie Trent's eyebrows rise fractionally and he glanced briefly towards her father, but it was Carrie to whom he spoke again. "I'll bid you good-day then, Miss Smithson. I hope we'll meet again."

Before she could utter a word, Jamie Trent had urged his horse forward and was soon cantering down the hill away from them. Carrie's violet eyes followed him.

"Come along, girl," Evan said roughly. Reluctantly Carrie turned and followed her father, but all the way up the hill she kept glancing back towards the now tiny figure of the young man on horseback.

Some three miles to the north of Abbeyford, at the top of a rise, they stopped to look down at the workings of the railway below. Like an open wound, the railway gouged its way through farmland, woodland, rock, over water, even through hillsides. The gang of navvies over whom Evan Smithson was the ganger, scurried about like a colony of working ants. As they neared the site, Carrie could see the men, some stripped to the waist under the hot summer sun, shovelling the earth and rocks into the carts which, when loaded, were pulled away by horses, five hundred or so men and over one hundred and fifty horses, working over a three-mile stretch. Like their ganger, they found shelter wherever they could – in empty village cottages, in barns, sleeping two or three to a makeshift bed, some even with their wives and families sharing the harsh life. They worked hard and yet throughout the country the navvies had a bad reputation for causing havoc wherever they appeared. Not only did the railway itself meet with opposition from the country dwellers as it tore its way through their lands and their livelihood, but the arrival of five hundred hard-drinking, swearing navvies in a peaceful village was something to be feared.

Only the contractor's men who held a position of some importance – the engineer, the engine drivers, the foreman and skilled men – could find comfortable accommodation in the village. For the rest, the labouring navvies, it meant finding a bed wherever they could.

Yet there was a strange camaraderie amongst these ruffians, built like an army of Goliaths. They ate meat in huge amounts and consumed vast quantities of ale. They fought and gambled and yet they worked hard – exceedingly hard – with great courage, seeming to have a contemptuous disregard for even the most dangerous work. Whilst they appeared to have little respect for the various communities upon which they descended, there was loyalty amongst themselves and when any of their number suffered fatal injury, his brother-navvies would suddenly become a group of silent mourners at the nearest church.

"I'll be off home, now," Carrie said. She did not want to go too near the workmen. Not that she was afraid of them, for Caroline Smithson feared no one, not even her swift-tempered father, but the men's whistles and calls caused her an embarrassment she would sooner avoid. More than once she had had to skip smartly aside to avoid their reaching hands and once, when a hulking brute had managed to lay hold of her she had had to fight, claw and scratch her way free of his loathsome embrace. She admired the tenacity and pluck of the navvies as workmen, but she had no desire to lead this life for ever. There must be a better life than this, Carrie told herself, somewhere, somehow, and so she kept a safe distance from the lusty navvies.

"Make yourself presentable, girl," her father said. "Lloyd Foster will be calling. Brush your hair – you look like a gypsy!"

"Ain't surprisin'," Carrie retorted boldly, "since we live like gypsies." She began to run down the hill out of reach of her father's hand as he raised it to cuff her. His eyes glittered with momentary anger and then he laughed aloud, the breeze carrying the sound to the ears of the running girl so that she turned, grinned cheekily at him, waved briefly and then ran on. Of all his family, only Carrie dared to oppose her father or speak her mind and only she could do so and escape his vicious temper.

Nearing the shack which was the Smithsons' present dwelling-place, Carrie slowed her pace.

Lloyd Foster! She wrinkled her nose and her generous mouth pouted. She could see his horse tethered outside the shack and knew he was waiting for her.

Lloyd Foster was an important man – he was the Boss. He was the man who held the contract for the building of the railway and yet he was still a young man. He was a flamboyant character, loud, brash, even vulgar and yet likeable. At least, most people liked him, responding readily to his never-failing good humour, his happy-go-lucky manner. All except Carrie. Even though she knew Lloyd Foster wanted her, she refused to let herself like him.

Carrie peeped through the small, grimy window. She could see her mother sitting at the bare, scrubbed table, her elbows on the table, her hands cupped to hold her weary head. Her knuckles were misshapen, swollen and painful with the rheumatism which afflicted the whole of her body. She was looking towards the man who stood in front of the makeshift fireplace – Lloyd Foster. He was tall with dark, tanned skin, fair, curling hair, bright blue eyes and a wide and ever-laughing mouth. He was standing, tall and straight, his chest thrown out, rocking backwards and forwards slightly on his heels, his thumbs stuck into the armholes of his gaudy waistcoat. A thick cigar was clamped between his white, even teeth. His clothes were always of the finest material. His shirt was sparkling white and his riding-coat and breeches well cut. His black leather boots shone and always there was a gold watch chain looped across his broad chest.

Carrie sighed and pushed open the door. Lloyd Foster turned at once and made an exaggerated bow towards her, then spoilt the courtly gesture by smacking her on the backside as she passed close to him.

"I'll thank you to keep your hands to yourself, Mr Foster."

Lloyd Foster's loud laugh threatened to bring the dilapidated shack tumbling down about them. But Carrie merely glanced at him and moved out of reach again as he made to put his arm about her waist.

"Ah, Miss Carrie, an' don't I be lovin' you the more when you're angry." His rich Irish brogue mocked her good-humouredly. It was impossible to offend the man, Carrie thought, and in spite of herself she found the corners of her mouth twitching into the beginnings of a smile. It was very difficult to maintain a mood of anger with him

when all he did was laugh and tease and pay extravagant
compliments.

Lloyd Foster was something of an enigma. No one knew
anything about his background, only that he was a railway
builder – one of the best in the country and he was a clever
man with people, Carrie thought. The gangs of navvies who
worked on the western railways were often made up largely
of Irish and to hear their own delightful brogue from the
lips of the Boss himself ensured hard work and loyalty from
them. The railway site rang with his boisterous laughter
and the workmen's faces, glistening with sweat, would
break into a grin at the sight of the tall man on his horse.
Also, he was reputedly generous to a fault towards his
employees, so much so that other contractors on rival lines
grumbled that he attracted all their best navvies into his
gangs!

"I'm supposed to be here on a matter of business wid
your father, me darlin', but 'tis all a devious plot, for me
eyes were hungry for sight of your lovely face."

Carrie raised her eyebrows cynically and glanced at her
mother.

Lucy Smithson sat at the table, leaning wearily against
it, her eyes dark pools of suffering and bitterness. The years
of itinerant living had treated her harshly. Her once black
hair was now grey and dull. Her body was thin and
shapeless, her hands wrinkled and work-worn. Lucy had
borne seven children of whom only four now survived. The
others were buried in different parishes, their unmarked
graves in churchyards alongside the railway line. One had
died of typhoid and two of consumption. And now Luke,
Lucy's first-born, suffered from that same terrible cough.
The two younger children, Tom and Matthew, only
fourteen and thirteen, yet already working on the railway
bed, were sickly too. Of all Lucy's children only Carrie,

now aged eighteen, was healthy, strong and resilient. And of all of them only Carrie was not afraid of Evan.

"Will ye be takin' a walk wid me, Miss Carrie?" Lloyd Foster was saying, bending towards her. Carrie opened her mouth to refuse but at that moment the door opened and Evan Smithson came in.

"Ah, an' now here's the man himself," Lloyd Foster said. "An' how is me darlin' railway comin' along under your guiding hand, Mr Smithson?"

Evan grinned and slapped Lloyd Foster on the back, for, although in theory, Lloyd Foster was his employer, in practice Evan enjoyed an unusual position of equality with him. Such was the amiability of Lloyd Foster that no one, not even the youngest navvy with the most menial task, was ever made to feel his inferior. He made each and every one of them feel that all of them together were building the railway.

Evan turned towards his wife and daughter, his face once more hard. He jerked his thumb in the direction of the door.

"Out – we've business to discuss."

Tiredly, Lucy levered herself and moved, without argument, towards the door, but Carrie, hands on hips, faced her father squarely. "Why? What's so secret?"

"None of your business, me girl. Get!"

"Ah, sure an' me lovely lass can stay if she'll sit an' hold me hand."

"Not *this* time," Evan said firmly. "We've men's affairs to talk on." He glanced meaningly at Foster, who shrugged, laughed, and slapping Carrie once more on the backside said, "Now don't you be goin' too far away, me girl."

Carrie moved towards the door of the shack. To her left hung an old brown curtain, dividing the small area where her parents slept from the rest of the shack. Carrie opened the door and then glanced back towards the two men. She was curious to know what lay behind her father's secretiveness. Their backs were towards her so she shut the door with a slam, as if she had left the shack, but instead she slipped stealthily behind the curtain. Her heart was beating rapidly as she sat quietly on the shakedown on the floor and pulled the worn blanket over her. Silent, she sat listening to the voices of the men, her father's sometimes low so that she had to strain to hear his words, but Lloyd Foster she could hear plainly.

"And what did ye find out then, me friend?" Foster was saying. She heard the rustle of paper and could only guess that her father was unfolding a map. She had seen them use one before to plan the route of the railway line.

"It's even better than I had hoped," Evan replied, and there was a kind of suppressed excitement in his tone. "The best route is right across the land which now belongs to the Trents. And Squire Guy Trent's tight for money. Drinks and gambles all his grandson's inheritance away. He's ripe, I tell you!" There was a dull thud as if Evan had thumped the table with his fist in his enthusiasm.

"Gambles, is it, you say? Ah, a man after me own heart! And where is it you think our railway should run?"

Again Carrie heard the rustle of paper and imagined their heads bent together over the map as she had seen them so many times. She heard her father's voice. "We continue south from where we are now, making a cutting through this small incline, then into Abbeyford valley, between the hills to the east and west. We'll need an embankment, but the best line would be between the Manor House and the stream and continue south out of the valley. We can get through the dip between these two lines of hills quite easily."

"Mmm," Lloyd Foster's tone was, for once, serious – the only time he was ever serious was when discussing his beloved railway. "I'll be needin' to survey the whole district. 'Tis me engineer's job by rights, but you know when 'tis me own livelihood I'm gamblin' I like to be seein' the cards for meself."

Carrie knew that, although a fine engineer by the name of Thomas Quincy, who also happened to be a surveyor, was employed on this line, Foster himself always surveyed the land and knew the workings of the line as well as any engineer. And she also knew that the money which built the railway was not his own but that of the Railway Board – men who invested capital into such schemes with the hope of becoming even richer than they already were.

There was a pause, then Foster added, "What about skirting these hills – avoidin' Abbeyford all together?"

"No!" Evan's tone was sharp. "To the east there's more hills and if you veer to the west you'll go through Lynwood's lands – not the Trents!"

"And will that be mattering?"

"Well – he'll demand a higher way-leave for his land. I reckon we'd be better to buy off a good deal of Trent's land – we ought to have a station or a halt hereabouts, anyway."

"Aye, maybe you're right as ever, me boy." Foster's ready laugh rang out. "You'll be takin' me job if I don't watch out. Tell me now, what is it about these Trents? Your face seems to change when you speak of them and you're determined the railroad shall run through their land, are ye not?"

"It's none of your concern," Evan growled.

Behind the curtain Carrie stifled a gasp. Despite Lloyd Foster's friendliness, he was still Evan's employer and she had never heard her father be deliberately rude to him before. But, even now, Foster took no offence. Reluctantly, Evan added, "I've an old score to settle. By rights, the Manor House should be mine!"

"Yours? How?" Foster's tone registered surprise, but that was nothing to the astonishment Carrie, in her hiding-place, felt.

"It's a long story," Evan muttered, his voice now so low that Carrie could scarcely hear. "Just take my word for it. I aim to ruin the Trents and live there mesel' – one day!"

"Well, now, me boy," Foster's hearty laugh rang out. "I just might be able to help you there. I have plans of me own, don't you know, and there's something *I* want – very much – that maybe *you* could be helpin' *me*."

"What's that?"

"Ah, now never mind for de moment. Maybe in time we'll both be gettin' what we want."

"Hmm, mebbe." Evan sounded doubtful. There was the rustle of paper again as he refolded the map. "Shall we go and have a look at the land?" It sounded as if Evan were trying to change the subject now. Carrie heard him move towards the door and the curtain shook. She froze, holding her breath, fearful her father would come behind the curtain and discover she had been eavesdropping.

Carrie heard the door slam and their footsteps move away from the shack and she breathed again. She waited some moments before moving from her cramped position till she was sure they had really gone. She thought about her father's bitter words. 'The Manor House should be mine ... I'll ruin the Trents and live there mesel'.'

The picture of Jamie Trent, the tall, handsome young man on horseback she had met but once, came before her mind's eye and inexplicably her heart began to beat a little faster at the thought of him.

TWO

Two days later, in the early afternoon, Carrie slipped away from the shack and, avoiding the railway workings, made her way across the fields and up the hill towards Abbeyford. She was determined to get to know her grandmother better, yet she had had the intuitive sense to keep her intentions secret.

Carrie tapped at the cottage door with some trepidation, remembering the unwelcoming figure of the hunched cripple in the corner – her grandfather, and yet he seemed to bear such hatred for his son, Evan.

The door opened and Sarah Smithson's wrinkled face lit up with pleasure at the unexpected visit from her grand-daughter. "Come in, my dear, come in."

Carrie followed her slow-moving steps into the small back scullery where they could talk freely without the malevolent presence of Henry Smithson's scowling face.

"Tell me about yourself, child." Her old eyes roved over the girl's lovely face, as if she would draw strength from Carrie's youthful vitality.

Carrie shrugged and smiled. "There's not much to tell. There were seven of us children, but three died in childhood. There's Luke – he's twenty, the oldest." A shadow flickered across her violet eyes, "but he's not strong. Then there's mesel' – I'm eighteen. Then there's Tom and Matthew – they're fourteen and thirteen. They all work on the railway – with Pa. I help Ma as best I can." She broke off and asked, "Do you know me Ma?"

"I might. Is her name Lucy?"

Carrie nodded.

Sarah Smithson sighed. "Yes, I thought so. Lucy Walters. She disappeared when Evan first left Abbeyford."

Carrie leant forward eagerly. "Grandma – will you tell me about me Pa? What caused him to leave home …?"

"No, no," the old woman cried sharply. "I cannot speak of it! He – he is not welcome here. People remember. He should not have come back." Her words were halting and painful to her, Carrie could see. She bit back the words of pleading which sprang to her lips. She could not cause her grandmother more pain by making her relive unpleasant memories, but she longed to learn the truth.

Some time later Carrie took her leave. The summer sun was warm upon her head, and in the quiet of the valley she felt a peace settle upon her. She wandered along the lane, reluctant to return to the shack she must call home. Her gaze roamed the hills on either side. The mansion to the east called Abbeyford Grange and then opposite the Manor House and above it, silhouetted sharply against the blue sky, gaunt and lonely, stood the abbey ruins. Intrigued to see them, Carrie took the lane leading towards Abbeyford Manor. As she drew level with the house she looked at it with interest. This was where Jamie Trent lived – and it was the house her father coveted. He had vowed to bring ruin to the Trent family because of some deep ill-will he bore them, some revenge he sought. His reasons, buried deep in the past, were a mystery to his daughter.

Even in the warm afternoon sun Carrie shivered, and

moved on up the lane past the gate leading to the Manor's stables and on up the hill towards the wood.

Beneath the trees it was cooler and shady and quiet save for the sounds of the woodland creatures. She took off her heavy clogs and delighted in the feel of the long grass on her bare feet. Joyously she skipped along, light-hearted and for once free from the cares of her harsh life.

As she emerged from the wood she stood a moment looking down on the valley below, her eyes tracing the line her father had suggested to Lloyd Foster that their railway should follow, entering the valley from the north and running alongside the stream directly in front of the Manor and on southwards to the natural pass out of the valley.

"Why," she spoke aloud in surprise, "the line will cut right through his pastures – and his cornfields!" She remembered her father's bitter words, 'I'll ruin the Trents', and she frowned thoughtfully. Perhaps he had planned the route to come through the Trents' land intentionally for the very purpose of ruining them.

She shaded her eyes against the sun. Carrie expected to see men working in the fields, but there seemed a strange lack in numbers. Certainly there were one or two tiny figures in the far distance, moving about their work in the fields. She saw a horseman cantering along the side of the stream and then turn up the hill towards her. As he drew closer she saw the rider was Jamie Trent. He reined in beside her and sat, tall and straight, upon his horse. He wore breeches and knee-boots and an open-necked shirt. His brow glistened with sweat and his shirt was stained darkly with the signs of hard labour.

Why, thought Carrie in surprise, he's been working in the fields alongside his labourers.

He was smiling down at her. "Miss Smithson. How good

it is to see you again." His voice was warm and deep, and Carrie's heart beat a little faster.

"Mr Trent," she murmured, almost shyly, though her eyes regarded him boldly, taking in every detail of his dark, handsome face, his deep brown eyes and rugged jaw line. He dismounted and stood beside her, the manly closeness of him quickening her pulses.

"I hoped we might meet again, but I had no idea where you came from – or why you came visiting Abbeyford."

"I – we – came to visit my grandmother, Mrs Smithson."

Jamie Trent's eyebrows rose a fraction. "Oh! I had no idea she had any children, let alone a granddaughter. Where do you live?"

"I – er ..." Carrie hesitated. Now she wanted to keep the fact that she was linked with the railway a secret from Jamie Trent. He could not welcome the railway which threatened the Trent farmlands – nor the people who built it! "We're staying, just temporary, over the hills there." She waved her hand vaguely in a northerly direction.

"May I escort you home? It's a long way and my horse will carry the two of us easily."

Carrie drew breath sharply, torn between the desire to remain in his company, close beside him on horseback and the wish to keep her identity a secret.

"I'd – be very glad of a ride, Mr Trent, but I don't like to trouble you ..."

"It's no trouble, Miss Smithson." His voice was low and his eyes were upon her face. "It will be my pleasure."

He lifted her easily on to his brown mare and mounted behind her. His arm circled her waist lightly, her shoulder was warm against his chest and she could feel his breath on her cheek. The horse moved on at walking pace, down the hill and then following the winding path of the stream.

Carrie, acutely aware of the whole time of his closeness, glanced up towards the Manor House – his home – as they passed before it.

"That's where you live, ain't it? It's a lovely house."

When he didn't answer at once, she glanced up at him, her eyes only inches from his face.

"It – could be," he said guardedly, offering no further explanation. Carrie bit back the questions on her lips, sensing that she could not probe into his life. Glancing again at the square, solid Manor House, she saw now that on closer inspection there was an air of neglect about it. The windows were dull, the paint peeling. The garden was overgrown with long grass and weeds. She didn't know what to say, so they rode in silence until Abbeyford was far behind them. Then Jamie Trent seemed to relax. He smiled down at her. "Are we taking the right direction? You still haven't told me where it is you're staying."

"Oh – er – about two miles further on. Are those fields yours?"

Again the frown was fleetingly across his handsome face. "Yes, and I'll see they stay that way."

Carrie's heart pounded. The railway! She guessed he referred to the railway trying to encroach upon his lands. But his brown eyes were looking down into her face, quite unaware that she belonged to the railway people.

"Tell me about yourself, Miss Smithson – Carrie, isn't it?"

She nodded. "There's not much to tell," her voice was husky. What could she tell him? Of her family's gypsy existence? Of their harsh way of life? About her father? No, no, she couldn't mention him – or the railway! And yet, that *was* her life!

He was smiling, interpreting her reticence as natural

shyness. "Oh I'm sure that's not so. You're – you're a very pretty girl."

She smiled a little shyly – she was unused to such gentle compliments.

"Please – tell me about your family?" she asked softly. Again his face darkened, but because it would be churlish to ignore such a direct request, he said slowly, "My parents are dead. So, too, is my grandmother – my father's mother. My own mother died giving birth to me. Now there's only my grandfather, Squire Guy Trent and myself."

"Oh, but I thought your mother ..." Carrie stopped, shocked that she had allowed her chattering tongue to slip.

"What?"

"No matter – please go on." But now her mind was in a turmoil.

"My father was killed in 1819 when I was only small."

"How – did it happen?" Her heart beat fast. She was almost afraid to hear his answer and yet she had to ask, she had to know.

"Oh, there was much unrest amongst the workers at that time, so my grandfather says, and one man who seemed to have a vendetta against the Trents led the villagers in revolt."

Carrie was not sure what the word 'vendetta' meant, but she could guess! Now she was silent.

"They threatened to march upon the Manor if my father did not give them better wages."

"And – and did they?" she asked faintly.

"Aye," Jamie Trent answered grimly. "But my father had been forewarned of this. My stepmother and my grandfather had, whilst out riding, come across a secret meeting of the village men in the abbey ruins. My father called out the yeomanry and as the village men marched upon the

Manor the soldiers galloped down upon them."

A vivid picture of the crippled old man – her own grand-father, she believed – flashed before her eyes. So that was how Henry Smithson had been maimed. And the revolt had been led by Evan Smithson, her own father. *He* was the man of whom Jamie spoke as having a – a vendetta against the Trent family. She frowned, vaguely remembering something else. It had been when her grandmother had been telling Evan that Wallis Trent – Jamie's father – had been killed that night. Now, what was it her father had said …?

"Was there a fire at the Manor?" she turned her violet eyes towards Jamie. His face only a breath away, his lips so close to her hair.

"Why, yes," there was surprise in his tone. "How did you know?"

"Oh – I – er – well," Carrie was flustered. There she went again, letting her curiosity outrun her. Why, why, did she not think before she spoke? "You said – you said they were marching on the Manor – I suppose they meant to do it damage – and fire …"

"Yes," Jamie agreed. "One of them – the leader – escaped, mainly, I believe, because my stepmother went to warn the villagers."

"Your stepmother?" Now it was Carrie's turn to show surprise.

"Yes. She did not agree with my father that the yeomanry should be called out. She tried to prevent the bloodshed."

"How very brave of her." Carrie said swiftly, and then once more regretted her hasty words. Perhaps Jamie had believed his father to be in the right.

"Or foolhardy – whichever way you like to look at it."

His tone gave nothing away.

"And – which way do you look at it?" she asked boldly.

She felt the sigh rise in his chest and then upon her hair. "I cannot judge. There was much bitterness. I understand my father was a hard man – hated by the villagers. Perhaps there was cause – I don't know. He was trying to rescue his favourite stallion from the burning stables. The animal was wild and killed him."

Carrie remembered now – that was what her grandmother, Sarah Smithson, had said.

"And your stepmother?"

Jamie smiled and there was a gentleness in his eyes. "She's Lady Adelina Lynwood now. She's very beautiful and has always been very kind to me. I'm very fond of her."

Adelina! Her father had spoken of her as if he had known her. But so he might have done, for she had been Wallis Trent's second wife and therefore mistress of the Manor for a while.

Now it was Jamie's turn to ask probing questions. "Your grandparents are Sarah and Henry Smithson?"

"Y-yes," Carrie answered guardedly, her heart beating fast again.

"Strange," Jamie murmured. "I had not heard of their son. He must have left home many years ago."

"I don't know," the words came out in a rush. "I didn't even know he came from hereabouts until the other day."

"Really? Has he never talked about his family or …?"

"You can put me down now, Mr Trent, I can walk the rest of the way. It's only over the next hill."

"Oh, please allow me to take you …"

"No, no," Carrie said, wriggling a little as if to slide from the horse. "Me Pa, if he sees me with you, he'll like as not beat me."

"Oh, I see." Suddenly Jamie grinned making his usually serious face seem boyish and mischievous. "I wouldn't like that!"

"Nor would I!" Carrie retorted with feeling and grinned back at him. Their shared secret meeting seemed to bring them close.

He dismounted and held up his arms towards her and she slid from the horse's back into them. He did not release her immediately but stood looking down at her.

"Carrie – oh Carrie," his voice was suddenly husky. "You've the loveliest eyes I've ever seen ..."

Without warning his arms were strong iron bands about her and his mouth was hot upon hers. Readily Carrie responded to his kisses, her heart pounding fiercely. At last they drew apart, their eyes shining, their hot breath mingling, startled by the suddenness, the newness of this emotion.

"I'll – see you again?" he whispered.

Carrie, innocent of all guile, nodded, her mind in a turmoil. Hastily, suddenly afraid they'd be seen, she broke away from him and ran up the hill.

"Tomorrow?" he called after her. She paused in her flight, turned and waved. He returned her wave and then she was running up the hill again, her feet hardly touching the ground, her heart singing. At the top she turned. He was sitting astride his horse now, but still watching her.

He waved again and she lifted her hand in farewell, then Jamie turned his horse and cantered back towards Abbeyford.

When he was a small speck in the distance, Carrie turned and began to walk slowly down the other side of the hill towards the railway workings.

Carrie's mood of joy was short-lived. As she neared the bank overlooking the railway workings she saw her three brothers climbing towards her.

Luke, the eldest, was in the centre, leaning heavily upon the two younger boys, who themselves looked scarcely to have the strength to help him. All three were thin, their clothes ragged and they were covered – clothes, skin and hair – in the grey dust from the stone they had hewn since early morning. It was early for them to be coming home, and Carrie ran to them in alarm, fearful that Luke must have been hurt in some accident.

"What is it? What's the matter?" she cried anxiously, swiftly taking the place of Tom at Luke's side.

" 'Ee's bin coughin' 'is guts up!'' volunteered Matt, and as Carrie searched the thin, sickly face of her elder brother, her heart gave a lurch. There was a thin trickle of blood at the corner of his mouth. She'd seen that before. One of the other children, who had died of consumption a year back, had coughed up blood!

"Dunna let on to Pa," Luke gasped, "that we've come away 'afore time."

" 'Course I won't," Carrie replied with affectionate impatience and gave his shoulder a squeeze. "What d'you take me for?"

As they neared the shack, a handsome gig pulled by a high-stepping pony and carrying two women came lurching down the cart-track towards them. The older woman, holding the reins, pulled the pony to a halt beside Carrie and her brothers. Carrie stared open-mouthed at the two women – ladies without doubt. She had never seen such finery – silk dresses and bonnets, with delicate lace trimmings. The older one, whom she presumed to be the younger girl's mother, was still a beautiful woman, with smooth skin, green eyes and lovely auburn hair arranged to frame her face. The younger girl, too, was undoubtedly pretty but there was a discontented pout to her mouth and a coldness in her blue eyes. She twirled the parasol she held and sighed with boredom. The older lady was returning Carrie's gaze with equal interest, almost as if she half-recognised the girl and yet could not recollect where or when she had seen her before. But Carrie was quite certain that she had never before seen this lovely lady – she would not have forgotten!

"Are you belonging the railway?" the lady asked, her voice low and sweet with a slightly strange accent. American, Carrie thought, for she remembered a Yankee who'd worked as a navvy for a time had spoken the same way.

"Yes, ma'am." The courtesy came naturally to her lips. "Me Pa's the ganger."

The lady's eyes were puzzled.

"He's in charge o' the navvies – workmen, ma'am," Carrie explained.

"Oh, I see. Then is he the man who plans the way the railway should go?"

"Not really. That's the contractor or the engineer an' surveyor."

"Then I guess it's one of them I want to see. Could you tell me where I might find them?"

"Well ..." Carrie hesitated and glanced at Luke.

Her brother's eyes were fixed, mesmerised, upon the young girl sitting beside her mother in the gig.

"Luke, do you know where Lloyd Foster might be?"

Luke did not answer. Carrie prodded him gently. "Luke ...?"

He jumped. "What?"

"I said do you know where Lloyd Foster is?"

Luke, his eyes still fixed upon the girl, said, "I dunno –
oh, down near the bed, I think."

"That's the railway workings, ma'am," Carrie said.

"Thank you, I ..."

At that moment there was a rattle behind them and the
shack door flew open.

"What the devil ...?" As Carrie heard her father's voice
raised in anger, she saw the lady's eyes move from Carrie's
face to look beyond her. The lovely woman's green eyes
widened and her lips parted in a shocked gasp. Her face
turned pale. She must have pulled, involuntarily, upon the
reins, for suddenly the pony whinnied and shied, tipping
the little gig dangerously. The young girl gave a delicate
shriek of alarm whilst her mother fought to control not only
the animal but also her own runaway emotions.

Carrie felt Luke shake off her supporting arm and move
forward to help, but already Evan Smithson had moved
swiftly and calmly to the horse's head and Luke's gangling
figure stood uselessly by, his gaze once more returning to
the girl's face.

Evan, stroking the horse's nose, grinned up at the woman
in the gig. Carrie watched, fascinated.

"You!" the woman breathed. Words seemed to desert
her, for she just said again, as if she could not believe it,
"You!"

"Aye, m'lady. It's me." Then, almost insolently, he
added, "I'm gratified you ain't forgotten me."

The colour was returning to her face. "As if I could!" she
muttered bitterly. Then her glance rested briefly upon
Carrie and her brothers. "Are these your – children?"

Evan nodded. "I married Lucy – you remember her?"

"I do."

Evan's grin widened and he laughed aloud. "She's changed – you'd scarce recognise her now."

"I don't doubt life with you has altered her," the lady said wryly. Then she nodded towards Carrie. "But she has the look of her grandmother – Sarah."

Evan's eyes hardened with bitterness.

"So," the lady was saying thoughtfully, "you're a railway builder now, are you?"

"Yes, my lovely lady, I am."

"And where – exactly – might your railway be going?"

Evan's eyes glinted. "You've naught to fear, m'lady. 'Twill not cross your land."

A small sigh escaped the beautiful woman's lips and she said flatly, with what Carrie thought to be exceptional insight, "Across the Trents' land, I suppose?"

Then Carrie realised the lady was not merely guessing. This lovely woman knew her pa, and her ma and grandma, and knew, too, that Evan was planning to cross the Trents' land with his railway, and the tone of her voice told Carrie that she knew, too, the reasons behind his plan. She knew why he planned to ruin the Trents!

"Can't you leave them alone? Haven't you had enough revenge – even yet?" she asked Evan in a low voice.

Slowly Evan shook his head, his mouth set.

"Then I'll bid you good-day, Mr Smithson." She slapped the pony with the reins at the same moment Evan let go of the animal's head.

"Good-day, my lovely Adelina," Evan murmured softly, more to himself, for the gig was already bouncing away from them over the rough track. His eyes followed its progress.

"Pa?" Luke and Carrie spoke together. "Who was that?" "Who are they?"

For a moment Evan did not answer, his eyes still upon the disappearing vehicle.

"Lady Adelina Lynwood."

Carrie gasped. So that was Jamie Trent's stepmother.

"And the girl? Who was the lovely girl?" Luke, with unusual boldness, persisted, his eyes too following the two women.

Evan shrugged. "Her daughter, I suppose."

Luke, still gazing up the track, began to cough, his thin body shaking. The sound seemed to break Evan's reverie. "What you doin' home so early, eh?" he asked roughly.

" 'Twas Luke," Matt piped up. " 'Ee's sick."

"Sick?" Evan scoffed. "We've no time to be sick, boy. We've a railway to build!"

Carrie flared angrily. "Don't be so heartless, Pa. Can't you *see* he's ill – like – like ..." She bit her tongue and glanced hastily at Luke, but he was oblivious to them all, his gaze even yet straining for sight of the gig, even though moments before it had dropped down a slope and disappeared from view.

"Ill – me foot!" Evan gave a click of exasperation, and his resentful gaze included not only Luke but his two younger sons also. "Why she can only bear me wreckling sons, I dunnot know." Then his eyes rested upon Carrie. "Still, there's you, me lass, ain't there." He pinched her cheek with a rough gesture which was the closest Evan Smithson would ever come to a sign of affection. "Mebbe *you'll* be the one to help me get what I want, eh?"

Without further explanation Evan strode away, his strange words bringing an inexplicable chill to his daughter's heart.

The following day Carrie was unable to slip away over the

hill to Abbeyford to meet Jamie Trent. Luke stayed in the shack, too ill to drag himself to the railway site, and Carrie, whilst wanting to nurse her brother, chafed inwardly at her enforced captivity. She was unusually impatient with him, fretting for fear Jamie would misinterpret her absence and would think that she no longer wished to meet him, when in truth her heart yearned for sight of him.

Luke lay on the straw shakedown with only an old coat as a cover and stared at the rough boards of the roof, his thoughts far away from the harsh surroundings. Carrie had a shrewd idea what – or rather who – filled his thoughts and this was confirmed when Luke said pensively, "I don't think I've ever seen such a beautiful girl."

Carrie sniffed derisively. "Huh! Anyone can be beautiful if they're rich. She looked right uppity to me."

Luke raised himself on his elbow. "How can you judge when you dunna know her?"

"Then how can *you* judge?" she retorted sharply.

"I ..." But whatever he had been going to say was cut off by an attack of coughing, after which he lay back exhausted.

"There, you see, you go upsetting yourself and making yourself worse."

"I just wanted to know – who she is – that's all," Luke said weakly.

"Yes – yes, all right," Carrie soothed, contrite now that her arguing with him had brought on a coughing fit. "I'll – see if I can find out more about her, but try to rest now."

Luke closed his eyes and slept.

So it was three days before Carrie's flying feet took her over the hills once more to Abbeyford.

As she topped the hill overlooking the village she scanned

the fields anxiously for sight of Jamie – but she could not see him.. Then she was running pell-mell down the hill towards the squat cottages where her grandparents lived. She had decided to visit her grandma each time she came to see Jamie, thereby establishing some kind of alibi for herself should her Pa ever hear of her visits to Abbeyford and question her.

The old woman's eyes glowed as she saw Carrie again. "My dear child, come away in!"

After she had spent a pleasant half-hour chatting with the old lady in the kitchen of the small cottage Carrie grew restless, anxious to be off now in search of Jamie. Then she remembered her promise to Luke.

"Grandma, a fine carriage came by the railway the other day. Pa said it was Lady Adelina Lynwood."

The pleasure died on Sarah Smithson's face, her eyes were suddenly once again wary and pain-filled and her shrunken lips trembled. "Oh – was it?" she murmured guardedly, now avoiding her granddaughter's eyes when moments before she had gazed fondly into Carrie's face.

"Yes. There was a young girl with her – a year or two older than me, I should think. Who would she be, Grandma?"

Sarah sighed heavily, then said. "I suppose it would be her daughter, Francesca."

"Oh, is she a Trent, then?" Carrie asked, interested in anyone who might be connected with Jamie.

After a moment's hesitation, Sarah said flatly, "No – she's Lynwood's daughter. I – used to be quite friendly with Adelina – Lady Lynwood – once. She came from America and had a daughter by Lord Lynwood before she was married."

Carrie gasped, but listened.

"Then she left Lynwood. They quarrelled — and she married Wallis Trent. But it was not a happy marriage. He was a hard, cold man who treated his employees — and I guess his wife too — as possessions and bent everyone to his will." She sighed as she remembered. "Then there was unrest amongst the farm workers."

Carrie nodded, compressing her lips. "Led by Pa?"

Sarah glanced fearfully at her but was obliged to nod agreement.

"Then I suppose," Carrie continued, guessing the end of the story before Sarah had finished the telling of it. "When Wallis Trent was killed, she was reunited with Lord Lynwood. How romantic!"

Sarah murmured bitterly, "Romantic, you call it, eh? Real life is not at all romantic. It's cruel and harsh and ..." She stopped, startled at herself for unleashing her own emotions which had been stifled for many years. "I've said too much," she muttered roughly. "It's time you were going, girl."

Surprised by her grandmother's swift change of mood, Carrie left. She had found out what she wanted to know and now she wanted to meet Jamie. She took the lane towards the Manor House, but the only sounds were the twittering of the birds in the hedgerows and the rustling of the creatures in the long grass. The sun was hot on her head and her bare feet became covered with the dry dust from the lane. She drew level with the Manor House and stood at the gate leading into the stableyard. Everywhere was still and silent — no sign of activity in the yard, no sound of stamping, restless horses in their stalls. No stable-boys cleaning up the yard — which it needed badly, Carrie thought. Even the gate was off its hinges.

As she stood staring at the neglected yard a man

appeared round the corner of the stables. He walked with a shambling gait, weaving first right, then left. Drunkenness was no stranger to Carrie. She frequently saw its effects upon the navvies after every pay-out. And her pa, too.

As the man neared her, Carrie could see he was elderly with white wispy hair. His complexion was florid, almost purple, and his eyes bleary. He was grossly, uncomfortably overweight, and his ageing suit – once of fine material and well cut – now scarcely fitted him.

This must be Jamie's grandfather – Squire Trent.

He caught sight of her standing there watching him and he stopped and blinked, as if trying to focus his vision. Then he lurched towards her until he was standing in front of her. His gaze was fixed upon her face, then his mouth sagged open as he whispered brokenly. "Sarah!"

Carrie smiled uncertainly. "My name is Caroline – Carrie – Smithson."

"Caroline – Smithson? No – no, you're Sarah – my lovely Sarah!" He stretched out his arms and made as if to catch hold of her, but Carrie stepped back quickly.

"No – no, don't be afraid. I'll not ..." he hiccuped and then belched noisily, "hurt you, Sarah. I'll not hurt you again."

"My name is not Sarah, it's ..." Carrie stopped as the realisation struck her swiftly. Her grandmother's name was Sarah. Maybe her likeness to her grandmother was such that this old man, in his befuddled state, had turned back the years and mistaken her for Sarah Smithson.

But why, Carrie wondered, should Squire Trent address her grandmother in such a familiar, intimate manner?

Now he was rubbing his eyes with the back of his hand, miserably confused. "Caroline – not Sarah, not my Sarah? Then who are you. Why do you look like my love?"

His love? Carrie recoiled. Surely he could not be referring to her grandmother, that shrunken little old woman, care-worn and with lines of bitterness engraved by the years upon her face?

At that moment there was the sound of a horse's hooves in the lane and Carrie saw Jamie cantering towards them. He slid from his mount and ran towards her, his dark eyes afire.

"Carrie – you've come, at last!"

Oblivious of his grandfather's presence he stood close to her, taking both her hands in his and raising them gently to his lips. The old man forgotten, Carrie gazed up into Jamie's eyes.

"I'm sorry," she said, excitement making her sound breathless. "I couldn't come – before. It was Luke – my brother. He was ill and I had to – look after him."

Jamie was smiling down at her. "I wondered why you did not come. But everything's all right now you're here."

"Yes," she whispered, their eyes still locked in a timeless gaze.

"Mus' be going," the old man muttered and shuffled away, his shoulders sagging with disappointment, but neither Carrie nor Jamie even glanced in his direction.

"Let me stable my horse and we'll go for a walk," Jamie said and Carrie nodded.

A little while later, their fingers interlaced, they were walking side by side up the lane towards the shady intimacy of the wood. Once beneath the sheltering trees, Jamie stopped and gently took her by the shoulders and turned her to face him. His lips brushed her forehead, her closed eyes and then found her mouth with a tender sweetness which thrilled her fast-beating heart. Never had she known such gentleness in a man. Certainly she had never seen it in her father, nor even in Lloyd Foster, who, despite his open admiration and desire for her, was brash in his approach.

Jamie's hands smoothed her long black hair and ran down her back coming to rest on her slender waist. Responding to his ardour, Carrie slipped her arms about his neck and pressed herself against his lithe, strong body. They could feel each other's heart beating through the thin clothes they wore this hot summer day.

Breathless they drew apart, their eyes afire with their new, overwhelming emotion.

"Oh, Carrie," he said softly, his fingers tracing the outline of her face. "My lovely, lovely Carrie," and he drew her once again into his embrace.

Much later they emerged from the wood, happiness shining from their faces.

"I must go back," Carrie murmured, but her words held no firm intention.

"No – stay. I can't bear to let you go now that I've found you. I didn't know one could fall in love so quickly." His eyes caressed her, making her heart sing. Never had she felt this way about any man before. So this was love and for Carrie, with her strong character, it was deep and lasting. "I didn't know it could be this way either," she whispered.

An hour later, Carrie, fearful her father's wrath would prevent further clandestine meetings with Jamie, said, "I really must go – but I'll try to come again tomorrow."

"I could come to your home ..."

"No!" she said sharply, and then for fear her brusqueness had given offence, she put her hands upon his chest and stood on tiptoe to kiss him gently. "Not yet – I don't know what my folks would say. I don't want to tell them – yet."

Jamie smiled indulgently. "Yes, that's how I feel. I want it to be our own secret from all the world."

"Where – where shall I meet you?" she asked.

Jamie pointed. "How about the abbey ruins, mid-afternoon?"

Again he kissed her and then she was running up the hill out of Abbeyford.

THREE

" 'Tis time we started on that little bit of a cutting to the north of the village and on the embankment through the valley itself, me boy."

They were standing at the edge of the woods, just above the Manor, overlooking Abbeyford village.

"Aye," Evan Smithson grinned. "Have you got the way-leave yet?"

Lloyd Foster rubbed his chin and laughed. "Yes – and no."

"What do you mean?"

"Yes, I've got the *way* planned, but not the 'leave'," and Evan joined in his laughter. "But I'm workin' on it, m'boy. The old man and me – we've got dis nice game o' cards goin'. Running up a peach of a debt to me, the man is." He shook his head. "Poor ol' divil, 'tis breakin' me heart, so it is!" But his grin belied his words.

Evan snorted. "Dunna waste your sympathy on *him*! He dunna deserve none."

Foster's eyes surveyed the line his railway would run. "And way over there," he mused, "to the south of the village, where there's that natural pass between the hills, we could have an unstaffed halt. Abbeyford Halt. I don't reckon it needs a station, for it'll only serve Abbeyford and Amberly."

Evan nodded with satisfaction. "Aye, an' it's still *his* land we'd be tekin'."

A girl was climbing the hill towards them, her head bent so as to avoid stubbing her bare feet on the rough ground.

"Isn't that me darlin' girl?" Foster narrowed his eyes against the bright sun.

Evan's mouth tightened. "Aye, it's Carrie. What the devil's she doin' here?"

Silently they watched her approach and it was not until she was almost up to them that she lifted her head and saw them.

She stopped and the joy disappeared from her face, her eyes darkened with fear and the smile faded from her lips as Evan stepped towards her menacingly. "Where've you been, girl?" Roughly he grasped hold of her arm.

Carrie winced but clenched her teeth against crying out. "To see me grandma," she lied glibly. Evan shook her. "Who gave you leave?"

"No – no one."

"You stay at home where you belong."

Carrie wrenched herself free and rubbed her arm. She turned to face him, her eyes blazing with anger now. "Home! You call that – that *hovel* – home?"

Evan's blow was swift and well aimed and before Carrie had time to spring back his hand had met her cheek like the crack of a pistol shot.

It was then that Lloyd Foster sprang forward, one arm went round Evan's throat in a vice-like grip, the other arm holding his arms behind his back. Evan gasped for breath as Foster, his mouth close to Evan's ear, all sign of joviality gone in a moment, muttered, "Don't you ever lay a finger on dat girl again, me boy. Not while I'm around. D'ya hear me now?"

Evan's face grew purple and he began to choke whilst Carrie watched in amazement at the sudden change in Lloyd Foster's manner.

"D'you *hear*?" he asked again, jerking his arm even tighter around Evan's throat. Evan's 'yes' was little more than a squeak.

"Dat's better," Foster released his hold and turned to Carrie, his face still unsmiling. "You'd best be off home, me lovely. I'll talk to yer da."

Carrie glanced once at her father – once was enough to read the malice in his eyes.

She turned and ran.

For a few moments Foster watched her until she disappeared amongst the trees, then he turned back to Evan. He laid his hand on his shoulder, now in a gesture of friendship. "Ach, I'm sorry about that, me boy. But – I have dis feeling for dat girl of yours, don't you know?"

"She's still *my* daughter," Evan said gruffly, more angry to have been made to look foolish in front of Carrie than over the physical hurt Foster had momentarily inflicted.

"I know, I know," Foster's tone was placating now, his hand still on Evan's shoulder. "But I have this plan in me mind. Maybe I'd better be telling you about it." He paused and then went on. "Ye see, I want that girl of yours. I've a mind to wed her."

He let his words sink into Evan's mind before he went on again. "And I want to strike out for pastures new. England's too small. There's a whole *world* out there waiting – just waiting for me railroads. You see, me darlin' boy, what I t'ought was dis. If you'll give me the hand of yer lovely daughter in holy matrimony, we'll be away across the seas to make our fortunes. And," he stood back facing Evan as he delivered the final coup, "And I'll be givin' *you* the contract I hold to build the rest of *this* railway! Now, what d'you say to that, me boy?"

Evan stared at him for several moments in total disbelief. "You'll *give* me the contract?"

"Aye."

"Why in hell's name should you give me anything?"

Foster spread his hands wide and cast his eyes heavenwards in a gesture of mock despair. "An' haven't I been tellin' you, you'll be givin' me your daughter. An' to my way of t'inking, I'll be getting the best o' the bargain. Oh," he rolled his eyes, "to see dat lovely girl dressed in silks and satins. She'll be like a queeen, she will, to be sure."

Evan's eyes glittered suddenly and he turned his gaze away from Foster to look down at the village of Abbeyford.

"Then," he murmured more to himself than to Foster, "it'll be *me* building the railway across his land!"

There was silence. Then Evan turned and held out his hand to Lloyd Foster. "It's a bargain!"

Foster clasped Evan's hand delightedly and his ready laugh rang out across the hills.

Carrie waited in fear for the return of her father that evening, trying to think of a way to avoid him. The shack was so cramped that unless she were to go somewhere right away there was no escape.

But Evan appeared in a very jovial, hearty mood, surprising not only Carrie but her mother and brothers too. Far from berating her further, he kept glancing at his daughter and grinning as if sharing some secret with her. Carrie and her mother exchanged looks and Carrie lifted her shoulders in a shrug, signifying that she, too, was mystified by her father's unusually good mood.

Since her father had not questioned her any more about her visits to Abbeyford, Carrie's desire and love for Jamie, which daily grew stronger, made her risk another visit the following afternoon.

She followed the lane up towards the Manor and as she rounded a bend she saw ahead of her the gig belonging to Lady Lynwood. Seated in the stationary gig was Lady Adelina and her daughter, Francesca, and beside the vehicle nearest the girl was Jamie Trent on horseback. He was smiling down at Francesca, who, with her head thrown back and laughter on her lips, was the picture of elegant loveliness.

Carrie felt an almost physical pain in her breast. Jealousy swept through her in an overwhelming wave, making her feel quite dizzy. Quietly she crept through a gap in the hedge and moved silently along until she was level with the gig, though hidden by the hedge. Now she could hear their conversation.

"We have not seen you of late, Jamie," Francesca was saying in a purring tone. "You have neglected us shamefully, has he not, Mama?"

Peering through the leafy hedge, Carrie saw Lady Lynwood smile gently. "I guess you've been real busy on the farm, Jamie?"

Jamie nodded and there was a trace of grimness in his tone. "I'm afraid so. We're losing workers to the towns, to say nothing of the land we've lost."

"Oh, Jamie, I'm so sorry. Is there anything we can do to help?"

Jamie shrugged and sighed. "No. I don't reach the age of twenty-five – when I can take over completely – for another two years. If only no more goes before then, we may pull through."

Carrie closed her eyes and almost groaned aloud. Lloyd Foster and her father planned to take more land from Jamie, she knew. But these thoughts were driven from her mind again as she saw him lean down towards the gig and take Francesca's hand in his.

"I must go, my dear. I'll try to visit soon – I promise." He raised her gloved hand to his lips.

"Now don't go breaking that promise, Mr Trent, or I shall be mightily put out!" The girl teased, laughing up at him flirtatiously.

Carrie knew nothing of the ways of Society, of coquetry or gentle, meaningless, flirting, so her heart twisted with pain and jealousy. There was something between that girl and her Jamie! Jamie rode off in one direction and Lady Adelina slapped the reins, and the gig moved off in the other. Carrie saw Francesca turn round to wave again to Jamie and saw his return wave and she closed her eyes to shut out the picture.

She sat down where she was, behind the hedge at the edge of a meadow and tore angrily at the long grass with her fingers. How dare he? How can he make love to me one moment and then be so affectionate towards that girl? Hate began to grow in Carrie's heart for the girl she hardly knew. A few moments later she sprang to her feet and ran and ran until her lungs were bursting, up the lane, through the wood to the abbey ruins. Only then did she sink down against the crumbling walls, panting and sobbing.

Impatient with herself for shedding tears, Carrie rubbed at her eyes with the back of her hand. Gradually her misery turned to anger against Jamie. She waited and waited. An hour went by and still he did not come. When at last she saw his horse appear out of the trees and canter towards her, even the sight of him, which caused her heart to beat a little faster in spite of her anger, could not wipe away the picture of him with Francesca.

"Where've you been? You're late," she greeted him crossly. "I've been waiting an hour or more."

"I'm sorry, my darling." He came to her and tried to take her in his arms but she pushed him away.

"I'm not your slave, your plaything to be picked up and put down just when you feel like it!"

"Carrie, Carrie ..."

"I saw you with – with – *her*!"

Jamie frowned. "What are you talking about?"

"With Francesca. Mighty friendly you seemed to be!" Carrie stood, her hands on her hips, her feet planted wide apart, her violet eyes flashing now, her wild hair flying, quite unconscious of how lovely she looked – a natural, untamed beauty.

Jamie gazed at her admiringly. "My dear," he said softly. "Lady Lynwood was once my stepmother, and Francesca and I are like brother and sister."

"Huh! It didn't look like that to me!" Carrie retorted. "Fluttering her long eyelashes at you, making up to you. You forgot all about meeting me here, didn't you? Didn't you?"

"Carrie, my dear love. I've come at the same time as always. It's only three o'clock. You must have been early."

Then she remembered. She had been so distressed by the scene in the lane that she had completely forgotten to pay her usual visit to her grandmother's cottage before coming to the abbey ruins to meet Jamie.

Suddenly her anger evaporated and she flung herself against him, throwing her arms about him. "Oh Jamie, I'm sorry. Forgive me."

"My darling girl. There, there," he said, stroking her

hair and, gently tilting her head back, he kissed her ardently.

Carrie felt him lift her into his arms and carry her the short distance towards the one small cell-like room left whole in the abbey ruins. They squeezed through the small opening. Inside it was dim and quiet.

They kissed with growing passion, lost in their own secret world, their embrace all the sweeter after the misunderstanding between them. His fingers gently unfastened the buttons of her coarse blouse and caressed her. Swept away on a tide of love they gave themselves to one another in mutual desire. Jamie's lovemaking was so gentle and thoughtful that – virgin though she was – Carrie felt no pain, only an overwhelming need to give herself to this wonderfully considerate man.

Afterwards they lay in each other's arms, the tempest of their ardour subsiding to a calm feeling of closeness.

"I know so little about you," Jamie murmured, his lips warm against her neck, "and yet I know that I love you, my dearest Carrie."

She ran her fingers through his brown hair. "You're the first man I've loved," she told him, almost shyly.

"I know," he whispered, "and I'm glad – so glad."

"My first love and my last love."

"Oh, Carrie, Carrie," and his mouth found hers again. "We must be together always. Marry me, my darling. Be my wife."

"Yes – oh, yes," she breathed and closed her eyes. There could be no greater happiness on earth, she thought, than this moment.

The weeks of that hot, ardent summer faded into autumn. Lloyd Foster made ready to begin work on the cutting needed about a mile north of Abbeyford and the embankment through the valley itself.

"We take on more men, Evan me boy," he explained. "See the village men. If what I hear is true, they'll be only too glad of the work. Seems the Trents only employ a few now and the next estate – Lord Lynwood's, is it?"

Evan nodded.

"Well, he employs men from his own village – Amberly. Is that right?"

"Yes, but I'd have thought he'd have employed Abbeyford men on the land Lord Royston left his daughter Francesca."

"Is that the pretty girl with an older but still lovely lady I see riding about in a foine carriage?"

"Aye. Lady Lynwood and her daughter. They were lookin' for you some time back."

"Were dey now? Now isn't that the greatest shame I missed meeting them? But, then, they can't hold a candle to me darlin' Carrie's lovely face. Ah – if she had dose fine clothes an' a carriage, wouldn't she be the grand lady too, I'm t'inkin'?"

"Takes more'n clothes and carriages to make a lady of someone," Evan growled, bitterness clouding his eyes. "Takes birth and breeding."

Foster laughed. "An' what would me navvy ganger be worryin' about that for, eh?"

"There's things you dunna know, Foster, even yet!" Abruptly, Evan Smithson changed the subject. "I'll see the village men – but then what?"

"We divide the men into three gangs. One lot to continue working on the flat bed where we are now, one lot to begin work on the embankment and the third gang to work a cutting through that little incline between the two. That'll

not take as long to do as the embankment in the valley and
by the time that's finished the line should be nearly ready to
join up."

Evan thought rapidly. He could not fault the scheme but
he knew he would be hard pressed to keep tight control over
three gangs of navvies working some three miles apart. As if
reading his thoughts, Foster said, "Start training two or
three to take over as gangers soon. I plan to see this little
scheme started and see you have no problems but I'll be
away with me lovely bride before it's done."

Evan found that Foster had spoken the truth about the
Abbeyford men. Many were unemployed now and
bitterness against the Trents – Squire Trent especially,
since it was his gambling debts which had caused their
possessions to dwindle – was growing.

"Aw, Evan lad," Joby Robinson, son of the village
smithy whom he'd known in boyhood, greeted him. "The
years 'ave proved you right. We should have won our battle
all them years ago, not given in just because Wallis Trent
called out the yeomanry. Lad, if we'd tried again after he
was killed, we'd 'ave won! But you'd gone – disappeared."

"Aye, I thought it best. I thought I'd not be welcome
after the bloodshed that night."

"Aye, well, 'appen. Straight after, we was all bitter –
that's true. But we're worse off now than ever."

Evan grinned. "Well – I've work for as many as wants
it."

"Aw, lad, that's great."

"It's hard graft, mind," Evan warned, "and since I'm
boss, I'll not stand for shirkers."

"They'll come, we'll all come, lad, and thank you for it."

So the Abbeyford men – the unemployed, that is – from
at first resenting the encroaching railway, now seized upon

its arrival as a gift from God. Hungry mouths could be fed once more and a man could have back his pride he had felt to be lost. Yet those who still worked on the Trents' land saw the railway as a further threat to their already insecure livelihood and began to look upon those village men who had become gangers as turncoats.

Abbeyford became a divided village.

There were just two matters left to settle before the new workings could actually begin — the acquisition of part of the Trents' lands, indeed the majority of the land still left in their possession, and Foster's acquisition of Carrie Smithson in exchange for giving Evan Smithson the rest of the contract.

The first came about quite easily, for Foster had prepared well in advance for that very event, though the aftermath was to cause such a turbulence that the ripples would be felt for years to come.

Foster had joined a card school where Squire Trent frequently played. By making himself a good friend to the drink-sodden, sad old man, Lloyd Foster had by now manoeuvred him into a helpless position. To repay his gambling debts to Foster, Squire Trent was obliged to sell off yet more of his land. And with Foster's blarney he made it seem as if he were doing the old man a favour instead of a disastrous disservice.

"Didn't I tell you I could do it?" Lloyd Foster boasted, waving a piece of paper under Evan's nose. "An' all legal-like too!"

"How much have you got?" Evan's eyes gleamed as he grabbed the paper out of Foster's fingers and scanned it eagerly.

"My God!" he exclaimed when he saw the figures

written there. "Twice as much acreage as I thought you'd get and at half the price I thought you'd have to pay!" He looked up at Foster admiringly. "You crafty devil!" he grinned.

Foster laughed and slapped Evan on the back. "An' it's all in your hands now, me boy. 'Course the land belongs to the Railway Board, they laid out the money, you know that, don't you?"

Evan nodded. "Of course."

"And now," Foster said softly, "the contract's yours."

"The Board agreed, then?"

"They did too. When I saw them in Manchester last week about that," he jabbed his forefinger at the paper Evan still held, "I told them I was wantin' to spread me wings and fly like an eagle."

"And they let you go — without working out your contract?" Evan showed surprise.

"Didn't I tell them you were me right-hand man; that you knew as much about the building of dis railroad as me, and that, as long as the engineer checks everything, they'll have their railroad on schedule, if not before? By the way, they want to see you next week — just to make it all official."

Evan nodded. He'd had little cause in his life to thank any man for favours, and now he found his gratitude to this man impossible to express. But the irrepressible Irishman needed no thanks. "An' you'll not be forgetting your side of the bargain, now, will you, me boy?" For a moment, beneath the banter, there was the hint of steel.

"No — no," Evan said swiftly, trying to sound reassuring, but even he could not be sure his wayward daughter would comply.

During the first weeks of autumn Carrie and Jamie, locked

in the bliss of their growing love, each living only for the next moment when they would meet and touch and hold each other close, had been oblivious of the world around them. For Carrie it was an escape from the harsh reality she knew into a dream of tenderness and joy she had never believed could exist. Even Jamie, entranced by Carrie – this wild beauty like no other girl he had ever known – forgot, for a time, his drunken grandfather, his sullen employees, the dwindling estate, and the threatening railway over the hill.

Now, cruel reality was crowding in upon their private world.

It was pay-out night and the navvies descended into Abbeyford like a band of marauding Red Indians. They wanted liquor and because Lloyd Foster was an employer who believed that he could extract better work from his men by giving them what they wanted from time to time he had arranged that a quantity of ale was on hand.

So it was a drunken, rowdy mob who ran, whooping and yelling, down the hillside into the peaceful village below, looking for sport of any kind. They were rough, tough men who worked hard and played hard too.

"Come on out, you village wenches," shouted one banging on the door of a cottage, whilst behind the door a mother clasped her young daughters to her, her eyes wide with fear. "Hush," she whispered fearful that the girls' terrified whimperings would be heard. "Be quiet and he'll go away."

After a few moments, unable to gain any response, the navvy staggered round to the rear of the cottage, where he found half a dozen hens in a run.

"Aha, lookee what we have here. You'll mek me a foine dinner, I'm thinkin'," and he began to chase the birds, which, feathers flying, ran hither and thither, squawking loudly.

"Come here, blast you, you silly critters," he muttered rolling from side to side, making feeble grasping movements.

"What is it you're doin', Joseph me boy?"

Three more navvies, hearing the commotion, had gravitated towards the noise and now stood, a little unsteadily, watching their friend.

"Tryin' to catch dees stupid birds, so I am!"

"Well, let us be helpin' you." And the three of them climbed into the chicken run. Drunk though the men were, the chickens were no match for four pairs of grasping hands and very soon all six birds lay in a twitching heap, their necks broken.

"Now – der's one each for us and two over – is dat right? We can sell them other two, I'm t'inkin'."

"Aye an' do you know what I'm t'inkin', Joseph?"

"No, Michael, and what might dat be?"

"If dis 'ere cottage has chickens, maybe der's others in the village too, eh? What d'you t'ink?"

Joseph blinked, swaying on his feet.

"I t'ink you could be right. Come on."

Between the four of them they killed fifty-four chickens that night and carried them off in sacks up the hill back to the dwelling-place.

Another small group of navvies smashed the windows of the Monks Arms because the landlord refused to serve them any more ale. So they hurled stones at his windows and then burst into the bar and helped themselves. With even more drink inside them they rampaged down the one village street, tearing up plants from the gardens, damaging fences and gates and hurling stones through windows. Not until dawn began to stretch its pale fingers over the skyline did the navvies stagger back up the hill.

The following afternoon Carrie waited in the abbey ruins for Jamie. She shivered and drew her tattered shawl more closely about her. It was a blustery, cool day with grey clouds scudding overhead.

She saw him approach and ran to meet him as he tethered his horse and dismounted.

"Oh, Jamie – is it only yesterday since I saw you? It seems so long ago." She flung herself against him and as he put his arms about her she could feel a fierceness in his embrace. She raised her head to look up at him. His eyes were dark with anger and his mouth was set in a hard line.

"Jamie, what is it? Something's wrong, I know it."

Jamie tried to smile. " 'Tis naught to do with you, sweetheart. It's those – those railway workers."

Carrie stiffened and her heart missed a beat. Sure though she was now of Jamie's love for her, still she had not been able to bring herself to tell him of her own connection with the railway. She had not dared to risk spoiling their idyllic happiness.

"What – what has happened?"

"They descended on Abbeyford village last night, an unruly *mob*!" He clenched his teeth. "They've caused damage to property and stolen hens and frightened the women and girls half out of their wits."

"Was – was anyone hurt?"

He hesitated then said, "One girl was raped."

Carrie groaned.

"The village men – those who are not involved with the railway themselves – are out for revenge. I can see trouble brewing. I'd like to get my hands on the men responsible for those – those drunken louts!"

Carrie shuddered and wound her arms tightly about Jamie, burying her face against his chest. She felt him relax a little. She raised her head and looked up at him. He cupped her face in his hands and looked deep into her violet eyes. "Oh, my darling – what should I do without you now? You are the only one who brings me happiness."

His mouth was upon hers, their bodies entwined and for the moment all other thoughts were driven from their minds save the sweet passion flaring between them.

When they parted some two hours later, Jamie to return to the Manor and Carrie to run, skipping and jumping with light-hearted happiness, she had almost forgotten his mood of anger and even Jamie was smiling once more as he waved farewell.

"I won't, I won't – *I won't*!" Carrie shouted and stamped her foot.

Only moments before she had been dancing over the fields from her tryst with Jamie, giddy with happiness and her love for him. And now she stood in the centre of the rough shack facing her father, her violet eyes flashing with rage, her hands clenched so that the nails dug into her palms.

"You'll do as you're told, my girl," Evan spat, grasping her long black hair and wrenching her head back, whilst he raised his other hand to deal her a stinging blow.

"Whatever you do to me," Carrie said through her teeth, "you can't *make* me marry Lloyd Foster."

"You'll obey your pa, my girl," Evan bellowed again giving her hair a vicious tug, "or ..."

"Never – never," Carrie screamed and twisting sideways, she sank her white teeth into his arm. His hold on her slackened. "You little she-cat! Why, I'll kill you ..."

But Carrie did not wait to hear any more threats. She flung herself against the door of the shack, wrenching it open with such force that the rotten woodwork trembled and splintered. But as she hurled herself through the doorway, she came up against something solid – something, or rather someone, tall and broad and strong, whose arms were about her lifting her off her feet and swinging her round.

"Ah, an' if it isn't me darling running to meet me with a welcome I didn't expect."

Then, as Carrie realised it was Lloyd Foster holding her fast, she began to beat down upon his shoulders and kick at his legs.

"Now, now, this was not the welcome I had in mind." Still holding her, he glanced towards Evan, who had appeared in the doorway of the shack, holding his arm.

Then behind Foster there came the sound of horse's hooves and all at once Carrie's flailing arms and kicking legs were stilled and Foster felt her body go rigid in his arms. He looked into her face and saw her violet eyes widen with fear. Huskily she whispered a name.

"Jamie! *Oh, no!*"

Lloyd Foster lowered her slowly to the ground and turned to follow the line of her horrified gaze. He saw a young man, tall and broad-shouldered, his skin tanned, his handsome face contorted with anger, leaping down from his horse.

Then Foster saw, as the young man caught sight of Carrie, the rage soften momentarily in his eyes, heard him speak her name in surprise.

"Carrie? What on earth ...?" An expression of bewilderment flickered over the young fellow's face as he glanced away from her, towards Evan Smithson still standing in the doorway of the rough shack, briefly took in Lloyd Foster and then returned to Carrie's face.

Carrie, breaking free of the paralysing shock, ran towards the young man, the tears running down her face.

Never, Lloyd Foster thought dully, in all the time he had known her – through all the misery of her hard life and her father's brutality – never had he seen her weep. And now the girl whom, in his own boisterous way, he loved, was running towards another man, her arms outstretched, crying out to him with an impassioned plea. "Jamie, Jamie – you must take me away with you. You must save me. He's trying to make me marry Lloyd Foster. Tell him ..." She flung herself against him and clung to him, but Jamie Trent, like a man in a daze, merely stared over her head at Evan Smithson and Lloyd Foster. "Tell him I belong to you."

Jamie's eyes were hard, his mouth a grim line as he took hold of her arms and released himself from her limpet hold upon him. He held her away from him by the shoulders. He looked into her tearstained face, not an ounce of sympathy in his expression.

"You belong here? To the railway people?" His voice was harsh.

The hope died on Carrie's face. She closed her eyes and groaned aloud. "I can't help that. Jamie – I love you."

He thrust her aside and walked towards where Lloyd Foster and Evan Smithson stood watching. Behind him – unobserved by any of them now – Carrie sank to the ground and buried her face in her hands.

"Who's the contractor?" Jamie Trent demanded.

Foster and Evan exchanged a glance.

"Well, 'tis like this, d'you see. I am – but I'm in the process of handing the remainder of the contract over to Mr

Smithson here. So – perhaps if you were to tell the both of us what it is troubling you, me boy."

"Are you Foster?"

"I am dat. Me fame must be spreadin' far an' wide," he grinned.

"Fame?" Jamie's lip curled. "Is that what you call it? Infamy more like!"

Foster, instead of being insulted, threw back his head and roared with laughter. For a moment Jamie seemed disconcerted and then his anger grew as he thought his grievance was not being taken seriously.

"You've swindled an old man – a drunken, confused old man – out of his – and my – inheritance. There's not enough land left now to be worth the working!"

Evan Smithson's eyes glittered and a slow smile spread across his mouth. He folded his arms and leant against the door-frame.

"Drunk as ever, then, is he?" he said quietly.

Jamie met his gaze squarely and for a moment there was silence as the two men stared at each other: one, young, angry and a little unsure of himself; the other, older by some twenty or more years, a self-satisfied expression on his face.

"You – you know my grandfather?"

Evan Smithson continued to stare disconcertingly into the young man's troubled eyes.

Quietly and deliberately, Evan said, "I should do. I'm his son!"

FOUR

The reactions to Evan's dramatic statement were varied.

"Well now," Foster murmured softly. "An' don't that be explaining a lot o' t'ings."

Jamie Trent was motionless, his stare fixed upon Evan. His tanned face turned pale.

Carrie raised her head slowly, disbelievingly, from her hands, her sobs stilled in shock. Her violet eyes, still brimming with tears, gazed at her father and then at Jamie's rigid back. "Oh, no," she whispered hoarsely. "No, no, *no*!" her voice rising to hysteria.

"His – *son*?" Jamie Trent's voice was no more than a whisper. "But how – who ...?"

The enormity of Evan's words seemed to dawn upon the bewildered young man. "You mean – you're illegitimate!" he said baldly.

Evan's mouth tightened and his eyes hardened. "Aye, Squire Trent's bastard by a village girl."

Slowly Jamie nodded as understanding came. "Sarah Smithson." And the way in which he uttered her name told the onlookers that the revelation of these facts answered questions which had puzzled him for years.

There was no need for confirmation – they all realised the truth of Jamie's statement.

Not that gentle little old woman in the cottage and that drunken old man – it wasn't possible! Carrie closed her eyes and rocked to and fro on her haunches. And yet they, too, must have been young once, must have laughed and loved in secret – just as she and Jamie had done.

"So," Jamie was saying, "you'd bring ruin to your own father, would you?"

Evan stepped close to him, his eyes filled with hatred, only inches from Jamie's, so close that Jamie could feel the spittle rain upon his face as Evan spat out the words. "Father? *Father*? What sort of father has he been to me? Look at the ruin he's brought to people's lives. Ruined a pretty young village girl. Ruined Henry Smithson's life – to say nothing of mine. I've waited years for this moment – all me life! So don't expect no sympathy from me. I'll see the whole lot o' you in hell first!"

He turned his back on Jamie and strode away towards the railway, as if he would push the line – single-handed – through the Trents' land, so deep was his bitter desire for revenge.

For a moment Jamie seemed too stunned to move, then suddenly he turned and ran to his horse and mounted. Ignoring Carrie's desperate cry, "Jamie, oh Jamie!" he rode away at a breakneck gallop.

Carrie watched him go through a blur of tears, the sobs shaking her body. She felt a hand upon her shoulder.

"Don't, me darlin', don't," Lloyd Foster said, gently comforting. He drew her, unresisting, to her feet and put his arms about her. Hardly realising who was offering her support, Carrie clung to him, still weeping brokenly. He stroked her hair and rocked her. Then suddenly she tore herself free and rushed into the shack. Lloyd Foster watched her go with misery in his eyes. Slowly he turned away and followed Evan's path to the railway.

The railway! There was still the railway ...

That evening, before Evan returned home, Carrie slipped away from the shack. Lucy, unable to help her daughter, for after years of misery and hardship she had no strength to fight any more, watched her go with unhappy eyes. Calm now, Carrie was resolved to seek out Jamie.

"It doesn't matter that we're cousins," she said aloud to herself as she tramped determinedly across the hills towards Abbeyford. "In Society circles lots of cousins marry. It doesn't *matter*!" She tried to convince herself.

There was a cold October wind blowing and, by the time she neared the Manor House, Carrie was shivering. She drew the old shawl closer round her shoulders and slipped through the stableyard gate. There was no movement in the yard, no light from the windows on this side of the house. She moved towards the back door which she guessed led into the kitchens. Her heart was pounding now. She was afraid she would meet with some servant who would bar the way of the gypsy girl, but no one came to impede her entry to the house. She pushed open the door and went in. She stopped a moment, waiting whilst her eyes accustomed themselves to the dimness. She felt her way through the kitchen and up the stairs leading to the upper house. Through the swing door cutting off the servants' domain from the main part of the house, and into the entrance hall. Here a candelabrum burnt, casting eerie shadows. A grandfather clock ticked heavily in the corner, but the whole place was as neglected inside as outside in the stableyard. Dust covered the furniture and the floor was dull and mud-stained. Carrie jumped as she heard a shuffling noise and turned to see an old man moving towards her, his back so bent he could hardly lift his head to look at her.

"What do you want?" He was dressed in a shabby black suit and Carrie guessed he must be a servant of sorts, probably the only one who remained in the service of the Trents now.

"I want to see Mr Jamie Trent, please," Carrie said boldly, drawing herself up and trying to sound as if she had every right to be there.

"He's gone," the old man sniffed.

"G-gone? Where's he gone?"

"How should I know? Went galloping off on his horse as if the devil himself were after him."

"Is – is Squire Trent here?" Her tone was more hesitant now.

"Oh, yes." The man stretched his mouth into the semblance of a grin. "Drinking himself into his usual stupor." He waved his hand towards the left-hand side of the hall and said, his tone heavy with sarcasm, "The Master is in his study, ma'am, if you'd care to step this way!"

Opening the door he indicated and peering round it, she saw Squire Guy Trent slumped over his desk, an empty glass in one hand and an empty bottle at his elbow. This room, too, was dusty and littered with papers, empty bottles and dirty glasses.

Carrie cleared her throat, but when there was no response from him she moved closer.

"Squire Trent?" Still no reply, so tentatively she put her hand on his shoulder.

"Wha' ...?" His movement was so sudden that Carrie snatched her hand away in fright and sprang back a pace.

Bleary eyes gazed up at her, his head rolling from side to side. "Who is it? Can't see ..."

"It's Carrie. Carrie Smithson." She bent closer now, desperation giving her courage. After all, he was only drunk and hadn't she seen *that* many times before?

"Squire – where's Jamie?"

"Carrie? Carrie Smithson?"

"Yes. Where's Jamie? I must see Jamie. It's – important!"

"Jamie?" he repeated stupidly, whilst Carrie grew more impatient.

"Yes. Where is he?"

"I don't know. Gone. Gone away. Left me."

"What do you mean?"

"Left me all alone. He was in a rage. Wouldn't speak to me. Looked as if he – he could – kill me. Never been frightened of Jamie before. Not Jamie. Wallis, yes. I was always afraid of Wallis. My own son – and I was afraid of him." The words were drawling and slurred but Carrie could plainly understand. She sat down in a chair opposite the desk. She would have to be patient with him if she were to learn anything. Perhaps if she encouraged him to ramble on like this, she would find out what she wanted to know.

"Your son, Jamie's father?" she prompted.

"Yes. He was a hard man, so cold and ruthless! I've been a failure all my life. Failed my parents, failed my wife and son and worst of all, I failed the only girl I ever really loved. My Sarah!"

Carrie said gently. "Jamie knows about – about you and Sarah. My father told him."

"Your father?" The eyes peered at her, red and puffy.

"Yes. Evan Smithson. Your – son by Sarah."

For a moment the room was still and silent. Then the old man let out such a groan that Carrie was afraid. He covered his face with his hands, knocking over the bottle, which rolled to the edge of the desk and fell to the floor, shattering into a dozen pieces. The glass dropped from his fingers to the desk, but Carrie grabbed it before it, too, fell to the floor. He was panting and moaning and Carrie thought the shock had brought on a heart attack of some kind.

"I'm sorry," she said swiftly. "I'm terribly sorry. But please – you must help me. I love Jamie. And he loves me, I know he does," she tried to convince herself, blotting out the picture of him riding away from her, ignoring her when he had learnt the dreadful truth.

The pathetic old man seemed suddenly, painfully sober. Slowly his hands fell away from his face, his moaning quietened and he looked at Carrie full in the face. "As I loved Sarah and she loved me."

There was silence. Moved by pity, Carrie reached out her hand and touched the old man's. He covered hers with his other hand. "If you love him, and he loves you, let no one stand in the way of your happiness. No one! Do you hear me?"

Carrie nodded, unable to speak for the lump in her throat. "But," she whispered at last, "he rode off without a word – after – after Pa had told him. Perhaps ..."

"It'll be all right. He was hurt. Hurt beyond words, but he'll get over it." Squire Trent, for a brief moment, was no longer the pathetic drunk, but an elderly gentleman offering comfort to a distressed young girl – his grand-daughter. That fact seemed suddenly to dawn upon him. "You're – you're my granddaughter, then?"

"I – suppose so," Carrie said and smiled faintly at him. His grasp upon her hand tightened.

"Don't let anyone or anything stand in the way of your love," he said hoarsely, "or you'll spend your life lost and alone – like I have done. I fell in love with Sarah, but I was the squire's son! My parents arranged for me to marry Louisa Marchant, the daughter of a wealthy clothing manufacturer from Manchester. I tried to fight them, tried to see Sarah. But they were all against us. Her father – Joseph Miller – arranged for her to marry a distant cousin – Henry Smithson. But I still might have won," he thumped the table with his fist, "but I was attacked in the wood late one night." He glanced at Carrie sheepishly. "I was drunk. Seems as if I've been drunk ever since," he muttered and then his voice grew stronger again. "I never saw who attacked me, but while I lay abed – my Sarah married Smithson and – and my father sent Joseph Miller to gaol!"

Carrie gasped. "Sarah's father? Why?"

Squire Trent groaned and closed his eyes. "He *said* it was because he believed it was Miller who attacked me."

"And was it?"

He shrugged. "We've never found out. He wouldn't admit it – nor would he defend himself. But he was a strong man, a man who stood up against my father for his rights, and my father hated him. Of course, he died in gaol, and Sarah's mother died soon after. Broke the whole family. They've hated me ever since. Your father – my own son – he's had the hate bred into him. He led the village against the Manor once. Wallis was killed."

"I know," Carrie said. "I heard about that."

"And now he's ruined me – and Jamie – completely."

There was silence again.

Carrie said gently, "Where do you think Jamie went?"

Sadly, he shook his head. "I don't know. I thought maybe he'd gone for good, but perhaps if there's you to come back for ..." He left the sentence hanging in the air like an unanswered question.

His head fell forward again. "I'm tired," he said heavily. "So tired of it all."

Carrie left him sleeping over the desk.

That night Carrie hid in the Manor stables, waiting in case Jamie should return. But at the first light of dawn, when she awoke from a fitful doze to move her cramped, cold limbs there was still no horse back in the stall, no sign of Jamie.

She couldn't – wouldn't – go home. But where could she go? Not her grandmother's – her father would think to look for her there. The abbey ruins! Jamie would come to her there. It was their meeting-place. The place where they had made love and spent their moments of bliss. Her cold, cramped feet moved faster and faster and she began to run both to warm herself and to reach the abbey ruins all the quicker. Why had she not thought of it before? she scolded herself. Jamie would come for her there – she was certain of it!

"Where is she?" Lloyd Foster demanded.

"How should I know?" Evan replied.

Foster's face showed none of its usual geniality. He grasped Evan's shirt collar and hauled him close. Though sturdy and strong, Evan was no match for the big Irishman. "Then you'd better be findin' her, me boy. A bargain's a bargain. I've no mind to lose that little girl, d'you hear me now?"

"She'll come back," Evan said confidently.

"How can you be so sure?"

"Because he's gone."

"Young Trent?"

"Aye."

"How can you be sure she hasn't gone with him?"

"Yesterday – after he rode off in such a tekin' – she was at home all day until just before I got home. Me wife said so."

"So? She could still have gone to find him."

Patiently, Evan said, "No, it was me went after Jamie Trent. In the afternoon he was at the workings talking to Luke, but I soon put a stop to that. I told him she was to marry you. That it'd be no good cousins marrying – enough bad blood on both sides to breed the devil himself!"

"What did he say?"

Evan laughed. "He looked sick – sick and beaten!"

"But what was he saying to Luke, maybe he was arranging to meet her – through Luke, eh?"

"Nay. I asked Luke an' he said he'd only just come as I got there. Trent hadn't said nothing."

"He could be lying. Lyin' to protect Carrie."

Evan frowned. "Luke – lie to me? He wouldn't dare!"

Foster gave a grunt of disbelief. "Frightened of you he may be, me boy, but he thinks a lot of his sister. Maybe more than his fear of you."

Foster said no more but strode away leaving Evan frowning thoughtfully.

"Luke, come here."

Luke Smithson glanced fearfully at his father. They were at the new workings of the Abbeyford embankment. He had put Luke in charge of the gangers on this section, but the sick, weak boy had no power to be authoritative over the men.

Luke slid down the bank and came towards Evan.

"You sure young Trent said naught to you?"

Two spots of colour appeared in the boy's cheeks and he coughed. "Nay," he gasped, "I told you, didn't I? You came up just as he got off his horse. He'd no time to say aught ..."

"You'd better not be lyin' to me, boy, or it'll be the worse for you. Now get back and shape these men up. You'll let 'em run riot over you, if you dunna."

Thankfully Luke turned his back on his father and hurried away, feeling, as he did so, the rustle of paper in his pocket. The letter Jamie Trent had given him for Carrie. How long he could keep it from his pa, he didn't know. He just wished Carrie would come home so he could give it to her and be done with it!

Then all thoughts of Carrie and Jamie Trent and even of his father's wrath were swept from his mind as his gaze travelled up the hill above the embankment.

Ranged in a line some hundred yards away, silent, watchful and menacing stood thirty or more men armed with a variety of weapons – picks, shovels, staffs, crooks and knives. The navvies had seen them and had paused in their work, looking up at the strangers above them.

The farmworkers, Luke thought, and shuddered. They've come to try to stop us building the railway through their village. For a moment he closed his eyes and when he opened them the men had begun to move slowly forward down the incline towards the railway workings. The navvies, too, had, by common, silent consent formed themselves into a defensive line and they stood waiting, watching the approach of their adversaries. It was like two armies in a battle, Luke thought, and then the two lines met and clashed. Screams and cries and the sound of wood on wood and metal against metal filled the air and there was no more time for conscious thought!

Lloyd Foster sat on his horse at the top of the hill over-looking the quiet, peaceful village of Abbeyford.

"Where could she have gone, where could she be hidin' herself?" he murmured aloud, his gaze roaming the countryside, taking in the squat, straggly cottages, the grand mansion, Abbeyford Grange and the neglected Manor House, and the mounds of earth already beginning to form the embankment which would run right across the valley. Then his eyes came to rest on the abbey ruins to his right, rising gaunt and black against the grey October sky. He spurred his horse and galloped across the ridge towards the ruins, feeling the first spots of rain on his face from the low, threatening clouds above.

Carrie crouched down in the small, cell-like room in the ruins. She had been there since early morning. She was cold and hungry and so miserable. If only Jamie would come! She had ventured out once or twice to peer over the crumbling walls, hoping for sight of him. But the fields were empty, devoid even of workers. She dare not show herself in the open for fear someone might see her. So the little room, cold and inhospitable it seemed now – so different from the sanctuary it had been when she had lain in Jamie's arms – had become her hideout.

During the late afternoon the room became darker as rain clouds gathered. Carrie crouched against the wall, dozing fitfully, worn out with the drama of the past few hours.

As if in a dream she heard the horse's hoofbeats.

"Jamie, Jamie! He's come!" She dragged herself, still dazed, but hopeful now, to the doorway. The rain beat upon her face, arousing her to full wakefulness as she saw a man climbing over the low wall. She watched him jump down into the ruins and come towards her.

She stretched out her hands and made to run towards him. "Jamie! Oh, Jamie!"

"Oh, an' there you are, me darlin'. An' I was thinkin' I'd not set eyes on you again, me lovely."

Carrie stopped and stared at the man walking towards her across the stone-strewn floor of the abbey ruins. Her arms fell limply to her sides.

Lloyd Foster! Not Jamie.

Lloyd's arms were strong about her and if she had not been so disappointed because it was he and not Jamie, she might have welcomed the support and warmth he offered.

"Go away," she said weakly.

"Aw, now an' you don't mean that, to be sure."

Exhausted, scarcely able to think rationally, Carrie found herself leaning against him. This last disappointment had swept away the last reserve of her strength and left her helpless and without hope.

"Come on, me darlin'." He lifted her and carried her to his horse. "I'll not let anyone be hurtin' you ever again, do you hear dat now?"

She heard his words, soft, comforting words, but did not comprehend them. She just knew she was unable to resist him any longer. She could no longer stop him taking her home. She had no will, no strength left.

He sat her on his horse and mounted behind her. He took off his jacket and wrapped it round her and held her close, warming her cold, aching limbs. The rain soaked his fine waistcoat and shirt, but Lloyd Foster smiled. He had found her! She had not gone away with young Trent. He had found her in time. But his smile was tinged with sadness, for he knew that it was mere chance that she had not gone away with her lover, for it had been Jamie Trent she had been waiting for in the ruins. But now he had her again, Lloyd Foster did not intend to lose her this time.

As they rode down the hill towards the stream, he saw suddenly the line of men – farm labourers – advancing with slow and deliberate steps towards the workings of the embankment. Foster saw the makeshift weapons they carried and, afraid of their intention, he spurred his horse forward. The sudden movement stirred Carrie and she clung to him. "What is it?"

"I t'ink dere's trouble ..."

He saw his navvies become aware of the advancing foe, saw them pick up their working tools and automatically form themselves into a line facing their attackers.

Carrie, now fully aroused, gasped in horror. As the two lines of men met, staves waved in the air, knife blades flashed and the cries of pain and triumph wafted to their ears.

Lloyd Foster leapt from his horse. "Stay here, me darlin' out of harm's way." Carrie narrowed her eyes, trying to see ...

"*Luke*!" A horrified shriek escaped her lips. "Oh, look!"

Lloyd Foster ran towards the fight whilst Carrie watched with terrified eyes. She saw a huge fellow lunge towards her brother, saw him raise his crook and deal Luke a vicious blow, saw him fall to the ground, the man raising his weapon yet again. Then Foster reached him, grasped him by the collar and twisted him round. His huge fist smashed into the man's face, felling him at once. Then he picked Luke up in his arms and moved away from the fighting. Carrie scrambled from the horse and ran towards them. "Oh, Luke, *Luke*!"

But the young man was unconscious.

"We'll get him home."

"What – about the rest?"

Lloyd shrugged. "Dey'll have to fight it out, won't they now? And may the best men win!" He grinned at her, confident that victory would be with his navvies.

As Lloyd Foster lifted Luke gently from the horse outside the shack, Evan Smithson opened the door.

"There's a fight going on in Abbeyford. The farm labourers have attacked the navvies," Foster said curtly to him. "You should be there."

"Luke's in charge there ..." Evan began, then seeing the still form in Lloyd's strong arms, he gave a click of annoyance. "Can't he do anything? Oh," he added catching sight of Carrie, "you're back, are you?"

Carrie's answer was to push past him into the shack. Holding the door open she beckoned Lloyd to carry Luke inside and lay him down on the rough shakedown behind the ragged curtain.

"I'll be getting back to the trouble. You comin'?" he demanded of Evan.

"In a moment," Evan was looking down at his son thoughtfully. "You," he said to Carrie, pushing her roughly, "get some water. I'll be with you in a minute." It was a dismissal of both Carrie and Foster. Evan wanted them both out of the way.

Alone with his son, Evan knelt down by his side and felt amongst the boy's clothing. Something rustled, and Evan drew out a crumpled piece of paper.

As Carrie returned with a bowl of water and rags to bind Luke's head, she saw her father rising from a crouching position beside Luke, his hand inside his own coat pocket. As he stood and turned to leave, she saw the gleam of triumph in his eyes.

"He's all yours now – but I doubt you'll be able to do aught with him!" His tone was unemotional, as one might speak of an injured animal, not a human being, not his own son!

Evan brushed past her and was gone. Carrie stood a moment, wondering at his strange actions, then, as a low moan came from Luke's lips, all other thoughts were driven from her mind save the care of her brother. She knelt and began to bathe his wounds.

On the other side of the curtain, seated at the table, Lucy sat motionless staring into space, totally resigned to face the loss of yet another of her offspring.

The fight was over and the navvies had won. The village men returned battered and beaten to their homes. Two were dead and three more seriously injured, and not one of them survived without a wound of some sort. The victorious navvies began two days of heavy drinking ending with a march through Abbeyford village, where they took their revenge by smashing property and fighting anyone and everyone, young or old, who got in their way.

Then they returned to work on building their railway as if nothing had happened! But the bitterness and hatred in the village was irreparable.

Carrie nursed Luke devotedly, pushing all thoughts of her own happiness aside as she tried to save the life of her brother. But her knowledge of nursing was scant, and her brother too ill with consumption anyway to survive for many more years. His wound had merely precipitated the inevitable!

For two days he lay on the shakedown, sometimes unconscious, sometimes mumbling incoherently.

"Beautiful lady. Never seen – anyone so – before."

"Letter – the letter. Carrie!"

"Not strong, can't fight him. Ruin us all ... The letter – give ..."

Carrie listened and heard but could not understand everything. Obviously his wandering mind was remembering Francesca, the lovely girl he had seen with Lady Lynwood. But the murmurings about a letter she could not understand.

On the third day after the fight, Luke died, quite quietly and quickly.

Carrie shed a few tears, but her mother, Lucy, was beyond tears, her emotions all used up over the harsh years of continual grief. Evan was unmoved, and the only comfort Carrie received came from Lloyd Foster.

Luke was buried in Abbeyford churchyard, so hurriedly it was almost indecent, Carrie thought. Several of the villagers gathered but only to stare with hostility at the three figures near the grave – Evan Smithson, Carrie and Lloyd Foster.

As they left the churchyard, Foster drew her arm through his own and patted her hand. "Carrie, me lovely, you know I want you to be me wife. I've a special licence here," he patted his coat pocket. "Been carrying it around next me heart these past few weeks now, so I have. I have a mind to go abroad – to build railways in far-off lands, an' I want you to be with me. Do you hear me now?" His voice was gentle, coaxing, quite unlike the brash Irishman she had always thought him.

"Oh, Lloyd, I owe you so much. You tried to save Luke's life from that – that mob," she glanced fearfully behind her to see the surly eyes of the villagers still upon them. "But – but I don't – I can't love you, you know that."

Again he patted her hand and sighed heavily. "I know, I know. But, me darlin', he's gone. Your pa told me. An' if you come with me, I'll be good to you – I swear it on your brother's grave, so I do." She glanced up at him and his eyes were on her, serious and full of love.

"Oh, Lloyd – I'm sorry, I can't."

But Carrie had reckoned without the determination of her father. "He's gone. Left you. His sort won't *marry* the likes of you. 'Specially now he's found out you're a blood relative!"

His words were like a knife in her heart, robbing her of all the belief she had held of Jamie's love for her. Her last memory of him had been as he had rushed past her and ridden off, ignoring her cry of desperation.

Somehow she found herself, as if in a dream, as if the events were happening around her and she had no will, no power to prevent them, agreeing to marry Lloyd Foster.

The marriage was performed – like Luke's funeral – hurriedly, early in the morning with only her father and mother present, besides Lloyd Foster and herself. Lloyd was dressed in his fine clothes whilst the bride stood, a pathetic, unhappy creature in her ragged skirt and shawl, making her promises in a mechanical tone.

As they came out of the church, far above them, unnoticed by any of them, a rider sat on his horse beside the ruined wall of the abbey.

Jamie Trent narrowed his eyes and though the distance was too great to recognise the tiny figures moving away from the church, somehow in his heart he knew their identity. He had returned that morning, riding through the night and going straight to the abbey ruins with the vain hope of finding Carrie waiting for him. He knew that, if she wanted to see him, that was where she would be waiting.

He watched, motionless, his eyes following the group of figures as they moved along the lane, lost from sight for a time amongst the hedgerows and then appearing again as they climbed the hill out of Abbeyford.

Jamie closed his eyes and groaned aloud and then turned his horse towards the Manor.

In the stable, hanging by the neck from a rope round a beam was the stiff, cold body of Squire Guy Trent. Jamie leaned his head against the rough wood of the door and gave way to total despair.

Foster could hardly get Carrie away from Abbeyford quickly enough. The Railway Board had accepted Evan as the new contractor, and with the marriage between Foster and Carrie, the private bargain struck between Evan Smithson and Lloyd Foster was complete. Carrie had no belongings to pack and so, only hours after their wedding, they were climbing into a pony and trap after a brief farewell to her mother and younger brothers and moving off down the rough cart-track to start a new life. Evan Smithson watched them go, his arms folded across his chest, a smile of satisfaction on his face.

Now for the railway!

As the trap rattled along the lane, suddenly a man stepped out into their path a little way ahead. Lloyd Foster pulled hard on the reins and brought the vehicle to a standstill.

"Jamie!" Carrie whispered. Then she turned pleading eyes upon Lloyd. "Please – let me – speak to him? Just – for a moment."

Lloyd hesitated and then sadly nodded his head in agreement, his heart heavy as she scrambled down so eagerly from her seat beside him and ran towards Jamie Trent. He did not reach out his arms towards her and his stillness stopped her flinging herself against him.

"Jamie?" There was uncertainty in her tone, but only for a moment, for then she saw the wealth of misery in his eyes, which matched the ache in her own heart. He loved her still! He had come back for her – but too late!

"I thought you'd gone – for good," she whispered.

Jamie shook his head, and his voice when he spoke was low and hoarse with emotion. "No – no. I went to Manchester to see the lawyers. To see if I could save my land."

"And – did you?"

He shook his head. "And I lost something far more precious in my absence. Oh, Carrie," he reached out and touched her cheek with his fingertips. "Why did you not believe in me? Didn't my letter convince you …?"

"Letter?" Carrie's voice was shrill. "What letter?"

"I left a letter with Luke telling you where I'd gone. Telling you I'd be back for you."

Carrie closed her eyes and groaned. "Oh, no, *no*! Jamie – Luke's dead. He was hurt. There was a fight between your farmworkers and the navvies. Lloyd," she gestured with her hand behind her towards the man sitting so silent and still in the trap, unable to hear their words and yet torn with jealousy to see them together, "tried to save him, but he died three days after. Jamie, he murmured about a letter – I couldn't understand. And there was no letter on him, I know …"

Grim-faced, Jamie said bitterly, "Your father must have found it."

Carrie gasped and the picture of Evan Smithson bending over Luke's still form as she had returned to tend his wounds flashed across her mind, his hand, as he stood up and turned towards her, inside his own coat pocket. In that moment Carrie hated her father.

"So, he's got what he wanted," Jamie said. "My land, Grandfather's death – and you married to Foster!"

"Your grandfather?"

Jamie's head dropped. "Yes – I found him this morning. He must have been dead a – couple of days. He – he'd killed himself."

"Oh, Jamie," Carrie whispered, horrified. "I'm so sorry."

There was nothing left to say. Their emotions were too deep for words. Gently, Jamie took her arm, turned her round and led her back to Lloyd Foster.

As Jamie helped Carrie into the trap the two men's eyes met. There was no animosity between them, more a look of understanding and mutual pity, for whilst one had lost her, the other had not won her love. There was an unspoken request in Jamie's eyes. 'Take care of her, be good to her', and an answering promise in Lloyd Foster's, yet not a word was spoken.

Lloyd Foster slapped the reins and the trap jerked forward. Twisting round, Carrie watched Jamie's figure grow smaller and smaller as she was carried away from him.

Just once, he raised his hand in a final farewell.

FIVE

They travelled for several days, stopping at wayside inns, making for London.

That first night, their wedding night, she sat in the bedroom, tense and fearful, waiting for him to come to her. She sat by the window, shivering and staring out into the darkness, seeing nothing, but determined to stay as far away from the big double bed as she could. She kept her eyes averted from it, trembling at the thought of what she must endure.

Carrie was no maiden, afraid of the unknown. Her fear lay only in that, having known the joys of loving with Jamie, she must now submit to the passions of a man she did not love.

They had been welcomed into the inn by the beaming landlord, who, though she could see the question in his eyes, politely ignored the incongruity of a well-dressed gentleman accompanied by a gypsy girl.

"I'll be wantin' a *double* room," Lloyd Foster had said firmly, and Carrie had felt a twinge of revulsion at the thought of what was to happen that night. "An' mind the bed is clean and warm for my wife, an' a fire in the grate."

"Of course, sir. Mary Ellen," the landlord had shouted to one of the kitchen maids, "away and prepare the room, girl – the *best* front bedroom." He had turned back to Lloyd. "And you'll be wanting refreshment, sir, I don't doubt. Now we have a nice roast veal, and some of the best wine this side the Channel, sir."

Bowing, he had ushered Lloyd and Carrie to high-backed bench seats in a secluded corner. Two brass candle-sticks with lighted candles stood on the table. They sat opposite each other and waited for their meal to be served. Carrie's violet eyes were dark, the soft candlelight highlighting her beauty, but she was unaware of her own appearance. All her senses prickled at the nearness of the man sitting so close, his knees accidentally touching hers beneath the table. Though the meal was such as she had never tasted before – tender veal, sparkling wine which tickled her nose as she raised the glass to her lips, a sweet of delicious meringue and fresh cream, and coffee, real, steaming hot coffee, fresh and fragrant – Carrie could not enjoy it. She felt as if she could never enjoy life itself again.

Now, as she sat in the bedroom, she felt such a loneliness that she had never before known. Always, she had fought for survival. She had been the strength her weaker brothers – and even her mother – had leaned on. And now, plucked from their midst, even with the promise of security and comfort, she felt bereft. Torn away from all she knew, all that was familiar and – worst of all – torn from the very first man with whom she had fallen in love ...

The bedroom door opened with a scrape and she jumped and turned to see Lloyd Foster standing in the doorway. He came in and closed the door behind him and stood looking at her. The silence between them lengthened until it grated on her nerves. She turned back to gazing out of the window, even though she could see nothing through the blackness.

She was acutely aware of him standing behind her. She felt a shiver down her spine as he crossed the room and moved close to her.

He reached out and touched her shoulder and she flinched from his touch. He sprang away as if burned. "So, that is how it is to be, is it?" His voice was low with emotion. "Rough I may be, but I'm no ignorant brute. But you're my wife, and, by God, you'll be my wife!"

Gone was his joviality. There was no mistaking the steel in his voice. Carrie shuddered. She had heard it before, but never directed at herself until this moment. He turned and strode from the room, banging the door behind him. As she heard his feet clatter down the stairs, Carrie could only feel relief.

Lloyd Foster made his way to the saloon bar, where he drank steadily through the night until drunkenness dulled his frustrated passion for his bride.

The following day, much to Carrie's surprise, Lloyd Foster seemed to have recovered his usual cheerful spirits. He laughed loudly with the innkeeper, tipped the stable boy lavishly for looking after the horse and was courteous towards Carrie. She avoided meeting his gaze and so did not see for herself the pain deep in his eyes, hidden by his outward show of good humour. She was quiet, withdrawn into her own private misery, repulsing all attempts Foster made to reach her.

They travelled on, Carrie sullen and silent, Foster singing Irish folksongs at the top of his loud and surprisingly tuneful voice. They stayed in a pleasant hotel in London, though where Foster slept Carrie never knew nor cared to enquire, for each night she slept alone.

He took her to the shops and insisted she should buy herself a trousseau, but Carrie had no idea how a lady should dress and was at the mercy of the dressmaker. All manner of clothing was laid before her, such items as she had never seen, let alone possessed. Flannel vests, cotton chemises, petticoats, corsets, cotton drawers, white thread stockings, coloured silk stockings, kid gloves, silk gloves, morning dresses and afternoon dresses of silk cashmere, black silk skirts and bodices, two evening gowns and a white lace ball gown, so beautiful it took Carrie's breath away. Shawls and cloaks and hats, even a parasol edged with lace. Neat button boots and shoes for day and evening wear which Carrie's feet had never known.

"I can't accept all this," she hissed at Lloyd Foster, gesturing towards all the garments being wrapped by the willing assistants.

"Ah, so you can find it in you to speak to me," Lloyd said, his mouth smiling but his eyes reproachful. It was the first time she had spoken to him since their marriage — except to answer his questions in sullen monosyllables. "And you will accept it. It is a husband's duty to provide for his wife, is it not, now?"

Her violet eyes flashed — the first time she had shown any spark of life since leaving Abbeyford.

"I'll not be *bought*!" She glared at him, standing facing him in the centre of the fashionable shop, her hands on her hips.

"Oh, an' I love you when you're angry," Lloyd Foster's booming laugh rang out, causing the dressmaker to 'tut-tut' and her young assistants to giggle to each other. Carrie stamped her foot, causing the girls to give little shrieks of horror. It was the behaviour they were not accustomed to seeing in their shop — not the behaviour of a lady!

"*I'm* serious — even if you're not," Carrie cried angrily.

"Oh, me darlin', I was never more serious in the whole of

me life." The hint of steel was in his eyes again. He took hold of her wrist, and though he only held her lightly with one hand, she could feel the strength in his fingers. "You will accept these gifts, my lovely *wife*!" The accent on the last word was audible only to Carrie.

Thwarted, she flounced out of the shop and stood waiting for him in the street outside. He sauntered out in due course, now seeming quite unperturbed by her outburst.

As they walked along she stole a glance at him. Wherever he was, she thought, he seemed at ease. Whether it was amongst the navvies, covered with dust, or with Squire Trent playing cards, or here in the fashionable quarter of London, he was equally at home and – amazingly – accepted. Whilst she felt a misfit, a dirty, dishevelled gypsy with no manners and no idea of etiquette.

She was quiet now and as they walked along she looked about her at the shops, at the grand carriages, at the coachmen and footmen in their smart liveried uniforms, and at the noblemen and fashionable ladies inside the carriages. Lloyd walked at her side, smartly dressed as ever in a well-cut suit, a brightly coloured waistcoat, his watch-chain looped across his broad chest, and swinging a cane.

Suddenly he reached down and took her hand and drew it through his arm. She could feel the curious glances of the passers-by and the colour rose in her cheeks.

"You see, me darlin'," Lloyd was saying in his lilting brogue. "I want to see you dressed in fine silks and satins. You've the beauty of a fine lady already, me darlin', all you're needin' is the fine feathers. Do y'hear me now? There's so many places I can take you. Now, wouldn't you like to play the fine lady?"

Carrie was silent.

She supposed she should feel gratitude to him for his

generosity, but she could not forgive him for having aided her father in tricking her into this marriage, tearing her from the arms of her lover. But as the days passed into weeks and months, she found she could not help being caught up in the excited bustle of the vast city. The shops fascinated her, the fancy carriages, the beautifully dressed ladies in the silks and velvets. She even had a maid of her very own now – a young girl who helped her dress her hair and bedeck herself in her new finery.

Away from Abbeyford, away from all the squalor and hardship of her former life, away from the anguish of losing her brother, Luke, of seeing her mother weary and beaten, away from her brutish, obsessed father and with so much that was new to interest her, she found the pain begin to lessen and her natural vitality slowly reassert itself.

Carrie Smithson Foster was a survivor. She was strong and blessed with a natural zest for life that could not, would not, be beaten or bowed for long.

In the company of Lloyd Foster's jovial spirit, she could not remain locked in her private misery for ever, so resolutely she raised her head, accepted his gifts and determined to make the best of the situation. She could not forgive him or give herself to him willingly – but between them, on the surface at least, there was an uneasy kind of truce.

Carrie still slept alone and never troubled to enquire where, or how, her husband spent his nights.

Lloyd was true to his promise. He introduced her to a life she had never dreamed existed. True it was not the life of aristocratic Society – those doors were closed even to Lloyd Foster. But they found their niche amongst the middle-class, well-to-do, 'respectable' Victorians. Carrie began to enjoy her new role, laughing secretly at the thought of the astonishment on the faces of these fine ladies if they knew of her past life – her impoverished childhood and harsh living. Now she mimicked their manner of speaking, their elegant way of walking, their affectations, yet she never lost her earthy honesty, her strength of will.

Yet, deep in her heart, she was lonely for sight of Jamie. *Gladly she would have forsaken all this luxury – and more – for one kiss from her lover.*

"Now, you sit here at this table, me darlin', and I'll be fetchin' you some ginger beer."

Carrie sat down at the table in the tea-garden to which Lloyd had brought her. It was April, over four months since she had left Abbeyford – and Jamie. Amidst the hustle of the tea-garden, Carrie felt the loneliness steal over her. She looked about her at the happy families – mothers in their beribboned bonnets, their wide crinolines spread about them, leaning down to tend their small children. The gentlemen in their pink shirts and blue waistcoats seemed to gravitate to one corner of the garden, where they smoked their cigars and leant on their canes, with their tall silk hats at a rakish angle.

"Here we are, me darlin'," Lloyd placed a glass of ginger beer on the table before her and a dish of winkles. "Now – you'll be all right for a moment, I just have a little business to attend to," and, weaving his way between the tables, avoiding two boys chasing each other across the grass, Lloyd went to join the other gentlemen.

Carrie saw them greet him like a friend – he was obviously known to three or four of them.

It was a huge place where they were, on the banks of the river Thames. Far in one corner, Carrie could see a crowd clustering round a balloonist who was making ready to begin his ascent. She did not join the crowd but watched with casual interest from where she was sitting. The spring day was surprisingly warm here in the sheltered tea-garden. In her wide-skirted crinoline with its numerous petticoats and the close-fitting bonnet beneath which her hair was arranged into a neat chignon, she felt uncomfortably restricted and hot. In that moment she longed for the freedom she had known last summer, her black hair flying loose, her bare feet running through the long grass to the abbey ruins to meet Jamie.

Tears prickled her eyelids and she sighed. Now it could never be. She was here in London, dressed in fine clothes, trying to ape the lady, married to a man she hated.

But did she really *hate* him? Carrie turned her gaze to where her husband stood. At that moment he threw back his head and laughed at something one of the other men had said, a loud, infectious sound that caused those nearby to smile too.

He was certainly a fine figure of a man, a man any woman could be proud to marry – any woman but Carrie, whose heart belonged to another!

She turned her eyes away again and watched the balloonist as he rose, a little jerkily at first, above the ground. The crowd 'oh'ed' and 'ah'ed' and then he was soaring above their heads and drifting away from them across the Thames.

You are married to Lloyd Foster, Carrie told herself sharply. He treats you well and your life is more comfortable and luxurious than you had ever believed possible for the gypsy Carrie Smithson. You had better make the best of it! But her heart longed for Jamie to see her dressed in fine clothes. How much more worthy of being *his* wife she was now than she had been a year ago.

That evening, back in their hotel room, Lloyd suddenly said, "Now, me darlin', how would you like to be goin' to Paris?"

Carrie swung round to face him, unable for once to prevent him seeing the joy shining in her eyes. "Paris? Do you mean it?"

"Now would I be jokin' about a t'ing like that?"

She put her head on one side and regarded him thoughtfully. "We'll be coming back, won't we?"

Lloyd Foster avoided her gaze. "Ah, well, now, an' that's a little difficult to be sayin'. You see, I've got to earn a livin' for us, haven't I now?"

Carrie's mouth tightened. "I thought you'd made your fortune at the expense of others. Twisting people out of their inheritance by taking advantage of a drunkard seems to be your way!"

It was the first time they had spoken of it, although always it lay like a barrier between them.

"I'll not suffer your reproaches the rest of our lives," he growled. Carrie said nothing and the silence between them grew as they glared at each other, challenging. Suddenly, as if unable to bear it any longer, Lloyd strode towards her and took her in his arms. His mouth was upon hers, his hands tearing at her clothing. For a moment she struggled, but he was too strong for her. He took her, not brutally as she had feared, but demandingly, possessively.

"You are *mine*," he muttered against her cheek, "all mine. God knows how I've waited this long!"

Afterwards he left her abruptly without another word. She lay in the double bed, her emotions in a turmoil. She knew now what it must have cost Lloyd Foster these past months to stay away from her bed. Since that tentative approach the very first night when she had cringed from him he had never again made any attempt to touch her. Not until now.

Now, finally, as they had quarrelled openly his passions had boiled over and he could no longer hold back.

"Possess my body he may," she promised herself, "but my heart – never! He took me away from Jamie," she told herself fiercely. But Lloyd is your husband, her conscience reminded her, and he has been good to you.

In Paris they stayed in a fine hotel. Lloyd took her dining in the best restaurants and courted her with gifts. "Didn't I say you'd be the fine lady, me darlin'? You're every bit as lovely as these Society ladies, so you are."

Paris was a truly romantic city. Carrie was caught up in the whirl of the life there. Everything she saw she committed to memory and learnt from it, so swiftly that soon she was able to move in the middle-class society with ease as if she had been born into such circles and not bred in a mud hut, with bare feet and scarcely a wrap to keep her warm in winter!

She heard no news from England. Not of her family, nor of Jamie Trent. Though Lloyd came to her often now, many nights she still slept alone. Occasionally, she wondered where her husband went when he was not by her side.

He took her through France and, as winter encroached, they moved south until they reached Cannes.

Cannes was fast becoming a place where it was fashionable for the wealthy British to buy a piece of land and build a villa. Then when the English winter became too chill they could travel to their 'winter resort' on the Mediterranean coast.

"Do you know," Lloyd pointed out the villas to her as they drove by in a hired carriage. "Do you know that they even have turf shipped from England – renewed every year if they need it. Can you imagine a fellow bein' rich enough to be able to do that?"

Carrie looked at the magnificent villas, white and shining in the sun, surrounded by groves of orange and lemon trees. "No," she said soberly, "I *cannot* imagine it!"

Lloyd laughed and put his arm about her slim waist. "Ah, me darlin', we'll be rich one day. You'll have everything you ever dreamed of!"

Carrie glanced down at the green silk crinoline she wore, at the fine gloves, at her feet encased in satin slippers. Already she owned more than she had ever thought possible. But how swiftly she would abandon it all to be back in her coarse skirt and bare feet, to be back in the abbey ruins in Jamie's arms. *That* was all she had dreamed of!

Lloyd rented a villa and they stayed in Cannes. Almost against her will, Carrie grew to love the pretty town nestling in a bay, the beautiful blue sea, the mountains. She blossomed in the warmth of the sun and in the clear air. Her thinness was gone, the pale, half-starved look. Her skin glowed with health and she matured from a young, passionate – yet undernourished – girl into a beautiful woman, serene yet somehow remote. Always, deep in her violet eyes there was a sadness.

"You know what dey'll be wantin' here, all these wealthy Englishmen, is a railway – a passenger railway from Paris to the south coast," Lloyd said standing on the balcony of the villa overlooking the blue sea. He glanced back into the bedroom where Carrie was lying on the bed, fanning her face vigorously. It was the first time the word 'railway' had been mentioned between them.

"Really," Carrie's tone was non-committal, bored almost, as she flapped at an intruding mosquito.

"There's only about four hundred miles of railway in the whole of France," he was saying, suppressed excitement in his voice. "And that's mainly for the carrying of coal."

"Really," Carrie said again and closed her eyes, not noticing the expression on Lloyd's face as he looked at her and sighed and then went back to gazing out to sea.

This life of high-living was all very well, he was thinking, but I'm beginning to miss me railways. He couldn't push the matter too far – not yet. He must give Carrie time to forget. But, some day, somehow, somewhere, he knew he must once again build a railway.

It was in his blood!

As the months stretched into years Lloyd Foster grew increasingly restless. Between himself and Carrie the uneasy truce remained. She was his wife in every sense now and yet always there was a shadow between them, the shadow of her love for another man and of Abbeyford and all its memories.

"We'll have to go back to Paris," Lloyd told her. "That's the centre of things. We've been here in Cannes three years and I'm missing what's happening. Louis Philippe passed an Act in 1842 for the construction of a great network of trunk routes from Paris over the whole of France. I could be part of all that. Damn it – I *want* to be part of it!"

So back they went to Paris. Unfortunately for Lloyd, things did not work out as he wanted. For another two years he tried to find employment as a railway builder, but once again there was confusion in Paris and although a network of railways had been approved in theory, the actual construction was a different matter. Economic difficulties in France and the air of unrest, which at any moment might erupt into revolution yet again, made investors wary and the capital required for the railways was not forthcoming.

"Damn it all!" Lloyd burst out, striding up and down the hotel bedroom whilst Carrie sat at the dressing-table, arranging her hair in readiness for a ball they were to attend. "There's nothing here for me. The whole city is in a turmoil! They're never at peace, these people! Now, they're wanting to be rid of Louis Philippe!" He paused a moment and then said, "They're so wrapped up in their political intrigues, there's going to be no progress for the next year or so. There's no railways for me to build *here*! We'll have to look elsewhere. I must find work!" And he punched one clenched fist into the palm of his other hand.

Carrie stopped brushing her hair, her brush suspended in mid-air, and turned to look at him, suddenly interested. "You mean you've come to the end of your 'fortune'?"

Lloyd's laughter filled the room. "Me darlin', there never was a 'fortune'. How do you think I've made us a livin' these past five years, eh?"

Carrie shrugged. "I thought it was the money you'd made building railways in England. You always seemed a wealthy man."

Again he laughed. "Ah, me darlin', there's still much you don't know about me. Where do you think I spend me nights when I'm not beside you?"

"I neither know nor care."

The pain was fleetingly in his eyes, then he said. "For your information, madam, the money which buys you all these fine fripperies," his fingers touched the lace on her white shoulder, "comes from gambling."

She swivelled round quickly on the stool to stare at him in amazement. "*Gambling?*"

"Aye, whilst you're sleepin', I've been playing at the card-tables here and in Cannes, earning us a livin'."

"Well!" Carrie was speechless. "*Well!*" was all she could say again.

"But I'm tired of it now. I've had enough of the high livin', the drinkin' and gamblin'. I want to get back to me railways."

Carrie's lips parted and her eyes shone. "If there's nothing here, then – then – we're going home? Back to England?"

Lloyd's eyes darkened with anger, his mouth became hard. "No, I don't mean dat at all," he said harshly, her joyful anticipation bringing back all the antagonism between them. "We're *never* going back to England, d'you hear me?"

As the look of hope died in her eyes now, Lloyd's tone softened a little. "I've met this man, a captain in the British Army in India. Stationed at Calcutta, he is. He's been on furlough – enjoying himself in Paris," he grinned. "Well – he tells me they're planning to build a railway from Calcutta. There's a lot of wrangling goin' on, so it seems, but I've got used to that this past two years in Paris. He reckons if I was to get out there, maybe have a look at the terrain, I could persuade the powers that be to hurry things along a little, y'know. Captain Richmond'll be at the ball tonight. Now, ye'll be nice to him, won't you, for my sake?"

Carrie turned back to the mirror and resumed brushing her hair with sharp, angry strokes. "India! That's the other side of the world. I don't want to go. I *won't* go!"

"Well, me darlin', we're going!"

"This is Captain Richmond," Lloyd introduced a gentleman in military uniform to Carrie.

"I'm happy to make your acquaintance, ma'am." The Captain took her hand in his, bent over it with a show of gallantry and raised it to his lips. As he lifted his head, his eyes looked into her face with bold audacity.

"Captain," she murmured.

He was undeniably handsome. Tall and slim, with fair hair, bright blue eyes and a small, neat moustache. He was indeed resplendent in his scarlet coat, with its white sash across the chest, the gold braiding and shining gold buttons. He was elegant and his whole manner and bearing exuded confidence – the kind of self-assurance that only comes from having been born into a wealthy family, of accepting the place in life as a leader of men as one's natural right.

"May I have the pleasure of this next dance, ma'am?" Carrie inclined her head and she moved gracefully on to the dance floor on his arm.

"You dance exquisitely, Mrs Foster."

She smiled at his compliment. How his face would alter, she thought mischievously, if he knew my background and my upbringing.

"I was fortunate enough to learn to dance here, in Paris," she told him.

"Ah, then that explains it."

They danced for a short time in silence, then the Captain said, "Your husband is a delightful fellow. Unique, one might say. I've played cards with him several times and don't he have the devil's own luck …?" He paused as the steps of the dance took them apart. "He never seems to lose!"

"Really," Carrie said with an air of complete uninterest.

"But, then," the Captain smiled, his blue eyes intent upon her, "perhaps it's the charm of all his Irish blarney. Is that how he came to capture such a prize as yourself, ma'am?"

The smile died on Carrie's lips, her violet eyes were dark with sudden misery and her steps faltered in the dance, causing her to miss a sequence. His question had evoked unhappy memories. The Captain seemed faintly amused. "Forgive my audacity, ma'am, but amongst these fair, milk-white maidens your dark beauty is so striking. Your eyes are like the spring violets ..."

"Pray, sir, your compliments are extreme!" Carrie, once more in control of her emotions, smiled.

His eyes were upon her face, his smooth voice low and intense. "Indeed they are not, ma'am, I assure you!"

The dance ended and he led her back to where Lloyd Foster waited.

Captain Richmond was the epitome of politeness, yet in his eyes there was danger when his gaze rested on Carrie. If it were not for the protective presence of the huge figure of her husband, Carrie thought, I should have need to fear this man. She put her arm through Lloyd's and smiled up at Captain Richmond, believing herself secure in the thought that a man of such good breeding would not encroach upon another man's preserves.

"Have you decided, Foster?" Captain Richmond addressed her husband but his gaze never strayed from Carrie for long.

"Well, now, I'm thinking I've nothing to lose by comin' out to India. Me only concern is for me lovely wife here. Will it be possible to find a comfortable place for her, d'ya think? Havin' never been to India, I just don't know what to expect. D'you understand me now?"

"Indeed I do," the Captain smiled. "There are many European inhabitants in Calcutta, wealthy merchants and the like. We should have no trouble in finding suitable accommodation for your good lady," he gave a slight bow in Carrie's direction and added, almost as an afterthought, "and for yourself."

At that moment another gentleman requested Carrie to dance and she left her husband and the Captain eagerly planning the proposed trip to India. Carrie sighed inwardly. Lloyd had become animated at the thought of being once more involved with the building of a railway. After all the disappointments he had met here in Paris these last two years, now his hopes were rekindled.

She guessed his self-imposed exile from the work he so obviously loved had been entirely on her account. He had wanted to remove her from the environment of railway building that would always remind her of Abbeyford – and of Jamie! But now, after five years of living off his wits and his dexterity at cards, the man hungered for useful, constructive work once more.

The dance ended and as the young dandy led her back across the floor to her husband and she saw his eyes seek out her face, for the first time since her marriage she felt a flash of genuine fondness for him.

If only, she thought half-regretfully, I had not already given my heart so irrevocably to another, maybe I could have found real happiness with Lloyd Foster.

The ship was moving, under the direction of the Pilot, the last forty or so miles through the Ganges delta towards Calcutta on the east bank of the river Hooghly. Carrie stood on deck between her husband and Captain Richmond. The three months which this voyage had taken, throwing the three of them into close proximity, had rendered a subtle change in the relationship between them. Carrie had, with each day that passed, come to fear Captain Richmond a little more, and in so doing had drawn closer to Lloyd for security. Her husband had seen nothing amiss and the Captain was careful not to let him see the lust which flashed in his eyes when he looked at Carrie, but she had seen it! Lloyd did not feel the underlying challenge in Jeremy Richmond's mocking tone. He accepted the Captain as a man who would introduce him to the right people in India, on whom his future depended. So Carrie remained silent.

"Will yer look at dose swamps?" Lloyd was saying. Carrie saw the treacherous swamps, with palms and mangroves and sticky mud. Birds rose from the trees and they could hear the sounds of the undergrowth. She shuddered. "I don't like it," she murmured. "It's so hot and – *eerie!*"

"Not many dare to venture in there, Mrs Foster," Captain Richmond glanced down at her. "There's all manner of snakes, tigers, monkeys – to say nothing of the crocodiles!"

Carrie glanced down over the side of the boat, as if fearful of seeing one of the monsters sliding by. She looked up again towards the bank, and then cried out in surprise. "Why, there's a village. I thought you said the place was uninhabited?"

"That's a *native* village, ma'am." His tone was condescending and Carrie pursed her lips.

"They're people, none the less," she replied sharply.

"A little farther on you will see a clearing where a European indigo planter has his bungalow and factory, and later still an area called Garden Reach, where rich European merchants and officials have their homes. It's quite the 'little England'," Captain Richmond added, his tone heavy with sarcasm.

Eventually, Carrie saw the place he mentioned – houses with verandahs and flower-beds and trees. She could see children running on the well-kept lawns with their ayahs – their Indian nursemaids. There were even one or two pet dogs barking playfully.

Then as they rounded the final curve Carrie's attention was caught by the busy harbour. It seemed crammed with boats of all descriptions – barges, fishing-boats, clippers, and all manner of small boats. Set high above were the ramparts of Fort William.

"Will that be where you are stationed, Captain?" Lloyd asked.

"It is indeed, sir," was the reply.

Carrie saw that amongst the Indian coolies on the dock side, amidst the bustle of bullock carts, camel carts and barrows, stood a few British or European people, men in top hats and women in fine crinolines. There were even a few British landaus pulled by shining horses. Behind the teeming dockside, rose a skyline of magnificent towers and domes.

After they had left the ship, Captain Richmond found lodgings for them in the Garden Reach district.

"This house belongs to – er – a friend of mine. He is away at present, but I know he would not mind you having the use of it."

"We are most grateful to you, Captain, to be sure," Lloyd laughed and slapped his new-found friend upon the shoulder, but the Captain's gaze was upon Carrie as if it were her gratitude alone he sought.

"Pray make yourselves comfortable," he said, bowing, his insolent gaze never leaving her face. "There are servants to do your bidding. I must report to Fort William, but I shall return tomorrow to see that you have all you need."

Carrie inclined her head, but she could not bring herself to enthuse over the Captain's seeming kindness. She felt instinctively that one day, somehow, he would demand repayment.

Her husband made up for Carrie's lack of gratitude. "I don't know what we should have done without the Captain, me darlin', in this strange land."

"But for the Captain, we should not *be* in this strange land!" Carrie retorted sharply and flounced out of the room.

That night Carrie lay in a huge bed under a mosquito curtain. England seemed so very far away now. She had had no word from her family since her marriage. Nor had she had any news of Jamie. Was he still in Abbeyford? Was he married, with children? Though her homeland and family were far removed, Jamie's face was still vivid in her recollection. His face was before her, tender, loving, and then finally filled with the desperate misery of their final parting.

Lloyd Foster lay a few feet from her in his own bed, flapping occasionally at a stray mosquito which had found its way in, but Carrie's thoughts were many hundreds of miles away. They had left England in the early spring – now it would be high summer there. She fell asleep dreaming of that wonderful summer when she had fallen in love ...

SIX

For the next few months Lloyd Foster seemed rejuvenated. He would return to the house bursting with news, his enthusiasm spilling over. "Ah, Carrie me darlin', such opportunities here. Such visions. Oh, 'tis hard work there's ahead of us, to be sure. There's so much that's new."

"New? How?" Carrie asked, attempting to show interest though she found her days dull. Now that she had a houseful of barefoot servants, silently padding about their tasks, she found the days empty.

" 'Tis different to railway building in England. The climate is so different, the heat, the rains, to say nothing of the river changing its course before we get the bridges built!" He laughed. "And you should see the length they'll have to be." He spread his arms wide. "The rivers swell so, that the bridges have to be much, much longer than in England."

England! Carrie felt a great yearning sweep over her. But it was no use. Her husband was happy now he was once more going to build a railway – so here she must stay!

The months passed and Carrie found her days filled only with the social life of the European wives resident in Calcutta – tea-parties and afternoon visits; dinner-parties and balls.

There were delays with the actual beginning of the railway construction – and Lloyd began to chafe.

"I t'ought they was all ready to begin building and what do I find now?" He flung his arms wide in a gesture of despair. "I find there's two, if not three, different companies going to build different parts of the railway." He ticked them off on his fingers. "There's the Great India Peninsula Railway going to be built from Bombay; the East India Railway from Calcutta, to say nothing of a third company – the Madras Railway."

"Well, since we are in Calcutta, I suppose it's the East Indian Railway you're involved with, is that right?" Carrie asked reasonably.

"Yes, but …"

"And where is the line from Calcutta going exactly?"

"Supposed to be westwards over the Ganges plain to Lahore, but …"

"Then where," asked his wife calmly, in contrast to Lloyd, who was visibly heated, "is the difficulty?"

He paced the room. "Oh, 'tis all politics and guarantees and contracts and shareholders – just what I came here to try and escape. The East India Company were on the point of signing contracts with both the East India Railway and the Great India Peninsula Railway – and *now* what do they tell me?"

"I have no idea. What?" Carrie asked patiently.

"There's been some sort of financial crisis in Britain and revolutions in Europe and the companies cannot find the deposit required before signing the contracts. Then rival companies leap in and investors lose confidence in ours and so," he shrugged his shoulders, "it looks like another hold-up. Oh, I don't understand it all – 'tis all high finance at government level – I only had to deal with directors of railway boards in England – an' I could handle them, but here ... 'tis out of me hands." He sat down looking dejected and beaten.

"Do – do you think Captain Richmond knew this when he suggested you should come here?" she asked carefully.

Lloyd shook his head. "I don't suppose so. I reckon he's genuine enough."

Carrie said nothing, but she did not agree with him. She watched Lloyd. Her heart leapt. Perhaps he would be obliged to leave India, to go home, back to England. They had come here to build railways and if there was no railway to build ...

But the irrepressible Irishman would not be deflated for long. Before Carrie could utter any suggestion of her own, he had bounded to his feet again and, his hand on the door, turned to her to say briefly, "But, in the meantime, while all the wrangling goes on, there's no reason why I can't be surveying the land and makin' out me own case, now is there?"

He was gone, once more bounding with enthusiasm and energy.

Carrie sighed. It looked as if she must resign herself to life in India for a while yet.

The months stretched to a year before the contracts were at last signed and work could begin. Lloyd rubbed his hands. "We're to site the eastern terminal of the railway at Howrah on the west bank of the river Hooghly," he told Carrie.

"Really? Why not in Calcutta itself?"

"It would need an immense bridge from Calcutta across the river – it's over seventeen hundred feet wide there, even though that's its narrowest point," Lloyd explained. "We could hardly begin with such a difficulty after all dis time it's taken even to get started building the railway."

"I suppose not," she agreed.

So at last Lloyd was actively employed, though even then the actual construction did not begin until another several months had passed, for the surveying was complicated in view of the nature of the unpredictable terrain and climate. They were hampered by the rains, by flooding, to say nothing of the difficulty in procuring the gang of navvies from the native population and sorting out who would work where and with whom, in view of all the differing religious beliefs and the strange caste system.

During all this time Captain Richmond was a frequent visitor to the house in Garden Reach where the Fosters continued to stay, though there were periods when he was absent on military matters up-country.

"Won't your friend mind us staying here all this time? Where is he?" Carrie asked him.

The Captain seemed amused. He coughed and then said, "My friend has no need of this accommodation at present and is most happy for you to stay in his house as long as you wish."

"Yes – but surely we should be paying him some rent?"

"My dear Mrs Foster, I – my *friend* – would not hear of it."

Carrie glanced at him curiously. Suddenly she began to doubt the very existence of the mysterious 'friend' who owned the property. Wisely, she thought it better not to press the matter further.

At long last, when they had been in India over two years, the actual construction work began and Carrie found she had to leave the comfortable house and follow her husband alongside the track of the slowly growing railway. But now her itinerant life bore no resemblance to that harsh life in England under her father's neglectful care. Whenever possible, Lloyd Foster found accommodation for her in proper houses, the homes of people either directly connected with the railway, or at least interested in its growth. If no house were at hand, the camp they set up was like a small village, for not only were there all the railway workers, but the entourage which Lloyd Foster had collected for himself and his wife, whom he was determined should be treated as a lady, was vast in itself. Carrie laughed at the difference between her life in a mud hut or shack in England to the one here surrounded by servants. But her laughter was tinged with sadness when she thought of the hard life her mother had led, how she had never known such consideration from her husband.

Carrie's tent was elaborate, being twenty feet high and twenty feet square, divided into sleeping quarters and living quarters. Meals were served by her servants with the same ritual as if they were in a palace, and at night the whole camp was surrounded by fires to keep away the tigers and other beasts which roamed the jungle.

Captain Richmond was a frequent visitor to the camp, as he had been to the house in Calcutta.

"Lloyd is not yet home," Carrie told the Captain one evening, meeting him at the entrance to the tent. She was determined not to ask him inside, for the silent Indian servants had a habit of disappearing if they thought their mistress had a guest.

His face was in shadow, but his voice, mocking and yet at the same time challenging, came softly through the darkness. "Perhaps you would care to take a walk around the camp-site, Mrs Foster?"

Silently, she put her hand reluctantly upon his arm and he led her away from her tent, towards the camp-fires set at intervals.

"Ah, what mystery and danger lurks beyond those flames, my dear Mrs Foster."

"Indeed, sir!" Mockingly she adopted his own turn of phrase. "There is much to be feared from the wild animal, almost as much as from civilised man!"

Captain Richmond's eyes were upon her face illuminated by the flickering firelight. She is the most beautiful, fascinating woman I have ever met, he thought. And her coolness towards me arouses my desire for her all the more. I'd like to crush her in my arms, feel her yield to my will ...

As they walked through the darkness amidst the jungle, he bent towards her. "You have nothing to fear, my dear Mrs Foster, from any *man*. All men would fall at your feet. Such beauty as yours demands adoration."

"I think you mock me, sir."

"Ah, madam, how can you be so cruel? If you were not a married lady, married to a man I most *earnestly* admire, we would not be walking like two friends, so chaste, so distant."

Carrie's heart beat fearfully. He was hinting at his feelings for her. Yet, instead of being flattered by his words, she felt an icy finger of dread amidst the heat of the jungle. She shivered and Captain Richmond was at once all effusive concern.

"Mrs Foster, are you cold? I forget my duty. Pray let me put my coat about your shoulders."

At once he began to unbutton his scarlet tunic.

"No, no, I am not cold. It is merely the jungle – the cries

of the birds and the monkeys. It seems so frightening here in the darkness."

"No – I insist," he said and draped his jacket about her.

"Thank you," she murmured, unable to refuse now. "Please, will you take me back to my tent now, Captain?"

Lloyd Foster was waiting at the tent. At the sight of them he started forward. "Carrie – Carrie, my love. Are you all right? What ...?"

"My dear Foster," the Captain bounded forward. "She is quite safe. We were merely walking when your wife became a little chilled."

Lloyd glanced from Carrie to the Captain's face and back again. "Oh, I see," he said gruffly, obliged to accept Captain Richmond's explanation, but Carrie could see the anguish in his eyes, the unspoken question.

"I will take my leave of you, Mrs Foster." As she gave him back his coat, the Captain took her hand and raised it again to his lips. "Goodnight – goodnight, Foster." He disappeared into the darkness.

As they prepared for sleep that night, Carrie was aware of the feeling of tension between them. At last Lloyd burst out, "I'm beginning to dislike that fellow, to be sure. I don't like to see you with him. I don't – trust him!" He paused and then laughed wryly. "But then, I suppose I don't trust any man wid you, me darlin', now do I?"

Carrie smiled a little sadly, for though Lloyd's words were spoken half in jest, she knew that there was a world of longing behind them. Suddenly she felt compassion for him. He loved her in his own rough way. He had been so good to her. And even though she found herself in a strange land, he saw to it that she was comfortable and lacked for nothing. She reached out suddenly in an unexpected gesture of tenderness, "You have naught to fear from him, Lloyd, for I dislike him myself – intensely, and have done so since first meeting him."

Lloyd caught at her hand, longing in his eyes. Slowly he pulled her to him and took her in his arms. "You never said."

Carrie, within the circle of his embrace, shrugged. "I thought he was important to you. I thought you needed him to help you meet the right people ..."

"Ach, Carrie me darlin', I can stand on me own two feet. I want to live in no man's debt. Aye, he's been useful, I'll not deny, but ..." his embrace tightened about her. "If he's makin' a nuisance of himself to you ..."

She put her fingers on his lips. "I'll not let him."

Lloyd laughed softly against her. "Aye, an' I believe that, me lovely."

That night his lovemaking was tender and gentle and for the first time Carrie felt herself respond to him through a growing fondness. He was a good, kind man and deserved her love, she thought sadly as later he lay sleeping beside her.

She closed her eyes against the tears. If only I could love him, but there's no room in my heart for anyone but Jamie!

The following morning, Lloyd explained that he was to be away from the camp for a week. "I must look at the land ahead, do another survey, for these damn rivers have a habit of changing their course. And I need to be findin' a new camp-site ahead." He looked down at her with concern. "Now you'll be all right, me darlin'?"

"Of course," she assured him, but she did not feel as confident as she sounded. Despite the fact that the camp was full of people, without Lloyd Foster's strong presence,

Carrie felt very much alone in this foreign land.

Two days after his departure the first Indian was taken sick with cholera. Carrie visited her servant, who was lying in his tent. He was vomiting and crying with the pain in his feet. Constantly he cried out weakly for water and yet when she held a cup to his cracked lips he seemed unable to drink. Within twelve hours he was dead. After that the fever swept through the camp so that soon the roles were reversed and the mistress was moving from tent to tent ministering to her servants and to the men who built the railway. Three died the following day and another two the day after that. Work on the railway must have stopped, she thought, but she could not worry about that. Those who were left, lugged the corpses to the river bank and unceremoniously flung them into the water.

The sight of the victims – their brown skin parched and burning to the touch, their already emaciated bodies becoming like skeletons, the dark eyes filled with suffering – touched Carrie's heart. She felt so helpless, all she could do was to keep sponging them down and offering drinks.

"Missus – we put hot rods on the soles of der feet," one servant told her. "Old Indian custom – very good – drive out pain."

Carrie snorted. "The only effect I can see that having is to cause even more pain!"

The Indian shook his head. "Oh, no, Missus – very good. You wanna try?"

"No," she said sharply, lifting the head of one of her patients and holding a wooden bowl to his cracked lips. "I do not – and don't let me hear of you trying it either."

The Indian shrugged philosophically, "They all gonna die anyways," he muttered and padded away.

Carrie felt no fear of disease herself. Had she not nursed her brothers? She had no time to attend to her own appearance, so that by the end of the week when Lloyd was due to return, her hair was ruffled and streaked with dust, her clothes stained, her face hot and her eyes red-rimmed with fatigue.

She longed for her husband's return, for his strength and help, as four more of her servants fell ill. Soon there would be no one left and she would be alone in the camp, alone amidst the horrors of the wild jungle! She lit the fires at night but there was little fuel left and courageous though she was, Carrie dare not venture into the thicket to seek more.

As she stooped to light the fire, she heard the sound of a horse approaching the camp. She stood up.

"Lloyd, oh, Lloyd, thank goodness!" she cried, greatly relieved at the thought of his return. She ran towards the man on horseback and then stopped suddenly.

It was not her husband who had ridden into the camp, but Captain Richmond.

Disappointment and a twinge of fear caught at her.

"My dear Mrs Foster," Jeremy Richmond leapt from his horse and hurried towards her. "Whatever is the matter ...?"

"I – thought you were – my husband."

"But – you look greatly fatigued. Are you ill?"

"No. No, I'm not. But there is cholera in the camp. The Indians ..."

"My dear lady, you must remove yourself at once. This is no place for you. If you should contract the disease ..." Instinctively, he had moved back a pace from her and she could not help a wry smile touching her lips as she noticed his action. She was not so desirable now, she thought, dishevelled and dusty and a possible carrier of disease.

"I cannot leave until my husband returns. Besides the sick need caring for ..."

"Your husband would not forgive me if I were to leave you here in such danger," Captain Richmond insisted. "Not only danger of contagion but – if all your servants die – what then? You – alone in the jungle? It is unthinkable!"

"I must admit to being a little afraid ..." then she added firmly, for she guessed what he was leading up to say, "but I cannot leave. I cannot leave these people to die."

Captain Richmond dismissed the matter with a wave of his hand. "They are dispensable. I can obtain you more servants in Calcutta."

Carrie gasped. "How can you be so heartless? They are human beings. They are suffering agonies with this terrible fever ..."

"Your husband would have no such scruples, ma'am," the Captain's tone was full of sarcasm. "I must insist you return with me to Calcutta. We will leave a message here for Foster on his return."

"I will *not* come with you, Captain Richmond," Carrie said quietly and added reluctantly. "Though I am grateful to you for your thought for my welfare."

"Oh, Carrie, Carrie," he stepped towards her, his eyes wild. He gripped her shoulders. Carrie grew rigid beneath his touch.

"Captain Richmond – you forget yourself!"

Behind them there was the sound of another horse. They both turned to see Lloyd Foster riding towards them. Captain Richmond released her at once and hurried forward to meet her husband.

"Foster! How glad I am to see you. I have been trying to make your wife see reason. The camp has been hit by a cholera epidemic in your absence, and Carrie – Mrs Foster," he hurried on swiftly to hide his slip of the tongue, but the look in Lloyd Foster's eyes told Carrie that he had noticed the Captain's use of her Christian name in a familiar manner. "Mrs Foster has been nursing them. I cannot emphasise too strongly the danger to herself in this. You should get her away immediately. Leave all your belongings – everything. I pray you, come quickly back to Calcutta, back to my house – my friend's house." Again in his agitation, he made a slip but now concern filled Lloyd Foster's mind so that only Carrie observed it.

Lloyd was down from his horse in an instant and striding towards her. "Ach, me darlin', what have you been doin' to yourself?"

Her head rose in defiance. "I've been nursing the sick, it's my duty, Lloyd. Our duty. We cannot leave these people to die alone – out here in the jungle."

"If you don't leave – and now," Captain Richmond's voice was insistent," you will all be dead!"

"I may already have the disease on me," Carrie said calmly. "Do you wish me to be the cause of an epidemic in Calcutta?"

The Captain shrugged, whilst Lloyd murmured, "But I should get you away from here."

"Don't be ridiculous, Lloyd," Carrie snapped, impatient with all the arguing. "Of course I shan't get the disease now. I must have an immunity to it. Good grief, haven't I nursed enough sickness with my own brothers?"

But their problem was solved for them in an unexpected way. That night the Indian servants who had not fallen sick fled the camp, and by the morning Carrie and Lloyd found themselves the only two healthy people in the camp. By evening the sick had died, and so there was now no reason for them to remain in camp.

"Leave everything," Captain Richmond, who had again come to visit them, insisted. "Just come home with me and we will engage more servants and workmen for you in Calcutta. No need to tell them you've had the disease here. They'll come back with you in due course."

"Aye, maybe you're right at that," Lloyd Foster agreed, though there was a reluctance in his eyes.

Back in the comfortable surroundings of the house in Garden Reach, Carrie found herself once more cosseted and waited upon. Neither she nor Lloyd contracted cholera and after a few days Captain Richmond insisted that they should use their enforced holiday to become acquainted with some of the Europeans in Calcutta.

"Many of the wealthy merchants are anxious to meet you, Foster," he told Lloyd. "They look upon your railway as a means of transport which will bring greater profits for them, and they wish to show you their hospitality."

So, thought Carrie, it still went on, even out here in India. Men using one another for their own ends. Even though her feelings towards her husband had mellowed considerably through his goodness to her, she could never forget how he and her own father had used Jamie Trent's grandfather — who was her own grandfather too, she remembered suddenly — a drunken, defenceless old man — to gain possession of his land for the railway.

"Ah, well, dat's good to be sure, but I should be getting back to me railway ..."

"Oh, surely not. You've not yet found all the men you

need, have you?" He glanced sideways at Carrie. "Besides, your wife deserves a change of scene from the nightmare of that camp!"

Lloyd's eyes rested upon his wife. "Well, you're right there, I'm thinkin'."

So they allowed themselves to be swept once more into the social life of the wealthy Europeans in Calcutta. But Carrie was not taken in by it. All this wealth, she thought, and there's people starving in the streets below, dying of dreadful diseases and living in squalor. She sighed. Life, it seemed, was unequal the world over.

"May I have the pleasure of this dance, Mrs Foster?" Captain Richmond was before her, his eyes challenging, his smile mocking. They were attending a ball given by one of the European merchants in Lloyd Foster's honour.

"Thank you, Captain." She gave him her hand and forced herself to smile charmingly at him.

They moved into the dance.

"May I be permitted to say how beautiful you are looking tonight," Jeremy Richmond murmured.

"Why, thank you."

Her ball gown was pale pink satin, decorated with tiny bows. The neckline was low and the wide, swinging crinoline emphasised her tiny waist.

As the dance ended, Captain Richmond said, "May I be allowed to escort you home? Your husband has become involved in a lengthy game of cards, I believe."

"Do you not play, Captain Richmond?"

"Occasionally, when it suits me."

When he needed to, more like, Carrie thought wryly, just like Lloyd, he would use his gambling instincts to swell his pockets.

Aloud she said, "Thank you, but Lady Benjamin, who

lives next door to your house – to your *friend's* house, I should say – has offered me a place in her carriage. Her husband, too, is involved in the same card game as Lloyd." She was glad to have a ready-made excuse, thankful for the kindness of Lady Benjamin. She saw the Captain's anger spark in his eyes, saw his mouth tighten. He took her hand in his and bowed low over it.

"Some other time, ma'am." His words seemed like a veiled threat.

Lloyd did not return that night and when there was still no sign of him the next morning, Carrie became alarmed.

She sent word to Lady Benjamin to see if her husband had returned and was informed that Sir Hugh had come home at about two in the morning.

Where, then, was Lloyd?

The servant, whom she had sent on the errand, bowed low once more. "Lady say to tell you, Missus, that Master go with Captain. Where, she don't know, but he go."

"With Captain Richmond?"

"Ya, Missus."

"Very well, thank you." Now she was even more anxious.

About mid-morning she heard hoofbeats and ran to the window at once. Captain Richmond was dismounting in front of the house, but he was alone.

Carrie bit her lip as she waited for the Captain to be shown into the room.

"Ah, my dear Mrs Foster."

"Where's Lloyd?" she asked without preamble.

"Your husband, ma'am?" The insolence was more apparent now. "I should not have thought you would be particularly worried about your *husband*!"

Carrie gasped. He moved closer, so close she could feel his rapid breath upon her face. "What do you mean, and how dare you speak to me in that – that manner?"

"Oh, I dare, Mrs Foster, because I found out a few things about the beautiful, aloof Mrs Foster last night."

He grasped hold of her shoulders. "Your dear husband was drunk and he started rambling, talking about his life – his married life with you. Oh, he loves you, that's not in doubt. What is in doubt, Mrs Foster," his words were lined with sarcasm. "Is *your* feeling for *him*. From his sometimes incoherent mumblings I managed to piece the truth together. At least, I think it's the truth. That's why I'm here, Carrie my darling, to find out about you, and your so-called marriage."

"Let go of me this instant, or – or I'll scream!"

"Much good it would do you. *My* servants would not come to your rescue."

"So it *is* your house?"

"Of course. I could scarcely tell you that, though, could I, or you would have refused to accept my hospitality?"

"Yes, I would."

"See how well I know you already, my dearest."

Carrie began to struggle but the years of refined living had robbed her of some of her strength. Under Lloyd's protection she had had no need to fight for survival.

Not until now.

"Where is Lloyd?"

"Mr Foster is on his way back to the railway site. I packed him into a gharry and bade three of my servants drive him back."

"He went – without telling me?"

The Captain laughed maliciously. "He had no choice, ma'am. He was dead drunk. By the time he is sober he should be back with his beloved railway."

"There are no navvies there since the cholera."

"Oh, that was taken care of days ago – a party were sent out and should be well settled into camp by now. All that was missing was their master. So I thought that should be rectified."

Carrie grew more angry and a prickle of fear ran down her spine. "Then I, too, must return to the camp."

"Ah now, I have other plans for you, my dear."

"You presume, sir. Whatever your plans are they shall not include me!"

His grip, from which she had been unable to wriggle free, tightened so that his fingers dug into her flesh. "You have kept me at arm's length, so cool and remote, playing the lady. And I thought it was because you loved your husband. But you don't, do you, Mrs Foster? 'If only she loved me', he said last night. 'Why couldn't she love me instead of that Trent fellow?' "

"Oh!" Carrie cried and began to struggle violently. But the more she wriggled, the tighter he held her.

"Ah, now that seems to have struck a chord, doesn't it, my dear Mrs Foster?"

"You are insufferable. Let – me – go!"

"Who is this Trent? Is he your lover?"

"It's – none of your damn business."

"Aha!" His eyes glinted with satisfaction. "So the ladylike mask begins to slip a little, eh?"

"I've never pretended to be a *lady*, as you put it. But Lloyd has money and he wanted to buy me clothes, and ..."

Jeremy Richmond was laughing. "Lloyd Foster has money? You're living in a fool's paradise, my dear. He owes me five hundred, and God knows how much more to others interested in his damn railway."

Carrie was suddenly still, horror-stricken by the Captain's words, for she knew he was not lying.

"But – but you're not interested in his railway, are you?"

"No," and his voice grew hoarse with suppressed emotion. "But I am interested in his *wife*!"

Carrie, her face only inches from his, said, "Well, Captain, now your cards are finally on the table, let me tell you this. Husband or no husband, I would never – ever – be interested in you. Now, will you kindly release me or I shall create the biggest commotion ever heard in Calcutta."

For a moment they stood locked in a battle of wills, then with a short laugh he let her go. "I can wait, my love. Now I know the truth about you – and your marriage – I can bide my time. But," he added, and there was menace in his tone. "You shall not escape me. I shall follow you wherever you go – to the ends of the earth if necessary. You shall not escape me – not now!"

He turned and was gone from the room. Carrie sat down, suddenly finding that she was shaking from head to foot. The revelation of her husband's financial state, the Captain's abhorrent advances and his threats, had badly frightened even Carrie's stout heart.

"Lloyd," she said aloud to the empty room. "I must go to Lloyd. I must tell him. He will protect me."

She managed to hire a gharry – a box-like vehicle without springs drawn by a scrawny horse – and soon Calcutta was behind her. As Fort William grew fainter in the distance, Carrie breathed more freely. They travelled for a distance of some thirty miles, passing all the places she had stayed alongside the railway as slowly it had stretched across the countryside during the last eighteen months. The horse was exhausted, but the railway bed was in sight.

As they drew closer, it seemed to Carrie that there was a great deal of shouting and yelling going on. Indian workers were running in all directions, their arms waving, their voices raised in a high-pitched babble. She narrowed her eyes against the glare of the sun. The work in progress was a cutting through a low hill and the railway track had already been laid so far into the cutting, but it stopped dead, hidden by what looked like a landslide.

She jumped down from the vehicle and, picking up her crinoline skirt, she began to run towards the workings. She grabbed an Indian running in the opposite direction. "What has happened?" she demanded, but she had learnt so little of the language that she could understand nothing of his incoherent jabber.

She hurried on, down the embankment, slipping and sliding in her anxiety. She could see Mr Thompson, the new engineer, near the fall, directing the workers, his voice loud and clear, his arms waving directions.

"Mr Thompson, Mr Thompson, what has happened? I'm Mrs Foster – Lloyd's wife."

He turned. His clothes and face were covered with dust, his face streaked as rivulets of sweat ran down his cheeks. Wearily he passed his hand over his forehead.

"Lloyd, where is Lloyd?" Her voice was shrill with fear. She saw him glance towards the pile of rubble, and her heart contracted. "Oh, no!" she whispered.

"There's six under there, ma'am. And I'm pretty sure one's your husband. We're getting to them as fast as we can but ..." His voice died away, then more briskly, he added, "If you'll excuse me, ma'am. I must help."

"Of course," she said and stood watching, feeling lost and helpless as the men dug and scrabbled at the fall.

How long could anyone live under that, she thought, supposing they even survived the first fall? It was sand and stone mostly. They'd suffocate. It would fill their mouths, their nostrils, their eyes ...

She gave a small cry of anguish and clasped her arms

about her body in a gesture of self-comfort.

After half an hour they retrieved the first body, then swiftly three more were found – all dead.

One of the party of rescuers gave a cry as another body came into view and Carrie's head jerked up. She saw them pull Lloyd's huge frame from beneath the sand and she stumbled forward.

"He's still breathing, Mrs Foster," Mr Thompson said, "but only just!"

They carried him a short distance from the fall and laid him down gently. At once Lloyd began to struggle to rise.

"No, no, lie back," Carrie insisted, kneeling beside him and cradling his head in her lap. He began to cough and splutter, gasping and wheezing. She brushed the sand and dirt away from his face.

"Carrie, Carrie, is that you?" his voice was a strangled whisper.

"Yes, now lie still. We'll get help."

"No, no time," he whispered desperately. "I can't breathe – I can't breathe." He began to choke.

He drew rasping breath then said, "Carrie, you must get home. Go straight home to England. Don't stay – here. He's dangerous. Get away!" She knew he meant Captain Richmond. "Do you hear me – now?"

"Lloyd, don't talk ..."

"I must – tell you. Go back to – to – Trent." As if he had only lived to see her once more, to speak to her again, to tell her what she must do, he fell back, his eyes staring blankly towards the sky.

"Lloyd! *Lloyd*!" she cried and shook him.

" 'Tis no use, ma'am. He's gone. The stuff must have choked his lungs. I don't know how he lasted that long in there," Mr Thompson said in wonderment.

Slowly Carrie lifted her face. She said nothing but silently she thought – you don't know the strength of this man. And now his strength was gone. His protection was gone. She was alone in a strange, hostile country at the mercy of Jeremy Richmond.

The dead were buried with little ceremony at the side of the railway. As Carrie stood above the grave marked by a simple, rough cross made out of railway builder's tools, she felt real grief for her husband. If only I could have loved him, she thought with remorse. Although she could not forgive many of the things he had done, she had to admit that his treatment of her had always been loving and thoughtful. Knowing she loved another man, he had married her, lavished gifts on her, protected her and tried to make her a lady. Her life with him had been one of comfort and luxury such as she had never before known. As she turned away she knew that, though her love would always belong to Jamie Trent and to no other, Lloyd Foster had earned her tender affection.

SEVEN

Carrie stepped down from the train at Abbeyford Halt. The train pulled away from her, thundering up the line, past Abbeyford Manor and out of the valley. She looked about her in wonder. How altered everything was. The railway line ran exactly where her father and Lloyd Foster had planned it, between the Manor and the stream, the common and farmland cut in two by the embankment supporting the track.

The Manor! Her heart missed a beat. Was he there? Was Jamie Trent still living there?

She walked along the small wooden platform, through the white-painted gate that marked the boundary of the railway property and began to walk towards the village. Now the cottages were stained black with the constant smoke from the steam engines. She neared the line of cottages where her grandmother, Sarah Smithson lived. A little nervously, she approached the door, but as she lifted her hand to knock she felt a sense of desolation sweep over her and knew there was no longer anyone living in this cottage, even before she wiped away the grime from the window and peered in. Then she tried the door and found it opened, scraping on the stone floor. She stepped into the dismal, damp cottage. The place was derelict. Odd items of furniture still littered the dirty floor, a broken chair, broken cups, old clothes and dust – dust everywhere. The cottage had been empty for some time.

Carrie felt the sadness sweep over her. Her grandmother was dead – she sensed it, knew it. And probably Henry Smithson too. There was nothing for her here. She left the cottage reluctantly, closing the door behind her as if closing the door on her memories of the little old woman who had lived there. She wished she had known her better, wished she could have known the truth of her grandmother's love affair with Guy Trent.

Carrie looked up and down the village street and then her gaze was pulled once more across the village green and up, up towards Abbeyford Manor. Her heart began to beat a little faster. She had to know whether or not Jamie still lived there – if he was married with a family of his own – or if he still remembered her.

She walked up the lane, over the tiny bridge near the ford and then over the new railway bridge – a slim young woman in a wine-coloured skirt and jacket of fine velvet material, edged with self-coloured braid. Her black hair was smooth and neat, coiled up on the top of her head, upon which perched a pretty bonnet.

It was autumn of 1853 and the golden leaves were falling from the hedgerows, and the air was clear and sharp.

Carrie breathed in the country air, savouring its freshness which even the presence of the railway and all its smoke could not spoil completely. It was so invigorating after the heat and humidity of India. It was so quiet, so peaceful – almost too quiet. She glanced back thoughtfully towards the village. There were one or two people moving about, but many of the cottages seemed deserted now. Perhaps, with the ruination of the farming land by the railway, many families had been forced to move elsewhere to find work.

So much had happened during the years she had been away, so much had changed and yet now she was back here again, the years between seemed to have gone so quickly.

Would Jamie have changed? Would he look the same? Would he *feel* the same about her?

"Go home," had been Lloyd's dying words to her. "Get away from here – go back to Trent!"

She had been lucky to escape from India in the way that she had done. After Lloyd had been buried she had returned briefly to Captain Richmond's house. Luckily, he was not there. She learnt he had been sent at short notice with a detachment of soldiers up-country. Silently thanking Providence, she had swiftly packed as much as she could carry. Taking her jewel box she had found her way to the markets in the streets of Calcutta and, after much haggling, had sold her jewels for enough money to buy her a passage home. Her only fear was that there would be no ship in Calcutta harbour bound for England. But once again she was fortunate. Threading her way through the busy dockside, she had heard the English voice of a First Mate shouting at his idle crew as they loaded cargo on to the ship.

Minutes later when she faced the Captain of the ship and requested passage, she knew a moment's fear as he said gruffly, "This ain't no passenger ship, lady. You'd best be waitin' till next week ..."

"Captain, I cannot wait till next week. I must leave India at once. My husband has been killed in a railway building accident, and I ..."

"Building the railway, was he?" Interest had sparked in the man's eyes. "Ah, well now, there's a man after me own heart. Me brother's a Hingineer on a railway back home in England. Now, I'd be right glad to help you, ma'am, but the cabin'll be a bit rough. An' I can only take you to France, ma'am.''

"I don't mind one bit, Captain," Carrie had smiled and silently had blessed the Captain's 'hingineer' brother. "I can find something else from there, I'm sure."

The passage home had taken over three months. Three months in which she had been able to rest and recover her composure after Lloyd's death and her hurried departure from Captain Jeremy Richmond's clutches.

Now finally – after several more weeks – she was back in Abbeyford and the years between seemed to slip away.

As she stood at the gate leading into the stableyard of the Manor, Carrie hesitated, irresolute. If he were still here, how could she just burst in upon him? What if he had a wife and children? Would it not be wrong of her to disturb the peace he had perhaps found for himself? And yet, her own heart ached for sight of him. She knew, deep down, that whatever his situation now, his love for her had been so deep that even the passage of these last twelve years could not have dimmed that love.

She walked through the deserted yard, everywhere was neglected and overgrown. The stables were tumble-down, the weeds growing through the cobbled yard. Jamie cannot live here now, she thought with sudden disappointment. He would never allow it to become like this – unless, unless he had lost all heart, all ambition with her going.

She knocked on the back door, but there was no reply so she walked round to the front of the house and pulled on the stiff bell-rope there. She waited for what seemed a long time until she heard shuffling footsteps approach the door.

It opened slowly and Carrie found herself staring at a

stranger – a woman of about her own age. She wore a low-cut silk dress which once must have been a fine ball gown, but now it was rumpled and stained. Her hair was piled up untidily on to her head, tendrils hanging down around her face.

"What d'you want?" Her voice was rough and her manner coarse.

Carrie's mouth felt suddenly dry. "Does – Mr Trent live here?"

There was a moment's silence as the woman eyed Carrie. "And if he does, what do you want wi' him?"

Carrie almost gasped in astonishment. Surely, surely not *Jamie*?

She squared her shoulders meeting the woman's hostile eyes calmly. "I'd like a word with him, if you please?"

"Oh, 'I'd like a word with him, if you please'," the woman mimicked mockingly. "What'd he want wi' the likes o' you?"

I might well ask the same question of you, Carrie thought but aloud she repeated, "I would like to see him, please," with far more confidence in her tone than she felt.

Oh Jamie, Jamie, her heart cried out. Not this!

"You'd best come in then," the woman turned, leaving the door open for Carrie to enter and follow. She flung open the door of what had once been Squire Guy Trent's study and stood aside for Carrie to enter the room.

"There he is – but I doubt you'll get much sense out of him jus' now. Been drunk for two days, 'ee has."

The smell of drink hit her forcibly as Carrie stepped into the small room. She blinked and as her eyes became accustomed to the dimness of the room, she saw the figure of a man sprawled across the desk, an empty whisky bottle on its side. His head was resting on one arm, a few inches from his limp hand. She almost spoke the name aloud – Squire Trent – for this is how she had last seen him. Then she checked herself. No, no, he was dead, by his own hand. Jamie had told her. Then who ...?

She walked round the desk until she could see his face and when she did she drew breath sharply in surprise. "Pa!"

It was indeed her father. At the sound of her voice Evan stirred and raised bleary, bloodshot eyes to squint up at her. Carrie's heart missed a beat. It was as if she were seeing a ghost, for now her father was the image of the defenceless, pathetic old man she remembered as Squire Guy Trent – Evan's own father!

"Oh, Pa, what are you doing here?"

The woman, who had stood in the doorway watching, now moved into the room. "Is 'ee your Pa, then? Well, I niver!"

Carrie looked up at the woman. "Calls himself Trent, does he?"

The woman looked surprised. "Yea. Why, ain't that 'is name, then?"

Carrie smiled sadly. "It used to be 'Smithson'."

The sound of her voice, or the use of his former name, roused Evan. "Me name's Trent. I've a right to the name of Trent – it's my birthright!"

Carrie leaned closer. "Pa, it's Carrie."

The blurred eyes squinted at her. "Carrie? Ha – told you I'd live here one day, didn't I?"

"Much good it seems to have done you," she said candidly.

"I got a right to be here." He banged the desk with his clenched fist and swept the empty bottle to the floor. The sound of shattering glass made the two women jump.

"You 'is daughter, then?" the woman asked Carrie. "Well I never knew 'ee was even married!"

"Where is my mother?" Carrie asked.

"Lord knows," the woman shrugged. "Taken me in proper, 'ee 'as." Her glance rested balefully on the sprawling form.

"Does anyone else live here?"

"No, only us two."

"Pa," she shook his shoulder. "Pa – where's Ma and the boys?"

"Gone, all gone."

"Where – where've they gone?"

"Dead – all dead," he moaned and slumped forward again.

Carrie caught her breath and she and the woman gazed at each other.

"Ee, love, I'm right sorry to hear that." For the first time there was friendliness in the woman's tone. "You bin away then? Didn't you know?"

Carrie shook her head. "I've been away for almost twelve years." She paused then asked. "Do you know who lived here before Mr – Trent?" Referring to her father by that name did not come easily, but it was the only name by which this woman knew him.

"No," she shook her head. " 'Ee was here when I came. I met him in Manchester, an' he brought me back 'ere."

Carrie sighed and looked down with sadness at her father. He'd achieved his bitter ambition – to ruin the Trents and to live in the Manor House himself. But it had not brought him any happiness. In so doing he had ruined himself also.

"There's nothing for me here," she turned away and walked slowly from the room, past the woman and out of the house.

"Come an' see 'im again – when he's sober," the woman called after her, but Carrie only smiled faintly and nodded. She passed through the silent stableyard, averting her eyes from the buildings – that was where poor Guy Trent had ended his useless, tragic life. Once in the lane she turned to the left and climbed towards the wooded brow of the hill. Sadly she wandered through the shadows, hardly knowing where her footsteps led her. So many memories came crowding back. Memories of those wonderful days of summer. Memories of the handsome young man she had loved and still loved to this day.

She paused at the edge of the wood to look at the abbey ruins and then was drawn towards them.

The ruins had changed little. The ground within the crumbling walls was still littered with rubble, and the little room was still intact. If she had been more of a fanciful nature she might have imagined she heard the echoing laughter of the happy, ghostly lovers. Herself and Jamie? Or Guy Trent and his Sarah?

She shuddered and turned away down the hill towards the village. The bright day seemed to mock her sadness. She was no nearer, now, of finding Jamie again than she had been when she had left India. If anything she was even farther away, for then she had pictured him still living here.

Fondly – romantically – she had imagined him still living in Abbeyford Manor. Her heart had woven the fantasy of a joyful, poignant reunion. Her arrival at the Manor, Jamie's strong arms about her, the haven of love she sought.

But he was no longer here.

He had gone, and all that was left was her drunken,

pathetic father, now the image of the man – his own father – whom he had hated with such venom all his life; on whom he had sought – and achieved – such a terrible revenge!

But his revenge had destroyed them all.

Where was Jamie now? Where could he have gone? Who would know?

Her steps led her automatically to the churchyard set in the centre of the village. She pushed open the gate and went in. Walking among the gravestones, without thinking she began to search for those of her mother and brothers.

"May I help you?" A kindly voice spoke behind her making her jump.

She turned round to see the smiling face of a young curate. "Oh – I – er – don't quite know."

"Were you looking for a particular grave?" he asked gently.

She nodded. "I've been away for almost twelve years. I have only just learnt that my mother and younger brothers are – dead. I wondered ..."

"Perhaps I can help. I could look in the Parish Register, if you like."

Carrie nodded. "That would be very kind of you. I'd like to know – where they are."

"Come along, then," the young man said briskly and led the way into the quiet dimness of the church and through into the vestry.

He pulled a huge book from a shelf and laid it on the table. "Now, can you give me some details."

"Well, there's Lucy Smithson and her two sons, Matthew and Thomas."

"And you've been left about twelve years?"

"Yes."

His finger was running down the pages.

"Smithson ..." he murmured. "Ah now, here's a *Luke* Smithson."

Sadness swept over Carrie at the memory of her elder brother. "Yes – yes, he died just before I left."

"Ah – so the names you are looking for would be later than that." There was a short pause when he said. "Now here we are – Matthew and Thomas Smithson. Oh dear me, their deaths are listed on the same date. Now, wait a minute, I seem to remember. Yes, were they working on the building of the railway?"

Carrie nodded.

"Yes, *now* I remember. There was an explosion – dynamite incorrectly placed, I believe. There were seven killed, I think." He counted the names in the register. "Yes, seven. And I'm afraid your brothers were amongst that number."

"And my mother – Lucy Smithson."

Again he searched. "Yes – here it is. She died only two months after your brothers."

Carrie nodded again, a lump in her throat. She could imagine poor, worn-out Lucy, finally beaten by the loss of her two youngest children. Of all of the seven children Lucy had borne, only Carrie now survived.

"Could you also look for a Sarah Smithson? She was my grandmother."

For several moments his finger ran on down the page. Slowly he shook his head. "No – I can't see any Sarah. There's a *Henry* Smithson. He died eight years ago."

"Yes. He was – her husband." Carrie hesitated for he had not been her grandfather. That was Squire Trent.

Suddenly, a thought struck Carrie. "Wait a minute. Go back a little. To the time when Squire Guy Trent died."

The young curate made no comment, but did as she asked.

"Why, yes, her name is directly after his. She died the following week." His eyes were upon Carrie, questioningly, but even though the young man had been so kind she did not want to confide in him.

Let the unhappy lovers' secret die with them, and she thought how ironic it was that they had been obliged to live out their lives apart and yet in death their names were close beside each other.

"Can you tell me where my mother and brothers are buried, please?"

"Ah, yes, now where are we?" He looked back at the list again, noted the numbers of the graves and then from the back of the book pulled out a plan of the graves in the churchyard. "Yes, they're all together over by the yew tree in the far corner." Again he turned, almost apologetically, towards her. "Their graves are unmarked, I'm afraid. No one requested any head stones and the parish cannot …"

"No, no, of course not," Carrie said swiftly. Her father would never have thought to spend his money on such things as gravestones! Sooner a bottle of whisky, she thought bitterly.

It was quiet and peaceful under the yew tree in the corner of the churchyard. Probably the only peace her mother had ever known, Carrie thought sadly, and wished she could have done more to make her mother's life easier. The grass was long and the area neglected, but she could just detect the gentle mounds showing where her mother and brothers were buried. At last she turned away, sick at heart that, at the moment, she could not afford to erect headstones either. "Some day, some day …" she promised the silent earth.

Then intruding into her quiet solitude came the sound of a train whistle as it neared Abbeyford Halt, then moments later it burst into view, puthering clouds of grey smoke. Fascinated, and yet partially appalled by the iron monster thundering through the quiet valley, Carrie watched it screech to a brief stop at the Halt and then, with much chugging, it pulled away and was soon gone, leaving only the tell-tale cloud of smoke drifting over the village.

It was beginning to grow dusk, she had allowed that train to depart without her, and she doubted that there would be another that day. Besides, she was not yet ready to leave Abbeyford. Surely there must be someone here who knew where Jamie had gone. But who?

"Of course," she murmured aloud and a small smile of fresh hope curved her mouth. "His stepmother – Lady Adelina Lynwood!"

She remembered Jamie's words all those years before – could almost hear his beloved voice; 'She's very beautiful and has been very kind to me. I'm very fond of her.'

Jamie would not leave without telling his stepmother where he was going. She would go and see Lady Lynwood, and with that thought her feet began to move eagerly up the lane, then she stopped. It was too late now to walk the several miles from Abbeyford to Lynwood Hall. She could hardly arrive there late at night.

Carrie decided she would stay here in Abbeyford and visit Lady Lynwood the next day. But where could she stay? She could not – would not – go back to the Manor. She wandered down the one village street and found herself outside the cottage which had been her grandmother's. It was empty and cold; she thought, but it offered shelter. There could be no harm in her staying there overnight.

The cottage was lonely, haunted with memories of the

old couple who had lived there.

Carrie found a few bits of wood in the coal-house at the back and built a fire in the living-room grate. Though the chimney smoked a little through lack of use, the fire warmed her. She drew the old rickety armchair towards the blaze and banged the cushions vigorously to get rid of the dust, then she curled up in it and despite the fact that it was now several hours since she had eaten, she soon fell asleep.

The morning found her cramped and even more hungry – and cold, for the fire had burnt down whilst she had slept.

She splashed her face and hands under the creaking pump in the small backyard and tidied her hair. Then, since there was nothing she could breakfast on, she left the cottage and began the long walk over the hills to Lynwood Hall.

At the Hall, the butler led her into the morning room. Carrie dropped a curtsy and said, "It is kind of you to see me, your ladyship."

"Please be seated," Lady Adelina indicated the wide window-seat near her, where she was sitting, some embroidery in her lap.

"Thank you," Carrie said and moved across the room and sat down. Now that she was closer she could see that Lady Adelina had scarcely altered since the last time she had seen her – over twelve years previously. Her rich auburn hair was just as beautiful with not a trace of grey and her lovely face showed not the faintest line or blemish. She was staring at Carrie, a slightly puzzled expression in her eyes. "Should I know you, Mrs Foster?" she murmured. "I can't seem to recall ..."

"My lady – we did meet once, but the circumstances, *my* circumstances, were very different then." She trembled a little inwardly, but met Lady Lynwood's gaze with an outward show of fearlessness. "I am Evan Smithson's daughter."

Hatred and fear swept across Lady Adelina's face, then she touched her forehead with trembling fingers and tried to smile. "I'm sorry, my dear, it was just a shock to hear his name again ..."

Carrie leaned forward, no longer afraid. Lady Lynwood did not resent her, though she obviously felt a deep, abiding hatred for Evan Smithson.

"Why do you hate him so much?"

Lady Lynwood met her clear, questioning gaze. "My dear, it would be very wrong of me to tell you. Just let me say that something he – he did, caused me a great deal of unhappiness. I cannot forgive him – though I know I should."

"It seems," Carrie said quietly, "his bitterness and twisted soul has touched many lives – and brought unhappiness to them all."

"I'm afraid so."

"You know he is living in Abbeyford Manor now and calling himself Trent?"

Lady Lynwood gasped. "No! No, I didn't. We have severed all connections with Abbeyford now – even though it is only a few miles away. We sold Abbeyford Grange – my grandfather's old home – so there is no need for me to visit Abbeyford now. I went there once, just after the railway line was completed, but to me the village has been spoilt."

Carrie nodded, then said, "Lady Lynwood, the reason for my visit is – to ask you – if – if you know," the colour rose in her cheeks and her heart beat faster, "where Jamie Trent is?"

"Jamie?" Lady Lynwood gazed at her for a moment then she smiled. "Of course, he told me. You and he fell in love, but your father and – another man, I forget his name …"

"Lloyd Foster," Carrie interposed. "They came between us, and I was tricked into marrying Lloyd."

"And now?" Lady Adelina asked.

Carrie's shoulders slumped. "I suppose it's too late. I expect Jamie's married, with a family."

"What of your husband?" Lady Adelina probed gently.

"He was killed – in India. I have only just returned to England myself. I came straight here – to Abbeyford – but my father, he's too drunk for me to make any sense of him."

Lady Lynwood's mouth hardened. "He doesn't seem to have found much happiness himself either."

Carrie shook her head. "But Jamie? Do you know where he is, how he is?"

Slowly Lady Lynwood shook her head sadly. "My dear, I wish I *could* help you. Shortly after you left, he came to stay here at Lynwood Hall for a while. Then he decided he would go right away – so he joined the British Army. I hear from him very occasionally, but it is over two years since I last had a brief letter, so I really don't know where he could be now."

Carrie felt the tears prick her eyelids. Her disappointment was acute. She had been so hopeful that Lady Lynwood would know where he was.

"I'm sure he's never married, my dear," Lady Adelina leaned forward and gently touched Carrie's hand. "He would have written to tell me *that*, I know."

Carrie nodded but she was not convinced. Two years since Lady Adelina had last had word from him. So much could have happened in that time …

Carrie stood up. "You have been most kind, my lady.

Thank you for receiving me."

"I'm so sorry I cannot be of more help. Where will you go now?"

Carrie shrugged, desolate and lost. "I don't know."

"May I suggest London," Lady Adelina said gently. "I believe there are many headquarters and officers' clubs and so on there. You may be able to get news of him. And if," she added, "you need help, we have a town house in Mayfair."

"No – no, I wouldn't presume. You have been so kind already."

"Well, send me word of your address and if I hear anything from him, I promise I will write and let you know."

"You are very good, my lady," Carrie said gratefully.

Lady Adelina smiled. "He mentioned you only once while he was here. He was very unhappy at losing you, I could see that. I'll do whatever I can to help you find each other again."

With Lady Lynwood's promise to cling to, Carrie left Lynwood Hall and returned to Abbeyford. She would catch the next train to London – the very next train! There was now no reason for her to stay in Abbeyford any longer.

Passing the Manor, she hesitated. Perhaps she should just see her father once more before she left. Have one more try. Perhaps by some chance he knew more than Lady Lynwood, though she knew it was unlikely.

"Oh, hello," the woman greeted her in a friendly manner. She was still wearing the same dress she had worn the previous day. "He's sobered up a bit this morning. But he don't remember you comin' yesterday." She held open the door for Carrie to pass into the dismal hall. "I've been tellin' him, but I don't reckon he believes me. Evan," she raised her voice shrilly. "Evan, she's 'ere again. Your girl. Come on," the woman beckoned her through into a room which had once been the drawing-room. It was large and could have been beautiful, but the furniture was dusty, the paintwork peeling and the carpet worn into holes.

Evan Smithson was sprawling on the sofa in front of a blazing fire. His head turned jerkily, and it seemed to take a few moments for his eyes to focus upon her. He still had the manner of a man in a permanent state of drunkenness, though Carrie could see that today he was a little more aware of his surroundings.

"My God! Is it really you, lass?"

Carrie stood before him. "It is, Pa."

"Where've you come from? Where's – what's 'is name?"

"Can't you even remember the name of the man you forced me to marry?" Carrie asked bitterly. "He's dead. He was building a railway in India and he was killed in a landslide."

"So you've come back home, have you? Well, we'll have to clear a room out ..." he made as if to struggle up.

"There's no need, Pa. I'm not staying. I've only come to ask one thing of you. Do you know where Jamie Trent is now?"

Her father slumped back against the sofa. His mouth trembled and his eyes darted from side to side. His shaking fingers plucked at the worn material of the sofa. "Trent? Trent? Tha's my name."

"No, it isn't, Pa. Your name is *Smithson*!"

"No, no," he shouted, breathing heavily.

" 'Ere, watch it," the woman spoke up. "Don't upset him. He's had one heart attack. I don't want him havin' another."

"That's *my* name," he mumbled. "Squire Guy Trent was my father. It's my birthright."

"I know, Pa. I know," Carrie said soothingly, with far more patience than she felt. "But do you know where his grandson, Jamie Trent, is now?"

"Grandson? Grandson? I don't remember no grandson. His son, Wallis – but he's dead, isn't he?" He grinned suddenly, showing blackened, broken teeth. "Killed trying to save his horse from a fire I started."

"You seem proud of the fact," Carrie said with disgust. Her father grunted.

It was no use, she thought. He couldn't even remember Jamie – or wouldn't! She turned to leave, then briefly looked back over her shoulder. "Pa – why does Lady Adelina Lynwood hate you?"

"Adelina? Ah, my lovely Adelina, my proud beauty!" He laughed cruelly. "Robbed her of her maidenhead, didn't I? Thought she was better than me. I showed her. Wallis Trent wasn't going to have her before me."

Carrie turned away feeling physically sick. His whole life had been spent in bitter resentment of his unfortunate birth. Instead of rising above his illegitimacy, he had allowed it to warp his mind and soul and had destroyed everything and everyone he had touched. Even himself.

Carrie left the Manor and went towards the tiny railway platform to wait for the next train to London.

She would never see her father again, for she guessed that, in that pitiful state, he could not survive for many more months.

EIGHT

London was a vast and lonely place and the small amount
of money she had had left after paying for her passage home
would not last very much longer. Her heart wanted only to
search for Jamie, but common sense told her she must find
shelter and employment first. But what could she do? Her
only experience had been of housework – and the keeping of
the shack was scarcely the same as working in a fine house
as a maid. She found cheap lodgings and then began
searching for work. Carrie applied for one or two positions
as housemaid but was turned away. She was even
unsuitable for the post of kitchen-maid it seemed.

Winter came, but Carrie had no money to buy warmer
clothes – clothes such as she had not needed in the heat of
India. New Year arrived, but except for the odd temporary
job, lasting only a few days at a time, Carrie still had not
found permanent employment. And still she had no news of
Jamie, in spite of numerous enquiries.

Then suddenly the cold weather was gone and a warm
spring arrived. At least now she was no longer shivering.

One evening when she returned to her dismal lodgings,
she found the house in a turmoil. The landlady, a fat, loud-
mouthed individual, was standing at the top of the stairs
banging on the door of a room opposite to the one Carrie
occupied.

"You bring that woman out o' there, Mister. I'll have no sickness here in my house." Again she banged on the door.

"What is it, Mrs Prince? What's the matter?" Carrie asked.

"Cholera! That's what," she panted, wheezing heavily. "I don't want no sickness in my house." She shook her fist towards Carrie as if she were personally responsible.

Carrie stood still on the stairs as the memories of the camp in India swept over her, the natives dying of the dreadful disease.

"Mrs Prince — let me try. I was among cholera in India. I'm not afraid."

"I want 'er out of here. There's a place run by a Miss Nightingale — a cholera house — in Harley Street. She can go there."

"Perhaps you'd call a cab then, while I try to talk to the husband."

"A cab? An' who's to pay for that, might I ask?"

Carrie raised her eyebrows. "Which do you prefer? The price of a cab against her staying here in your house?"

Grumbling, the woman turned and waddled downstairs.

Carrie knocked on the door. "Mr Smith — please open the door. It's Mrs Foster from across the landing." There was no response. "Mr Smith — I know something about cholera. I've been amongst it. I want to help you. Please — open the door."

Nothing happened for a few moments, then Carrie heard the key turn in the lock and the door opened a fraction. Two frightened brown eyes peered round the door.

"Has she gone — Mrs Prince?" He was thin and under-nourished himself, dressed only in trousers and a dirty striped shirt and waistcoat. He still wore his cap even in the house.

"Yes, let me come in. I want to talk to you."

Once inside the cramped, airless room, Carrie quickly saw that the woman lying on the rough bed in the corner was very sick. She was writhing and moaning and dribbling. The whole room smelt sour with sickness. Swiftly, Carrie explained in whispers to the man that his wife must have some proper care. "Mrs Prince knows of a cholera house. Let your wife go there. It's her only chance!"

"No, no, it's the workhouse she means."

"Nonsense – but we will go with her to make sure Mrs Prince is speaking the truth."

The door of No 1 Harley Street was opened by a maid in a black dress with a frilled white apron and cap. "Yes'm?"

"We have a woman sick with cholera," Carrie said. "We have been told we might bring her here."

"Oh, no, madam. This is an Institution for Sick *Gentlewomen*. We can't take – just anyone!"

Carrie opened her mouth to protest but at that moment a quiet voice spoke behind the maid. "What is it, Mary?"

The maid turned and curtsied. "Begging your pardon, Miss Nightingale, there's someone at the door with a woman sick with cholera. She thinks she can bring her here."

The door opened wider and Carrie looked up to see a tall woman, slim and dignified, dressed completely in black. Her calm face was surrounded by short brown hair and her grey eyes were alert and bright. "I am Miss Nightingale. May I help you?" Her voice was pleasant and her pronunciation beautiful. She was undoubtedly a lady of quality, Carrie thought instantly.

Carrie repeated her story.

"I am so sorry, what my maid tells you is perfectly correct. This establishment is for gentlewomen only, and I couldn't take the risk of a cholera patient here either. Take her to the Middlesex Hospital. She will be well cared for there."

"Thank you. We'll do that." Carrie turned away and hurried back to the anxious little man in the cab.

"What'd she say?"

"They can't take her here. We've to take her to the Middlesex Hospital."

"Oh, no!" the little man groaned. "She won't come out of one of them places!"

Grimly, Carrie was forced to agree.

But little Mrs Smith did recover – though she was one of the very few people who survived the dreadful sickness. Perhaps she owed her recovery in no small measure to the devotion of one particular nurse – Mrs Carrie Foster. As soon as Mrs Smith had been admitted to the hospital, Carrie had applied to become a nurse there and was taken on immediately.

"It looks as if we could be at the beginning of an epidemic," the Matron sighed. "Inexperienced though you are, I can make good use of you. I shall be glad to have someone who is not afraid of infection. It will make a change!" she added wryly.

As the spring of 1854 turned into summer the cholera epidemic which had threatened broke out in earnest. The hospitals were stretched to bursting point. Several nurses fell victim to the disease and others fled, fearing for their lives. Carrie worked long and hard amongst the crowded wards – so crowded that some beds were occupied by two women. Others lay on palliasses – or, as more and more patients flooded in, on the bare floorboards – between the beds and down the centre of the ward. There was little the nurses could do to cure the victims of cholera. They could only try to alleviate their discomfort by washing them, offering drinks, or holding the hand of the dying.

It was here at the Middlesex Hospital that Carrie met Miss Nightingale again, for in August that lady came to help organise the nursing of cholera patients. So hectic were the days, so exhausted was she at the end of them, that Carrie had little time and even less energy to continue her search for Jamie. She had written to several officers' clubs, enquiring if he were a member, she had even written to army officials, asking for information as to his regiment and posting, but all enquiries had proved useless.

Then, as weariness and desolation threatened to break down even Carrie's strength of purpose, a letter arrived from Lady Lynwood.

'*I have just learned that Jamie's regiment has been posted to the Crimea. I understand he sailed last week.*'

Carrie sat with the letter in her hand, loneliness and misery sweeping over her. He had left England, he had been here, somewhere quite near perhaps, and she had not known, and now he was gone, away across the sea to fight a war they had only just begun to hear of.

The weeks passed and the cholera epidemic abated and the hospital began to return to something like normality.

It was ironic, Carrie thought, that now that she had a little more time, there was nothing she could do. Jamie was in a far-off country and she was a virtual prisoner here in England.

At the beginning of October, Carrie received a terse note from Miss Nightingale.

'Please come to see me tomorrow at No 49 Belgrave Square at 11 a.m.'

Carrie was shown into the dining-room of the home of Mr Sydney Herbert, Secretary at War, at two minutes to eleven the following morning. Miss Nightingale was seated at the dining-table, papers spread out before her, her pen poised in the act of writing copious notes. She was plainly dressed, her brown hair, parted in the centre and looped in two plaits over her ears. The grey eyes in the oval face regarded Carrie searchingly.

Without preamble, she launched into the reason for her summons. "I have been asked to take a party of nurses to the Crimea. Will you come?"

Carrie gasped. The Crimea? She was being asked to go to the Crimea? It seemed like a dream. She could find Jamie, or at least, her reason told her, she would stand a better chance of hearing news of him than stuck here in England.

"Oh, yes, yes. I will." She could not stop her eagerness from showing on her face.

"It will be demanding, back-breaking work, it will tax your strength, your resolve and your courage to the utmost. You will see sights you had never thought existed. I know of your work at the Middlesex Hospital – it does you credit. But I know nothing of your experience before that?" The statement was a question.

"I nursed my brothers when they died from consumption. Last year I returned from India – my late husband was a railway builder." She paused as Lloyd's laughing face was in her mind's eye. "There was much sickness in India – particularly cholera. I helped out when necessary."

Carrie was not one to boast of her self-sacrifice and yet Miss Nightingale's shrewd eyes seemed to read on her face that here was a woman who had had experience of life. It was written in her eyes.

"Have you any ties in England? Any family or – attachments?"

Carrie shook her head and answered quickly, perhaps too quickly. "No – there's no one here now."

Miss Nightingale's eyebrows rose fractionally but she asked no more questions on that point. She went on to explain the work which would be required of Carrie, finishing with the words, "I am a strict disciplinarian and any transgression from my rules will be severely dealt with. Do you still want to come?"

"Yes – I do."

Miss Nightingale smiled and her face altered immediately, the stern lines relaxing, but only for a moment then she added seriously, "I don't know what we're going to find out there, Mrs Foster. I hope you will have the stomach for it."

Carrie smiled, remembering the harshness of her life as it had been before she had married Lloyd Foster. "I think I shall, Miss Nightingale."

"Good," Miss Nightingale said briskly. "We leave on Saturday, the day after tomorrow. Can you be ready?"

Carrie felt a surge of excitement. "Yes, ma'am, I can."

She was on her way to find Jamie!

It was a motley selection of women who finally staggered ashore at the Scutari landing-stage. The *Vectis*, in which the party had travelled, had docked at Constantinople and the last mile of the journey, across the Bosphorus, had been made in two caiques. Carrie, least affected by the *mal de mer* of all the party, helped her companions.

"Gawd luv us," exclaimed one 'nurse', a woman recently

released from prison, "w'ot 'ave we let ourselves in fer?"

"What indeed," murmured Carrie. Some of the younger girls sank to the ground, whilst the Sisters, Roman Catholic nuns, accepted the trials in silence, but they were white-faced and, Carrie noticed, their hands were shaking.

Carrie looked about her. The whole shoreline was a vast cemetery. In the rough ground were row upon row of grave-stones of various sizes.

Near the landing-stage were a few Turks and, scarcely recognisable, their uniforms were so torn and dirty, were some British soldiers. All pride was gone, their faces were grey with sickness and suffering. Two walked on crutches, one trouser leg hanging loose and empty. Another nursed an empty sleeve, his eyes staring and vacant. Another ranted and raved, weaving about as if drunk until he slumped down on to the ground. No one went to his aid, no bearers appeared to carry him to the hospital. The man just lay there.

Carrie shuddered. Was her Jamie here – one of these pathetic creatures?

The hospital? Carrie's eyes lifted towards the huge, square building, three storeys high, with a red-tiled roof and a tower at each corner, set high up on top of the hill above the landing-stage and the small village.

They began to climb the muddy, winding track leading to the British Barrack Hospital – their home for the next few months at least!

It was not what they had expected. Nothing ever was, Carrie thought ruefully. The party of nurses, not at all welcomed by the officials, were housed in the north-west tower. The party had been here several days and yet they had scarcely set foot outside their cramped quarters. Miss

Nightingale remained adamant that she would do nothing until asked to do so by the Senior Medical Officer of the Hospital, a Dr Menzies.

"But men are dying whilst we sit here," Carrie had dared to argue. "Why can't we begin the work we came here to do?"

Miss Nightingale's face had softened. "My dear, your sentiments are admirable, but I fear misplaced. If we set foot in the wards without invitation, without permission, we shall be regarded as intruders, unwelcome ones at that. We must wait – we must!" Her mouth was firm, her voice resolute, but there was a haunted look in her eyes. She was convinced of the rightness of her own actions and yet the necessity for it tore at her heart. Carrie had turned away, sickened. Out there men lay dying, suffering untold miseries. Perhaps Jamie was amongst them. Her heart twisted in panic and silently she prayed. 'Don't let him be out there. I want to find him, but not this way, not *here*!'

The days passed and the nurses grew resentful. Whilst they continued to sort linen, to mend and darn and count provisions, they could hear the screams and cries of the wounded and sick. Miss Nightingale remained tight-lipped and resolute. And the nurses began to think she did not care. Only Carrie understood the reasons for her actions, and yet even she began to think Miss Nightingale was wrong.

"The only thing we're allowed to do is cook extra food in our own kitchen," grumbled one of the nurses, "and then only if a doctor has requested it."

"Why aren't we allowed near the patients?" asked Ellen, a scullery-maid who had been dismissed from her last employment without a reference for having a follower.

"Don't they trust us?" She grinned at Carrie cheekily, the suggestion in her tone implying that her ministrations to the soldiers' comforts might exceed those rules set by Miss Nightingale.

"I'm sure Miss Nightingale knows best," Carrie said, bending her head over her sewing of an arm-sling to hide the anger shining in her own eyes.

Less than an hour later she was bending over the rickety table Miss Nightingale used as a desk, repeating the very same question the young girl had asked. "Why aren't we allowed near the patients? We can hear them — dying in agony! We can smell the stench of death. The conditions out there," she waved her hand towards the part of the building which housed the wards, "must be intolerable. If we have lice and rats in our quarters — and we have — what on earth must it be like in there? You've seen it. You've toured the wards, haven't you? Well? You can't tell me we're not needed — desperately — by those men?"

Miss Nightingale's grey eyes regarded Carrie steadily, silently reproaching her for her display of temper.

"I'm sorry," Carrie said swiftly, even before Miss Nightingale had uttered a word. "But — but, oh it seems so pointless our being here if we are allowed to do nothing — absolutely *nothing*!"

"We shall be — soon. I'm sure," Miss Nightingale said quietly, but with conviction. "We must wait until we are asked."

And that was all she would say.

It seemed to the impatient nurses a long time that they waited in idleness whilst only yards away men died for want of attention, but in fact it was only a few days, for on the 9th of November, four days after their arrival, there came such an influx of sick and wounded following the Battle of Inkerman, that in desperation the doctors and officials turned to Miss Nightingale and her nurses for help.

"At last," she told her nurses, her grey eyes alight with the fire of the challenge, "we have been asked for help. We can begin our work ..."

At once excited chatter broke out amongst the women, but Miss Nightingale held up her hands. "I must ask you to remember – at all times – that we are under orders from the doctors. No one – not one of you – is to undertake to do anything without a direct order from me or from a doctor. Neither must you give commands to the ward orderlies. We shall find much to be done, you will work until you want to drop, and even then you will carry on, but you will work quietly and efficiently and – submissively. Do I make myself clear?

"Very well, then. Now, the first task is bedding. Many of the men have no beds to lie on, so we must make some straw palliasses ..."

So their work began. The wards were overflowing so that men lay in the corridors on the stuffed sacks, with just enough room to pass between them. Then the bags of straw were all used up and the men lay on the bare boards. The floors were filthy and verminous and the men no better. They were surprised to see the band of women moving quietly amongst them.

"I shouldn't come near me, lovey," one soldier, his face caked with mud, his hair and beard matted, said to Carrie. A filthy bandage wrapped his head and his left trouser leg was torn to the knee to reveal an open wound in his leg, the blood oozing from it on to the floor.

"Why ever not?" Carrie asked bending towards him. She could not kneel beside him, for the wooden floor was running with stinking liquid.

"I'm not fit for a lady to come near me."

Carrie laughed. "I'm no lady, I can tell you."

"By, you're from home!" The man's eyes brightened and for an instant the suffering, the pain, the filth, were forgotten as he was reminded of England. "I'd know that tongue anywhere, b'God. Aw lass, 'tis good to hear your voice!"

"*Now* wut thou let me help?"

"Ay, an' I reckon I will, at that." Then he looked at the bundle of clothing in her arms. "That's not some clean clothes, is it?"

"It is. Now, let's be gettin' those off you and these on."

"Aw well now, I dunno, I mean ..." Embarrassment spread across his face.

Carrie smiled. "What's this? A bashful soldier. I never thought I'd live to see the day!"

He grinned sheepishly and allowed her to help him, for he could not manage without her help.

"Where are you from?"

"Near York, miss. And you?"

"Now that you ask, I don't rightly know. Me Pa was a railway builder, so we moved about the country. We finished up near Manchester." She chattered on, asking him questions about his family, his home, anything to keep his mind off the job in hand – the changing of his clothes.

"There now, it wasn't so bad, was it?" she asked straightening up when they had finished.

"Nay, you'm a grand lass and no mistake."

"You – you don't happen to have heard of a Jamie Trent out here, do you?"

The soldier thought for a moment. "Nay, can't say I have. Why, he a relation of yourn?"

"Well, yes. My – my cousin. I – heard he was out here. I just wondered ... Well, I must move on. I'll see you again."

The man lay back on the rough straw bed, but his eyes were fixed upon Carrie's slight figure as she moved amongst the other patients.

Carrie had thought her experiences, the harshness of her childhood, the years in India, had equipped her to face anything that life had to offer. But even she was appalled by the conditions at Scutari. She worked, as Miss Nightingale had predicted, until she wanted to drop, and then she still carried on working until fatigue enveloped her and she stole a few hours' exhausted sleep, to rise and begin again. It was worse, far worse than the cholera wards at the Middlesex Hospital. The sick and wounded poured in and of each one whom Carrie attended she asked the same question.

"Have you met anyone called James Trent out here?"

Day after day the answer was always no, and then one night she came upon a young boy of no more than sixteen or so who had been brought in that afternoon with a sabre wound in his chest. His breathing was rasping and obviously the boy was in great pain. Carrie washed him and made him as comfortable as she could. She was about to turn away, omitting to ask the boy her usual question, for obviously talking would exert him further, when he caught hold of her skirt. She turned back and bent down.

"What's – your – name?"

"Carrie Foster."

The boy smiled and closed his eyes, but his fingers still gripped her dress. Then his eyes fluttered open. "Carrie. That's funny. I got friendly with a chap in our camp. He talked about a girl back home called Carrie. Delirious, he was, with the cholera. He was callin' her name. When he got a bit better I asked 'im about her. But he wouldn't tell me nothing. Said it was all a long time ago."

Carrie's heart was thumping madly. "What – was your friend's name?" she whispered tensely, steeling herself against disappointment.

"Name? Oh yes, his name. James Trent, that was it."

The boy had fallen asleep and Carrie could ask no more questions. She stood up and moved away as if in a trance. Jamie was here! She had met someone who had known him.

Cholera! The boy had said Jamie had cholera. Carrie's heart contracted in fear. Very few men had cholera and survived. But then the boy had said Jamie had got better. No, no, what he had said was that when Jamie had got a *little* better, he'd asked him who Carrie was. He had not said that he'd recovered completely. Then, why wasn't he here in the hospital? She was sure he could not be here. Every evening, she followed Miss Nightingale and her lamp through the wards, searching, always searching for Jamie and yet dreading to see him lying in this hospital.

How could she find him, how could she search for him? She had come as a nurse, she had hidden the real motive for her desire to come to the Crimea from Miss Nightingale. How could she now desert Miss Nightingale and betray the trust she had placed in her? How could she deplete the number of nurses so badly needed by the men? True, another batch of women had arrived, much to Miss Nightingale's dismay, for she found difficulty in uniting the diverse members of the first party and forming them into a hard-working band, without doubling the number.

Hour after weary hour, Carrie washed and bathed and bandaged, scrubbed and cleaned, held the hand of dying men, comforting those about to face the butchery of the surgeon's knife and all the time her thoughts were filled with one name. 'Jamie, Jamie, how can I find you?'

Her opportunity came unexpectedly. When the hospital ships arrived from Balaclava, much to Miss Nightingale's horror they were often anchored in the Bosphorus for a week or so before the sick were landed.

"It's appalling," she told Carrie, in a rare moment of confiding in her. "The men tell me that the wounded are often on board ship for fourteen days or so before they even leave the Crimea, then they have the ghastly sea voyage across the Black Sea of four or five days and then to think that they lay out there," she waved her hand in disgust towards the sea, "before they are brought to us. Is it any wonder the death rate is so high?"

"What can we do?" Carrie asked.

"Very little, I'm afraid," replied Miss Nightingale caustically. She glanced down at a letter she held in her hand.

"I've received a note from a major aboard the ship now lying in the Bosphorus. He's not among the wounded, I understand. I'm not quite sure what he's doing aboard – some official business, no doubt. He says he has heard of our arrival and asks if I could send my very best nurse out with some supplies '*so that she may attend the sick and wounded, and lessen their suffering, I am sure.*' Will you go?" Miss Nightingale looked up at Carrie.

Carrie's heart leapt. Here was the chance she had been waiting for, to get away from the hospital, even if only for a short time. That way she might find out more positive news of Jamie.

"Of course," she breathed, scarcely able to hide the joy from showing in her eyes. "When do I leave?"

"Make up a first-aid kit from our stores. Take all you can

manage. In fact, take one of the younger girls with you too. We can spare two of you, and it sounds as if your ministrations are badly needed out there."

"How – how long do we stay aboard?"

"You will leave at first light tomorrow and be away from the ship by dusk."

"Only one day, ma'am? That will scarce be time to attend to a quarter of the number on board."

"You may go back again the following day."

"Wouldn't it be more sensible to remain on board overnight?"

"It would – but think of the danger you would be placing yourself in."

"Among sick and starving men," Carrie said scathingly.

"The loss of your reputation ..."

"Madam, if I ever had any such *reputation*, then it was lost many years ago," she added softly.

"Oh, well," Miss Nightingale sighed. "You had best use your own judgment, I suppose."

Carrie turned away to hide the light of triumph in her eyes.

"Oh I'll be seasick again, Mrs Foster," wailed Ellen, trudging after Carrie down the muddy track towards the landing-stage. "You knows how bad I was when we come."

"Nonsense, Ellen, the sea's as calm as a millpond, look at it."

Carrie soon found a caique to take them out to the ship lying at anchor in the Bosphorus, and despite Ellen's continuous wailing, they boarded the ship quite safely.

"The Lord save us!" Ellen cried, her mouth dropping open, her eyes wide as she gazed around the deck of the ship. Grim-faced and silent, Carrie's eyes, too, took in the dreadful aspect.

Men lay on the open deck, mostly with no bedding, not even a covering blanket. Their clothes were unrecognisable as the British uniform, so torn and tattered and filthy were they. Some had open wounds with no kind of dressing, others with dressings so dirty that they undoubtedly did more harm than good to the wound they covered.

"Good day, Mrs Foster." A voice spoke close behind her.

Carrie gasped and her whole being stiffened. Slowly she turned and looked up at the man standing behind her, a smile of satisfaction upon his face.

"Captain Richmond!" Her voice was a hoarse whisper.

"*Major* Richmond, ma'am, at your service." He bowed mockingly. "I had hoped my letter might bring you. I guessed that amongst Miss Nightingale's motley band ..." he glanced meaningly at poor Ellen, "that you would stand out as a jewel amongst the rest."

"You – knew I was there?"

"Oh, yes," Major Richmond replied with confidence. "I have followed your every move, my dear, since you left India – in such haste!" His eyes glittered dangerously. Carrie swallowed the fear that rose in her throat. He has not forgiven me for escaping from him, she thought.

"But how – how do you come to be here – in the Crimea?"

Major Richmond tapped the side of his nose. "It pays to have relatives in high office, especially when one wants a transfer in a hurry." He laughed. "And I managed a promotion out of it too – though it cost me a pretty penny, I can tell you. Still ..." His hand reached out and caressed the sleeve of her dress. "It was worth it for sight of you again. You see," his soft tone was full of menace. "I told you you could not escape me."

Carrie felt a shudder run through her as she shrank from his touch, but she would not let this man know the fear he brought to her heart. Defiantly, she tossed her head. "You will excuse me, Major, we have work to do aboard this ship."

"Of course, ma'am." He bowed again. "I will not detain you – *now*!"

He turned on his heel and walked swiftly away, passing through the lines of wounded men lying on the deck without even glancing down at them. Carrie stared after him. Ruthless as ever, she thought, and shivered again. It became even more imperative that she should find Jamie, for he was her only protection against Major Jeremy Richmond.

"Who is 'ee, Mrs Foster?" Ellen whispered. "How do you know him?"

"I had the misfortune to meet him in India," murmured Carrie wryly. "I had hoped never to meet with him again, but it seems ... Come," she said, shaking herself, "we have work to do."

The following hours were taken up with the task of trying to make as many of the wounded and sick as comfortable as possible. Men with cholera and dysentery lay alongside those with wounds, so that very soon the wounded men had not only the pain of their injury to suffer, but the sickness too. They had lain on the bare decks, so that their backs were red raw. They were cold, filthy and starving.

"This is intolerable!" Carrie muttered angrily, straightening her aching back. She looked about her and then glanced towards the setting sun. Dark clouds were gathering with the threat of rain. It was obvious the men on deck would have no shelter.

"Where is Major Richmond?" she demanded of one of the crew.

The man shrugged uncaringly. " 'Ow should I know," then he grinned, showing blackened teeth. "But if you'm lookin' for a man, darlin', I'll ..."

Carrie turned away, disgust upon her face. She glanced towards the bridge and her eyes met the gaze of the man she was obliged, out of necessity, to seek. She crossed the deck towards him, stopping now and then to help one of the injured. Major Richmond descended from the bridge and came towards her.

"Ah, your work finished for the day, my dear? Then will you come below to my cabin ...?"

"Major Richmond, this work will *never* be finished," she began angrily. "Is there no shelter for these men? Look," she gestured towards the darkening sky. "It's going to rain soon. What are you going to do about it?"

"Ma'am, I am a man with power at my fingertips, but even my influence does not extend to the elements!"

"Don't treat me like a fool, Major," she snapped.

"Never that, ma'am, I assure you," he said sarcastically. "If you will permit me to give you a little refreshment after your labours," he held out his hand to her, "then we will discuss the matter."

"I don't think ..."

The Major made as if to turn away, shrugging his shoulders, "Then there is no more to be said."

Carrie glanced back at the men lying on the deck. Then she felt the first drop of rain upon her cheek. In desperation she turned back to him. "Very well, then," she said resignedly, trying to ignore the triumph which leapt into his eyes.

Below decks, in his cabin, the Major had evidently anticipated her acceptance of his invitation, for the meal on the table was the nearest to a banquet which Carrie had seen since leaving England.

"How do you come to have all this," she gasped, "when the men out there are starving?"

"I told you I had power at my fingertips. Pray be seated, my dear."

"No," she said sharply, "I couldn't, not when ..."

"My dear Carrie, this small meal would be as nothing to the number of men out there."

She whirled to face him. "How can you sit here gorging yourself, knowing your men are wounded, sick and starving?"

"There's no point in getting emotional about the situation. The officers in command must keep themselves fit and well, as must you, their nurse. Now, be sensible and eat."

"No," Carrie replied defiantly.

Major Richmond gave an exaggerated sigh. "Still as stubborn, I see. Still determined to play the heroine as you were in that campful of cholera-ridden natives."

"What are you going to do about those men on deck?"

"Absolutely nothing, my dear." Major Richmond seated himself at the table and spread his napkin across his knee. "If you will not join me, then there is nothing further to discuss."

For a moment Carrie stood irresolute, staring at him in disbelief. She had recognised him for a hard, ruthless man who would do anything to get his own way, but she had not thought that even he would stoop as low as this – to neglect his soldiers' well-being, to use them as pawns to blackmail her into submission! His passion for her – for it could not be called love – must be far greater than she had imagined. He had carried out his threat to follow her from India, to follow her wherever she went in the world. 'You will not escape me', he had promised, and now that promise – or, rather, threat – had been fulfilled. As she watched him begin to eat, her loathing for him overflowed. Then she remembered the men on deck, the encroaching darkness, the threatening storm.

Reluctantly she sat down opposite him. He grinned at her. "It's really very good, my dear, do try some."

Sick with revulsion she picked at the food upon her plate, merely to satisfy this man's whim. She must get him to do something for those men up there.

"Major Richmond, please ..."

"Ah, now that is more the tone of voice I like to hear from you." He reached out and touched her cheek. Though she cringed inwardly, Carrie clenched her teeth and restrained herself from slapping his hand away.

"Please – will you do something for those men?"

"Ah, yes, the men." He raised his voice. "Sergeant."

The cabin door flew open. There was a stamping of feet as the man came to attention with a sharp "Sir!"

"Arrange for the wounded on deck to be taken ashore. See what covering or shelter you can afford for those waiting."

"Y–yes, sir," the man's surprise was evident. "Right away, sir."

The door closed behind him.

"You see," Major Richmond said smilingly, "what it means to have power? I usually get my own way in the end, you know."

Not in everything, thought Carrie determinedly.

"Do have some wine, my dear, I'm sure you'll find it to your liking."

Major Richmond seemed determined to savour every mouthful of his meal and every sip of his wine. The minutes lengthened into hours and Carrie, weary, not only from this day's work, but from the weeks of hard, grinding labour, found her limbs grow heavy and her eyes drowsy from the warmth of the cabin, the headiness of the wine, the comfort of the chair.

She was unaware of the Major lifting her on to a couch, of him covering her with a blanket and then stealthily leaving the cabin.

When Carrie awoke, at first she did not realise where she was. It was so blissfully comfortable, so warm, so restful. Her aching body luxuriated in the soothing softness of the couch. She became aware of a gentle rocking motion and as wakefulness came, she looked about her. The remains of the Major's dinner still lay on the table, though light streamed in through the porthole. Bright light! Daylight!

Carrie was fully awake in a moment. She must have slept the night through. She sat up and swung her legs to the floor and stood up. Smoothing her crumpled dress and ruffled hair, she went to the door of the cabin. Twisting the knob she found she could not open the door. It was locked!

Stunned for a moment she could not think properly. Then she became aware that the ship's motion was far greater than the previous day when they had been at anchor.

She went to the porthole.

They were moving. The ship was out at sea, the shore a speck in the distance.

"Oh, no, no," Carrie cried and covered her face with her hands. How could she have been so foolish?

He had planned this. From the beginning, from the moment he had sent that letter to Miss Nightingale — perhaps even long before that for all she knew — he had planned this abduction.

Anger flooded through her. What of the wounded? Then she remembered. He had given the order last evening for the wounded to be ferried ashore. No doubt this had gone on all night whilst she slept in a locked cabin, and now with the morning they were out into the Black Sea.

"Jamie, oh, Jamie. I need you so much!" She closed her eyes.

During the previous day she had had little time to ask her usual question of the men on board and whilst she had attended to many she had not seen all of them. Ellen had descended to the lower decks to tend the men below.

The situation held more irony than Carrie knew.

At the moment when she awoke to find herself a virtual prisoner aboard the ship and sailing back across the Black Sea towards the Crimea, the wounded were being carried up the steep slope to the Barrack Hospital. Amongst them was a soldier with his arm badly smashed by a musket ball. Like his companions he was more dead than alive, dirty, half-starved, unshaven and cold.

His name was Corporal James Trent!

NINE

James Trent lay on sacking on the floor of the Barrack Hospital. He was slipping towards death. His eyes were closed against the sight of his companions and their suffering, but he could not shut out the sound of their moans, or the shrill cries as they were carried towards the small room where the doctors now operated instead of on the floor of the ward in full view of all the patients.

Perhaps he would lose his arm. Not that he really cared. How he had survived until now he didn't know – but it could not be for much longer. He was luckier than the many who had lain in that place before him, for now – slowly but surely – Miss Nightingale's influence was beginning to take effect. The floors were clean, the beds reasonably so. There was clean clothing and food.

Jamie Trent had a chance of survival – if he had the will to take it.

He was by no means a coward, but it was so like the time in Abbeyford – what was it now, thirteen years ago, or more? There had been nothing left worth fighting for, not after he had lost Carrie, after he had watched her ride away from him for ever, as another man's wife. How he had loved her wild, gypsy beauty, her bright violet eyes, her black, flying hair. He had loved her strength, her passionate

nature – even her jealousy when she had spied on him
talking to Francesca. How angry she had been. And then
that anger had turned to love in a moment and they had
become as one.

Jamie smiled faintly as he remembered and the pain
lessened a little. His memories of her were still so vivid. She
was part of him. He would never be free of his love for her.

How many times during the years since had he gone over
and over the events in his mind and wished his own actions
so very different. If only – he had not ridden away in a
moment of senseless, wild anger, ignoring Carrie's
desperate cries. If only – he had not entrusted his letter to
her brother. If only – he hadn't galloped like a mad thing on
a pointless journey to the lawyers in Manchester. If only – if
only – if only …

Someone was bending over him, shaking his arm gently,
trying to arouse him. "Sir! Sir! Corporal Trent. It's me –
Boy. Don't you remember?" No one knew Boy's real name.
Not even he knew it, for he had been an orphan living on
the streets of London until at the earliest possible moment
he had taken the Queen's shilling and joined Her Majesty's
army.

He was a wiry little fellow, unaccountably cheerful and
willing. The name officially given him was 'John Smith' but
he had become known as 'Boy' to men and officers alike.

Jamie was drifting, slipping into a world of memories,
dreaming of Carrie and he did not want to be aroused back
to the pain and suffering. He just wanted to drift away …
away … But the voice was insistent, it would not let him go.

"Sir – I've got some'at to tell you. Do wake up, sir.
Please!"

The pain was throbbing in his arm again, the noises of
those nearby were pressing upon him once more. Jamie

sighed and grimaced, shifted his sore and aching back a little and opened his eyes. "Hello, Boy," he said flatly. "You here too?"

"Aye, bin here abit, I 'ave. Gettin' better, I am now, sir, thanks to these nurses. Eh, that's what I want to tell you, sir."

Jamie's eyes were beginning to close again. "Sir!" The tone was reproachful. "Do listen, sir. I reckon it's important."

"Go on, then," Jamie said resignedly, his eyes still shut. "I'm listening."

"Well, sir, you know when you had that bout of cholera, an' I helped look after you, you was on about a girl called Carrie."

"Mmmm?"

"Well, she's here," Boy said triumphantly. "She's one of Miss Nightingale's nurses!"

Jamie's eyes flew open in an instant. "Here? She can't be – she … Boy – are you sure?"

Boy nodded gleefully. "She was asking about you. She's been asking everybody who's come here nearly – so I've heard – an' it was me who knew you." He was so proud to be involved.

"Where is she?"

Boy's face fell a little. "That's the only trouble. Since you've been here these last three days, I ain't seen her. I've been burstin' to tell 'er, and I can't find 'er nowhere. An' you've bin lyin' here half dead since you come." He sniffed in a matter-of-fact manner. "I was afraid you was goin' to snuff it 'afore I could tell you."

Die! Oh, hell! Jamie thought, not now! I'll not die now. Only moments before he'd been close to it, allowing himself to slip over the edge into blissful oblivion. But not now, not any more if Carrie were here. If she was somewhere close again, if he could just see her!

His hand reached out and clasped Boy's arm, trying to raise himself up. "Boy – who d'you say is in charge of the nurses?"

"Miss Nightingale."

"I must see her."

"She comes round at night – goes all over the hospital, carrying one of those Turkish lamp things. It's dusk now. She'll be along soon."

Jamie sank back again. "You're sure Carrie's here? She's not gone away again?"

"I dunno. I can't find anyone who seems to know." He paused. "Except Ellen. When I asked her she wouldn't seem to answer me proper. Looked upset, I thought ... Oh God," he glanced down at Jamie the words spilling out before he thought to check them. "I hope she ain't ill. Some of the nurses get cholera."

Jamie groaned aloud, whilst Boy watched him, biting his lips anxiously. He stayed with Jamie, squatting on the floor beside him, watching the long corridor for the pale, flickering light which would herald Miss Nightingale's approach.

"She's here – she's coming!" Again he was shaking Jamie into wakefulness.

"What? Who? Carrie?" Jamie tried to pull himself up.

"No. Miss Nightingale." Boy began to scramble up.

"Miss Nightingale – Miss Nightingale," he said in a loud whisper. "Please, ma'am, would you step over here a moment. Corporal Trent wants to speak with you urgent."

Jamie saw the tall woman stop, hold her lamp high and look across in his direction. The light moved nearer and she was standing beside him.

"How may I help you?" Her voice was soft and reassuring, yet firm and confident.

"I'll get you a camp-stool." Boy fetched one and returned to place it beside where Jamie lay. Miss Nightingale set her lamp upon the floor and sat down. "Well?"

"Ma'am, have you a Carrie Smithson – no – no, wait a minute – a Mrs Carrie Foster here as one of your nurses?"

There was a moment's pause, but Miss Nightingale's face showed no change of expression. "May I ask why you want to know?"

For a moment Jamie closed his eyes, unable to answer. Why, she asked. If only she *knew*!

"You must understand, Corporal Trent," her voice was gentle yet there was authority there. "That I must exert a strict discipline over my nurses, and ..."

"Yes, yes, of course. I appreciate that, ma'am," he assured her hastily, "and I can promise you I do not in any way wish to cause you any trouble or embarrassment, only – I – beg you – let me see her – just let me speak to her."

He was silent, the words would not come. He could not explain to this quiet, composed woman all the craving in his heart which had been locked away there for thirteen lonely years. Would she – could she even – understand? Did she know what it was to love? Had she ever loved and lost, and then been given the chance of finding her beloved again?

Boy, hovering near, was bending forward, whispering to her. "He loved her, ma'am, a long while back – only they was parted, I reckon. He won't say much, but – if you could help him, ma'am, I reckon she's all he's got to live for – if you sees what I mean."

Her gaze was upon Jamie's gaunt face, accentuated by the pale lamplight. "She is one of my nurses – yes," Miss

Nightingale said slowly, "but I'm afraid she's not here at present."

"Why? Is she ill?" Jamie asked, afraid of the answer.

"I – trust not. I was asked to send a nurse aboard the ship you arrived on whilst it lay at anchor off Scutari. I sent Mrs Foster and a young girl, Ellen, with her." Miss Nightingale sighed. "Ellen returned with the wounded when they were brought ashore – but not Mrs Foster."

"What happened to her? Did the girl say nothing?"

"I have questioned Ellen closely and it seems there was a major on board – she didn't know his name, though I've since learnt from the soldiers his name was Richmond – the same man who wrote the letter to me asking me for my help. Evidently he had met Mrs Foster in India."

"India?" Jamie's surprise was evident.

"She had been in India with her husband – did you not know?"

"I – knew she was married," his eyes were filled with pain, "but not where they had gone."

"Her husband was killed in India. Didn't you know that either?"

"No. No, I didn't."

There was a pause whilst Jamie took in this information and all its implications. He raised his worried eyes again to Miss Nightingale's calm face. "But what can have happened on board the ship? Who was this – this Major Richmond?"

There was bleak misery in his eyes, which Miss Nightingale could not fail to see even in the dim, fitful light. Had he found Carrie only to lose her again?

"If it's any comfort to you," she said gently. "Mrs Foster did not seem at all pleased to see the Major – in fact, Ellen says she seemed afraid of him."

"Carrie – afraid?" Jamie almost smiled at the thought of his wild gypsy love being afraid of anyone. But that had been thirteen long years ago. He knew nothing of her life since with her husband, in a strange land. His expression was haunted.

"Ellen last saw her arguing with this Major about shelter for the wounded from an approaching storm."

Jamie nodded. "Yes – I remember. It rained like hell when we were being brought ashore. I beg your pardon, ma'am," he apologised swiftly, "army life has robbed me of my manners."

Miss Nightingale nodded slightly and said, "Corporal Trent, you do wish to know *everything* I know?"

"Why, yes, of course. There's – more?"

She sighed. "Yes. And it may be distasteful to you to hear it. Ellen heard the Major refuse to discuss helping the wounded unless Mrs Foster went below with him."

"And?" His face was dark now with anguish.

She lifted her shoulders fractionally, almost sadly. "She went."

He groaned, unable to stop the sound escaping from his lips.

After a few moments Jamie said quietly. "They began taking us ashore and even tried to rig up some improvised shelter for those waiting on deck. Whatever happened, she evidently succeeded in persuading the Major to help the wounded." There was bitter sarcasm in his tone as his imagination played cruel tricks on him, forcing him to picture her in the unknown Major's arms in exchange for the well-being of the wounded.

"Has the ship sailed back to the Crimea yet?"

"Yes, it left as soon as all the wounded had been put ashore."

"To think she was on that boat – and I didn't even know," he murmured. "If only ..."

"I'm sorry – truly," Miss Nightingale said with compassion.

Then, as if filled with a new purpose, Jamie said, "My arm? How bad is my injury?"

"The doctor thinks it may have to be amputated. Tomorrow he ..."

"No. Leave it. I will not be operated on. It'll heal. It'll have to. I'll be out of here. I must go in search of her. I won't lose her a second time!"

"Corporal Trent." The firmness was now more in evidence. "You will, whilst you are my patient, do what is best for your recovery." Then her tone softened. "For the present – concentrate on your own health – I will do what I can to help you in – the other matter."

Then she was gone, moving amongst the other patients, giving a drink to one, covering another and holding the hand of a dying man.

Jamie lay back. The pain was back in his arm with a vengeance but now he didn't care. Now he had something to live for – he had to find Carrie again!

Now there was a future for them together.

"What is the meaning of this?" Carrie demanded of her captor when finally the door of the cabin opened and Major Richmond entered.

"I should have thought that was quite clear, Carrie my love," he drawled. "I have no intention of allowing you to escape from me again. As soon as we get to my quarters, I shall arrange for the chaplain to marry us!"

"Never, never!" Carrie screamed at him.

"Oh, I think you will agree, my dear," he said

menacingly, moving closer to her. He reached out and pulled her towards him, pressing his mouth upon hers. Carrie struggled, but his arms were strong about her, his body trapping her against the wooden wall of the cabin. She fought and clawed her way free until they stood back from each other panting, the one from exertion the other from frustrated passion.

"You *will* agree to marry me," he gasped, his eyes dark with hunger for her.

Carrie shook her head. "No – I'd rather *die* first!"

His laugh was humourless. "You probably will do, my dear, if you refuse my protection." He moved closer again. "Not all our soldiers are weak and ill. Whilst they may not enjoy the best of health or conditions, they are strong and lusty." He paused a moment to let his words sink in. "A beautiful young woman alone amongst a herd of men who have not held a woman for months …"

"You are *despicable*," Carrie spat at him, but the Major only laughed.

Carrie remained a prisoner in his cabin for the five days the voyage took. Not that she wanted for anything. Food was plentiful and even fresh clothing was provided – a velvet gown and a black velvet cloak. But his outward show of generosity only confirmed for Carrie the thought that he had planned all this so carefully in advance.

The ship docked at Balaclava and Carrie found herself conducted to a house not far from the dock area, and there the Major left her.

At once Carrie tried to escape, but immediately found that not only had the so-called housekeeper – a slattern of a woman, dirty and fat – been instructed to keep watch on her, but two soldiers had been posted outside the door.

Carrie sat in the room and tried to compose her

emotions, tried to remain calm and rational, to plan her escape sensibly. But every moment that passed brought her nearer to the time the Major would return with the army chaplain. She could not bribe the woman and the two soldiers, for she had no money.

She heard footsteps on the stairs and felt her flesh creep as she knew he was returning. Major Richmond was alone but in a vile temper. He banged the door behind him.

"There's not a chaplain to be found. All up near the front line, performing their *admirable* duties," he said sarcastically. Carrie breathed a sigh of relief and some of that relief must have shown on her face, for Major Richmond pointed his finger at her. "Don't look so pleased with yourself, madam. I'm not finished yet!" He stepped towards her and grasped her shoulders. "But what need have we of a parson, my lovely. I've waited long enough to taste your sweetness for myself. You've taunted me long enough, held me at arm's length when your husband was alive to protect you. Escaped me after he died. But now there's no one here – no one to help you. Not even your precious James Trent!"

He felt her go rigid beneath his grasp, her eyes widen, her lips part. "Jamie – you know where he is?"

His anger grew. He shook her fiercely. "Why can't it be me? Why, at the very mention of his name, do you look like that?" He was almost weeping with frustration. Then he flung her from him so that she fell to the floor whilst he stood over her. "Yes – I know where he is. He was shot in the arm. Badly wounded." He leant over her, menacing, gleeful. "*Fatally* wounded. He's dead, your hero, your beloved. Dead, do you hear me?" His voice rose to a high pitch. He raised his hand to strike her, but his words, his venomous anger galvanised her into action. With the inborn tenacity for survival, she sprang to her feet and flung herself at him, her fists and feet flailing. Surprised by her sudden retaliation, he fell backwards, but Carrie did not wait to see what happened, for she wrenched open the door and fled. Down the stairs, out of the house, she began to run wildly without thought for direction or purpose. She must just escape from him.

The two soldiers had relaxed their vigil now that Major Richmond had returned. In fact they were in the housekeeper's kitchen, flirting with the woman and drinking.

Carrie ran on. Fortunately, her flight was in the right direction and within moments she saw ahead of her the mast of the ship she had so recently left still anchored near the dock. She glanced fearfully behind her, but there was no one in pursuit. Not yet.

Her heart was pounding, her breathing laboured, but on she ran, her legs weak and shaking. As she neared the landing-stage she saw that more wounded were being carried aboard the ship. Thankfully she threaded her way amongst them, glancing behind her every now and then. She reached the gangway and was obliged to pause whilst the stretcher-bearers carried their sick and wounded on board. She waited, panting heavily, almost sick with fear. She began to climb aboard and was halfway up the gangway when she saw Major Richmond running towards the landing-stage, followed by the two soldiers.

"Oh, please let me pass. I am a nurse. Please let me reach the Captain."

" 'Ere, who are you pushing?" snapped one stretcher-bearer. At that moment the burly figure of the Captain of the ship appeared at the top of the gangway.

"Let her through," he bellowed. "She's one of Miss

Nightingale's nurses." Then he pointed to the running men below, to the Major and his two followers. "And stop those men coming aboard!"

Five or six of his own crew plunged down the gangplank and with bloodcurdling yells they rushed towards the Major and his men. She saw Jeremy Richmond stop and hesitate. Then he glanced up at Carrie, who had now reached the top of the gangway and was standing close beside the burly, protective figure of the Captain.

He shook his fist but once, and then, as the sailors drew nearer, both he and the two soldiers turned and ran.

Relief flooded through Carrie so that her legs gave way. She felt the strong arm of the Captain about her waist, but it was only offered as a comfort, a support.

"Let me help you, ma'am," he said politely.

"Oh, Captain, how can I ever thank you? You don't know how much you've helped me."

"I think I do, ma'am," the big man said quietly.

"You – you do?" Carrie was surprised. As the Captain led her below to the comfort of the cabin she had so recently vacated, though this time no longer any man's prisoner, he explained. "I watched you, ma'am, all that first day, tending they poor fellows, the wounded soldiers I have to bring by the thousand." He shook his head. "Ma'am, it fair breaks my heart to see it and I'm given no help to tend them, no help at all. I was right glad to see you come aboard, ma'am. Then I thought it strange that the Major ordered them put ashore in the dark of night, but I made no argument, seein' as how it was gettin' them to hospital the quicker. Then, when they was all ashore, he starts chafin' me to go about and start back for the Crimea. Well," he shrugged his huge shoulders, "I had no reason to linger, and the conditions bein' right, I did as he bid. It wasn't until we was a day at sea that I learnt you was still aboard. I swear that's the truth, ma'am. I had no part in his plan."

"I believe you, Captain," Carrie said softly. His actions a few moments ago had told her this fact.

"I thought there'd been a genuine mistake, that you'd fallen asleep after all the long hours you'd worked. You deserved some rest, if you don't mind my sayin' so, ma'am."

Carrie smiled.

"I said to him, 'Shall I put back to Scutari, Major, and take the young lady ashore?' 'No, my man, you will not,' ses he in that haughty way of his. 'There's been no mistake, I assure you'. Well, I didn't know what to think. An' then a member of my crew said the cabin door was locked, an' I didn't know whether you'd locked it against intruders or what was goin' on. Then when we docked at Balaclava and he hustled you ashore, I could see you wasn't goin' willingly, so as soon as I saw you runnin' towards the ship just now, I knew you needed my help real bad."

"Captain, I can't thank you enough!"

"Well, ma'am, it'll be a week or more till we can sail back to Scutari. I have me orders – not," he bent forward in a confidential whisper, "that I always agrees with them, but there it is. I'm not allowed to sail till I have a shipload of wounded and sick, so I can't see but that you'll have to stay aboard. But I'll see you come to no harm, ma'am, I promise you that. You and that there Miss Nightingale are doin' a fine job, and you have my admiration."

"Thank you, Captain. I shall be only too glad to stay on board. In the meantime, until we sail, I shall do whatever I can to help the wounded."

The Captain, bearded and burly, patted her shoulder with his huge hand in a fatherly gesture. "Good, good, and

I will do what I can to obtain some medical supplies for you, if you promise not to ask *how* I obtained them!" He tapped the side of his nose and winked broadly.

Carrie laughed. "Oh, I promise you that, Captain."

The big man laughed heartily and left the cabin. Carrie sank on to the couch, listening to his laughter still resounding as he returned on deck.

It was only then that the full realisation of Major Richmond's words hit her.

'Jamie Trent is dead!'

With a deep moan, Carrie flung herself face downwards on the couch and gave way to an uncharacteristic storm of weeping.

The emotional storm passed but left her feeling exhausted and drained. She bathed her face and went on deck resolved to bury her own misery in hard work helping the wounded. But her whole world had disintegrated with the Major's words. 'Jamie Trent is dead'. Her very reason for living was gone. The thought of finding him again one day had kept her going through all the sorrow of parting, through the long years of a loveless marriage. And now, when she had followed him half way round the world, to find that he was dead was almost more than she could bear.

But her fighting instincts, her will to survive, would not let her give in, even yet. Instead she threw herself into her work, scarcely noticing whether she ate, or washed, or slept, whether it was day or night. She was only aware of the dull ache in her own heart and of the men in her care. Still she managed to smile, to comfort, to bathe and bandage, whilst all the time her heart was breaking.

On the day following his conversation with Miss

Nightingale, the surgeon chopped off Jamie's left arm and with it all his hopes for a future with Carrie.

Physically he recovered, but emotionally he was plunged once more into the bottomless pit of despair. For a time he lived in a crazy half-world somewhere between dreams of past happiness and the nightmare of the present. At last the only thought left in his now fully conscious mind was the torment of the decision he must make.

He opened his eyes to find Miss Nightingale bending over him. "Are you feeling a little stronger, Corporal Trent?"

His sigh was long and deep, almost as if he wished it could be his last breath. His voice was hoarse and expressionless. "Miss Nightingale, I no longer wish to see Mrs Foster. In fact, I'd be obliged to you – should she return here – if you …" he paused hardly able to force the final disastrous words through his unwilling lips. "If you – could keep my presence here from her."

Miss Nightingale was thoughtful for a moment. "I understand the reason for your decision, but I think you are wrong. However," she straightened up, "that is not my concern. I may tell you that, should Mrs Foster return here, I shall be obliged to send her home to England – in the interests of discipline. So – she will not be on these wards again."

Jamie closed his eyes. It was the right decision. She would be better with her Major – a whole man. He was sure it was the right decision.

But, oh, how it finally shattered his already broken spirit!

TEN

London offered little hospitality for its wounded heroes. The meagre temporary pension Jamie was granted of sixpence per day could not buy lodgings, food and clothing – and it could be stopped at any time! Day after day he trudged the streets but no one wanted to employ a one-armed war casualty. At night he joined the tramps and vagrants along the Embankment and was embittered to see many of his companions were old soldiers.

But what shocked him even more was that they were not the only homeless. There were whole families, women and children huddled together in almost every available corner on the Embankment and in every recess across London Bridge!

Unable to sleep for the cold and the bitter misery in his heart, he stared at the dark shadows of the Thames. Beneath its cold waters he could seek oblivion. But then the remembered picture of his own grandfather dangling purple-faced, eyes and tongue bulging, from the stable rafters made him turn away from such a course with a shudder of revulsion. Suicide was not the answer.

Abbeyford! The name crept unbidden into his mind and memories stirred. That was were he belonged. The Manor was still his. At least it would be a shelter of sorts.

Restlessly he moved his cramped and frozen feet.

Abbeyford! The place called him, set him yearning to be among the familiar fields and lanes. And there he could relive memories of the time shared with Carrie.

His mutilated body and his tattered emotions sought the only haven of happiness he had ever known.

Abbeyford! He would go back to Abbeyford.

As the train pulled away from Abbeyford Halt and the smoke drifted away, Jamie Trent looked about him. Grimly, he saw how the railway line tore through the very heart of the valley, an ugly scar across the green fields and quiet country lanes. His eyes, somewhat reluctantly, were drawn towards the Manor House. From this distance it looked surprisingly unaltered.

Without realising he had consciously moved, he found himself walking along the platform, through the white-painted gate – already hanging off its hinges – and down towards the village.

Two women passed him, staring at him and then whispering together as they went on. A man was limping towards him, his left leg swinging stiffly at each step so that he moved along with a rolling gait. He stopped a few feet in front of Jamie and stared at him. Jamie continued walking.

"Why, 'tis Master Jamie!" The man's face was altered in an instant from lines of fatigue by the grin which stretched his mouth. "Eh, Master Jamie! I'm glad to see you – we thought you was dead."

His glance fell upon the empty sleeve of Jamie's coat, and the grin faded. He gave a quick nod towards it. "You've bin hurt bad, I see. I'm sorry, Master Jamie."

"Thank you, Joby," Jamie said quietly. He had recognised Joby Greenfield at once, though the limp was something new. In turn, Jamie nodded towards Joby's left leg. "You too?"

"Aw, that's a legacy from that there fight we 'ad years back wi' t'railway navvies."

"How – how are things here now, Joby?"

Joby Greenfield shrugged with the philosophical acceptance of a man born to expect hardship. "Could be worse. A lot of the villagers have gone. Moved to towns to find work in t'factories." He paused, seeming to want to ask a question and yet not knowing quite how to phrase it. "You – you back for good, Master Jamie?"

Jamie's smile was a little thin, his eyes still mirroring the heavy weight of sadness in his heart. "I expect so, Joby. I've nowhere else to go."

He moved on again with a casual word of farewell. "Be seeing you again, Joby."

Jamie did not look back and so did not see the grin widening upon Joby's face as he watched him walk up the village street and take the lane towards the Manor House.

"Good to have you back, Master Jamie," he called after him, and Jamie waved his one hand in acknowledgement without turning round.

"Aye," Joby Greenfield murmured to himself. "You'm home now, m'lad, an' I reckon you'll be stayin' when you find out who's up at t'Manor!"

Jamie paused, his hand on the sagging gate-post leading into the stableyard from the lane. The gate was off its hinges, lying in the grass a few feet away. His eyes roamed over the stableyard, at the weeds pushing their way up between the cobblestones; the buildings, the timber rotting and some of the brickwork beginning to crumble. Slowly he moved across the yard and, avoiding the back entrance, he walked round the side of the house to the terrace.

The long windows stood open to the sunshine, the floor-length curtains billowed softly in the light breeze. Jamie stepped over the threshold and stopped in surprise.

The room was freshly decorated – the old chairs and sofas had been dust-beaten to a respectable condition. The carpet – worn and faded – had at least been scrubbed to cleanliness and the oak floor shone with polishing that must have taken a week!

Someone lived here. In his home!

He moved across the room and opened the door into the hall. It was still dimly lit, but no longer dismal. There was not a cobweb nor a dirty footprint to be seen.

Jamie sniffed. Was it possible? Baking bread? The smell drew him towards the kitchens. Now he could hear a woman humming softly to herself and the sounds of dough being slapped and kneaded. Quietly, he pushed open the door.

She was standing at the bare, scrubbed table, her hands busy with the dough, her slim body enveloped in a huge white apron. A white scarf tied back her black, curling hair and a smudge of flour lay upon her cheek.

For a moment he thought – man though he was – that he was going to faint.

He whispered her name. "*Carrie!*"

She was suddenly still as if turned to stone. Then slowly, as if almost afraid it would not be true, she turned her violet eyes upon him.

He wasn't conscious of having moved towards her, but the next instant she was reaching up to touch his face, leaving traces of flour upon his cheeks too.

Wonderingly, her hands passed over his face, his chest,

his waist, unable to believe he was real, whilst he stood drinking in the sight of her.

"I – thought you were – dead!" she breathed and then with a sigh of thankfulness she laid her head against his chest and wound her arms tightly around his waist. "What kept you away from me so long?" she murmured.

Jamie shook his head but could not speak. The time for explanations was later. Without asking, he knew why she had come back here. Back to Abbeyford. All roads led back to Abbeyford.

Now his mouth was hungry for the taste of her lips. His one arm held her close and they clung together, swaying slightly, lost in the ecstasy of their reunion.

He had come home – and so had she. Home to Abbeyford, home to happiness and to the hope of a new tomorrow.

And the ghosts of unhappy lovers past finally found their long-sought peace.

It had begun in Abbeyford and it ended in Abbeyford. And yet, it was not really the end, rather a new beginning.